After Amba

Stephanie Shields

First published in Great Britain by The Sheep Shed Press
2025

Cover image and illustrations: Copyright © Jacky Fleming

Edited by The Wishing Shelf (www.thewsa.co.uk)

Typeset by: Hilary Pitt

Printed and bound by: IngramSpark

This book is a work of fiction. Any references to historical events, real people or real places are used fictitiously. Other names, characters, places, and events are products of the author's imagination, and any resemblance to actual events or persons, living or dead, is entirely coincidental.

A CIP catalogue record for this book is available from the British Library.

ISBN: 978-1-9998182-4-1

"The past is the present, isn't it? It's the future, too.
We all try to lie out of that but life won't let us."

Eugene O'Neill, *Long Day's Journey into Night*

Acknowledgements

My late grandfather Francis Robert Chapple, a cavalry man, who fought in Egypt and Palestine in The Great War (1914 -18). His tales left a profound impression on the imagination of his favourite granddaughter.

Diane Park, of Wave of Nostalgia, Haworth's wonderful independent bookshop, for her unwavering belief, encouragement, support and friendship.

Jacky Fleming, artist and cartoonist, for capturing the character of Amba in the cover image.

James Nash, poet and writer, for his encouragement, kindness and reassurance.

Contents

PART 1

Flying Home

Chapter 1

Frasey Hannah Fisher
Research Librarian, The Mount, Menston, West Yorkshire, November 2018

I'm trying to imagine what it was like for Amba Atha that day, the fourth of July 1948. I picture her poised to board the plane at Stockholm's Bromma Airport. A brand-new aircraft, the *Agnar Viking*; a Swedish airport, the first in Europe to have paved runways. Amba herself would carry the confident air of a seasoned traveller, a travel and fashion writer of repute; a woman of the world.

What a figure she must have cut. I've studied her portrait, looked through her photo albums, pored over her portfolios, immersed myself in her writings. I've been through her wardrobe and admired, touched and even tried on her outfits. Her suite at The Mount has been kept intact, just as it was then, seventy years ago. I've tried to enter her world.

Tall for those times, she will have been dressed to the nines. She will have worn her sable cape draped nonchalantly over her shoulders, for although the temperature might have equalled a warm summer's day here, Amba wouldn't have trusted her cape to the trunk. And flying in those days could be a chilly affair.

Amba prided herself on an eclectic mix. Dior above the belt, and Katherine Hepburn below – New Look meets

American Look. She would never relinquish her trousers for some ghastly long, full skirt. She had an enviably svelte figure and her choice of trousers would emphasise this – high-waisted and wide-legged, without turn-ups. Above these, a Dior-style jacket with a nipped-in waist.

I've seen this outfit in a later style book; her sketches with small swatches pasted in. There are notes too, ideas, suggestions and modifications. She noted it was perfect for travel.

Ron, her father's tailor in Bradford, created this slacks suit for her, to her own pattern and under her own stipulations. She had chosen a gorgeous wool cloth, dark grey with lilac pinstripe. So soft to the touch, light yet warm. Rationing did not thwart Amba. There were ways and means and Amba's family had grown rich on worsted. Ron had risen to the challenge. He had enjoyed this commission, especially after the interminable demob suits for returning heroes. Amba released the artist in Ron. He was easy in her company. She allowed him to be himself. No pretence. They recognised something in each other.

In a diary entry Amba confesses that her clothes are her carapace, they mask her vulnerability. Since starting my research I've fallen under Amba's spell. I've combed her letters and articles for clues. I feel I almost know her. Of late, I have wondered if I might have become obsessed with her. Sometimes when I look up from my desk, or rather her desk, I could swear I feel her presence, see her watching me. I see her standing on the far side of the lake, sometimes closer.

This strange sense of connection with subject has never happened to me before. I have always been a facts and figures sort of researcher; a stats person. I have never been credited with imagination. But something about Amba has seeped under my skin.

I see Amba stroking the nape of her neck. She loves her silken shingle cut which emphasises the elegant contour of her head. So easy to maintain. She wears her thick chestnut hair slightly longer now, on top, but still in a boy's cut. The almost quizzical arch of her dark brows is emphasised by two artful kiss curls, one either side of her forehead, each curling inwards, a mirror image of the other. These are teased and secured by a generous application of lotion. Hers is an arresting, androgynous look. It stops both women and men in their tracks. Forty-one years on the planet yet there is still something of the girl in her appearance, a certain petulance, and pure devilment in those mocking, copper, dancing eyes.

The Amba of my imaginings will smirk ruefully at the thought of being carried off by a Viking, for she's never had much time for men. The exception is her brother Andrew. She has all the time in the world for him. Generally, Amba prefers women.

As she pauses at the base of the aircraft's steps, she will see her beloved trunk trundle past on its way to the hold. She might imagine which expletives the tall, blond Scandinavian men may use as they try to lift it. She carries her world in that trunk.

"Serious luggage is the true traveller's choice." That's what Amba has written. A costly choice in those earlier times of commercial aviation, but she believes the traveller is more receptive to new experiences if cocooned in things familiar, cherished, practical, and pleasing items, creature comforts alongside the exotic.

Amba carries with her emblems, talismans, charms - an eclectic selection from her favourite places and peoples: an owl hewn from the grey volcanic rock of Reykjavik; a palm-sized spirit with a burden from The Gold Coast; a Peruvian alpaca manta with geometric patterns; a tiny white marble

Ganesh with inlaid flowers in precious stones and a ruby brooch – paste – from Aunt Rania's casket. She swears she will never be separated from these, nor from her other treasures. Wherever she lands, these precious things she carefully unwraps from their packing silks. She sets them out as a shrine to her soul. And the centre piece, always, a fragment of driftwood from the Seine. For Paris is where Amba abandoned her broken heart.

No, Amba Atha never travels light.

"Pack for the predictable, pack for the possible, then, pack for the improbable." This is what she told her readers. "Pack as if you'll never come back."

Her editor scratched that. "We mustn't unnerve the readers, Miss Atha."

Amba wasn't happy. She has always hated people messing with her words.

But on that day, boarding that ill-fated aircraft, did she think the unthinkable? Did she have any presentiment that this would be the day she herself would not come back?

Chapter 2

Coming Home
The Fourth of July 1948

Time to remove the cape. It's so warm. Here comes the purser eager to lift it to the locker for me.

'I thank you.'

He's very smiley. I hope he won't be too attentive. I can't be doing with fuss.

This plane is so much more substantial than some of the aircraft I travelled on before the last war. Perhaps there will come a time when flying will become less sophisticated, and too accessible. If this ever happens, I fear the world will shrink and become less mysterious. But then it's wrong to think this way. Everyone ought to have the chance to fly, surely? It should not be the province of the privileged few, people like me who travel the world and interpret it for those less fortunate and less free.

But I've never minded discomfort, or even a tinge of fear. Once, we crossed the Channel, Ida and I, both sitting on the floor of a small plane. It was The De Havilland Fox Moth, designed to carry a pilot and four. We begged a lift from some madcap friends and, despite the absence of seats, they allowed us on. The pulse of the engine thrilled us both to the very core. Delicious vibrations. We hung on to each other so tightly, enjoying this truly erotic sensation.

We made Paris in record time. Ida, my lost love, the love of my life…

I enjoy flying, and in truth, dying in the air holds no fear for me. There are worse ways to leave the planet. But I'm trying not to think about Ida, or death.

So, I'm coming home at last. But what is home? Where is home? My home is in my trunk. This is my line, but it is not the whole story. My birth home is The Mount, Menston, in the West Riding of Yorkshire, home of the Athas with our wool wealth and lots of it. Thank heavens that Father hasn't cut off my most generous allowance for what I earn through my writing would never support my lifestyle. The way Father sees it, I've certainly provoked such a severance. I'm a disappointment, a stain on the good name of Atha; unnatural. Spare me.

I hope it will be different this time.

Flying always makes me reflective. Perhaps it's time to embark upon a memoir? Too soon at forty-one, I wonder. But not so fast, for so much has happened and I must save my memories from the distortion of the elderly mind. People go soft in the head. They gradually grow respectable, then mushy in the mind. Oh, I've seen the sanitising effect of being too long on the planet, certainly in my parents. I'd like to tell my tale as freshly as I can, whilst I'm still able to taste the moment of being with all its pains, terrors, embarrassments, heartbreak, and indeed, the occasional delight and pleasure.

If I ever write it, mine must have the truth of a proper memoir. A veracity of feeling, what it was like to be me, not fact, not some tedious 'then I did this, then that' autobiography, but how I felt 'in the moment when'. A fictional non-fiction told through the memorable moments of my life, my milestones. If I could tell my tale through vignettes, dramatised scenes, snapshots, and spools, then it might be worth my readers' attention and their precious time. Failing this, I'll merrily forego the memoir and be forever forgotten.

"Spools." A wonderful word. Spools like whirlpools. Jerky spools and spiralling pools. The Hindenburg disaster footage creeps into my mind unbidden – the Pathé News, the urgency of the received pronunciation commentary fighting the swirling momentous soundtrack, the aroma of popcorn and the dried sweat crustiness of the cheap velvet covered hard cinema seats. No, I don't want to think about The Hindenburg.

I banish this vision of flames. Instead, I will reflect on pools. The small lake at The Mount. That's what I'll focus on. Cupping my hand, trying to catch a ripple on the surface, scooping the crystal-clear water, letting it seep slowly between my fingers, sun spangling the droplets. Sitting on the raised stone rim of the pool, sandwiched between Lilith and Leda, the serpent and the swan.

Lilith and Leda were Aunt Rania's wedding gift to my parents. My mother loved them. Father wasn't quite so sure. Mother once told me this.

'There'll be some damned message in these two,' said Father when the two statues were delivered to the newly completed house. The Mount was ready for the newly-weds in 1902.

'Better not to over think these things, my dear. I love the two figures. It's a generous gift from my sister. The sculptor might be young, but Rania says she is held in exceedingly high regard. I can see exactly where they should go. We'll place our two ladies on the rim of the pool.'

'I suppose this sculptor is one of your sister's bohemian lady friends.' Father's initial hostility to Aunt Rania will deepen over the years. It will transcend her death.

I am transported back. The warmth of the sun on the crown of my head, heating my heavy, wound round hair.

The delicious aroma of the roast for Sunday luncheon. The summoning boing of the brass gong with the brown leather strap, mounted at the bottom of the oak-panelled stairs. "Home. Going home. Going home. Going home."

It's warmer than I expected. Time to remove the gloves. I have this down to a fine art. I push the leather down over the wrist, then pull each finger gently until the glove slips off. I'd better get my scribbler pad out just in case I have any ideas that seem worthy of note. What times and territories might I cover by Schiphol? By RAF Northolt, mid-afternoon, who knows where I might be in my memories? It's unlikely I'll make Menston in person this very day. But by tomorrow, surely, I will be back home.

Memories, eh. How trustworthy are our memories? We modify them through the prism of the present. But does this devalue them? I think not. Let's start with my own earliest specific memory as opposed to the impressionistic ones of the very young me. For this I'll summon my five-year-old self onto the stage of my recollections.

It's Christmas 1912, and for the family's entertainment Father bought a magic lantern and a selection of plates. The plates were beautiful, images exquisite and colours perfect, all hand painted.

One afternoon, Mother was reading the script as Nanny operated the projector. The fairy tales came alive, and I was thrilled, entranced. They did Alice in Wonderland and a selection of the Arabian Nights. Then Father entered the room and insisted on the box called "Titanic", sixteen plates and a script to evoke the first and last tragic voyage of the great liner. Father took the script. He insisted a sonorous, powerful, male voice was essential to reflect the gravity of the content. Mother looked apprehensive but took over the projector and Nanny was given the job of lowering the needle onto the spinning record, Be British, a jaunty lament sung by Stanley Kirkby.

There was a sequence of false starts for Father had the effect of terrifying Nanny, and her hand trembled so much she was in grave danger of scratching the Zonophone 78. But then, they were off.

Nothing in my young life had ever held my attention like the tale of the Titanic. "Be British was the cry as the ship went down…" The pacy, upbeat song belied the slides. There was the liner with lights ablaze, tilting a little into the midnight blue ocean. Two of the boats had already pulled away. Next there was the liner almost at the perpendicular. More boats filled with passengers in their finery pulled away in the swell of the inky waves.

'Mama, there are still people on board – women with children and babies!'

'Ambrose, this isn't quite the thing for the child.'

'Nonsense! The girl needs to know about the perils awaiting her. Life isn't a fairytale.'

'But what happens next Papa?' I just had to know.

'This next slide is about the anxious relatives. They will soon be sporting black, mourning their dear ones departed. And see now, people are giving to the relief fund on this one. The generosity of people always warms the heart, does it not?'

'"Nearer my God to Thee" – but if God's in heaven, Papa, the drowned people are further because they are at the bottom of the sea?'

'Heaven isn't a geographical destination child. It's more a spiritual place, don't you know?' He turned on Nanny. 'Don't you teach this child anything sensible?'

'Can we see it all again, Papa? I like the lady in the white dress with the pink cheeks and roses, the pretty one with her arm up. Did she die and go to God?'

'Ambrose, enough! You will unhinge our daughter.'

Chapter 3

The Bedstead Cacophony

When we recall the past, some characters we deify and some we demonise. Is this the full and fair story? But this is my story and I'll tell it how I like.

Kate and Ambrose, Mother and Father, were the significant characters in my early life, along with Nanny. My mother was cut from a finer cloth than Father.

My earliest memories are of the softness of a woman's neck, the cushion of an ample bosom and the fragrance of fine French parfum. If I let my mind ease back to the beginning, it would be to the silken dark ringlets that spilled over my mother's shoulders and down her breast. The lustre of mother's pearls was diminished only by her delicate skin's tone and feel.

Silk, satin, velvet, and exquisitely embroidered flowers. Nottingham lace. Ruched ribbons. As a very young child I could not sleep without mother's silk hair ribbon twined between my fingers. This ribbon is tucked in my trunk to this day. Mother taught me that silk was the kindest to the hair. Not that I have any practical need for silk hair ribbons now.

Mother had favoured mauve, a relatively new colour then and much worn by Queen Victoria. Jewels were nasty, glittering, sharp and unforgiving. Unpleasant pins. Boned stays. But choose the spot with care and rest there, rocking softly with Mother. Mother's eyes were violet and fathomless, her lashes dark and curled and her brow precision perfect, as if etched in soft charcoal. Mother's singing was sweet, low, soothing. My tiny eyelids would droop and slumber would overtake me.

My own eyes are drooping at the memory. I catch myself in time. It will not do to be seen to sleep in public. My mouth might fall open. I might snort or dribble. This would be the antithesis of elegance. What point in sporting such an outfit, only to be undermined by human frailty. Heaven forfend. Where was I?

'Put her down. Let the nanny take her now. Come Kate. My need for your company is far greater than that spoilt child's.'

My early recollections of Father are shady and far from favourable. Father, Ambrose Atha, did little to recommend himself to me. It never occurred to him to try. And in the battle for my mother's attention, there could only be one winner.

Ambrose was not a traditional Atha family name for the male child. Where it had come from I can only speculate. My later research suggested Saint Ambrose, a Roman and Bishop of Milan, a Doctor of the Church and scourge of paganism. Father certainly held no truck with paganism or any other 'ism' that might suggest the mystic, the exotic, the erotic, the libertine – or anything else delicious washed up on the wilder shores of life.

The tradition in the family was to model the first-born daughter's name on that of the father, hence my own name Ambrosia. Ambrosia, food and drink to the gods, heavenly nectar. Was it not with ambrosia that Hera cleansed defilement from her flesh? But then my own flesh has never been defiled, by man at least. And nor will it.

Father brought a biting wind from the north. Wherever he was in the house, curtains billowed, even the heavy Italian tapestry drapes and the opulent rugs rose. Nanny said his appearance was enough of a gust to part her hair. Certainly, a chill seeped into the nursery when he came to claim mother for "company" as he so often did.

Yes, Father's disappointment at my birth was difficult for him to contain. He continued this grievance with me throughout my childhood, teens and twenties. Full-scale war broke out in my thirties. Separation has softened relations a little, but even now, it is an uneasy peace. A cold war is perhaps a more accurate term.

'Ambrose, there will be others, my dearest,' cooed Kate, as I sat on her knee. 'We will keep on trying.' And try they did.

I recall the gross groans and grunts on Sunday afternoons, after luncheon. Replete and refuelled by fine wines, Father would demand the company of my mother. 'A little after luncheon nap, my love?' or 'forty winks, eh?' My parents would adjourn, up the wide, oak panelled staircase, arms linked and eyes locked. This activity was not reserved for Sundays. Repeatedly I would wake in the night to the monotonous grinding of bedsprings and the rattling of the brass bedstead beating a tattoo against my parents' bedroom wall.

'He's at it again,' I would confide in my beloved cat Aubrey. Aubrey liked to sleep spreadeagled on my quilt – a grey fur softly snoring coverlet. Aubrey resented disturbance deeply. He would tighten his lips across his gums, bare teeth, and deliver a hiss in the general direction of my copulating father. I would nod in agreement and run my knuckles softly down Aubrey's spine to calm him. Other times I would pull a similar face and hiss too. Neither Aubrey nor I could ever hold Mother responsible for such unseemly episodes.

In my later teenage years, I would whisper, 'Fornication,

Aubrey. Iniquitous. And in the sanctity of my poor mother's bed. It's just so distasteful, unhygienic – absolutely not on. Believe me, I shall never keep a man company. This I promise.'

My reverie is interrupted by a child's shrill voice. My eyes scan my fellow passengers. A rough headcount – twenty-five not counting the crew. Mainly men. A few women, two young children, and a baby. I hope that the children and baby will not cause a nuisance. I'd prefer them to make no noise at all. I can't abide a rumpus. I'm not keen on children, with one exception. Only one has found a place in my heart, my beautiful Andrew. Andrew Horatio Atha. He was such a Baby Bunting, so plump and jovial. But he is hardly a child now. Can he really be almost twenty? He's very much my own creation.

Was it wrong for me to want to take Andrew for my own, to shape him to be the opposite of our father, to make him love me and want to be with me always? "Vengeance is mine". Father had wrenched my mother from me. All he wanted was a son. He had no love for me. I only counted as a reminder of his failure to produce an Atha heir. A boy child to inherit the mill and the factories.

"Blessed are the meek, for they shall inherit The Mount." An appealing thought. Quite an amusing one in truth. We never know how things unfold, unravel.

After my own birth it took well over two decades before my parents' assiduous love making would pay off again. Andrew was born in 1928. Of course, The Great War proved a significant interruption. The Egyptian Expeditionary Force needed Father. And then there was the tapeworm episode.

The tapeworm – the hardest thing is not to giggle out loud. This would be so unseemly. Ida had declared 'The Tapeworm' an absolute hoot and asked for the tale over and over again. Ida embraced anything that might ever have caused my father discomfort. She had absorbed my hostility towards him. On each retelling I stretched the unfortunate worm's length another couple of inches.

'Go on Amba, tell them all about the tapeworm!' Ida would plead, and with a staged reluctance I would begin to set the scene to whatever company was present.

Chapter 4

The Tapeworm

How did I know Father had returned from the war? The greatcoat gave him away. The butler had draped this voluminous, stiff, green, woollen army coat over the tailors' mannequin in mother's dressing room. This dark and decapitated form haunts me still. I could see it as I climbed the stairs. I could hear voices in my mother's bedroom – two voices. I peered into the room. The butler intercepted. He stepped in front of me and closed the door quietly. Shaking his head, he discouraged me from going further. He endorsed this with a wave of his hand. Gently, Nanny steered me away from the landing. More sounds. The bedstead cacophony had begun again, after over four years of peace.

It was Valentine's Day 1919, my twelfth birthday, a Wednesday as I recall. I had been allowed to take the day off school, but this was not the birthday my mother had promised. I spent the rest of the day in the nursery with Nanny waiting for - waiting for I don't know what. It was as if the rest of the household had entered a state of paralysis.

Later, in the early evening, my mother called for me to greet Father. I had put on my new velvet dress for the occasion – deepest blackberry, with a cream sash in satin, and a matching collar.

I must confess I was shocked to see Father. He looked like

a cadaver. His face was hollow, his skin stubbly and jaundice-sallow and his body so reduced that I almost felt pity for him. Mother batted me a warning. Her eyes urged caution. 'Say nothing untoward, my child!'. That's what those eyes said to me. Her instinct was always to protect me.

Yes, Father was back. I must have made some pretty little speech for I can't recall any incident or ugliness on his part. I do remember I was required to kiss his cheek. I had to brace myself. Up close it was dry, cold, gaunt and scaly. His eyes protruded from their dark sockets. These eyes were fixed on me until I was ushered away. I'm sure he would have looked kindlier on the Turk.

We didn't see too much of Father in the days that followed. Clearly, he was worn out, from the prolonged fighting in Egypt and Palestine and then the long and arduous journey home.

'Open-topped cattle trucks. The length of Italy. Freezing conditions, appalling wet. A home coming for heroes, my arse!' He snarled this in variations, over repeated Sunday luncheons.

It seemed that Father had insisted on coming with his men and eschewed the more luxurious transport befitting his rank. This is how he had acquired the great coat, the model issued to the lower orders. One of his men had died and the coat was passed over to him. His men had pitied his fragility. I suppose, looking back, Father's act of loyalty and comradeship should have spoken something about my father's character. Ah, the arrogance of youth. Perhaps it is only now that recollections begin to chip away at my own assumptions about him and his motivations.

Gradually Father began to make more daily appearances and resume his role as head of the household. Even with the first signs of proper Spring, as the dense carpet of snowdrops in our wood gave way to wood anemones, and then to bluebells, The Mount became a colder, darker place. I felt a profound sense of loss, and I grieved for the closeness and warmth of my mother. We had been everything to each other in his long absence. I soon felt myself hoping and praying for another war.

Mother became increasingly concerned about Father's health. He suffered no loss of appetite; quite the reverse. He was voraciously hungry. He devoured his meals, but he didn't put on even an ounce. In fact, he was losing more weight. There were concerned voices from Cook and her kitchen staff. All talk hushed as I entered the kitchen, but I caught something about him "going home" – as in, "he looked as if he was going home". But surely, he had just arrived home. Another war perhaps? My hopes soared. It was a mystery to me, but I knew something odd was happening.

Saturdays and weekday evenings, Mother and Father dined alone. I dined in the nursery with Nanny. I no longer needed her services as I had started to attend The Leeds Girls' High School, but my mother was soft-hearted and Nanny was like a family member, so she was kept on. Perhaps this was as much for my sake as hers. On Sundays I was required to take luncheon with my parents. It was a tradition. On these Sunday luncheons I was able to observe my father. As well as Father's huge appetite, I soon became aware of his compulsion to re-enact the Battle of Megiddo. He made free with the glass and silver cruet set on the ornate Art Nouveau stand – oil for the infantry, vinegar for the tanks, mustard for the artillery and salt and pepper for the cavalry. Father was a cavalry man. Aeroplanes – yes, they were there too – were represented by a linen serviette cunningly folded by Father into the shape of a dart. A messy plate with leftovers represented the Turks. In fairness to my father, he always retained a grudging admiration for the Turk as a fighting man.

The history books might tell you it was the combined use of each of these units that won the day at Megiddo. Not so. Father demonstrated how the infantry and artillery closed on the enemy positions, but it was left to the mounted units to encircle the enemy, thus preventing escape. The Turks were annihilated. It seems it was my father who brought about the fall of the Ottoman Empire. Few people know this.

Of course, Edmund Allenby was quite important too. Father was generous in his praise. Allenby, the Bull, was efficient, organised and disciplined. According to Father, Allenby's formidable energy re-vitalised the campaign. Like Henry of Agincourt, he made morale boosting visits to the front. Keeping closely in touch with the mood of the men was pre-requisite.

Father was more cautious about the Bull's enthusiasm for irregular warfare, especially the role of Colonel T E Lawrence. About him, Father's expletives were unrestrained and largely unprintable. Abomination was one, seditious another and charlatan another. There were others.

'Was he on our side, or a friend of the Arabs?' When Father posed this question, he neither expected nor required an answer.

When I commented, in all innocence, that surely the British and the Arabs were on the same side, Father exploded like a shell. The cruet scattered. Mother soothed Father who would continue to snarl all the way upstairs. I suspected there was more to it and, even then, I wondered what Lawrence got up to, to provoke such an extreme reaction in Father.

Where was I? Ah yes, the tapeworm.

It was Doctor Gilbert who diagnosed the tapeworm, about three months after Father's return. You might wonder why Father had waited so long to seek help, but he believed himself immortal, and that doctors were there for lesser beings and poorer specimens. Eventually Mother prevailed. She badgered him into submission and the family doctor was summoned to The Mount.

It wasn't just the weight loss that had been causing alarm. Father was seen on occasion to double over with severe abdominal pain. I noted this myself and I had a fancy he might die. While the cramps were on him, he would turn ashen. I remember the sweat breaking out on his top lip and across his forehead. He would sprint to the lavatory whilst fumbling simultaneously to shed his braces and undo his trouser buttons. Then there was the vomiting, and the gunshot cracking of explosive diarrhoea reverberating round the porcelain bowl.

Doctor Gilbert gave Father the once over. It seems that under questioning, Father conceded he had noticed some oddities in the content of his stools – he described the things that the doctor identified as tapeworm segments. The doctor diagnosed Taenia Solium, the pork tapeworm.

'Exceedingly dangerous Ambrose. Procrastination has not been wise,' Doctor Gilbert chided him. 'There is the added peril that you might have passed it on to those closest to you. I hope you have been washing your hands.'

Father's indignation at the mere suggestion he might not have washed his hands boomed around the house. The doctor continued, undeterred. He was used to my father. He batted off Father's rage and soldiered on.

'Basically, this tapeworm has been eating you alive. Let's hope you haven't passed anything on to your wife and child, or to the servants. They all need to be vigilant and warned about the hygiene aspects. Well, we're going to try to shift it. I'll need your full cooperation in this, and I need to talk to your wife and daughter. Ambrosia seems a sensible girl, so tall and mature for her age – quite a beauty. She needs to know what is happening.'

Doctor Gilbert reported back separately to Mother. True to his word, he asked for me to be present too. He told us that it would have been the conditions – the poor sanitation, the bad waste management in the camps, contamination through unwashed hands.

'But Ambrose is a fastidious man, Doctor. He always washes his hands.'

'That may well be Mrs Atha, but we cannot say the same for those preparing his food. This worm comes from pigs; pigs that have eaten human faeces.'

'Oh my dear Lord, no!' Mother sank to the chaise, her left hand clutching her throat.

'Oh yes, Mrs Atha. It wouldn't have been like Menston out in Arabia. What's more, the pork from these pigs will not have been cooked properly, I'll wager. The larvae of the parasite will have entered your husband's body one way or another – the cook's dirty hands or the poorly cooked pork, or both probably.'

Mother swallowed hard. 'What can be done? Can Ambrose be saved?'

'We will administer an anti-parasitic powder, to be taken orally. This will paralyse the worm which will then, we hope, let go of the intestine wall. It will begin to dissolve and pass from the body via bowel movements.'

Doctor Gilbert did not look entirely confident about this, but he continued, 'Now, here's the thing. I need you to supervise your husband on this matter. I know he is not an easy patient. He veers towards the cavalier. Men who have once faced death do tend to do this. You know, I should have been summoned the moment he returned.'

The doctor waited and Mother, biting her bottom lip,

nodded slowly.

'Of course, Doctor. What must I do? My husband must be saved.'

'Capital, first of all, I need you to be sure he has swallowed the medicine. Make sure he takes it all, in front of you. Don't let him water the Aspidistra with it. Then I need you to ensure he collects the worm.'

'What?' asked Mother, through her cupped hand.

My eyes were on sticks. I was silent, horrified. I was still reeling from the thought of pigs eating soldiers' "business". Would I have to handle the worm coming out of Father's bottom? Too terrible a thought. I suppressed an impulse to gag.

'Yes, we must be sure that your husband has passed all parts. This is essential to his future health. I will furnish you with a diagrammatic representation of the anatomy of a tapeworm from its hooks and sucker, knobby head, neck, and body segments right down to the final tapering. And I will need to know its length. Believe you me, this type – the pork one - can be surprisingly long. Please record length and diameter – oh, and do save me the worm for inspection.'

'Oh, my dear God.'

'Take heart, be courageous. Not for the squeamish, true, but you, Mrs Atha, are more than capable. I know you are made of stern stuff. Your husband's future well-being will depend on ridding his body of this foul intruder.'

'Oh yes,' whispered Mother, her courage returning. 'We'll get the worm, be assured.' She stood, as if to demonstrate her resolve.

'Splendid. We are fighting for his future, don't you know? The real danger is that the larval cysts can infect the brain. Cysts in the brain can cause headaches, lack of attention, confusion, dark moods, seizures.' The doctor lowered his voice. 'Dementia even.'

My mother sat back down, heavily, now in full shock.

'That's why we need to check this blighter's fully out.'

'When will we know the worm has left him - properly?' she whispered.

'I'll need to recheck his stool samples one month after treatment and again after three. I'll be on the lookout for further evidence. But I have to be honest, the symptoms can occur months or even years after infection. Then the problem comes when the cysts start dying, and the brain begins to swell.'

'You haven't shared this brain business with him, have you?'

'Oh no, not the thing to do at all. Such information is inadvisable to be shared with the host. He'll think he's a goner from the start.'

The doctor took a deep breath. 'And you, young lady – this is our secret. You must care for your father and be kind to him. Be a dutiful daughter and do nothing to provoke him. No matter how unreasonable he might seem, do not provoke him. You understand me?'

I nodded. I wasn't intending to go anywhere near him.

'And look after your mother. I chose to include you in this confidence because your mother will need your support. I urge you both, be vigilant.'

'Thank you, Doctor,' we uttered in unison, like a Greek chorus.

Mother's thanks sounded thin. The Doctor left the room. Mother stared wanly at me.

'Whatever is to be done, Amba?'

'I suppose we better dose him?'

'Amba, your father is not a horse. We will administer the powders – that's how we describe it. Doctor Gilbert said he would send them directly.'

'So, what does a worm look like? And what if it comes out,

but isn't fully dead? What's to be done then? Will we have to club it to death?'

'Of course it will be dead if it emerges. Otherwise, it wouldn't have come out. And Doctor told us, he will send a diagram. We will study it. I think we'll know it when we see it, dear. A violent intervention will not be required.' Mother paused. 'Surely not?'

I wasn't convinced either.

As promised, the powders soon arrived. I stood beside my mother as she mixed them briskly, in a tumbler of water. Father swallowed the potion with minimal complaint and delivered a salvo of burps. This seemed to be it for a day or two.

My adolescent imagination ran wild. My father became "the host". I speculated about the battle going on inside the host. Would the worm scream when the powders hit the spot? Would there be a death throes convulsion as the worm relinquished its hold on the host's intestine? How soon would it make its appearance?

We didn't really know how to proceed from this point. Mother affected serenity but I knew she felt anything but calm. Father felt insecure, I suspect, for every time he got up from his seat he glanced round and down anxiously in case he'd ejected it.

Father spent an age in the water closet too. Mother said he would be inspecting his stools, probing and perusing.

For me, the worm became the serpent. I dreaded using the water closet. I feared it might have slipped out unnoticed and would rise from the bowl when I was seated and attempt to enter my bottom, or worse, far worse.

Other thoughts troubled me. Would I ever be required to be present for the probing of the stools? Please God no, I prayed.

I was spared. Three days later, a bizarre ceremony took place. Mother and Father stretched the worm, in four fragments, along the Yorkshire Stone veranda, in front of the pool. I emerged through the French doors to see Mother, on the side of Leda, and Father, bent over, near Lilith. They had a tape measure on full stretch, and still needed more. Nanny had to keep her finger on the join spot.

'Summon the good doctor. Eight feet four inches! Amazing.'

'Oh, my dear. And it has grown this long inside you!' Mother was clearly shocked, and, of course, relieved at the worm's passing.

I lurked in the shadows, watching, not eager to approach the dead worm. Doctor Gilbert showed no such hesitation and arrived in double quick time with a suitable receptacle.

'What a monster! A brute. Quite magnificent.' He shook my father's hand vigorously. 'Well done, Sir! And most deftly passed.'

The butler emerged with the fine tulip glasses for champagne. There was even one for Nanny and for me. He emerged a second time with the bottle in a bucket of ice. We toasted my father's health and longevity. Father preened. Mother gazed up into his eyes. Our own Saint George of Menston, indeed.

I sighed. From that moment, the soft pop of a released champagne cork, the effervescence of the fizz in the glass, the first nose of flowers, the sharpness on the palate followed by the ripe fruit richness – these prized sensual delights would evoke in me a strong sense of revulsion.

Chapter 5

Salome

The *Agnar Viking's* engine drones on. I note a patch of purest blue between the seemingly weightless clouds.

The past flows through my mind in unnavigable channels. Remembering triggers remembering. Let the worm, Menston saints and champagne slip away on the flow. Yes, I will happily wave away the champagne tray forever. Now wine for me is divine. My first ever sip – Viognier, soft, lush, peach, pear, and violets. Prized by Probus, the Roman emperor, I taste it now. This clear recall of Viognier leads me to Salome. Viognier, in The Peach Room. Salome in the boudoir.

'Come on Kate. A tiny tipple for the girls won't leave them "tol-hol". A young girl needs to find her palate.'

"Tol-hol" was our family's term for inebriate.

Mother looked anxious, but Aunt Urania's arguments carried the day. Mother blushed, already flushed from her third glass. Aunt Urania, oblivious to her younger sister's discomfort, instructed us first on pronunciation.

'Viognier girls. Répète après mois "vee oh nyay". Say it right and sip with delicacy. Don't slurp and burp, Ambrosia. And you are not trying to strangle the glass. A glass must be held by the stem, otherwise your palm will warm the wine.'

I relaxed my hold on the glass and adjusted my fingers down to the stem. My aunt nodded for us to proceed.

'Inhale with sensitivity before you taste, girls. And make sure you are seen to do this. Do not appear desperate. It's not good form. A girl must never be judged a lush.'

Viognier transformed a nice chicken salad lunch into something memorable and delicious.

'It is said Viognier draws its name from the Roman pronunciation of the *Via Gehennae*, "the road of the Valley of Hell".'

Aunt Urania, Rania for short, your fingerprints are on the rope that has tugged and twisted my fate all along my own *Via Gehennae*. If mother was my sun, you were my moon. Mother brought warmth, joy and sustenance to my young soul. You brought the mysteries of the night sky. Your name evoked the heavenly – art, literature, song, dance, music and theatre. You played muse to poets and mentor to me.

'If you feel different, seek out the different. Just be different. Remember my words, Amba.' That's what you told me. You followed your own advice, and I have too.

Rania was driven by curiosity; she wanted to know, to dip her toe. She moved in different circles to my mother. But then she wasn't wed to Ambrose. Mother had chosen her own snicket to hell.

In earlier years Aunt Rania followed Aleister Crowley. Encouraged by him, she joined The Order of the Temple of the East, a German occult order. It was Mother who told me about this brief interlude in Rania's life. In 1912, Rania had become quite infatuated with that odious Crowley man, as Mother called him, and he with Rania. She was one of the women he chose to attempt to beget a "Magical Child." This entailed drinking, drugs and some sort of sexual magic. I understand that a third party was to be involved, Satan. Crowley initiated Rania into the vibratory qualities of special words to aid consummation. I've puzzled about which words these could be. But I digress. It seems this interlude did prove a step too far, even for Rania. Shocked at such goings on, Rania returned home to Cadogan Square with her tail between legs alongside a touch of gonorrhoea, and a drug habit, albeit a light one, but without a Magical Child in her arms. She had to make do with the six-year-old Seraphina, her own dull, pasty daughter, begat by Uncle Robert without the assistance of either magical words or the intervention of Satan.

Like Mother, Rania had wealth and charm. The elder of the two, she had married well. Husband Robert was rich and rarely there. I once heard my mother refer to him as a "hands off" husband. I supposed next to her own he must have seemed such. Uncle Robert was high in the British Foreign Office, this much I knew.

At first, he was a flickering, faint presence on the periphery of my memory, a lesser ghost in the cast of many, except for one brief period from Spring to Autumn of 1918. Then he did fall into sharper focus; but I'm getting ahead of myself. Where was I?

The Peach Room, the place where my first sip was taken, was the spacious main room in Rania's London home, a rather fine mansion flat on the east side of Cadogan Square. I remember it as being a red brick building, a thrilling contrast to the old, soft, seasoned stone of The Mount. It had a balcony and there was a residents' garden to enjoy. Just being in Cadogan Square made me feel sophisticated.

In my memory, The Peach Room is bathed in sunlight and filled with flowers. Rania had a feel for lilies and orchids, and yet loved the humble violet best of all. She would often return with a posy of violets wrapped in damp moss, selected from a street seller's basket. She often quoted Wordsworth. "A violet by a mossy stone / half hidden from the eye!" I found out later the poem's title was "She dwelt among the Untrodden Ways." How apt, I thought, for my aunt's taste in flowers. But in no other way could my aunt be likened to Lucy Gray.

Taste, comfort and elegance. Rania could afford the most exciting designer in London, at the time. Her choice was a woman whose taste and vision were highly compatible with her own. The agreed concept was a metaphorical casting of corsets. I now have grounds to suspect that for the two of them, this might have been more than a metaphor, as side by side, they poured over plans, catalogues, and swatches. Shimmering peach walls, with sumptuous apple green rugs, white window frames and exquisite floral drapes. Light touch combined with an easy, wanton dishevelment.

Rania had assembled an eclectic collection of furniture – from high-end antique dealers to junk shops to local flea markets. She collected exotic items from Greece or the Orient. I drew in her style and vowed I would follow Rania's lead. For me, Cadogan Square united the realms of the spirit and the material.

Rania's daughter Seraphina combined caution with an inexplicable desire to do the right thing – her father's daughter. But unlike Uncle Robert, she was open to persuasion and easily led astray. She was a year my senior, but in all other respects I had the upper hand. Her mother frequently said that I should have been her daughter, and Phina, Kate's. Sometimes Rania referred to me as her true "Magical Child". How Phina felt about this I never queried. We got on well enough as children. I quite liked Phina. There was little to dislike, and once I'd hooked her, she entered into my schemes with enthusiasm. She hated to disappoint me. Thus it was with Salome.

I first encountered Salome hanging on Aunt Rania's

bedroom wall. My aunt's voice rings out sharply above the infernal Viking's engine drone.

'Ambrosia, please. Boudoir! Bedroom is such an unpromising word, so very West Riding practical. You might well have a bedroom at The Mount in Menston, dear, but here, in Knightsbridge, oh no, no, no, no!'

This correction is followed by a dying, mirthless laugh. And I'm flying through the clouds and back in Rania's boudoir at Cadogan Square. This day I was privileged to be initiated into some of its mysteries.

'But Aunt, who can this be?'

Rania swivelled to follow my gaze across her haloed boudoir. The large, intricate gilt frame could not detract from the gorgeous subject.

Rania's head tilted, lowering gracefully close to my ear. 'Salome,' she whispered, her fine, sharply etched crimson lips smiling, enjoying both the name, and my clear wonderment. 'Have you encountered Salome, Amba?'

'She's in the Bible. She demands John the Baptist's head on a tray in return for a rude veil dance. We did it in scripture at Sunday School.'

'Ahh. The bare bones, I suppose, but again, a very Menston interpretation of the biblical tale. And 'tray' will by no means do. The noble, severed head of The Baptist deserves so much better. Salver is appropriate. It was a golden salver, so I am led to understand. Furthermore dear, never confuse rude with the erotic. Rude turns the episode into the burlesque. Burlesque and biblical make uneasy bedfellows.'

Rania sighed. 'Come. Let's look at the painting more closely. Follow my observations and take something from them.'

Rania took my hand and led me over to the pale apple green, silk covered chaise longue. She seated herself and tapped the space beside her. And so began my first initiation not only into art appreciation, but also, I suppose, the erotic. I already feel quite warm recalling this episode.

The painting had been commissioned by Aunt Rania after she had first seen Maud Allan perform at The Palace Theatre in London, around 1908. Aunt Rania had been to see Miss Allan's performance, more than once.

'One time I saw her sharing a bill with "The Juggling McBains". Imagine that. Another time she was on with Professor Macart's troupe of athletic monkeys. Dear me, talk about the sublime to the ridiculous. Exquisite art and genius rubbing shoulders with circus acts. Variety, eh? I suppose all tastes must be catered for. The theatre is a broad church, Amba. Alas."

She said Maud was the sensation of the season; she was always a sell-out. Maud had inspired my aunt so profoundly that she approached Maud to sit for an artist friend of hers. I now realise Rania was desperate to get closer to Maud, to become her friend, and she saw this as a means to an end.

'I used to attend the sittings as often as I could. I admit, even from our first meeting, there was a frisson, a recognition. We found ourselves reaching for each other, metaphorically, well, mostly. We shared an exalted intimacy: ideas, preferences, matters of the spirit, matters of the couch, and then the boudoir. Ah, we were so very close for a while. Our souls, our very selves, entwined.'

There was a pause.

'Maud sat on this very couch, you know. We were as close as I am now to you, my dear Amba.'

Aunt Rania gazed at the painting. 'See the rapture on the face, the transporting to a different plane of feeling, existence, being. But a painting could never do justice to such a creature. There are things that cannot be committed to canvas.'

Maud certainly seemed transported in ecstasy, as did my aunt, who was now deep in her recollections and beginning to breathe rather heavily, almost to the point of rapture. She was panting.

I studied the painting. Somehow, I sensed that sitting on the same silk couch that Maud had graced, afforded me a deeper understanding. Maud's pale shoulders were thrown back, her head tilted back too, and her pearl-looped headdress echoed the waves of her abundant, dark hair. But I was transfixed more by the costume, or rather the absence of a costume. Our lady's top half was to all intents and purposes, naked. But, her nudity was veiled by a surfeit of jewels: gems and pearls, strings of pearls, and a gauzy navy harem style skirt. A bare, well-turned and fluid foot featured, hardly making contact with the floor. Maud appeared to glide.

Oh my goodness, something in that painting captured me. I wanted to be Maud Allan, to express what was in my soul, to dance freely. It was as if the painting had awakened and unleashed a serpent within me, somewhere deep down in my core. I felt very warm in what I would then have referred to coyly as my private parts. I wanted jewels on my nipples, and long ropes of pearls dangling from my hips. I yearned to slough off all constrictions and constraints, be they clothes, behaviours or Menston thinking. I wanted to dance for women, with women.

I became aware that my aunt was studying me intently, a wicked smile of triumph playing on her lips, a delicious delight shining in her eyes.

'Hmm, Ambrosia, you do show great promise. I believe we are very alike in so many ways. Be assured my dear, one day, perhaps not far away from now, you too will kiss The Baptist's lips.'

Rania lowered her face to mine, and kissed my lips, as if to illustrate her meaning.

The spell was broken by my mother's voice, calling me to dress for the morning's excursion to town.

Later that very week, a Sunday morning in early February, the strangest of coincidences occurred. It was after breakfast and we were taking coffee in the Peach Room. My mother and Rania were scanning the newspapers. They liked to read out the odd titillating titbit, snatch of society gossip, or miry morsel. Their eyebrows danced.

Phina and I were knitting mufflers for the soldiers at the front. My intended contribution to the men had been to knit scarves of vibrant colours, to cheer them and to raise their spirits, but mother had explained that the purpose of the muffler was to warm the wearer whilst not attracting the attention of the enemy, or the envy or ridicule of fellow soldiers. My first attempt at a soldier's scarf had provoked a comment about rendering the wearer a sitting duck. Mother instructed me to start again in more suitable hues and tones; camouflage colours were the thing. It was with a singular lack of grace I started to cast on again.

I confess I found the knitting of these muted mufflers tedious but had the good sense at least not to let on. I did not wish to provoke one of my mother's censorious lecturettes on patriotism, and the privations of our boys, all seemingly called Tommy, and the sacrifices being made by most in this country. This always led on to a tearful, hand wringing eulogy to my father out in Palestine. This I needed to be spared.

Where was I? Ah, the coincidence. Well, Rania favoured The Sunday Times. She gasped; an advertisement had snatched her attention.

'Kate, imagine. So exciting. She's back! My darling has returned to these shores. She's going to do it again. Maud is to reprise her role. Listen to this: Oscar Wilde's Salome. Maud

Allan in private performances by J. T. Grein's Independent Theatre. Ooh. This coming April. Why that's just three months away. We just have to go. For old times' sake, eh?'

'Oh. Aunt Rania, please can I come too? I'm desperate to see Maud dance. I must come with you. Please, may I?'

'What?' My mother looked from me to Aunt Rania. 'What on earth, Urania? With what inappropriate nonsense have you been filling my daughter's head? And you know you vowed to Robert you would not be in contact with Miss Allan ever again; not after that business.'

Rania remained unperturbed, completely serene, in truth. She blanked mother's last comment, but answered, 'Ambrosia admired the painting of Salome in my boudoir, and I explained a little about it, hmm, very little really. But your daughter has the appreciation and good taste to recognise beauty, originality, and genius. You've developed quite a crush on Maud, haven't you Ambrosia? For this you should be proud, Kate.'

I nodded enthusiastically, but my mother looked stricken.

'We will not fall out, Rania. It will not even be an issue, I'm sure. A child of eleven will not be allowed into a private theatre for such a risqué show.'

'Oh dear.' Aunt Rania pulled a rueful face. 'Like mother, like daughter. "Risqué show" is so very Menston. But, I fear you may be right, Kate.'

I dropped my half-finished muffler along with needles to the floor and ran from the room. I was crushed, inconsolable.

Rania was not long in following me. She sat beside me on my bed, running her soft, elegant fingers through my hair. Then she scooped me up, pressing my head to her plush bosom.

'Darling girl, my silly goose, my true Magical Child, there will be time enough for you to be initiated into the finer ways of we women. In the meantime, there's a new play by J. M. Barrie coming out this year. It's called *A Well-Remembered Voice*. It is to feature a séance with a dead soldier. I think you and Phina might enjoy this. Séances are such fun. The medium does the dead in a deeper voice. And, you will both see more clearly why you're knitting those ghastly mufflers.'

I sniffled. 'I'm sick of mufflers, and I did so want to see Maud do the Salome dance. What if I never get to see her? I'll just die.'

'I'll tell you what, Amba. Here's the deal. I'll take your mother – she will come round - and then I'll try and recreate the dance for you. I promise, I'll take special note of the movements, steps and music – the whole routine. Yes, Kate can concentrate on the score and I shall tackle the dance. We'll try to secure the sheet music for piano, but anyway, your mother can play by ear. I'm assuming the music will be the original Marcel Remy – so evocative, sensuous, captivating. How's that?'

'What about the pearls and jewels? What about the see-through bloomers?'

'Well, I might not go the whole hog as it were, but I can give a suggestion of, how shall I say, of Maud's freedom from the constraints of costume. I'll try to capture the essence of her performance, next door, in The Peach Room. We'll push back the furniture and roll up the rugs. Such fun we shall have, eh?'

'Oh. Well, if you promise to be as close as possible to the real thing. But I wouldn't want you to put your back out...'

'Ambrosia! Are you anticipating this injury will occur through the movement furniture, or the act of dance? I'll have you know I'm a classically trained dancer, which is more than Maud can claim. And I'm younger than she is. I'm supple. Why, I could reach attitudes she could only dream of. So have no fears on that score. Mrs. Betson can help with the furniture.'

'What about John the Baptist's head?'

'Hmm. Leave him me. I'm sure we can come up with something suitable. A shame Ambrose is still in Arabia…'

My aunt's smile was hard to read.

'So, dry your tears, Goose. The ball shall come to you, my sweet Cinderella. Perhaps you can take a break from the soldiers' mufflers and start to work on my diaphanous harem pants? And, remember, they are not to be called bloomers. Why, we are going to need gems and sequins, lots of them.'

Mother and I were back in London in time for the April performance. Aunt Rania came back from the performance in raptures. Even my mother caught the mood of the moment. Aunt Rania declared the dance to be delicious, captivating and truly seductive. Mother expressed anxieties about the scheme to re-enact. Was such a performance suitable for two young girls? Was the entertainment quite the thing for war time? Had times not changed since Maud first performed?

'Absolutely appropriate, Kate, and in the comfort and safety of our own home. What possible objections could there be? After all, the story is in the Bible. Maud performed the dance for our late King Edward, in Marienbad back in 1908. On Maud's own testimony, he congratulated her warmly; some say too warmly. Later, in London, she performed her exquisite Visions of Salome in front of the Prince and Princess of Wales.'

Mother's objections thus dismissed; serious preparations began. Phina was eager to accompany my mother on the tambourine. Cadogan Square was soon filled with the exotic keyboard accompaniment, and Phina's perfectly timed light drumming and clashes of bells.

I was to do wardrobe and to improvise with the lighting.

The lighting was quite a challenge, but I was given help by Aunt Rania, who supplied candles, torches and a tilting banker's lamp – The Tiffany Astoria model. Then, Rania produced a pair of flambeaux she had brought back from a New Orleans' Mardi Gras. These would certainly help set the scene.

Rania was right, the creation of the harem pants was so much more to my taste than mufflers. One day, as I was embellishing the pants, Rania returned home in triumph and presented me with a large, rusty, pale blue tin. It felt unexpectedly heavy. The scene depicted on the deep red tin lid was a classical one: a parched landscape, a villa with a terracotta pantile roof and pale blue shutters, nestling in the shade of a spreading tree branch. Opposite, a naked woman stood on a tall plinth. Caught in a moment in time, and alabaster, she seemed to be trying to flee from a danger unseen. Her body seemed shrouded in gauze. I was already entranced and excited, even before lifting the lid.

'Amba, aren't you going to look inside, for heaven's sake?' Rania prompted. Patience wasn't her forte.

I opened the lid, and there I beheld such riches. It was a veritable casket of jewels, gewgaws and appliqués. I was transfixed by a feast of bright colours. It was like a sparkling vision in stained glass.

'Oh my goodness; where on earth?'

'Well, dear one, these are only fake gems, mock jewels and paste. They are of little value, but they will do the trick, surely. I found them in our local haberdashery shop. It seems they came from a lady, a widow, the other side of The Square. She died of a broken heart following the telegrams about her two sons. These came in rapid succession. Too much sorrow for her to bear.'

'Oh, dear God, that's so sad. The poor woman,' said my

mother. 'Do you think it a little disrespectful to use her gems for such a purpose as ours?'

'What tosh, Kate! There you go again. Think about it. These aren't going to help the woman or her poor sons now. I'm sure she would have loved to see them put to good use. Remember this, Maud saw her creation of The Visions of Salome as a Passion Play. She insisted she brought the Bible story to life, and kept the reverence intact. Maud did not set out to be erotic, sensuous or even sensual. People criticise her for these elements, but this is to misunderstand…'

'Just as your husband did when he caught you and Maud on the couch, *in flagrante.*'

'Case in point, Kate. I was helping Maud rehearse a seduction scene. How could a man understand? Maud is an ideas woman, quintessentially, and an artist. She brings originality of thought, instinct, and interpretation. She interprets music through her graceful and fluid body. She has studied dance ancient and modern, and art, and her apparent abandonment to impulse, and the spontaneous, is the result of carefully executed ideas. In short, she is a triumph of the cerebral over the wanton. The wanton is in the minds of the more lascivious beholders - the Herods of this world.'

'So, you style your husband a Herod?'

'Let us say that Robert has never understood the closeness that exists between women. It is not his territory. Exclusion breeds suspicion and hostility. Show me a man who hasn't wished to control a woman. There are things that he could not appreciate, things that would be wasted on him. Men often resort to the term 'unnatural' if it lies beyond their comprehension. In short, Robert was wrong. Now, back to our own private performance.'

Mother looked as if she was trying to come to terms with her sister's thinking. Before she had time to respond, Rania set off again, changing her tack.

'What is more Kate, the scene is set in that very theatre of war in which your beloved Ambrose is camping currently with his men. Our performance could be interpreted as a nod to the sacrifices and endeavours of the Allied Egyptian Expeditionary Force, especially our own mounted troops.'

Aunt Rania paused for breath, and then looked grave. 'Know this, The Visions of Salome is a tragedy. We share Salome's rapture, and then we ache with her, no, through her. We feel her profound regret, grief and atonement, to our very cores. Why, in this one amazing dance she explores the mysteries of existence.'

'If you say so,' mumbled my mother, carried along by her sister's passionate defence, and yet not entirely convinced. And in truth, I'm not sure I was too. Why, if Maud was so cerebral, did the painting make me feel so strangely warm and physical. The thought of her made my inner thighs tingle in an entirely novel way. I wanted to withdraw to my boudoir to touch myself where I'd been told not to.

Two days later Aunt Rania returned from town in triumph. 'Now Amba, what do you think about this?'

She held aloft a garment, another of her finds. It was a gold and pearl lace appliqué bodice. The metallic sequins had been stitched onto an off-white mesh. The bodice was topped with sequinned epaulettes. Aunt Rania had found it in a theatrical costume emporium. It seemed it was surplus to the theatre's needs.

'It's perfect!' was all that I could say. The vision rendered me almost speechless. And you could see straight through it.

'Come Amba, help me try it on.'

I had just put the finishing stitch into the harem pants, so I carried these with me as I followed Aunt Rania into her boudoir. Aunt Rania positioned herself behind the Chinese screen for the fitting. I passed the pants coyly over the top.

'They're done. You are quite the little seamstress. A clever girl indeed.'

Then she summoned me to join her behind the screen.

'I'll need help with this fitting, and with the pearls and ruby shoulder brooches.'

My aunt stood naked before me.

'Come on round, Amba. Don't blush so. Why, I should be shyer than you, and yet, believe me, I'm not.'

Aunt Rania's body gave off the sweetest scent of verbena. I felt almost intoxicated. I helped Rania with each item. We giggled rather, adjusting her voluptuous breasts into the bodice. And then she was ready. Rania looked magnificent.

'Not too tight, Amba, for I'll need full freedom to move.'

She executed a Maud-style shimmy.

'Let me out here a little, dear.'

I loosened the ties between her shoulder blades. She then took my palms and smoothed them over her breasts.

'This is how it should feel. And again. Familiarise yourself with my form. Be sure to get it right on the night!'

She looked straight into my eyes and held my gaze for seconds that seemed forever. I felt I might swoon.

'Call your mother and Phina. I'm sure they will love my outfit.'

But I didn't want to leave her side. I just wanted to hang on to that moment, to take everything in. For the first time I realised how beautiful my aunt was, and how, in a way, my mother could never compete. It was to do with her sensuality, her sheer enjoyment of her own body. In helping her dress, I felt I had shared a delicious and intimate experience, a secret, an initiation, but into what I could not guess. Not then.

'The pearl girdle, Aunt Rania. Don't forget the pearls.'

I wrapped the pearls around her slender waist and

smoothed them down over the harem pants. I felt her hip bones protruding a little.

'Silly me, I must have been distracted. You know, Amba, I'd like you to help me dress more often. Yes, you shall be my dresser.'

'Oh, I'd like that too. I feel I could learn so much from you.'

Truly, I was in thrall.

Chapter 6

The Quest for the Clitoris

Ah, the bitter taste of disappointment. There was to be no performance. Fate, the Germans and The British Foreign Office conspired to thwart our delicious plans.

That spring, my father's shadow was stretching out to us across three thousand miles. Following the capture of Jericho in February, things had gone quiet in Palestine. But in March, the Germans launched their spring offensive on the Western Front. General Allenby was required to send reinforcements back, including his tank force, along with two divisions, infantry battalions and dismounted yeomanry regiments – in total, sixty thousand officers and men. The Force was significantly depleted, albeit temporarily, but the commander was to keep up pressure on the Ottoman armies. My father's mounted division was being sent repeatedly into the attack.

Throughout that April, an absence of news was leaving my mother increasingly anxious, distraught even, about my father's safety and well-being. This might not have scuppered our performance, for I'm sure my aunt would have continued to marshal excellent reasons why the show should go on. But then, the coup de grâce, my Uncle Robert unexpectedly returned home. He was to take up high office in Lord Hardinge's newly created Political Intelligence Department.

Uncle Robert's arrival changed the mood of the household overnight. The light seemed to be sucked through the windows, the very air we breathed became closer, and Cadogan Square lost its lustre. The faint, flickering figure came sharply into focus. The shadow became a stain.

I recall that first breakfast of his return.

'Rania, my love, I think the time has come to remove Miss Allan from your boudoir wall. I had hoped she would already have gone, for you did promise. But now there is a fresh imperative, I fear your heroine has become a little non grata. A back of the attic job for her if ever there was one. I'm sure Betson can find an old sheet.'

Uncle Robert sat back in his chair. A thin, cruel smile played beneath a thick moustache. He was watching Aunt Rania with seeming detachment. Aunt Rania was anything but detached:

'No! Never! Why ever should I do such a thing?' She was clasping her hands between her bosom in a dramatic pose worthy of Maud.

'We are at war my dear.' His syrupy voice maintained an even flow. 'Things have moved on. To have such a painting might be compromising to a man in my position; in my new position especially.'

Aunt Rania's magnificent bosom heaved with indignation. 'Surely, Robert, I deserve more explanation than this? Compromising? What utter tosh!'

'Do you not read the newspapers, Urania? I can't believe you have missed The Cult of The Clitoris?'

There was a prolonged, stunned silence. It was uncomfortable. Phina and I exchanged furtive glances. Then, I plucked up the courage to pose the obvious question. 'What is a clitoris, Uncle Robert?'

At this, Uncle Robert looked apoplectic, Mother shot

unkind and silencing glances in my direction, and Aunt Rania instructed Phina and me to withdraw to our rooms and to: 'Go and discover your clitorises for yourselves, girls! Be off with you.'

Phina and I left The Peach Room at speed, but I had the presence of mind not to fully close the door, to enable our lingering pairs of young ears to follow the escalating scene.

'You can't have missed this Vigilante business, surely?' snarled Uncle Robert. 'That infernal Pemberton Billing is laying waste.'

'Robert, as you know, I never read anything disagreeable. But from what I hear, mere gossip of course, Maud has been wrongly accused, reviled, and she should, most assuredly, be exonerated. Pemberton Billing has besmirched her character and all she stands for. He is a twerp, an odious man, and yet like so many on the extreme right, he trades in glib and evil falsehoods, misinformation, and he stirs hatred through working popular prejudice. He works the crowd! Sapho, Salome, Cult of the Clitoris, women who love woman, unnatural practices. Absolute hogs' wash. Baloney. Tommyrot. And to accuse Margaret Asquith too! I am speechless that you, of all men, heed such vile nonsense. I have always believed you to be above all this, a man of independent mind and intelligence.'

'Rania, you are clearly more informed than you were at first prepared to admit. I thus assume you are cognisant with the 'Black Book' and its implications for men in my line of employment?'

'But Noel Pemberton Billing will never enter my boudoir, Robert. I can guarantee you this. Maud stays.'

'Oh no she doesn't. Don't you understand? I cannot be seen to be connected with this dancer, even through you and your outrageous bohemian ways. That cad Billing has accused your beloved Miss Allan of being part of a group of those determined to undermine our war effort; a veritable conspiracy.'

'But there are no grounds to …'

'Who needs grounds? He alleges they work through sexual perversion, blackmail and espionage. He has suggested that Maud Allan herself is a German sympathiser and connects her with The Berlin Black Book. Forty-seven thousand names. He is targeting anyone of influence whom he and his ilk do not approve. He's in the business of ruining the careers. Naturally, no-one has seen this book. They don't need to, so powerful is the voice of the far right. A hint that you are in it; that's all it takes.'

'It doesn't exist. Someone should stand up to him, surely? Someone should call him out. And this is what Maud Allan is doing. She is my heroine.'

'Urania, the current mood is one of paranoia. Yes, Billing stirs the crowd with his hints and innuendos. It is a witch hunt and, believe me, these rarely go well for the accused. May his finger never point in my direction,' he paused, then added as if an after-thought, 'or yours for that matter.'

There was silence. Then, finally, Uncle Robert spoke again. This time he was calmer, but there was a hint of menace.

'So, the matter is settled. The painting will be taken down this morning. I will speak to Betson directly. The attic beckons. May your dear friend Maud find peace 'neath a dust sheet.'

When our two pairs of snooping ears heard the scrape of Uncle Robert's chair, we set off down the corridor at speed. Uncle Robert's anger was not to be provoked further. And anyway, we'd heard enough. We regrouped in Phina's room.

'But what could it be, this clitoris thingy?' I was desperate to know.

'Sounds Greek to me,' said cousin Phina.

'Well, we need to investigate. Your mother told us to find our own.'

'An investigation! Oh my, like the great detective and his friend Doctor Watson?'

'Indeed. And I've bagged Sherlock Holmes, so you are my Watson.'

Phina could only sustain a petulant pout for a few moments. She never fought her corner. I couldn't help but notice what a silly dimpled chin she had when she pulled a sulky face. But this wasn't the moment to point this out and tease her. We were going to have to work as a team. And mother had repeatedly requested me to be kinder to my cousin. Now was the time.

'Come on Watson, we need a plan of action. What is it? Where is it? Why is it? We should start with what we already know.'

'I think it's a ladies club.'

'That's interesting. You mean like The Somerville, The Pioneer, or The Grosvenor? Hmm. Didn't Aunt Rania join The Pioneer?'

"Yes, but my father wasn't happy about it. Mother herself told me that her joining was a move against toxic masculinity and male oppression, whatever these things are.'

'Hmm. Your father mentioned 'cult'. Cult suggests beliefs, a religion, a sect or something.'

'So, what can it be? A passionate devotion to something not to be spoken of? Something like the Methodists? Father has always disapproved of them. He says Methodism smacks of enthusiasm. Or,' Phina paused for effect, 'some sort of secret sect. Did you notice Aunt Kate's reaction to the word? She almost choked and she went quite puce.'

'True Phina. Even your own mother looked uncomfortable. Rare for her. I think it's something rude. I think it's rude and to do with women. And you might be onto something with the ladies' club notion. A club which is to do with rude goings on. We'll get to the bottom of it, have no fear Watson. We always do.'

'In the Sherlock books, perhaps. Not in real life.' Cousin Phina's mouth and chin were at it again, working together in a wobbling moue.

'Don't be such a pessimist, Phina. We haven't even started yet.'

And so, the Quest for The Clitoris commenced.

In the first instance, we combed the available dictionaries. References were sparse and baffling: a key, a latch, a hook.

'Shall we visit the ironmongers and ask for one?'

'No, Phina, I think not. Not much rude comes out of the ironmongers, not from the one I visited in Menston anyway. But then Mother was after ordering one of the newfangled washer-wringers for the scullery. She didn't think to order a clitoris, as I recall.'

Then we found "a small organ", but it was unclear as to whether it was anatomical or musical. Further investigation uncovered: a little hill, a small pillar, and a bulb, or, more specifically, "A bulb of the vestibule?" We liked that one.

'Like a hyacinth in a pot? Like the one on our inlaid console, the one with the Prince of Wales Feathers?' offered Phina.

'No, that can't be right. There is nothing embarrassing about a pot of bulbs placed on a table in the hall, surely?' I paused.

'I think we need to seek advice, further afield. Let's try the reference section of a library. We'll pretend it's for our school work.'

Aunt Rania, Uncle Robert and Mother seemed pleasantly surprised to note our new diligence, and our enthusiasm for study. We made a loose reference to a project that Phina needed to complete for school work. We were given some money, a little pep talk on behaviour, and personal safety, and lots of encouragement. We were poised to embark on our first independent trip.

The British Library was deemed far too far and too grand for us, but we were encouraged to explore some of the public libraries. Rania had told me previously that study liberated the mind. Clearly this was true of the person too, for a mere visit to the library allowed us to go out unchaperoned across the city. I made a mental note of this. It could be useful.

We planned our excursion with care. We chose the Public Library at Ladbroke Grove. The Ladbroke Grove Library had been conceived as an educational resource for the working-class communities of North Kensington. A children's room in the basement was opened just before the war. Chelsea Library had been operating a children's service since the early 1900s and was much closer to Cadogan Square. But we were known there and this might prove a problem, given the delicate nature of our quest.

We decided to take advantage of the tram. Our mothers discouraged us from using the underground railway because it was doubling as an air raid refuge – the German Gotha bombers had taken over from the zeppelins and people were seeking the safety of the station platforms. But these places weren't entirely safe. Mrs Betson said there were some hair curling tales about the behaviour of soldiers on leave, especially towards young women and girls. "Tube babies." Mrs Betson's phrase. I wasn't entirely sure what this implied, but, Phina and I decided to avoid any such encounter.

The trams were more exciting anyway. Many tram conductors had left to join the armed forces. The men had been replaced by conductorettes. But there were to be no women drivers because tram driving was a reserved occupation. At the time, it was believed that a woman would not be physically capable of operating the brakes. What tosh.

Phina and I were all mouth and eyes as the tram glided on. We passed food queues of women with empty baskets and old prams, and raggedy children. There were some scruffy people slumped in doorways, quite a lot of them. People looked gaunt, pallid and dirty. Some young men struggled along on crutches. It all seemed a very long way from Cadogan Square, or Menston for that matter.

Then the tram slowed to allow a modest military procession to pass by. The conductorette announced that this was a group from The Women's Auxiliary Army Corp and like her, these 'gals' were doing their bit for the war effort. The travellers on the tram burst into applause and the old man behind us started to sing Roses of Picardy. He'd just delivered the line about the roses dying with the summertime when his hiccups started. Phina looked aghast and declared the man to be a drunk. I had to concede there was a distinct smell of sick and scotch each time he hiccupped.

The women, commonly known as Queen Mary's Army, were marching four abreast. Their heads were held high, and their shoulders thrust back. They wore dark fedora-style hats and ankle length coats with neat dark collars and deep pockets. I was thrilled to see them. They looked so resolute. But it was as if Phina was reading my thoughts.

'Well I think they look stupid.'

'Why?'

'They look ugly. It isn't even a proper uniform they're wearing, just coarse long coats. They aren't allowed on the frontline to die. They just do things from a safe distance. What is the point of them?'

'But Phina, the point is, they release the men who then go

to the frontline. It's like the poster says, "The girl behind the man behind the gun". This is something, surely? At least they are involved. Do you want those poor women to be killed? Would you wish to be killed?'

Phina shrugged, as if none of it was of any consequence to her. I felt irritated with her over this. I found her sneering perplexing and part of me was spoiling for a fight. Still, we were supposed to be a team, Holmes and Watson, so I decided to ignore her. Why, my own mother had declared a great admiration for these women. She had read out some details about them from the paper. So many had volunteered in the first year that there were now fifty thousand, or even more. Mother said that if she hadn't home and family commitments, she would certainly have joined up. Aunt Rania had said it was splendid to see these groups of women marching together as a powerful collective. She'd declared them to be fine women indeed, and then likened Queen Mary and her Auxiliaries to Boadicea and her daughters. Then Mother made a rare joke about it being a pretty big family Boadicea had. Well, if Rania and Mother both approved, who was I to object?

As the women disappeared from our view, and the tram started up again, I couldn't resist saying, wistfully, 'I wish I was old enough to join Queen Mary's Army.'

'You? Ha! You wouldn't last five minutes. You couldn't even stick with knitting mufflers for our men at the front. Too boring for you. No, you had to be sewing sequins onto fancy knickers. And you'd be complaining about everything and rushing off to your room to sob. Mother's "Magical child" – I don't think so. You'd be charged with insubordination. You would be shot. And who would grieve for you? No sane person.'

I was stung. Phina and I turned away from each other for the rest of the outward journey. I pressed my warm forehead against the cold tram window. I gradually persuaded myself she had spoken in haste. Mother had told me Phina had just started her periods, so it could be what our cook had called, "That time of the month".

Eventually, we reached The Library at Ladbroke Grove and our spat was forgotten – well, almost. Phina and I stared up at the building, awestruck. It was an impressive early Arts and Crafts style red brick building, late Gothic and quite irregular in design, with eye-catching bands of cream stone. It was grander than either of us had expected.

'My father insists it's too good for the poor people. Wasted on them is what he told me. The poor need to help themselves. He said up north, where you come from, people make do with modest institutes and improve their minds with Samuel Smiles.'

'Phina! That's so pompous and on more than one front. I am shocked and surprised at you.'

'These are not my own words, Ambrosia. I merely repeat Father. But I do agree with him.'

Our discussion was interrupted by a sudden shouting. A scruffy man was standing, jittering and gibbering in the road just by us. He was right in the path of an on-coming horse and cab. He had a mad smile on his face, almost demonic. The cab driver was showing no signs of slowing the horse or taking evasive action. Passers-by were screaming at the man to get out of the way. But he seemed frozen to the very spot.

I sprang forward, grabbed the man's arm and pulled him onto the pavement. It was then I realised he was crying, shaking and it seemed as if he was trying to say something to me. I took him to a stone step and guided him to sit down. To my own astonishment, I realised I too was crying. Not only this, but I was holding the man's hand, stoking his knuckles and whispering endearments, just like I always did to Aubrey back home in Menston, especially when puss was out of sorts.

Phina's presence re-entered my consciousness, looming above us. She wasn't smiling. Her mouth was tight and tilting downwards at the corners.

'Phina, don't just stand there gawping and looking censorious. It's unbecoming. Go into the Library and get this poor man a glass of water. Bring it to me. Now!' I snapped.

Phina did as she was bid. Well, she disappeared into the library entrance, at least. At that point, a constable came up to me and said that I'd acted well. He thanked me.

'We know him, Miss. It's shell shock. Albert here was on the Somme, you know. Bright as a button as a lad, he was. But when bombardment hits a bloke's nerves, it's worse than losing a leg or an arm. You lose your mind, you see. I'll get him back to his mother's place. She has to let him out, of course. But, there's no knowing when he'll get an attack. And when it's on the streets – well, now you know, don't you?'

'Will he ever get better?' I whispered. I was still stroking Albert's hand. Albert's eyes were still locked on mine.

'He might or he might end up in the asylum, if he's considered a danger to himself, or to others. There's cruel people out there who say men like Albert are malingerers or cowards. But we don't know what they've seen – that's the thing. We go about our daily business, and we don't know the half of it. Best not to judge, eh? Yes, you did alright there, Miss.'

When Phina arrived with the water, Albert and the constable had already disappeared round the corner of Ladbroke Grove.

'Well. You've wasted my time, haven't you? I'll have to take this glass back inside. And look at your skirt. You're filthy. We can't be seen in a fine building like this with you in such a state, that's for sure.'

'A small price to pay, Phina, for a man's life.' I took the glass from her and drank the water myself. I needed it.

'So, you think you did the right thing? A heroine, eh? And how do you know he wished you to prolong his precious life? If I'd been left like him, I too would prefer to be crushed by a horse and cab.'

'Well, now.' I was too taken aback to muster a smart retort. The best I could do was: 'I think it is time to go home.'

That morning something had shifted between the two of us. I'm not sure if this ever happened to Holmes and Watson, although I do recall they had the odd tiff. True, we two cousins had never been close, but a chasm had opened and lava was bubbling up to the crater's rim. It was as if a smell of sulphur had hit me like a blow. I stepped away from Phina. She was certainly the personification of bad egg gas. I realised that I'd underestimated her. Now we were getting the measure of each other, sizing up, and the sum of it all was clear. We didn't like each other at all. Even in the cosseted world of women in Rania's apartment at Cadogan Square, resentments had been bubbling away.

I snap out of my reverie. My eyes are drawn to the Agnar Viking's wing. Consternation, a strange feeling, a sixth sense, a thought of flames. The Hindenburg noses its way back across my consciousness, the jerky newsreel images of the great airship on fire, people fleeing across the runway from the inferno.

At the age of nine I had my own zeppelin trauma. It was on an earlier visit to Cadogan Square. Mother had taken me to town. I have the most vivid recollection of the bangs, the crashes and sound of breaking glass. Screams and panic, but first there had been the throbbing. It was a strange, unearthly, positively eerie and oppressive noise, way beyond a hum. Sinister it was, and stealthy. I froze in terror at the dark, sly, sausage entity, the malevolent cylindrical shadow emerging over the London roof scape, the frantic crowd stampeding, women screaming and children squealing.

I was terrified and yet, in truth, transfixed; both repelled and intrigued. Strangely excited. People were rushing by, passing me, pushing me and pressing on regardless.

Then Mother let me go.

I was scooped up by a constable. He raced me to safety, cradled in his strong arms. Children of the quality were always saved first. Mother had lost her grasp of my wrist in the mayhem and I had been carried along by the crowd. She was distraught. We were reunited swiftly, thanks to the young constable. No harm done he said. And yet the zeppelin's shadow has haunted the landscape of my subconscious since that moment.

I feel a chill. I wrap a tartan blanket around my knees, tightly. I still find myself gazing out at the wing, trying to banish this fancy of flames.

Chapter 7

Decamp

More turbulence. The plane lurches. Where was I? Ah yes, making for Menston. Going home.

When Phina and I got back to Cadogan Square, I found mother packing our cases. We were returning to Menston the next day. An unexpected development. On the train home, Mother confided in me that she felt a prompt withdrawal was appropriate. Things were becoming increasingly awkward between her sister Rania and Uncle Robert. Mother had been embarrassed by some of the scenes she had witnessed. Mother quoted Benjamin Franklin's words on guests and fish beginning to smell after three days. Our position was a twist on this. Uncle Robert had been back just three days and Mother insisted that, for him, we'd both begun to smell.

'Perhaps he found us less smelly than he found his wife.'

'Ambrosia!'

I was saved from a scolding as my mother was overcome with giggles. I have to confess, it was wonderful to have her all to myself again. We had our carriage to ourselves too, so I snuggled into her. She seemed to relish a return to our old closeness. She stroked my forehead, and I might have dozed a little. I think she did too.

The Quest for the Clitoris was placed on hold. My own search would go on later, but not with Phina. Although we didn't know it, all our lives were in flux. October 1918 had witnessed the second great wave of Spanish flu. When Phina became ill, Aunt Rania rarely left her bedside. No nurse by nature, Rania somehow transcended her innate self-absorption and focused on her child as never before. Her attention turned to every detail of her daughter's care, every alleviation she could imagine, every small comfort she could provide, to try to reduce the raging fever, the pain, the girl's delirium. Even Uncle Robert couldn't fault his wife's performance. The period of Phina's suffering was short and intense. She died, and Rania crumpled. She gave in to grief and then she herself succumbed to the flu.

When I heard Phina had been taken by the Spanish flu, I tried to feel some sort of guilt. But I'd never actually wished her harm, and I could afford to spin some fond reflections of our earlier days, our childhood; those days before we began to know each other properly.

My mother hastened back to Cadogan Square to offer support and care. Mother would not take me. She was fearful I too would go down with the flu. Rania died in my mother's arms later that month. My mother was devastated.

Uncle Robert made the right noises and paid a lot of attention to the detail of the funerals of his daughter and his wife, and to the design of the exquisite mourning cards to commemorate their passing. Something simple and elegant for Phina with a daisy border. For his wife, a thick, embossed card in ivory with script in silver italics. And Calla Lily flowers, signifying rebirth and resurrection. Aunt Rania had always loved Browning, so Uncle Robert turned to *A Toccata of Galuppi's* for some apposite quotation. He chose:

"What of soul was left I wonder, when the kissing had to stop?"

His choice left Mother uncomfortable, but she believed it prudent not to protest.

Robert threw himself into his important work for The Foreign Office anticipating the Armistice, and thus appeared to place his grief on hold. That's how Mother explained his total composure. The Armistice was agreed on 31st October 1918. The following month he would be over in France for the signing in the carriage in the clearing in the woods near Compiègne.

For the first time in my life, I was stunned and overwhelmed by a sense of profound loss. Rania, my beloved aunt, my role model, my muse was gone. Who would be there for me, to school me in the true ways of women? I'd wanted to dress her, to become her. I'd loved her. More than this, for a little while, I was in love with her. What would become of me without her?

Shortly afterwards I began to find out that Aunt Rania had plans for me, even beyond the grave. The reading of her will would change the direction of my life. To me, she left her Parisienne apartment in Montmartre, its contents and a handsome sum left in trust until my twenty-first birthday. She also left me the portrait of Maud Allan.

Praise be to St John the Divine of Menston.

To me Christmas will always be December 1918, at The Mount. I was soon to be twelve. It was to be just Mother and me, and Nanny and Aubrey the cat of course. The Mount cocooned us from a troubled world. Even the pool froze over and Leda and Lilith looked decidedly underclad.

War was over. The Spanish flu still held sway, which kept unwanted guests away. Mother and I settled down to days of modest treats, seasonal celebrations and diversions. We had a tree and decorations, the first time since Father left.

The two of us ventured out of the grounds only to church, and, more memorably, to Forty Thieves at the Princes Theatre. We took the train to Bradford for this. I wore my new red coat, a matching muff trimmed with fur, and shiny, black-laced ankle boots. Mother wore full furs and a gorgeous winter fur hat. Her outfit was dashing. I always felt proud to be out and about with Mother. She carried all her outfits so well. As we left the Market Street Station, people parted on the pavement to let us pass. In the stores we visited, men would rush forth with chairs for her to sit. But back to the Princes Theatre.

The stars were Winifred Ward, Lottie Govel and The Brothers Obo, namely "The Popular Laughing Comedians". Mother loved The Brothers Obo. She started to giggle as soon as they appeared on stage. They were comical, but for me the real star was Miss Ward who made such a convincing Ali Baba. I loved the notion that a girl could be a boy, but still be a girl. Winifred Ward carried off the role with the swagger of a man, and the grace of a girl. Lottie Govel, as the loyal servant girl, was very good too, brave in the face of adversity, and Kamil the camel was such good fun.

We'd made quite a day of it. Lunch at The Great Victoria Hotel. Afternoon tea at Brown Muffs. The cake trolley never disappointed there, even with rationing. The drapery department commanded our full attention for at least an hour. The gorgeous bolts of material, the swatch cards for special orders, the patterns, the embroidery silks.

I have always seen colours like letters, some are vowels, some consonants. Their combinations make different words and create different feelings, emotions. To see the colours of the embroidery silks displayed together in their different shades gave me immense pleasure and joy. I tried to explain this to Mother, and she seemed to understand. Nonetheless, she said I was a funny creature, and stroked my hair.

Coming home from Bradford on the train together, a late supper and then sitting by the fire - I don't think I ever again felt so close to my mother as then. It seemed we were the centre of each other's worlds. This mood continued the following day, Old Year's Night. We brought in the New Year together, reminiscing about Aunt Rania, Phina, and how we'd probably never go back to Cadogan Square, but we would always have our precious memories. Mother was quite emotional, and I caught her mood.

Mother was unusually open. She said how she had loved her sister dearly, how Rania was different, not at all like most women. She was put together in a different way. She leant towards women. It was as simple as that. It wasn't as if she couldn't love a man too. But a husband had to understand that he would never be able to meet all her needs. Rania needed women.

Rania had not wished to marry Robert. Her resistance fanned the fire of his desire. He thought he could win her over, for how could any woman resist him. When he failed, well, that was when he started to bandy about terms like unnatural, or worse. Rania had been forced into marriage by her father. Robert was heir to a fortune. Rania never pretended to be other than what she was.

'It was not her fault, any of what happened. It is important that you know this Amba.'

Mother then confided in me that she had been increasingly anxious about Rania's interest in me. Whilst she trusted Rania, she was uncomfortable with the way Rania's eyes dwelt on me. She confessed she had worried every time we disappeared into her boudoir.

'In retrospect, I was being very silly. Perhaps I was just a little jealous of you both.'

I assured Mother than nothing untoward had ever happened. It seemed to be what she wanted to hear. How could I ever begin to explain.

It was that night I told Mother about Albert and my sorrow and sadness for those who had suffered during the war. In my mind, Albert had become more than the gibbering husk of a man I'd guided onto the stone step. He was an emblem for so much more. I confessed that I hadn't really thought about the awfulness of war until I met him, and had my strange encounter. Mother was surprised I hadn't shared this with her before. I explained that it was hard to put into words, but that I carried Albert in my heart, like a war wound of my own.

'Why, you know, I felt there was a change in you, my darling. Since our last stay at Cadogan Square you have become more melancholy, more thoughtful, a little more subdued. Perhaps a little less silly, although this is no bad thing in a young girl. If you can't be silly then, you'll never get the chance again.'

I bridled a little at "silly". Mother continued.

'This sadness in you pre-dated Rania's death. I'd put it down to the changes girls experience at your age. I know you have grieved so much for your Aunt too. You had a very special relationship. Oh, my dear Amba. You are so like her. What will become of you?'

I had no idea, but I did not wish to dispel the magical mood of these intimate moments.

Mother opened a bottle of Viognier in memory of Rania, Phina, and I added Albert. Mother poured me a rather generous glass. Then we toasted the future and to Father's safe return. Little did I know what I was raising my glass to.

Mother tucked me up in bed, sat on the edge, stroked my forehead, and kissed me. Aubrey nuzzled close. I began to drift off to sleep. I always ended my day with the prayer:

Lord keep us safe this night,
Secure from all our fears.
May angels guard us while we sleep,

I liked the idea of angels round my bed, taking care of me and Aubrey. I liked to imagine them with swords and long golden hair. This prayer was shorter than the Lord's Prayer too, and it seemed to cover the essentials. There was also the idea that we needed help through the night, but we could look out for ourselves during daylight.

I was just drifting off when I had a thought. Had anyone written to Maud to tell her Aunt Rania was dead? There had been an obituary in the Times, and the usual notices. But what if she hadn't seen them? I resolved to think more about this. I started to think about the right words to use. I had never even undertaken such a task and had no idea where this impulse had come from. Perhaps from Rania herself. A message from beyond. I made a resolution, my first. I would write to Maud.

And perhaps I should let Mr Crowley know too.

It was not a good Christmas and New Year for all. There was rationing. There were food shortages: flour, sugar, potatoes, margarine and even cigarettes, not that this last item would inconvenience me and Mother. There was unrest and calls for equal food, and the equal distribution of it. Be assured, we people of quality never went short. One way or another, we always got what we wanted.

But there was sadness throughout the country, irrespective of who you were. Few families remained untouched. Even though the war was over, the Horsemen of the Apocalypse still roamed freely claiming more victims through hunger and flu. Those soldiers who had been spared were not always welcomed back. Many would be trapped in the living hell of their bodies or their minds. Sometimes both.

Despite all of this, if I could have bottled this Christmas I would have done so, and I would have taken out the bottle every year just for one sip to take me back there, to my mother, and to The Mount.

Chapter 8

See, The Conqu'ring Hero Comes!

At the time, I knew my father would one day return, but it was clear from his letters and postcards that this wasn't imminent. Letters were sporadic. They appeared in battered bundles tied with twine. He was safe, somewhere, which was all my mother and I needed to know.

Early in 1916, Nanny had given me the new Stanley Kirkby recording of "Tell My Daddy To Come Home Again". I'd so loved the Titanic song "Be British", but even at the tender age of nine, this one was less appealing. Mother loved Mr Kirkby's baritone and Nanny admired the sentiments. But I preferred a household of women. I made a polite response but found it difficult to sit through to the end of the song. I digress. Where was I? Ah, yes, Father's return.

Father's admiration for Allenby shone through the clipped moustached lines of the latest batch of letters. Because of Allenby, the men were better provisioned, and the water allowance for each man had been substantially increased, a big thing in those parched conditions. Allenby was in touch with his men, wrote Father. He would always stop his Rolls Royce to give encouragement to the troops he passed, as he swept by the dunes, the rugged rock covered hills, the coast. When the Turks surrendered, the capitulating columns of prisoners spilled into makeshift barbed-wire compounds.

Father was heavily involved with making arrangements for the prisoners of war.

Our men were allowed, encouraged even according to Father, to do some sightseeing, especially to visit The Holy City. Jerusalem had been looted by the Turks, but the men were eager to go and see, to celebrate their salvation and to take in the sights. A unique opportunity, all hoped, for they prayed they would not be returning.

If I'm honest, and I confess this a little grudgingly, it was my father who lit the fire of my desire to travel. He wrote beautifully. Christmas 1918, mother received a letter in which he wrote of his own leave in Jerusalem. He'd left camp in the early morning and motored by military lorry from Ramleh to the Holy City. The route traversed the Plains of Philistia, wound up into the deep valleys and through precipitous mountain slopes. I recall he mentioned that the six miles an hour speed limit of the lorry was swift enough to lend great excitement to the journey. But then he was a cavalry man and distrusted this newfangled transport.

Father wrote that he was shocked to see gangs of female labourers along the roadside – girls and women of all ages breaking stones and rocks and repairing the roads. Syrians and Armenians, mostly, he said. The women stopped work as the lorry passed, their eyes locked on the soldiers. Some waved, called out, perhaps for help or water, he wasn't sure. For a man with a wife and a daughter, he wrote, it was particularly disturbing to see women used in this cruel way. Quite unacceptable.

Father entered the Holy City through the Jaffa Gate, by the Tower of David. He included a little history, but not too much to be tedious; names I knew well from church and Nanny's history lessons - Solomon, David, Joseph of Arimathea, Herod, Mary Magdalene, Veronica, Saladin and the Crusaders. Through Father's detailed descriptions, Mother and I followed Jesus to The Cross and beyond. Father's descriptions took us on a tour of churches, tombs, key sites of scenes from the Old and New Testaments. He brought it all to life.

Then it was onto Bethlehem in a gharry. Through the Valley of Rephaim, Father passed the small village of Bethor. He said he was following the route of the Ark of the Covenant when it was taken away from Jerusalem. He passed The Well of The Magi where the wise men, whilst resting, saw the bright star. This road was the old roman road which was rebuilt in 200 BC. He said it had been in existence since time immemorial. The very idea of this thrilled me.

I had followed my father's war through his post cards. I became familiar with Cairo: the grand stretch of the Sultanieb Palace with its tall railings and twin sentry boxes, guards on duty; the Pyramids of Gizeh – a tasselled camel caravan passing as the photograph was taken; the Sphinx so patient; the Badrachein Pyramid – I loved this one of the magnificent, stepped construction, the two donkeys in the foreground giving perspective, along with a touch of humility. There was one postcard of tramways to the pyramids. I marvelled at this. I imagined taking a tram to The Pyramids. The Kasr et Nil Bridge was on another, guarded by two stone lions sitting up on their haunches, perched on top of twin stone pillars. Mosques, palaces, hotels, the curious, domed tombs of the Kalifs, the palm-trees on the shore of the great Nile. Here there was grandeur. Here was romance. I would go one day. I promised myself this, and I did. I have stayed at Ghezireh Palace Hotel. I have even taken the tram out to The Pyramids, and I have taken my readers there too.

But back to those sepia postcards. Many featured The Canal of Suez and Port Said. I see them in my mind's eye;

the stillness of the water of the Bitter Lakes; a panoramic plan of the canal; a view of the canal from Port Said. Through the cards we follow a single-funnelled ship with three masts round the Tussun curve, and the curve of El-Guersh, along and into the port itself, past the Offices to the Company. Such grand offices, they were. There were views of the harbour, and even a dredging-machine. So typical of Father to send us a photograph of a dredging machine. But he was always intrigued by such things, the way things worked, the way things kept on working.

We saw the Quay with its lighter local craft, the docks, and the imposing statue of Ferdinand de Lesseps, father of The Canal. There was a card of the Square of Ferdinand de Lesseps. One card called High Water showed a view of the town with local people standing thigh deep. Why they were standing in the canal isn't clear, unless again, to give us a clue about the depth.

The fine buildings on The Street of Commerce show the prosperity of the town, two or three storeys, elaborate wrought iron balconies, sign boards in French. The native quarter was much more humble and homely. Onto Ishmailia, with the floodgate downwards featured; Kantara village, and The Fountain of Moses. As a young girl I devoured these images, made up stories of my adventures to come. These were so much more to my taste than the postcard of the massed troops assembled in front of the Moustapha Pacha Barracks.

In retrospect, I realise Father had written so little about his life as a soldier, battles, hardships and death. Perhaps this was because of the army censorship rules. But I believe he was trying to spare us, or to spare himself. All three probably, but he wrote about places and people so beautifully that Mother and I never questioned this at the time. We were privileged to travel in his footsteps.

To me it was as if Father was on a long holiday trip. It was only when he came home to Menston that Mother and I realised what was stored up inside, and I don't mean just the tapeworm. That's when he became obsessed with reliving the battles, especially the Battle of Megiddo.

Father's last card was mailed from Salonika. He was on his way home. Mother said that he could even be as close as Naples by the time we received it.

I watched the clouds skim over the sun, and the lake at The Mount darken to a gun metal grey. I preferred my father as a postcard from Palestine.

It was very early in the New Year, just before I went back to school, that something quite unexpected and unpleasant occurred. My mother received a letter from Uncle Robert. Mother read, then reread this. She poured us both a second cup of coffee before commenting on its contents.

'Well Amba, this is upsetting. I believe this communication from your Uncle Robert is vindictive.'

These were strong words from Mother, who was always reluctant to judge, and rarely roused to anger. She was now looking quite pink and tearful.

Mother gave me a potted version of the contents. Uncle Robert was instructing my mother to remove the portrait of 'that infernal' Maud Allan from his attic at Cadogan Square, before the end of the month. Failure to comply with this would result in its destruction. She then read out the conclusion.

'In short, the attic is too good for it. I want it away from my home!'

'Do you think he's in "The Black Book", Mother, and the powers that be are coming to look for evidence?'

'Good heavens, Amba, what an imagination you have. No, I don't think that at all. I think he is angry with Rania and wants to expunge anything from the apartment that reminds him of her.'

'Do you think he will remarry, Mother? Perhaps he is afraid that his new wife will find Maud in the attic and suspect he has a past.'

'Again, fanciful. What have you been reading, Amba? The penny dreadfuls? But then, you never know. "Out of the mouths of babes and angels?" Hmm. You might be nearer the mark than I first thought. But it's barely two months since Rania passed. To remarry so soon would be deemed indecent, indelicate and unfeeling. People would talk.'

We both fell into silence. But then the urgency of the situation hit me.

'Mother, we have to rescue Maud for Rania's sake.'

'Well, we can't bring her here. Your father will have a fit if he comes home from Palestine and finds her hanging here. I know my brother-in-law shared information with your father about Maud and Rania that I would have preferred him not to have done. Your father came out on Robert's side. Of course he did. Men share these things you know. They close rank. Reputations once lost, are lost forever. Bear this in mind, Amba. Always tread carefully.'

'Can't we send her to the Paris apartment, Mother?'

'Dear me, that sounds an expensive solution dear. But I could make enquiries.'

'Mother, Rania left me a little money outside of the trust. I haven't touched it. Could I not pay for the transporting of the portrait?' I adopted my most wheedling tone.

'Dear one,' she melted, 'that won't be necessary. Leave it with me.'

Mother hugged me to her bosom.

'We both miss her, don't we darling?'

'More than I can say, Mother.'

Term began again at Leeds Girls' High School. This was the second term of my second year in the Senior School. I'd joined at eleven. My first year had flashed by in a flurry of new experiences. I wasn't used to attending an institution for I had had my beloved Nanny at home at The Mount. If I'd been a boy I would have been sent away to school, no doubt to Marlborough College, my father's old school. But this was considered a waste of money for a daughter, so I went to the local fee-paying high school.

The school had seemed huge and complex at first. I also had to get used to travelling alone on the train to and from Menston station to Leeds, a train line I learned to love through the changing seasons. The stretch around Kirkstall was my favourite, with dense woodland opening to the beautiful sweep of the River Aire, and the ruins of the Abbey. At this time, I was beginning to enter my religious phase, albeit short-lived, and I felt a life of the spirit spent in quiet contemplation had great appeal. I longed for a cell in a sisterhood, a community of women. I contemplated the sort of order that enjoyed a vow of silence, because some of my classmates seemed so silly with all their daft talk about boys and crushes. I could certainly learn to live without this.

Sometimes, in idle moments at home, I arranged items of table linen from the hot press to form a nun's headdress: coif, wimple and veil. I then adopted a suitably pious demeanour. I practised holy poses and made up tales about my piety, virtue and gift of prophecy. I admired my profile in my dressing table mirror. I concluded I would make a stunning nun.

The only drawback was the food issue. I combined a ravenous appetite with a refined palate.

Returning this second January, I felt much more confident. I was more familiar with everything. I felt I knew the ropes. The school's motto: "Do what you do" pleased me greatly.

It reminded me of my late Aunt Rania and her advice to me. Every time I looked at the carved wooden motto scroll, I smiled. I'm not sure the school's founders had the same interpretation of the words that Aunt Rania had. But the motto's wording was left deliberately loose, surely. And each girl must make her own sense of it.

Later in my life I became more acquainted with the words of Aleister Crowley. I found "Do what thou shalt be the whole of the law" enjoyed an uncanny resonance with our school motto too.

The school's four houses were named after the patron saints. I was in Andrew House. I thought this was the best one. I'd always liked the name Andrew. At the time, I didn't know that the year I came of age, I would have a baby brother, and that he would be called Andrew, Andrew Horatio Atha, my beautiful boy.

School life was quite competitive between the four houses in the arenas of sport, arts and music. My favourite subjects were art, literature, dance, drama, history, and geography. I applied myself to French too, with a greater enthusiasm than in my first year, for I was now the owner of an apartment in Paris. This I kept from the teachers and from the pupils alike. They wouldn't have believed me anyway. Mother always told me to avoid stirring envy in others. Keep your cards close, she always said.

I had become quite studious and spent a lot of time in the school library. I loved the feel of the place, the wood and polish, and the stacks of books. I stroked the mice on the Mouse Man's furniture. I was drawn to the travel section. They had such a fine collection of books featuring celebrated women travellers of the past, those plucky, wealthy women who tackled the great rivers such as the Amazon, the Euphrates, or the Zambezi accompanied by natives and serious luggage carried on a flotilla of light craft. There were travellers like Nellie Bly who travelled around the world in seventy-two days, Harriet Chalmers Adams, Laura Bingham and Gertrude Bell. Even Calamity Jane had a place in my heart. This was probably the influence of Aunt Rania again, because she just loved the wild west shows. She never missed one when they toured. She took me and Phina to see one in London.

Mademoiselle Mai our French tutor became quite close to me. She always found her way to my table to take lunch. We conversed entirely in French, as if by mutual agreement. She seemed fascinated by my passion for France and the French way of life. I quizzed her particularly about Paris, especially Montmartre. She was gratified by this for she was a Parisienne.

She was petite and yet comely, and quite pretty. I felt stirrings of affection, and I believe it was mutual. My grades soared. She introduced me to Guy de Maupassant and his short stories. We would sit together in the library in one of the small study rooms and I would read a passage to her and she would correct my pronunciation. Then we would discuss the story.

The futility of war as suggested by the Maupassant stories was a theme that made sense to me. I shared my reminiscence of Albert, and she told me of the loss of her brother. We sobbed in each other's arms and comforted each other. No-one was surprised by this apparent intimacy, for many pupils had lost fathers and brothers, and emotions at school often ran high. But this interlude did mark a turning point. I felt there was something quite bonding under the surface here, and I found it hard to resist the desire to kiss her, on the cheek, the nape of her neck, and on the mouth. But we had to be discreet and behave with propriety in places public. Miss

Lucy Lowe, our headteacher, was a stickler for propriety and seemed to have a sixth sense for any untoward goings on. The girls respected her and feared her.

Dance was a passion. In the third year, an additional end of school class was made available to girls who were interested in modern dance. This caused me great excitement. Auditions were held. It wasn't just a case of being able to afford the additional tuition fee, it was a pre-requisite that you were suitable. You had to be graceful, lithe and strong and not too tall, and not too small. As far as I could make out from the chosen few, you also had to be rather beautiful, or at least good looking. I felt privileged to be included. The teacher for this class was Miss Angela Devine. She was also our teacher for keep fit and had placed a strong emphasis on posture and beauty, as well as swimming. I had already shown I was a strong swimmer. The pool at The Mount, Leda and Lilith held some responsibility for this, as well as my nanny.

Miss Devine lived up to her name for me. We shared a passion for dance in the modern style. At the introductory session she had asked what we knew of this. I volunteered my enthusiasm for Maud Allan. Miss Devine encouraged me to say more and so I did. I even mentioned my Aunt's portrait of Maud and their friendship. Well, a potted version.

'There, girls. Observe Ambrosia's sheer enthusiasm. I wish I could bottle it and sprinkle it on all of my pupils. May you all come to experience what Amba already knows. See her eyes and how they shine. My goodness Amba, I never realised that those fine copper eyes shine green in the sunlight. And I hope your movements, and grace, can match your spirit.'

I recall one or two of the girls were smirking at this, but I smiled and fluttered my eyes at Miss Devine.

It was then that Miss Devine declared herself to be in the Isadora Duncan camp. I felt a little crushed when she said that Isadora had accused Maud of stealing her dances. Miss Devine continued, 'Modern choreography is such a hotbed. I find Isadora's complete freedom of movement compelling. She flouts convention, be it in dance, or life. She is Bohemian, you see.'

There was a pause whilst the group digested "Bohemian". At that moment, we all desperately wanted to become Bohemian too.

'Some would argue, and you might well be amongst this number Amba, that Maud is more than a mere student, or apprentice, of Isadora's. Some would concede that she has become a very strong contender for the title Queen of the Dance.' She paused, held my eyes, then went on, 'But then some say, Maud lacks the poise of Isadora. Others say she more than makes up for this with her pure passion.'

I nodded sagely. I had already been introduced to Maud's pure passion by proxy.

Then Miss Devine moved onto what we would need to wear to be part of her dance group.

'Girls, Modern choreography requires a garment that will permit full freedom of movement and flow, in short, a Greek tunic and sash. I will provide these tunics. You will be barefoot when we dance. As Isadora said, you do not play the piano with gloves on.'

There was a mounting sense of excitement in the group.

'At first, we will focus on skipping, running, jumping, leaping, and spinning to music. It will require a high degree of physical fitness. We will learn to breath and relax into fluidity. You must practise all of this at home. When you are better versed in the basics, we will introduce improvisation. This is where your creativity will be unleashed.'

'Will our group have a name, Miss Devine?' I asked.

'An interesting question Amba. Girls, any suggestions?'

There was a silence, so I leapt in. 'Something Greek, perhaps?' Then, tentatively, I added, 'Or, something to suggest freedom, or a casting of inhibitions.'

'Oh Amba! Well. We might be entering dangerous territory here. What had you in mind?'

'Divinity. You see it suggests that together we are a force that transcends human capabilities, or we have a special relationship with the divine. And you are Miss Devine, our teacher, so it's a nod to you too.'

'Oh, my goodness. Girls, what do you make of Amba's suggestion?'

The girls nodded with great enthusiasm. Who wouldn't want to be divine? And clearly Miss Devine was exceedingly gratified.

'Well girls. If you are to aspire to divinity, you are certainly going to have to pull out all the stops, aren't you?'

On the train home, I reflected, and not without smugness, that I had firmly secured my position as Miss Devine's favourite girl.

Dance class became my obsession. I loved the concept of expressionism, the triumph of spirit, and feelings over virtuosity. Improvisation was key. Inhibitions were to be abandoned. Dance should inspire and provoke. Dance was my new religion.

My dream was to dance naked outdoors. When I confessed this to Angela – we were, by my fourth year, on first name terms in private - she had a strange look in her eye. She said nothing for a while as if deep in thought, and then she leant towards me and whispered, 'Oh, you will do this. And you will be wonderful. And I will be there. I see you dancing on the seashore, like Isadora. Or through the woods, as a green woman, a spirit of the trees.'

For two years I was the lead dancer of Divinity. We

performed for the school, for exhibitions, for Arts Festivals. I felt I had found my vocation. Miss Devine entered me for a dance scholarship for advanced study at a newly opened, avant-garde, dance academy in the south. I was successful. My parents were called in to discuss my future and what it would mean for me in terms of lodging in London, and the future career possibilities. Miss Devine believed I could move on to a school for the art in Switzerland, or Dresden, to become a teacher of the new dance. The headteacher, Miss Lowe, had watched my development over the years with fascination, and she too was eager to enlist my parents' blessing and support. To be an exceptional dancer would reflect well on the school.

It was Mother who came to school to hear about my scholarship and successes. Mother knew how important dance was to me. She loved to watch me dance around the pool at The Mount. She was gratified to hear Miss Lowe and Miss Devine speak of my talent. They declared me to be in a class of my own. But mother was also a little reserved, cautious perhaps. She thanked Miss Lowe and Miss Devine for the wonderful support they had given me, but at that time, she explained, she could not give any promises, for she would have to talk it through with my father. It was at this moment I began to feel unease, a fear, a petrifying of my excitement.

It was the next day, mid-morning, when the raised voices drew me out of my bedroom, to the top of the staircase, where I lingered. I strained my ears to catch everything said. I descended very slowly, silently, and then sank down on the bottom step. An argument between my parents was a very rare thing.

'No! No! No! No daughter of mine needs to work. And no daughter of mine will prance about in public view like a common whore. A harlot. A dancing girl. Enough. Those women should not have encouraged her. They had no right.'

'But Ambrose, dancing is her life.'

'Her life has barely started. She is sixteen, for God's sake. What does she know? What will a scholarship to an expressionist dance academy do for her marriage prospects? Expressionism my arse. Exhibitionism more like. She's missed a strong hand during the war years. We now reap the consequences. You spoilt and indulged her. She may already be ruined.'

'What can you mean?'

'If she goes down to London again, she'll be off the rails in no time. Just like your sister. Bad blood will out.'

'How dare you insult my sister and my daughter in this cruel way?'

I heard Father clear his throat. He modulated his voice, softening it a little but the anger was hard for him to suppress. 'Kate, do I have to spell it out for you? Your sister indulged in unnatural practices. She was a lesbian. Surely this is not news to you?'

'Ambrose! You must never say such a thing.'

'As Brabazon so eloquently put it to parliament, lesbians have abnormal brains and should be locked up as lunatics or hanged. I can't say I can argue with the Lieutenant Colonel. Damned fine fellow, Brabazon.'

'You think my sister should have been hanged? What sort of man am I married to?'

'Robert wrote to me, you know, whilst I was still away – December 1918 it was. He warned me to watch out for similar tendencies in Ambrosia. He told me that Urania had exerted an unwholesome influence on our girl.'

'And you took his word for this? You took against your own wife and child? That man is poison.'

'Poison or not, he is a very perceptive person. Explain to me then, my dearest wife, the leaving of the Paris apartment to our daughter? What sort of abominations did our daughter have to perform with Urania to secure such a bequest?'

'Ambrose. This is despicable. We will not continue this conversation. Rania and Amba were close, that's all. Rania was Amba's aunt. A closeness between aunt and niece is anything but unnatural, and next to me, Rania was the only adult companion there for our daughter – those four war years. At the time of rewriting her will, Rania had just lost her own beloved daughter Phina. Who was she to leave her property to?'

Mother's voice was getting more assertive, more confident.

'Of course, Robert was going to resent Amba and make trouble for her. He wanted the apartment for himself, and presumably so did that new love of his life, Winifred, or whatever she calls herself. You didn't see this? And you didn't think to discuss his odious, insinuating letter with me, your wife? You just absorbed it as the truth, stored its contents away and harboured a simmering resentment against our beautiful girl. You just took his side! I can hardly believe it.'

Father might have been chastened, but he had to have the last say. 'No good will come of this bequest, mark my words. Paris will undo her, if she chooses to reside there. Heaven forfend! A tainted inheritance, if ever there was one.'

Father had cursed my good fortune.

Father had been wrong-footed by Mother's last argument. I felt proud of her. She had been brave and gone into battle on my behalf. It was a battle neither of us could win. I silently withdrew to the garden, and entered the woods. I wept copious hot tears.

Later, I dressed in my Grecian tunic and slipped off my shoes. I made for the lake. I danced a slow, mesmeric set of movements around and around the rim, gliding between Leda and Lilith, again and again. Both looked on in sadness.

In my mind I could hear Dido's Lament, "When I am laid in earth…"

I was oblivious to anyone or anything. Mother and Father came out and stood together riveted to the spot, on the veranda, both rendered half-fascinated, half-fearful, by my dance. Mother recalled later that it was as if I was a creature incorporeal. She told me of the interchange she had had with Father, as they stood together. He asked her what the hell I was playing at. Mother said I was dancing for the loss of my dreams, of hope, of everything I held precious.

Even when the rain set in, I was oblivious. I could not stop. On and on I glided. The rain became heavier. Father turned on his heels, military style, and made for his study, tutting "tosh" as he disappeared. Mother came down to me, scooped me into her arms and held me close to her whilst I sobbed. Not a word was exchanged between us. There was no need, so strong was our bond. She didn't even try to explain his position.

I knew it would be a long time before I danced again.

Chapter 9

Freedom on Wheels

I left school that summer of 1923. I had no plan. Plans seemed pointless – the things that make God laugh, as they used to say. I realise now I must have entered some form of mild depression. I lost my appetite, my bloom, my usual optimism. All gone. I'd entered a sort of half-life. My only solace was my painting. I favoured water-colours and pastels. I filled pads with visions of the pool, of Leda and Lilith. I tried to capture reflections. Reflections became my thing. I also loved to paint plants and flowers. Mother thought these were exquisite.

Mother was concerned about me. She did everything she could to coax me back to my former self. Even Father put a little more effort into engaging with me. As I attributed most of my miseries to him, I was hardly receptive.

'No daughter of mine will ever have to work.' How often had I heard him say this? I was sad and bored. But it is often at the times of despair that things do start to happen to re-engage you with life. My new raison d'etre appeared in an unexpected form. Where to begin? Perhaps with my seventeenth birthday present.

February 14th 1924 was a Thursday, as I recall. Father was unusually late going into Bradford, to his work. I came downstairs to a rather large, wrapped item propped against the panelling in the hall. Mother and Father came out to wish me Happy Birthday. Mother hugged me closely and kissed me. Father interrupted with, 'Aren't you going to open it then?' He was unsettled by shows of affection.

I began to tear off the wrapping paper. It was a bicycle. It was the Raleigh All-Steel Bicycle, no less. "Rigid, Rapid, Reliable." It had stout, knobbly Dunlop tyres and a Sturmey-Archer 3-speed gear. Attached to the frame was a ticket that proclaimed that it was guaranteed forever, along with a testimonial from one Reverend S. W. Bazalgette, who had written: "I have used the Raleigh daily through the recent wintry months and I feel more than pleased with my machine, for it has proved a real friend in need. It is the best I have ever ridden."

Indeed, a friend in need was just the thing for me. And friends appear in many guises. I must confess a quickening when I saw it, a sense of potential pleasures to come.

The bodywork was a glossy black. The bike had presence. It was a smart looking machine.

'Aren't you going to have a go?' Father was impatient.

'Ambrose, let the girl have her breakfast, at least.'

'No Mother. I want to try it now, please.'

'That's the spirit. Of course she does, Kate. Try it on the drive, before venturing out on the open road. Come on now.'

'Have a care, darling,' Mother called to our disappearing backs.

He led me out of the front door, helped me on and held the saddle whilst I steadied myself.

'You'll have to get your sea legs. But once you get the hang of it there will be no stopping you.'

I wobbled off. I got back on. I repeated this again and again. By the time I reached the gates of The Mount, I was smiling – the first time in months.

'That's the spirit, girl.' Father called after me: 'Try it further afield. I'll tell cook to hold the toast. See how you get on going down to the station and back.'

It was exhilarating. It felt like freedom on wheels. I loved the sensation, the speed, the fleeting verges, the breeze in my hair. When I got back, Father declared me a natural. I thanked him profusely. He allowed himself to receive a kiss. I think it was the first time he'd ever shown pleasure in something I'd done.

Over breakfast he handed me a second present. It was a book: 'Cycling for Health' by Sir Frank Bowden.

'This will put the roses back in your cheeks. And when I get home, we'll see if you need the bicycle adjusting in anyway, height of saddle, handlebars. I'll see if I can pick you up a bell in Bradford. You'll need to let 'em know you are coming.'

With this he was off to catch the train to work. There was a spring in his step too.

'Your father is excited for you, Amba. He's been in such a state over that bicycle. He feared you would reject it.'

'I love it, Mother. I'll be able to go out to so many places. I'll be able to ride out onto the moors and into the dales. I'll pack my sketch pad. When you ride along, well, it's just how I imagine flying.'

'Now Ambrosia, you must not be reckless. Be careful. I know what you're like. But first, go and get ready. I'm taking you out for birthday lunch in Bradford.'

'Brown Muffs?'

'No. An innovation. We're going to Betty's on Darley Street. It has been opened over a year now and I've heard such good reports about it. They say the chicken salad is exquisite, and the cakes are out of this world – petit fours. We might even take a celebratory glass of Viognier – but only if you promise to behave yourself on that bicycle. It was your father's idea, not mine. I was always told by my mother never to get on one. She said that the saddle, together with overzealous pedalling, could compromise a young woman's virginity over time. We wouldn't want that, would we?'

'Mother, I promise you I will remain virgo intacta forever.'

'Really Amba!' Mother tutted, but in a good humoured way.

'And you know what I've read in a magazine: "Cycling will kill the corset!"'

With this I breezed up the stairs, suppressing my giggles. Perhaps things were looking up.

But the bicycle was just the beginning.

Two weeks later, at the beginning of March, mother told me to smarten myself up for we were going to have visitors for afternoon tea:

'Mrs Rose is calling with her daughter Ida. Ida is just your age. I'm hoping you "gel" – as the young ones say now. You don't see enough of people your own age, especially since leaving school, and you are out so much on that bicycle. It is not good for a girl to be so solitary.'

'Ida Rose?' I repeated the name, with incredulity. 'She sat on a pin and Ida Rose!'

'Please don't be silly dear. How would you feel if she was at home this moment making fun of your name, Ambrosia Atha. It is wrong to judge a person by their name. It isn't as if any of us has much choice. It's all fixed up before we are born, or just after. No one thinks to ask the recipient.'

'But Mother, it is a silly name – Ida Rose – isn't it? She sounds like a floral counterpane.'

'Amba, please do not be churlish. You are really going to have to pull yourself together, to step away from the shadows.'

'I bet she's not my type at all. Where's she from?'

'The Roses are a good family - quality. They have just moved in further down the road, into The Gables. You remember old Mrs. Rowbottom who died? It's her place, God rest her soul. They have had to do a fair bit of work on it. They have come from the south. You should take Ida under your wing and show her the locality.'

'Under my wing! Mother, that's even funnier. Like Mother Duck and Ida Duck.'

Amba! You are so facetious! What am I to do with you?'

It was in this frame of mind that I descended the stairs to be introduced to Miss Ida Rose. Then all my silliness disappeared. What a vision she was.

How best to describe Ida Rose?

She was almost my twin in age, being born in late January 1907. She hadn't quite reached my height, being about two inches shorter, at five foot four. She was wearing a stylish, slim-line, light purple herringbone Harris Tweed skirt, revealing the couple of inches above her well-turned ankles. A rather dashing thigh-length, nicely tailored blackberry wool velour jacket, a cream silk blouse, plum leather court shoes, and a plum musketeer hat with a pink ostrich feather. Her outfit showed off her slim figure to real advantage.

I'm embarrassed to confess that I froze halfway down the stairs and stared at her in an impolite manner. Well-dressed though she was, it was her face that stopped me in my tracks. She had such refined features. Her brows formed two perfectly matched arcs. Her eyes were a pale fizzy blue, and well-lashed. Even the whites had a slight blue tinge. Her gently upturned nose was short and beautifully sculptured with a light sprinkling of freckles, and her lips were moist, slim and sloping upwards at a pleasing angle. They gave her the appearance of smiling even when in repose. Her skin was dewy, pale pink and even in texture with a rose blush to her cheeks, and her hair a dark gold.

'This is Ambrosia, Ida, but she will want you to call her Amba, I'm sure. Don't just linger there on the stairs darling. Do come down and say hello to Ida.'

Mother's words snapped me out of my evaluation of Ida. All I can really say from this distance in time is that I had never seen such a stunning girl. Later, in our increasingly intimate discussions, I would find out that Ida too was smitten from the moment she set eyes on me. But I'm getting ahead of myself.

Introductions were made. Mrs Rose was a pretty lady, probably eight to ten years older than my mother. Mother had wed at such a young age. Like Ida, Mrs Rose was well dressed. Her outfit exuded elegance, taste and money. She was wearing a smart, belted, winter coat – all wool velour - mid-thigh length in navy, with matching dress and an intriguing pair of spat-style lace-up ankle boots. Mother and daughter were both exceedingly fashionable. Cook described them later as "the cat's pyjamas", a phrase that intrigued me:

'Cat's pyjamas? Do cats have pyjamas? Does Aubrey need a pair?'

'No Miss Amba. Can you imagine trying to coax that big cat of yours into a pair of silk pyjamas? You and whose army? No, it's just something silly that people say. It merely means new and stylish, but I think it goes back to the last century.'

The four of us enjoyed our afternoon tea, and afterwards I took Ida for a walk round the pool, introducing her to Lilith and Leda. We shared enthusiasms, and it soon came out that we were both keen cyclists. Ida had the Swift Cheylesmore Ladies Bicycle – the 'all-weather' model – a present from her parents from the previous Christmas.

'Shall we ride out together?' I asked.

'Of course, we shall. You will be able show me the delights of this area. I've been a little apprehensive about setting off on my own, taking the wrong turn and getting lost. With you by my side I will feel safe and secure.'

As she said those words, she raised her eyes to mine, and I felt a tingling in the bottom of my spine. I felt protective and couldn't wait for our first excursion.

Our families were delighted about our new friendship. On our first expedition, Cook made up a picnic and our mothers waved us off, instructing us to take care and watch out for motor cars.

Our mothers had bonded too. The four of us went off on shopping trips, first to Bradford, Leeds, Harrogate, York and eventually to London. London wasn't the same without Aunt Rania. Mother and I felt her loss so sharply.

Before long, Ida and I had become almost inseparable.

That first summer together we travelled further afield, taking our bicycles on the train, and cycling all the way home. We loved the hills. We often had to get off and push, wobbling until we could stand the incline no longer. And we loved the sheer exhilaration of travelling downhill at speed.

I made so many sketches of Ida. It gave me an excuse to gaze at her for long periods of time. She loved them. I was beginning to fall in love with her.

One day we were caught out by a sharp shower near a place called Arnecliffe. We'd cycled down a beautiful valley to get there, by the River Skirfare. We'd cycled out from Skipton, passing under the intimidating crags of Kilnsey. We dismounted and took shelter under Ida's Swan Umbrella. This was always fixed to her cycle with a Terry Stick Clip. I confess I'd coveted it since I'd first spotted it. It put me in mind of Leda by the pool.

Anyway, we had to snuggle together to avoid the great globs of rain. We started to giggle at our predicament. Ida had a rain drop on her nose. It sparkled like crystal and it came into my head that I should like to lick it off. It was just too tempting. As my mouth neared her perfect nose, she must have imagined I was going to kiss her. She raised her face, her lips to mine and we shared our first full-mouthed kiss. I think it shocked us both. We gazed at each other. I'd like to claim that it was a chaste experience, but it wasn't. It was an awakening. We both knew we were entering uncharted, dangerous territory.

The next time we were together, it was as if nothing had happened. It was better that way. The close friendship of girls was encouraged, but not too close. I knew my father would be watchful, thanks to Uncle Robert's hateful letter. But Father couldn't control my thoughts, my dreams and my fantasies. At night, in my imagination, I showed no such restraint. Ida had become the measure of my dreams.

But a sixth sense warned me to take time and see how things developed. I was schooled for rejection. But our friendship deepened as time passed. We shared our joys and our disappointments, and our ambitions. We shared too our resistance to our families' desire to see us well married – but not to each other unfortunately.

I will move forward to New Year 1928. My twenty-first birthday was fast approaching, and Ida's was even closer. Mother came up with a proposal that thrilled both Ida and me. It seemed that Mother and Mrs Rose had been thinking of a suitable outing to celebrate their daughters' coming of age. Even Father agreed to it, a fact that I found surprising, given his earlier comments about a poisoned inheritance. The proposal was for the four of us to spend Easter in Paris. We would be staying at my apartment. Yes, my apartment, for I had now reached the magical age at which I could claim ownership and access my funds in trust. I was 'to host' the outing, as a young woman of means.

Mother had justified the plan to Father by saying that there were legal issues to sort in Paris, things that required my signature. Also, we needed to go and visit to check the property was being maintained according to Aunt Rania's instructions. We needed to assess any further maintenance needs and to organise some redecoration, and possibly some new furnishings – nothing too extensive, but she reminded him that places did eventually need a facelift. She also said to me, privately, that we would be able to oversee the hanging of Maud's picture.

I was surprised and delighted by this proposal and so were Ida and her mother. We set to planning a fortnight of delights – shopping, shows, galleries, the sights, delectable dining – oh joy unlimited. Would it be possible to see a performance by Josephine Baker, I wondered. I'd read so much about her. Seeing beyond the scandal and prurience, I sensed a rare genius. And she was only my age.

Josephine had first arrived in Paris in 1925 and joined the Revue Nègre at The Theatre des Champs-Elysées. She had danced the Charleston, half-naked and caused a sensation. This she followed at the Folies Bergère wearing her banana skirt. Here was a woman of style, imagination, courage and irrepressible humour. An icon and a rebel. She inspired the avant-garde artists.

Thinking about Josephine made me wistful. Could I ever have achieved such? I'd shared with Ida my disappointment about the abrupt ending of my dance aspirations four years earlier. Ida said she'd love to see me dancing fully naked. I was delightfully disconcerted by this. I promised her it could be arranged. I suppose we were both enjoying a form of flirtation at this time. Things would hot up soon enough, but not yet. And Josephine herself was on a world tour, so we were left with the anticipation of a future encounter.

As we sauntered through Montmartre, I remember Irvin Berlin's 'Blue Skies' playing over and over again – tinkling piano keys in the minor key pulling the rug from under the brave words of optimism. But I wanted to believe in bluebirds all day long, truly I did. For this first trip to Paris proved delightful. It seemed to serve as a taster to the future. Although we were under the care and supervision of our mothers, Ida and I both sensed excitement, opportunities, and greater fun to be had. It was all there to be experienced when we came back on our own, unchaperoned. We would be back, and Josephine Baker would wait for us. We both knew she would.

Chapter 10

Follow Your Dreams, Lady

My parents had commissioned a portrait for my twenty-first birthday. I was to sit for a reputable local portrait painter.

The artist, Reginald, was younger and more interesting than I'd dared hope. We spent quite a time in each other's company, and we talked in a free and easy way. He made me laugh and gave me ideas. He asked me what I was going to do with my life now I was about to come of age. I told him most emphatically that there would be no husband, and no family. My intentions did not lie in that direction at all.

'In that case you'll need something to do with yourself. What are your thoughts? What are you interested in?' he asked.

'I told him about my enjoyment in sketching and painting and showed him some of my work. Perhaps it was just politeness, but he seemed impressed. I told him about my father's intervention in my earlier dancing intentions. Reginald said that this should not hold me back, that I was old enough to live away from home and do some proper training. He said a young woman like me could be anything she wanted for I had 'the boldness, the brass and the brains.'

'Anyway, your father might have been right,' he said, 'for sixteen is very young. But twenty-one, the world is your oyster, as they say. Choose a subject and a place to study and leave home. Follow your dreams, lady. Go to London. Things are so different now.'

He paused and dipped his brush:

'Ever heard of the Women's Pioneer Housing? I know about it because my cousin has been involved in setting it all up. It's been on the go since 1923, but there's about forty houses for women opened now, mainly in North Kensington and Earl's Court. Rents are reasonable. The rooms are clean. There's a lot of women like you, middle class women. There are teachers, nurses, architects, lawyers and accountants. The professions are open now since that Sex Discrimination Act Lloyd George passed just after the war. From what you have told me you should go for applied arts: costume design, theatre sets, interior design or dance. You are a creative, I sense. So go out there and create. My cousin says they've even got a lady journalist as a resident, and a palaeontologist – a bone lady – who works at a museum. She's self-taught. Imagine that.'

My mind was on fire with possibilities. A lady journalist! A bone-lady!

'Hold still. Ants in your pants? What's got into you Miss Amba?'

'You have. I can't pretend I'm not excited.'

'Well don't leave home until I've finished this. I won't get my fee. Just sit still and think about what I've said.'

'I am doing. That's the problem. Oh Reggie, I could kiss you.'

'Restrain yourself, dear heart. Neither of us are that way out, I reckon.'

Before Reginald arrived, I was determined not to like the portrait, but I loved it. I still do. There's hope in those eyes and I'm smiling from the eyes and the heart. I look like a creature about to try her wings, ready to fly. Reggie captured me at that moment in time.

My parents were not happy about my scheme to leave for London. By the time I announced my intentions, I had researched my plans well. I had already secured a place on the course and a room in a Women's Pioneer House in North Kensington. I wasn't going to have Father put any impediment in my way. In short, I was of age and a young woman of independent means.

It was one breakfast time, shortly after the completion of the portrait. My father had returned to the marriage subject. 'We'd better try and get you a suitable husband, Ambrosia, now you are twenty-one.' He shook out the paper, folded it, placed it carefully beside his empty plate and cleared his throat. 'I've just been reading there are one and three quarter million surplus single women in the country at this moment. Imagine that. It's the result of the war, of course. So many fine young men lost. This means there'll be stiff competition for the ones remaining. And the sort we want for you: good family, decent income, prospects …'

'A leg on each corner,' I cut in.

'Amba, this is not helpful. Your father only wants the best for you.' Mother was looking uncomfortable. She knew we were heading for a skirmish. Father was glowering at me, formulating a suitable response.

I nipped in quickly. 'And what, pray tell, is a "surplus woman"?'

'You know very well what a surplus woman is. One who can't get a husband. One who doesn't have anywhere to live. One who has no visible means of support. They range from ugly spinsters and the widowed to the delinquent, disturbed and the sexually deviant, like your Aunt Rania, but without her resources.'

'Ambrose, please stop that. Do not speak ill of the dead.

Show some respect to me, too.' Mother was beginning to look tearful. Every time father and I argued, he usually managed to take a sideswipe at Aunt Rania.

'And which category do I fit into, Father?'

'You don't fit any, I hope. You are a rich, good-looking, intelligent, healthy young woman. Your only downside is your attitude. When young men come calling, you just watch your lip. At least try to seem charming. You could take a page out of Ida's book. She always seems a quiet, amenable young woman. I've never seen a hint of contrariness in her.'

It was at this point I decided to announce my intended departure for London. Father was beyond himself and Mother distraught. The next few weeks were a challenge, but I held my ground. Then we were overtaken by events.

Mother fell pregnant.

My father was ecstatic and could not contain his delight. He had prayed for this since my birth - a son and heir to the Atha fortune.

My reactions went through many phases. My initial response was embarrassment and mild revulsion. You never like to think of your parents doing the sort of thing that makes a woman pregnant. The bedstead cacophony had eased off of late so I couldn't imagine when the baby was conceived.

Ida summed it up succinctly. 'Oh my goodness, that means your parents are still at it! I just can't imagine mine,' she struggled for the right phrase, 'well, you know. Too gross for words.'

It all seemed inappropriate. And Mother, surely, was too old to be having a baby. She was forty-one after all – my age now, but somehow it seems older when it's your own mother. And Father was forty-six. It was a wonder he hadn't had a stroke whilst doing it!

To me, it wasn't just that it was unseemly. I was very

aware of the dangers to my mother's health and well-being. Childbirth was so hazardous, especially for the older mother. I was genuinely worried on her behalf. If anything happened to her, I thought, what on earth would become of me? Me and my father were too toxic a pair to be left together on the planet.

I was so relieved that I would not be around for these coming months. I know this might seem selfish, but Father's desire for a male heir had always upset me, and I knew he would be clucking and cooing over Mother then, should the infant arrive safely, clucking and cooing over it too.

And what would it be like for the household if it was a daughter? Twenty-one years had passed, and he still hadn't forgiven me for not being a boy. Heaven help the new baby if it was another "surplus" girl. No, I knew I was better well away from The Mount in the run up to birth, and the aftermath. I would just cause trouble for all concerned.

I promised my parents I would be back early for Christmas. Mother's due date was Sunday, December 15th. I would be there for the Christmas break and be on hand to help should there be any difficulties. In truth, Nanny was still with us and would take up her duties again. I assured myself that I really was superfluous. I sincerely hoped so.

In late August 1928, I packed my bags and left home for London to study fashion and design under Muriel Pemberton at The Royal College of Art. And what heady days were these to be studying fashion.

We design students were not at the forefront. The foundation stones of the clothes' revolution for women had been laid throughout the decade. We would build on the achievements of those who had come before. As Virginia Woolf pointed out, clothes were a symbol of something underneath. Fashion was the emblem of the emancipation of women. Freedom of style reflected the wider freedoms in society. We wanted to push things further.

Since The Great War, feminine curves had given way to a straighter silhouette. Corsets had been abandoned. Underwear had become lighter and offered few constrictions. Hemlines were rising and dresses were designed for movement and dance. Legs were on display and stockings were natural in tone, with a little added silk gloss to entice, perhaps to encourage, touch.

But these new freedoms should never compromise quality. I was totally committed to the fusion of craft and art. I delighted in exquisite fabrics: printed silk voile, velvet, chiffon, bead work, appliqué, embroidery, pure wool, fur, leather. I was learning how to work each fabric, and how to work fabrics together to stunning effect.

Strength, vitality, and youthful defiance were the order of the day, and I had plenty of these qualities. We were encouraged to take our inspiration from all over the world. Chinoiserie – Shanghai was the Paris of the East – Orientalist, mythical Eastern influences. I loved it all. Every morning I awoke with purpose and the anticipation of learning new things. I learned about form and flow, fabrics and colour, style and design, pattern and sewing. I was building my portfolio.

My ability to write, to articulate my vision, was recognised early by my teachers, and I was singled out and commended for this. I was encouraged to write pieces for the college magazine, about sources of inspiration that I'd come across. I loved to attend fashion shows and pick out the style that had made the greatest impression on me. I confess I had been particularly excited by Victor Margueritte's 'La Garconne' and I loved the Lesbian chic epitomised by Tamara de Lempicka – a liberated, cheeky, mannish and perhaps a little severe style. "Tamara in the Green Bugatti" was an inspiration. The thought of speeding up the drive to The Mount in a green Bugatti was too delicious for words.

Since arriving in London, I had taken to wearing my long, lustrous hair in a floppy, tweed, baker boy hat. I began to think my hair would have to go. I knew this would not go down well in Menston.

One day I wrote a semi-confessional piece about how I longed to dress women, and the beauty of the female form over the male. As I wrote, I felt the ghost of Rania take over my pen. I seemed to enter a trance state. It was as if I was twelve again and back in the boudoir at Cadogan Square. I began to feel quite warm, aroused, erotic. When I had finished, I read what I had written and was shocked. I could hear my aunt's voice in the words. I submitted it anyway and didn't think any more about it, until...

I was called in by my personal tutor to discuss the piece. She was younger than most of our tutors. I would put her at around thirty. She was pretty, fair and carried herself with grace and confidence. I'd been drawn to her from the start, and I was eager to win her approval. What would she make of my words. I hoped Rania hadn't got me into trouble.

I need not have worried. My tutor declared my essay to be excellent. She said I had a rare appreciation for the female form. She asked me if I had had help. I said not. To mention my dead aunt might have raised eyebrows. She then said that I had the skills for fashion journalism and should consider this to be a possible route forward. 'New, avant-garde magazines were starting up for women, and their editors would be delighted with the sort of pieces I was writing,' she said.

I said I'd bear that in mind, but first I wanted to understand all I could about fashion itself. She said that this was wise, and then she asked a bold question, one that did surprise me.

'Are you a lesbian, Amba?'

I thought for a moment or two and then I told her I was unsure, but that I had leanings and feelings towards women that I believed I could never hold towards men. Her eyes held mine and she thanked me for my honesty. She said, 'Now Amba and, by the way, please call me Imogen, never deny your true self. Heed your inclinations. Listen to your core being, and never quell your impulses. You are amongst women here. You are amongst friends. If you ever want to explore your feelings further, I am always here for you. You now know your way to my room. My door will always open for you.'

I thanked her and we shook hands tenderly, perhaps leaving our hands entwined for a little too long. Imogen leant over and brushed my brow lightly with her lips. I inhaled her warm perfume.

I felt the stirring of sensations in me that I hadn't felt since parting from Ida. But I also felt caution. My fantasy Ida would expect fidelity. But would the real Ida? And who knows who Ida's new friends were at the teacher training college in Bedford? And what freedoms and new intimacies was she now enjoying?

But I took hope from this interchange. My writing had been singled out, and I was the object of female desire. I found myself smiling all the way back to North Kensington. Try as I may, I couldn't help but fantasise how it would be to lie naked with Imogen. She was rather lovely, and, I reflected, she might be quite useful to me.

Chapter 11

There's Room In My Heart For You

Imogen had set me thinking. Fashion journalism was not something I'd ever thought about. At the time, one of my favourite journalists was Lady Grace Hay Drummond Hay. I was following her articles on travelling around the world in a zeppelin.

I find my eyes drawn to the wing again. I remind myself sharply that Grace was on board the Graf Zeppelin, and her journey took place nine years before the Hindenburg disaster.

Grace was the first woman to travel around the world by air. Reading these pieces fired my imagination and whetted my appetite for travel. Grace and Imogen between them sharpened my desire to write. I was beginning to see a way forward.

For me, Lady Grace was the epitome of glamour, a young aristocratic widow of wealth. She had taken a husband fifty years older than herself. I was never inclined to marry, but if marriage had been obligatory, I could see the merits of such a plan. A flag of convenience, a hands-off husband, and an income for life. Lady Grace's four stepchildren all older than herself might have posed a challenge, but what the hell. Conveniently, after six years of marriage Sir Robert, Lady Grace's husband, was dead, and she was free to make her own choices, most amply resourced. Journalism was her choice, and she wrote with wit, imagination and flair. Fashion and travel journalism could suit me well.

Two years ago, I read the report of Lady Grace's death. I was truly saddened. Grace had been interned in a Japanese camp in the Philippines. She died shortly after her release. Of course she did. To hold such a free spirit captive is to kill, even if death does not follow instantly.

Term was over. It was early December 1928 and, as I had promised, I returned home. The train journey from St Pancras to Leeds was a pleasant one. As I arrived at Menston Station the snow was just beginning to fall. It was around five o'clock and the lights were lit on the platform. The snow had already settled, and took on a pure blue tinge. I felt a quickening of excitement to be home. I arranged to leave my trunk for collection at the station office and strode off to The Mount.

I lingered at the gate at the bottom of our drive, looking up to our house. Snow silence. The soft yellow lights from our windows cast yellow patches on the smooth white gardens. The trees were bare, and snow was already perching along the branches. I marvelled at the beauty of my home, so unlike my London digs. The Mount looked quite enormous.

Mother was delighted to see me. I was surprised at her size, so full a form I had not anticipated. She looked radiant, quite flushed in fact. Her eyes shone. I complimented her.

'Well, I'm due in a week. Baby could come anytime now. He kicks so.'

'He?' I gave her a quizzical look.

'Everyone says so. I'm carrying baby all on the front. It was different with you. I was so much broader in the beam.'

A little snow flecked my father's moustache as he bent down to kiss me. 'Well, what do you think to my beautiful wife?'

'Mother is as stately as a galleon in full sail. I don't think I've ever seen her looking so well.'

'Well, never mind how I look,' said mother. 'I am ravenous. As soon as you are ready, Ambrose, I'll ask Cook to serve. Amba must be famished too. I bet you haven't eaten since you left London, my dear.'

This wasn't entirely true, but I was basking in my mother's concern.

Next morning, Father left early for Bradford. I was getting myself dressed when I heard my mother calling from the lavatory. Her waters had broken. I was to summon Nanny, Cook and Doctor Gilbert. Labour had begun.

Cook appeared with towels, a bowl and a boiled kettle. Nothing ever ruffled her. 'I knew Baby was due when I saw your mother polish off those braised kidneys last night. She had that there look. It's not like your mother to wipe her plate with bread and to call for seconds.'

'But they were so delicious, I did the same.'

'You are as skinny as a lath, young lady. They won't have been feeding you down there.'

Nanny took command of the situation, mother pushed, and I held her left hand, and Cook the right. Nanny issued instructions to my mother as to when to breathe, when to pant, and when to push. The pulse of events quickened.

First the baby's enormous head.

'It's a very red head. Is it alright?'

'You'd have a red head Miss Amba if you'd just pushed your way down the birth canal. It's many years since you blazed the trail. Keep holding your mother up, support her, start encouraging her and stop peeking.'

'Well, is it a girl?'

'Wait, Miss. You'll have to wait till it's popped out proper! We can't see its private parts yet. It's too soon to tell.'

I had the distinct impression Nanny was scolding me for impatience.

The baby arrived in record time, beating Dr Gilbert to The Mount. The doctor burst into the room just as baby took its first gasp of air, then let out an ear-piercing scream.'

'Nothing wrong with the lungs, that's for sure. So, what's the score?' demanded Doctor Gilbert.

'It's a boy, a big bonny boy!'

Doctor beamed his approval.

They'd placed the baby across my mother's breast. I will always remember the way she gazed at him.

I found myself so caught up in the moment and it took me many moments before I realised I was crying. My feelings were complex. There was immense relief of course, for my mother had survived. But I was perplexed by the strange feeling of kinship, the bond I felt towards this creature. I had a brother. At twenty-one years old, I had a newborn brother. I had anticipated I might resent the birth of a boy, but at that moment I felt only tenderness and delight.

Doctor Gilbert made his checks on mother and baby, and then departed. Mother was under instructions to rest. Baby was bathed and then Nanny brought the baby to me. She placed him, all wrapped up in his white crocheted shawl, in my arms.

I felt proprietorial. I nuzzled down onto his delicate, pointed crown and kissed his sweet-smelling brow.

'My baby,' I crooned, in a conspiratorial way. 'You will be my baby now.' I couldn't take my eyes off him. The look of him, the smell of him, the very feel of him – perfection.

Mother was woken to feed the baby, but then she slumbered on. The birth had taken it out of her. I made myself as useful as I was able. I swear at one point he smiled at me but Cook insisted it would just be wind. I still choose to believe that I won his first smile.

A message had been sent to father, and he returned home

early afternoon from the mill. When he entered the bedroom, he found mother sound asleep, and the baby slumbering in my arms. I stood and presented him with his longed-for son and heir. I watched him weep for joy. Me, I enjoyed mixed emotions.

'God has answered my prayers,' he whispered. 'Andrew Horatio Atha, my son.'

A male heir. Someone to carry on the Atha name. A tiny captain of industry wrapped in wool. Someone to inherit the mill, the factories, The Mount.

I smiled up at Father. At the same time, I was thinking to myself, I was the one who held him first, loved him first, and I would have him. Yes, Andrew Horatio Atha would be mine.

Chapter 12

Birth and Death

This was to be a special and most memorable Christmas. Andrew's safe arrival on 7th December drove the whole household wild with relief and excitement. I was caught up in the joy and the anticipation. Little did I suspect that New Year would bring treachery and tears.

Ida, home from her teacher training college, brought her mother round to visit my beautiful new brother. I placed the swaddled baby carefully in her arms and advised her to support his neck. I could have saved my breath. Ida was a natural.

'Your time will come girls,' said Ida's mother. Ida and I exchanged furtive glances.

Mother was recovering well from Andrew's birth, but her milk was slow to flow. On Doctor Gilbert's insistence we were supplementing Andrew's feed. Dr Gilbert had advised a newly introduced speciality formula milk powder. This worked well. Andrew had a voracious appetite and played fast and loose between bottle and breast.

Whilst Ida was holding him, Cook entered with his bottle.

'Time for his titty-bottle ladies.'

I took the bottle from Cook. It was a banana-shaped glass bottle with a rubber teat. I handed it to Ida who looked alarmed.

'But I've never fed a baby before,' said Ida.

I had already had my feeding and winding lesson from Nanny, so I gave a potted version of proper procedures to Ida. Again, she took to it like a duck to water – an eider duck. I giggled to myself at my early reaction to Ida's name.

I sat back in my chair and watched Ida feeding Andrew. The poignancy of this vision hit me hard. I tried to focus on the beauty of the vision and not think about the cruelness of our situation.

Like the baby Jesus, Andrew was showered with gifts. Father, rarely so superstitious, had waited for Andrew's safe arrival before he would allow Mother to order items beyond the basic baby necessities. Once he beheld his robust baby boy, he pulled out all the stops. A special order was placed for Ludo, a beautiful Sportiboy rocking horse from Lines Bros. This was a magnificently carved horse suitable for a toddler, or for his teddy. It was dapple grey with a flowing mane that reached mid-frame. Ludo had a red blanket, a stout leather saddle, stirrups and a very pleasing demeanour. Mother thought that Father should have gone for the next size up, but he retorted that by that time Andrew would have his own pony and be done with childish things.

Before leaving London for home, I had visited "The Finest Toy Shop in the World", Hamleys, on Regent Street, the "joy emporium" we called it. I remembered Mother and Aunt Rania taking Phina and I there when I was very young. I wanted a bear for Andrew. I chose a dark brown mohair jointed teddy bear by Steiff. It growled at me, but I didn't take offense. I loved it.

Ida had bought a present for Andrew too. It was a fluffy toy kitten - quite adorable.

'I thought about you Amba, and how much you love Aubrey. So I wanted Andrew to have his very own kitten.'

This was so typical of Ida, so sweet and thoughtful. Neither Ida nor I were aware that father had entered the room.

'One bally cat is enough for any household! I hope you are taking yours away back to London with you, Amba. Cats and babies do not mix.'

My first reaction was embarrassment. I was upset that Father might have hurt Ida over her choice of gift. I also felt uneasy about what he was saying, but dismissed it as being the result of his increasingly irascible and unpredictable mood changes. I responded breezily:

'I'm sorry father, but pets are not allowed in the Women's Pioneer Housing. Cook is eager to look after Aubrey.'

Father grunted and the moment passed.

A traditional Christmas at the Mount with a delightful, many coursed, Christmas lunch. Roast goose, prune stuffing and game pie. Cook had made a black chocolate, cherry and brandy yule log, with clotted cream. This was my favourite pudding. Cook liked to spoil me. It was set off with a light dusting of icing sugar and always topped with the stag rampant. I could never be doing with Christmas pudding. Then Wensleydale and Scottish oatcakes. Perfection. After months of inferior dining down in London, I appreciated this special lunch as never before.

The day before I left to return to London, I was in my room, preparing items for my case. Nanny was assisting me. I became aware of a commotion at the side of the lake. I glanced out of the window and saw my father on his knees, down on the rim of the lake. He seemed to be struggling to hold something down under the water. Cook had heard the commotion too and raced out, followed by my mother.

I caught a glimpse of grey. My heart went cold. I have never descended the stairs at such a pace. I bounded through the French doors and hurled myself towards him.

'Stop!' I screamed 'Stop, you cruel hateful man.'

Aubrey was being held under the surface; his paws were thrashing the water. He appeared to be holding his breath. I started to pull Father off by the neck. He swore at me and shrugged me off with great force. I staggered backwards and fell. Aubrey's eyes were flashing with terror. He was forced to take a breath and when the water flooded his lungs, the wild paddling of his paws ceased.

I crumpled and wept. My beautiful Aubrey, my childhood companion, my confidante, my solace, my faithful puss. My father stood up and regarded me with utmost contempt.

'I told you. Cats and babies don't mix. Cats lie on babies' faces and smother them. Everyone knows this. I haven't waited two and a half decades for a son and heir to have him despatched to Our Lord by your silly bloody old cat. I gave you the chance to take him. You declined. He was on his last legs anyway. I've done him a kindness.

'I hate you! You are an evil, vile man.'

'Take that hysterical woman to her room. She doesn't know what she's saying. If I wasn't holding this wet corpse I'd slap her face for her, talking to her father like that.'

This was addressed to Cook. Father was standing between Lilith and Leda with the sodden bedraggled body of Aubrey dangling down beside his leg. I lunged forward on my knees and grabbed my cat. I slumped to the cold ground and sobbed over his body. I rocked him as tenderly as a baby.

Father left the scene. He was complaining bitterly to Mother that the beastly cat had scratched his wrists. She followed, ever eager to tend to his wounds.

Cook knelt beside me. She took me in her arms and held me. I realised she too was weeping:

'It's not right Miss Amba. It's not for me to say but drowning that cat of yours is just not right. He was too old and arthritic to leap up onto a pram or cot. I've always looked after Aubrey since you've been down in London. He's started to sleep on my bed. I loved him too.'

'I know you did. I never imagined Father would do such a thing. Without Aubrey in my life, I would have been so lonely. He was always there to listen and to love me.'

'Oh Miss Amba, there wasn't one of us in the household who didn't watch over you and worry. We used to call you our girl on the stairs. Come. Let's go and find Douglas to get this poor old lad buried. We'll choose a spot in the flower bed. Oh my dear one, I am so very sorry. My heart aches for you.'

Cook lifted me and Aubrey and guided me away from the lake. Nanny joined us. She too had been crying. She squeezed my arm. Douglas found a wooden crate in the potting shed and had filled it with fallen leaves. We laid Aubrey out and placed some sprigs of the flowering Witch Hazel across him. The scent of sulphur was overpowering. I led our prayers for Aubrey.

The next morning, I awoke to Mother sitting on my bed. She was holding Andrew who was a picture of contentment. She kissed my brow.

'I am so sorry Amba, I don't know what to say. Your father isn't quite himself.'

We said our goodbyes.

I left for London without a word to my father.

Chapter 13

Kiss Curls

My project for the last term of the year took an interesting turn. We students were asked to come up with something original – the design and creation of a garment of our own choosing. Swimming for women was gaining popularity as a sport, and I was already a keen swimmer. I was inspired by Gertrude Ederle. She was my age, and at nineteen, three years before, she was the first woman to swim the English Channel, from Dover to Cape Gris-Nez. Through storms and swells she fought on, damaging her hearing to achieve her goal.

My proposal was a swimming suit. Imogen approved the idea. She said it was an exciting area to tackle and that she would be intrigued to see what I came up with. The project required a full rationale, along with a design, and a mock up product. She said that it was quite ambitious, but she would be prepared to help me with the fitting, for in a project like this, the perfect fit would be key to success.

I accepted her help graciously. Why ever not?

I described my vision. A garment fit for purpose, enabling freedom of movement, of retaining shape when saturated, a costume that would double as a sun-bathing costume and a swimming suit – suitable for either the French Riviera or the English Channel. Chic modernity, svelte and yet serviceable.

In the early twenties, The Jantzen Swimming Suit had revolutionised swimwear. But I wanted to take things further. I wanted more stretch. I wanted to reveal more flesh, more of the spine, more of a woman's thigh, buttock and as much of the groin as I could get away with. The modern swimsuit still had those silly little legs which I considered an unnecessary restriction, and unflattering. These legs ruined the line and made the average-sized woman look dumpy, too wide of thigh, and inelegant. I felt no need to nod to modesty. Freedom was the key.

I decided to take advantage of the new artificial fibres that were becoming available. A degree of elasticity would be essential. I had come across a new woven satin finish silk and elastic material. It was intended for foundation garments, such as girdles. I saw its potential for swimwear and got hold of a sample in a rather attractive oyster colour. I loved the idea of the wearer appearing naked on the beach or at the poolside. I enjoyed a vision of a sunlit beach with female figures all in different attitudes of relaxation and recreation, all wearing my swimming suit creation. A beach populated by seemingly nude female forms.

My creation would have to be tested by prolonged saturation in seawater. The garment must not 'give' but instead remain true to the body's form. No bulges, no sagging. Ideally, it would improve the body's contour by smoothing and supporting.

I devised the pattern with great care, cut it out, sewed it together, and then cut away some more.

I was ready to reveal my work to Imogen and let her help me with the fitting. I was eager for her approval, of course, but if it wasn't appropriate, I wanted her advice on a modification of my concept. Imogen invited me to call at her apartment on Saturday afternoon with my garment.

Two days before, Thursday, 30th May 1929, was the general election – the one we now call The Flapper Election. News was breaking the Saturday of my appointment. It was headline news. Women had got the vote on the same basis as men. My goodness, the celebrations we had at college over this. We were all smiling that day, and on the days to follow. It seemed to cement our power. Our world was changing, and the pace was quickening.

But I have good reason to remember this day for another significant, personal encounter. Perhaps it was the euphoria of the election result; perhaps it was the enthusiasm with which Imogen embraced my work. As the day unfolded, my own world shifted; it tilted on its axis.

We were to begin with afternoon tea, but Imogen felt the occasion should begin with a celebratory drink. She poured two pink gins. I was a little shocked for in Menston, and even at Cadogan Square, alcohol was rarely taken in the afternoon. Lunchtime, yes, and after six o'clock, but mid-afternoon was a departure. And yet a victory of such a magnitude required a little more than afternoon tea.

I had never sipped a pink gin before. Imogen prepared our drinks in pink cocktail glasses and presented these with boudoir biscuits on a floral plate.

'Let's toast the women of this country,' she said.

I raised my glass. Delicious, it was. When we had enjoyed our first glass, she declared:

'Come Amba, time to reveal all.'

She ushered me into her own boudoir – there was no way it was a bedroom – and showed me where to change. She directed me to go behind her embroidered four panel chinoiserie screen.

Visions of Aunt Rania flooded my mind. I removed my clothes and shimmied into my swimming suit. When I emerged, I found Imogen sitting back on her bed against a stack of gold velvet pillows. Her feet were tucked under her. She gasped when she saw me and sprang to her feet.

'Amba, this is the most incredible creation. I love it. How on earth have you managed to do this? This makes the Jantzen look positively Edwardian. Clever girl!'

She stepped back to get a better view, to take in the whole of me.

'Let me see how it works. Is it alright if I trace how you have styled it? If I get too intimate do say and I'll stop. But I need to get the feel of it against you.'

'No, please do feel the cut. I appreciate it is essential. I need to know if improvements can be made, and how will you be able to advise me if you don't get the full feel of the fit?'

I might have appeared the model of innocence, but, in truth, I loved her touch. I loved what she was doing. I stood silently and relaxed into her exploration.

Imogen's face was also a picture of serious intent. Her fingers traced the line of my buttocks, over the top of my thigh and down into my groin.

'The fit is excellent. How have you managed to get so far without assistance?'

She then moved her palms around my body, cupping my breasts and stroking my hips. She moved me over to her full-length mirror and asked me to talk her through my thinking.

This I did, referencing the features of the garment to my rationale.

'And do you have any suggestions to improve your work, Amba?'

She delivered this with delightful gravity.

'Yes, I do.' I paused and looked her directly in the eye.

'I think I need my hair to be cut short, to complement the look. If I am to model this garment, I need to enter the spirit of the whole. I need a tight cut. I don't want The Clara Bow Bob. I want to look like Josephine Baker. I want a proper crop.'

Imogen smiled:

'You are so right. Of course you are right. A close crop would look stunning. With your features, you could certainly carry it off.'

'Where on earth would I get such a cut outside Paris?' I sighed.

'Shall I oblige? I do cut and style the hair of my friends. I confess I have never done a Josephine Baker, but I have a picture of her in a magazine. You would have to trust me. And what if you didn't like the result?'

'I will absolve you of all responsibility, Imogen. Please cut my hair.'

'But first, my dear, another gin. We need some Dutch courage to do this, both of us.'

'Oh, yes please.'

'You must take off your costume. I'll get you a robe. We can't have hair all over your exquisite creation.'

I disappeared behind the screen to remove my handiwork. Her beautifully embroidered, gold silk robe felt seductive next to my skin.

Imogen had positioned a chair in front of her large gilt mirror in the hall.

'Shout if you want me to stop. Remember, I can't stick it back on. We'll have to take it off in stages. First I'll take it down to a long bob, and then we'll go up to a Clara Bow Bob length. At either point tell me to stop if you don't wish me to go further.'

I would not stop her.

'Leave me two kiss curls on either temple, that's all I ask.'

The sensation of her fingers working through my hair was

stimulating, gratifying, sensuous. She teased and tweaked the fronds and clipped away. I was trying so hard not to smile. But I must confess I was far from calm. I had this curious desire to intercept, to take her hand and suck each of her fingers. I resisted.

When she had finished, I gazed at my reflection and she gazed at me. She stroked my bare neck with tenderness:

'You have the neck of a swan.'

She ran her hand though what remained of my hair. She moved her hand slowly.

'Now, you won't get the best effect until I've applied the lotion, flattened your remaining hair, and teased the two curls. But first I must wash your hair. I'll run a bath for you.'

Then she led me to the bathroom and left to pour us another pair of pink gins. I lowered myself into the pleasingly warm water in her enormous roll topped bath.

Imogen insisted on washing my hair for me, what little there remained to be washed:

'Well, you must have the full treatment!'

I'm not quite sure how it came to pass, but as soon as she returned with the drinks, we both agreed this washing would be easier if she got into the bath too. She had already removed her clothes down to her chemise, so she didn't get too splashed. She slipped off the rest with ease.

I will not dwell on the rest of the day, that night, and next morning. In truth, I can't remember that much about it. Suffice it to say we reached a level of intimacy that would have surprised me at breakfast the previous morning, just before I had set out for the fitting, with my costume tucked underneath my arm.

In the early hours of the morning, I awakened. I needed the lavatory. Imogen was sound asleep beside me. She had left a small lamp on in the hall, no doubt anticipating such an eventuality. I negotiated my way carefully. When I got into the hall, I was astonished to see my hair in long locks still lying on the floor. It bore an unsettling resemblance to a nest of vipers. Moreover, the floor seemed to be on a tilt. It was at that moment I realised that I was probably "tol-hol". I hadn't appreciated the impact of pink gin. Viognier had never done such damage. I was now entertaining a profound headache, a raging thirst, but what was worse, I was feeling surprisingly morose.

'The piper must be paid.' I told my reflection in the mirror above the basin. I determined to fight off the dark cloud of gloom that had engulfed me. I would need Imogen on side and to be anything less than cheerful would be churlish and unforgivable. But was this strange gloom the price of several pink gins, or, I wondered, was it guilt? Had I anything to feel guilty about? I gazed at my reflection and resolved that Ida must never know of this encounter.

Imogen met me in the hall. She too was staring at the locks. Her eyes, a little anxious perhaps, met mine.

'Any regrets?'

I smiled to reassure her.

'No regrets at all.'

She took my hand, kissed it, and led me back to her bed. She wrapped her arms around me and I took so much comfort from her closeness.

Following breakfast, Imogen styled what remained of my hair. She applied the setting lotion and flattened my hair down to my head. When she had teased both kiss curls into place, she kissed me chastely on the forehead, and less chastely on the lips. She then handed me the fat plait of my own hair that she'd collected from the hall floor.

'Until out next encounter. Let it be soon, my sweet Amba.'

I nodded and then presented her with my hair in a gesture

of supplication. She held it to her bosom, as if I'd given her the sweetest of rose buds.

On my way home to my room, I troubled a little over this last interchange. Again, the perplexing question presented itself. What exactly had taken place between the two of us? I barely remember getting out of the bath. I recalled a sensation of being wrapped in warm and fluffy white towels. But what then? Had I been so inebriate that I'd missed a most memorable life experience? To carry the guilt without the sin would be quite insupportable. I refused to do this and decided to give myself the benefit of the doubt. There was no point in introspection.

I smiled and patted the back of my head. The neck of a swan is what Imogen had said. I gazed with delight at my reflection in the tram's window. Imogen had done a perfect job; a true Josephine Baker. And I felt free.

At the end of term, I was thrilled to be awarded the top score for my first year's project, 'The Swimming Suit'. And I was on my way home to see my darling Ida, my adorable baby brother Andrew and Mother. "My cup runneth over".

Chapter 14

Baby Face

'A woman's hair is her crowning glory! What the hell have you done to yours? This is a tragedy.'

This was my welcome home from Father. His face suggested cardiac arrest. Nonetheless he found the strength to continue, 'You have certainly blown your chances now. There will definitely be no marriage. You look like what you are – unnatural. No man will come near you.'

He executed a perfect clipped turn, then marched away from me.

Mother's bottom lip trembled. Her eyes brimmed.

'Oh Amba,' she whimpered, 'you look just like your father when first we met. Your beautiful hair, all gone. Oh no.'

Mother too turned tail to follow Father to comfort him. I was left in the hallway to go and find little Andrew in the nursery.

It would take four weeks for Father to speak to me again. If he needed to converse with me, he communicated through Mother.

But Ida's response was quite different. 'I want to touch it. I want to stroke it.'

And so she did, whenever we were alone and away from prying eyes.

That summer of '29 swam by in a soft focus of sweet

pleasures. Ida and I ventured further afield on our bicycles. We explored the moors and dales. We were so close and affectionate, and as tactile as the times and the north would allow. Close women companions were common because of the impact of the Great War losses, but too close would raise brows.

When we lingered nearer to our homes, we spent so much time with Andrew. Ida doted on him.

On rainy days especially we loved to entertain Andrew. By eight months he had become our bonny laughing boy. His character was already emerging. He delighted in the world around him and began to explore. He loved music and there were no two ways about it, "Baby Face" was his favourite. We had the 78 recording of Jan Gerber and his orchestra, with Benny Davis doing the vocal refrain. Ida and I always joined in, pointing at Andrew. We played this over and over again on our Columbia Cabinet Gramophone.

Baby Andrew soon learned the word 'more'. I devised dances to delight him. Ida and I had a special dance for Baby Face – an energetic sequence of movements. The routine that included elements of The Black Bottom. Then we'd go all out for the Precision Charleston.

One cooler summer's day Ida and I performed a new pool side routine. We placed our body's together, delicious, both facing forward and then fitted our arms into the sleeves of Grandmama's fur coat. Secured together we then embarked a jaunty Grizzly Bear – both taking the woman's steps. To the ragtime syncopated beat, we joined in the song by Irvin Berlin, set to the George Botsford music. "Hug up close to your baby" – never had the words been taken quite so literally. We certainly moved round the pool like a deranged bear. It was so hot in Grandmama's fur, and we were giggling so much, we were tempted to throw ourselves into the pool.

Andrew was squealing with joy and Cook came out to clap. Instead of the pool, we fell onto the veranda, which was as well, for the coat was an expensive model.

Mother too used to sidle in and watch the pair of us in action. She found it hard not to giggle. Once I caught Father watching. He'd returned home early from his mill. He appeared, torn between horror at us making an exhibition of ourselves, and delight that his precious son enjoyed this spectacle so much. It might appear petty, but it gave me great joy that Andrew could say Amba before Dada. There was so much for which I couldn't forgive my father. And what he did to Aubrey remained an open wound in my heart.

Ida loved to walk along with me, and our sweet babe propped up in his handsome baby carriage, a Silver Cross, of course. On fine days we attached a lace parasol. There had been no expense spared – coach built, springs to give a gentle cradle motion. The hood was reversible, to protect our little angel from the heat of the sun, or the sharpness of the wind or squall. Ida and I liked to pretend he was ours; our very own child.

'But this is the closest we'll ever get to having our own child. We'd better make the most of it.'

Ida's observation, true though it was, stung me. But I had learnt the art of dismissing disagreeable thoughts many years before. I couldn't find a response, but I can't pretend her words didn't trouble me. It was as if she had raised a spectre, but of what I couldn't then tell. It was as if she was reproaching me for something that was beyond my control, as if it was my fault I was not a man.

Always, when we were together, there was the desire for greater physical intimacy, but we held back, as if there was an agreement that we would wait for the moment of total commitment. Our love was too precious and too profound to squander on furtive and fleeting fumbling.

September came, and Ida and I embraced and then parted tearfully, each to our colleges. 1 was surprised too how difficult it was to leave Andrew.

Chapter 15

Sew Your Own Couture

The purser has been most attentive. He's approaching again.

'Would you like any refreshment, Miss Atha? Tea, coffee, a juice?'

'I think I should like a tomato juice. I thank you.'

Where was I? Ah yes. My return to London.

In the second year of my course, my focus changed entirely. Perhaps I was changing. The Depression was coming. Fashions were finally reaching lower middle-class women and even working-class women. I had never considered myself elitist, and now I wanted to work towards safeguarding the rights of all women in my own chosen area – women's fashion. I believed, fiercely, that all women should have a right to self-expression. Couture, the province of the rich, could influence everyone, even those who had little spare income.

I turned my attention to pattern design, the sourcing of beautiful yet affordable materials and home dressmaking. My studies focused on simplified pattern making with clear instructions, and my writings became a war cry for women to "sew their own couture."

Imogen recommended me to a representative from McCalls, the pattern company. This company commissioned me to design styles and pattern blueprints. I embraced this opportunity with a pioneering zeal.

The following summer I was thrilled to be invited to teach advanced dress-making classes at a local institute in Shipley. Someone influential at the Institute had read one of my articles in the Telegraph and Argus and had been excited by my approach.

I soon realised that I loved teaching. My reputation as a teacher spread and I found myself in high demand whenever I was back home in the north. Women seemed drawn to me. They said I gave them confidence.

My new lines of activity required me to keep up to date with the fashion scene and I made repeated pilgrimages to Paris. The fashion houses of Paris and their designers – Coco Chanel, Madame Vionnet and Elsa Schiaparelli – did not share my egalitarian outlook. Collections were exclusive and presented at clients only events.

One had to be there, and infiltrate. I could see a design and click it with the camera in my head. Real cameras of course were not allowed. Couture was a closely guarded secret. But, once seen, the image locked in my mind would be embellished, interpreted and improved. What the designer really meant was … and that was what I presented to the women back home.

After graduation, I turned to travel. I had lots of contacts through Imogen and a veritable support network. I had the means. It was important to keep abreast of the trends in the capital cities of Europe and the wider world. I loved tracking down beautiful materials. But my impulse was also to immerse myself in different cultures. I needed to know how people lived outside the rarefied world of couture.

I even managed to visit Shanghai – a most prosperous and exciting city and so important for fashion. I travelled to India, Nepal and Africa. It was during this period I followed in my father's footsteps in Palestine.

People fascinated me. How women dressed, traditions, cultural and religious factors and limitations, colours, adornment, concepts of beauty – there was so much to discover, and my pen teamed with ideas and impressions.

Then, when Ida graduated, we decided to celebrate and where better to take Ida than to my beloved Paris?

But here's the purser again, with a most generous goblet of tomato juice.

'Ice?'

"No thank you, but do you have Worcester Sauce?'

'Most certainly.'

He returns with the Lea and Perrins, and a small bowl of moreish cheese straws.

The juice is delicious. It often occurs to me that tomato juice is that rare thing – a drink that tastes better in the air than on the ground. There must be a reason why it tastes fruitier and more flavoursome. And not quite so earthy.

But where was I? Yes, Ida and I were bound for Paris.

Chapter 16

The Glow Worm

Summer, to me, will always be Paris, 1933. These were the best of times. These were the good days.

"'Si J'étais Blanche" – "If I were white" – sang Josephine. It was the song of the summer. The piano accompaniment rattled our bones in a most exquisite way. It rolled along the boulevards and curled through doorways.

Ida and I together, truly together as we had always wanted to be. We were finally alone. These were the days of freedom and fulfilment. We followed our instincts, our inclinations. We became as one. How could this be "unnatural"?

This is how it happened.

We took up residence in the 18th arrondissement, Rania's apartment in Montmartre, which was now mine. Well, on paper anyway, for I have to confess, it was still Rania's in spirit and there's no two ways about it, Rania's spirit still inhabited that beloved, beautiful space. Believe me, she was there with me.

By the time I brought Ida over, I'd already grown to love every inch of the apartment. It had a balcony over a grey cobbled tree-lined street, and you could gaze out over the flower markets, grocery stores, boulangeries, patisseries, bars, cafés and restaurants with their white and pink walls and red awnings. The people, the artists, the musicians, the writers, the forward thinkers. They were all there.

Ida and I hardly had time to unpack. We were off to see Josephine Baker at last, at the Casino de Paris – Paris Qui Remue – we were to see her perform with Chiquita the Cheeta. We had tickets; we had to make haste. We had waited so long to see her in action.

Josephine sang, "J'ai Deaux Amours".

Then it started. Drums. Her body seemed to unfold to the rhythm. I could barely keep to my seat. My own body felt as if it was moving with her. I felt the very pulse deep within me. I could feel it through my pelvis. Such fine big legs, such wide hips, such faces she pulled, such total abandonment. "The Ebony Venus", they called her, was sending herself up. She was sending us all up. She was shameless, so deliciously and totally without shame. She sprinkled just a hint of decadence and showered us with oodles of joy. She sent me into ecstasy. She glittered in my head – and long after her performance had finished. She glitters there now, just remembering her.

Afterwards, Ida and I dined at La Couple, that temple of Art Deco. Josephine entered with her companions. They sat close by us. I could barely eat. I could not take my eyes off her. What had she unleashed within me?

That night Ida and I truly become one. All inhibitions fell away. We tore at each other's clothes and explored each other's bodies. What we did took us both by surprise. But how could such feelings, sensations, knowledge ever be deemed unnatural?

Our first night of full intimacy was a frenzied affair. The joy generated by Josephine and the relentless drums pulsed on through our bodies. This was a night of casting off – our embarrassments and our clothes. We emerged from our chrysalids as butterflies. We gazed at each other, touched each other, breathed in the scents of each other. That night

Ida told me I smelled like newly baked bread. I must have expressed perplexity. She started to laugh and said it was her favourite smell on earth.

'You make me feel like a baguette,' I protested.

'Perhaps we need a baguette?' Ida had that suggestive sideways look that she had always saved for me, when we were alone.

For me, Ida's touch and massage in my most intimate recesses were enough to send me into the ecstasy of orgasm.

'Amba, why do you always laugh when I feel your clitoris? Am I not doing it right?'

I reassured her with a kiss, and then recounted my own earlier quest for the clitoris with my departed cousin Phina in the guise of Holmes and Watson. I outlined our findings – the key, the small organ, the bulb of the vestibule.

'So, it's evolutionary, my dear Watson. Eureka! I think I've finally found one: yours.'

'Elementary, surely?'

'Ida, my lovely, I suspect it's both. But you know, I don't think it's enough to dismiss it as a small organ or a little hill. "Key" might be more accurate, but I'm not sure. I think that what is on the surface is only the tip of the iceberg, so to speak. For once you start to work mine, the whole ground floor becomes alive, hot with desire, and this reaches right round to the postern door.'

'I agree entirely. I just want to swallow you whole.'

Ida's desire for deeply penetrative sex took me by surprise. At first, I was at a loss as to how to give her satisfaction in our love-making sessions. Inspiration comes in many forms. Let me tell you about the glow worm. There are two stands here, and these came together rather neatly.

Ida had become obsessed with science fiction during her first year at college. She had become an avid reader of Clare

Winger Harris and brought with her copies of *Amazing Stories*. Ida always read beautifully and introduced me to this new world. She read to me as I sewed, or painted, or just lolled languidly on the chaise on hot afternoons.

She read me tales about the *Menace of Mars* and *The Miracle of the Lily*. This was mystical science fiction and thrilled me to the core. Also, I loved the fact that it was science fiction written by a woman. Clare Winger Harris was a pioneer. She was the first woman to publish science fiction under her own name. Male territory. Many editors believed that women did not make good writers of science fiction because their grasp of scientific matters would be limited; that alongside the fact that their education would be insufficient. Total tosh.

These stories fired my imagination. I was in the mood for an alien invasion, excited by the very possibility. I even developed a way of speaking in a Martian's voice, well, what I imagined one would sound like. This made Ida laugh. She called me "half-cut". I used to tease her about her acquired grasp of the Menston vernacular. Again, I digress.

Then, early that first summer we got in with some artists and their followers. The artists were surrealists and dadaists. I felt I needed to know more about both movements. I delighted in revolutionary ideas, the fusing of the familiar with the unknown. Ida and I were particularly fond of a vivacious young girl called Adeline who was on the edges of the surrealist circle. Adeline was a fine artist in her own right, but although the surrealists loved women, it was as creatures of erotic desire, inspiration or for the elevated few, muses. Later, women would carve their own space as surrealists, but in the summer of 1933, they were relegated to the periphery.

Adeline invited us to meet Victor Brauner. He was a Romanian artist who had settled in Paris in 1930. He was living in a building on Moulin Vert Street in Montparnasse.

This place also housed Yves Tanguy and Alberto Giacometti. Victor was a few years older than me. He was intense, dark and brooding. I felt an immediate connection with him; cerebral of course.

Victor told me that his latest surrealist works were not well-received but that this would not deter him. He showed me his new painting "Le Ver Luisant", The Glow Worm. I was transfixed, arrested, thrilled and excited by this piece.

He studied my face and smiled. 'Je vois que tu comprends, fille anglaise.'

I nodded enthusiastically. I certainly got it. In a honeycomb landscape against a jet-black sky, an alien form from outer space, with a single eye was beaming into or sucking out the core a naked woman. The two-legged alien form was slim, long and pale olive green. A glow worm indeed. The woman appeared to have risen from her chair to see what was happening and was left powerless. Her hair followed the line of the creature's beam. She was caught in the moment of astonishment.

I too was left in that moment of amazement. I felt that quickening in my deepest core, my perineum. I always feel this in the face of great creativity. The Glow Worm's effect on me was both erotic and exotic. It continued to haunt my imagination.

One afternoon, after an anxiety that I had not quite satisfied Ida in our lovemaking, I was visited by inspiration. I leapt from our bed. I left Ida lying there. She embodied a curious mix of the languid and the insatiable.

'What has got into you, Amba?' She had begun to sound a little peevish after our sessions. I was sure she felt a degree of frustration.

'I have an idea. It's a surprise. You wait and see.'

I went through Aunt Rania's drawers and found just the

thing – a pair of kid leather mint green opera gloves. I cut both gloves off at the wrists, to be hemmed up later. It was the long arms of the gloves that were my immediate project. With the glow worm in mind, I adjusted the width of the prototype and styled a slightly bulbous yet smooth head. I stuffed the tube with kapok and then sealed the base. I ruched a rear cuff with lily petals made from the off cuts.

Ida had fallen into a doze. I opened a bottle of Viognier and poured myself a generous glass. Dutch courage. I then poured two glasses and placed these, with the glow worm and a dish of olive oil on the tray, or should I say salver.

I placed the salver on the bedside table and gently woke Ida. I did this through body massage, becoming more and more intimate. Ida was making sounds of ecstasy and arousal. I suspected she wasn't entirely asleep. I oiled the glow worm and prepared for gentle penetration.

Ida opened one eye. I smiled reassuringly and adopted my Martian voice: 'Permission to enter the vestibule requested, Earthling.'

'Granted, space traveller. Proceed apace.'

I encountered no resistance. The worm slipped into the vestibule easily. Now both Ida's eyes flashed open. She looked down at the glow worm and squealed. 'What the hell, Amba? What the devil is that? It's green – verdigris meets gangrene.'

'Whilst you rested, I have been industrious. The Devil makes work for idle hands, as Nanny always told me, Ida. This is my present to you. The Menace from Mars, The Glow Worm. You just lie back and enjoy an alien visitation.'

And she did, although she found it hard to stop giggling.

We celebrated the ensuing and prolonged ecstasy with a glass each of Viognier, still chilled but not too chilled, by the time she'd reached her climax.

'So why didn't you make me a pink one?' Ida looked almost

reproachful. She often adopted a petulant way of talking.

'Why should I? It's not a penis, or a phallus. It's an alien probe, a Martian's proboscis. Who says there are men on Mars? And anyway, I didn't want my creation associated with penises. I have only ever had two penis experiences in my life. One was in my mid-teens when, lurking on the stairs, I glimpsed my father's erect member crossing my parents' bedroom – with him in tow. It was as they prepared for one of their Sunday afternoon nap sessions. So gross – red, huge and taut. The other was something told to me by a fellow student in London. She recounted the tale about Nancy Cunard and Aldous Huxley. Nancy had such a brilliant Eton Crop, and some fabulous turbans. I digress. Nancy said that love making with Aldous was like being crawled over by slugs. Imagine that.'

'That's a horrible image, Amba. Well, they both are.'

'No, we'll have no truck with male members, agreed?'

'Absolutely not. Agreed.'

She kissed me passionately. Then she picked up the Glow Worm, pushed me onto my back and declared, 'Your turn now, Amba.'

What had I unleashed?

A few sessions later, Ida was beginning to feel a new element of dissatisfaction. It was during one of those sweet sessions of post-coital reverie:

'It's a shame.'

'What is?'

'You know,' she was smiling sweetly as she said this, 'that we have to take it in turns, that we can't come together.'

I reverted to my Martian voice: 'What, like simultaneous spontaneous combustion?'

'Precisely.'

There was no satisfying Ida. It could always be that little

bit better if… But she had set me thinking. The left sleeve of Aunt Rania's mint green opera glove was still nestling in my sewing basket, neatly rolled.

I devised a new model, a "dildo double". I cut into the sleeve then threaded my glovers' needle and set off with a neat saddle stitch. My new aid would be in three parts, two like the Glow Worm, for penetration, and a more lightly kapok-stuffed central section to form a linked bridge. My thinking was that this version would allow us to be joined in consummation. And the raised ribs and seams of this bridging section would lend some friction that could be additionally stimulating.

I completed my task and admired my work. I was excited by what I'd come up with, but it was by no means as aesthetically pleasing as the original Glow Worm with its sweet petal base.

More Viognier and olive oil. I presented the new version to Ida. We tested it immediately. I must concede it wasn't an immediate success. The insertion technique had to be refined. There was something quite silly about it all. But gradually, once we'd stopped laughing, we got quite a momentum going.

'I think we'll rub along together famously with this, Ida.'

'Amba, you are so ingenious. You should patent it.'

'I think the "dildo double" might already have been invented. I believe the Romans got there before me. In fact, archaeologists may have found such objects that may be even older – from time immemorial.'

That summer established a pattern for the four that followed. This was our time, our heaven on earth away from those who would judge us, separate us, or be disgusted by the way we were. This was our time away from Menston.

We two good looking and rich English girls soon found ourselves in a full circle of friends, privileged young, and some not so young, people who chose to live on the outer edges of conventional society. Americans, English, German as well as the French – bohemian types, political refugees, writers, actors, photographers, artists, musicians and people just like ourselves with the wealth and leisure to be there and part of it all.

Ida and I, we were known as les filles de l'été. I'd continued to cultivate my gamine look with my sharp shoulders, bob, heavily kohled eyes, jutting collar bones, and deliberately firm set jaw. Ida was softer, sweeter, so much more biddable, approachable and so eager to please. She was the perfect foil to my sullen, truculent and contained boyish pose. Father called it my deviant, delinquent and devious look. He loathed it. I loved it.

We were invited to parties, carried off in fast cars, and rarely returned before dawn. We drank too much of the green fairy, smoked Sobranie and learned to enjoy a touch of morphine. What visions that stuff induced. My passion for dance was unleashed by my excesses and, under the influence, even I could have let my hair down, if I'd had any. I danced on tabletops. Imagine. And my friends demanded more. I was good, but I wasn't anywhere as good as Josephine. No-one could be.

In our second summer together Ida and I already felt quite at home in the Montmartre apartment. We started to explore Rania's armoires. Racks of the most exquisite outfits were taken out, admired and tried on. My figure was similar to Rania's but I lacked Rania's opulent bosom. Ida was shorter and a little comelier than me.

The outfits recalled an era before the war, a time of taste and opulence. The influence of The Ballets Russes was clear – especially "Schéhérazade". There were even some Maud style pantaloons. Paul Poret's influence was clear. Rania was drawn to the column silhouette. I marvelled at the fabrics, vibrant colours and workmanship, and Rania's style and discernment shone through her choices. Gorgeous silks, pearls, rhinestone trims abounded. We even found a hobble skirt.

'This,' I declared, 'Is the most preposterous style ever. No woman should ever have worn such. You might as well tie the ankles together. People disparage the Chinese practice of foot binding, but surely this is similar if not worse. Both are, well, as the name suggests, they are hobbling!'

'So why were Chinese girls' feet bound?'

'Some male erotic business – men desiring women with little feet. It was all about obeying men, stopping blood and diverting the flow to the vagina.'

'Amba!'

'Well it was a fertility thing. Chinese culture is fascinating. I've more time for culture than quirks of fashion. This skirt is just downright silly.'

Ida insisted on trying it on and immediately fell onto the enormous Louis XV walnut bed, giggling. I took advantage of the situation and dived on top of her.

I'm trying not to smile too much at the memory. The Purser is almost too attentive and will bear down on me to see if I need something. Back to Montmartre.

Another day, when a heavy rain shower kept us indoors, we continued our explorations. In the base of Rania's bonnetière, below a selection of feathered hats, we found a locked wooden box decorated with exquisite floral carvings. We were intrigued by a small front brass plate. "The Teaser Box." Ida and I were determined to open it. We started to search for a key. We finally located it at the back of Rania's dressing table drawer. We poured ourselves a glass of Viognier each and opened it up. We were not disappointed.

What had Aunt Rania and Maud been up to? The Belle Époque indeed. At first we were too convulsed with embarrassed giggles to fully appreciate our find. Some of the lingerie would not have been out of place on the Rue Saint Denis. Clearly my aunt and her companion, or companions, had a taste for the erotic.

'This stuff is so rude!' gasped Ida, her eyes wide and seemingly innocent.

At first Ida and I felt very "Menston" and censorious. But on our second glass of Viognier, we realised we were being hypocritical, and so we each selected an outfit to try on. Then we began to explore Aunt Rania's own implements of gratification. These were quite different to my own creation, the Glow Worm. The greatest curiosity was the "Macaura Pulsocon Hand Vibrator". The instruction manual recommended it as a cure for female hysteria. It claimed five thousand vibrations per minute. The diagram indicated you should place the vibrator in the body whilst manually turning the crank handle yourself. Ida and I were incredulous:

'Do you think Doctor Gilbert ever prescribed these for his patients?' Ida asked. The thought of the women of Menston being subjected to the Macaura Pulsocon Hand Vibrator was too much to contemplate, for either of us.

'Cook has often accused Nanny of being a bit "cranky". You don't think she meant…'

'No!'

I draw the veil over further revelation, but suffice it to say, from that day, Ida and I were never at a loss when the rain kept us indoors. We called our escapades "dressing up".

Rifling through Aunt Rania's drawers for the key had also revealed that my aunt was a fully paid-up member of "Les Rieuses" – the Merry Women. This exclusive lesbian women's association had monthly meetings with sumptuous dinners from dusk to dawn, and heaven knows what else. I couldn't help reflecting what a force of nature Aunt Rania had been. Ida and I were still so inhibited about revealing our relationship publicly, we'd passed Le Monocle many times before we had the courage to enter. Aunt Rania had no such inhibitions. We drew courage from her memory and began to lose our own.

One outfit Ida found in Aunt Rania's wardrobe astonished and perplexed me. It was the Salome costume, including the harem pants sewed by myself, aged eleven.

'But Ida, how can this outfit be here in Montmartre? It doesn't make sense. Aunt Rania and I were working on this in early summer 1918. My aunt died in the autumn. The war was still on. I don't understand why it is here. This is so baffling.'

I took the costume from Ida and buried my face in it, hungry for any lingering scent of my aunt. My fingers traced the seams I had sewed as a young girl. I stroked the bodice, the pearl girdle and traced the contours of the pearls, jewels and paste gems. Scenes from the boudoir at Cadogan Square were flashing across my mind. I was lost in that past. Ida's voice called me back.

'Aren't you going to try it on?'

I shook my head.

'It wouldn't be right.'

In my head Aunt Rania was guiding my palms over her breasts. I could hear Aunt Rania's voice: "Amba. This is how it should feel. And again. Familiarise yourself with my form."

I longed for her. I was eleven again and I longed for my aunt. I longed for her body. Again, Ida called me back.

'But Amba, you could recreate the Salome dance, just for me. I should so like to see you do "The Dance of the Seven Veils."'

Instead, I crumpled, holding the costume tightly to my chest. I buried my face into it again and I couldn't stop the tears. I wept for Aunt Rania, The Peach Room and the boudoir. The sheer longing and loss overwhelmed me as if it were yesterday and not sixteen years previous. Perhaps I was weeping also for the child I once was.

When I returned to Menston much later that summer, Mother explained what had happened. It seemed that her sister was in Paris that summer on a short visit. She and Phina had accompanied Uncle Robert to the capital city. Uncle Robert needed to be there in his new role, for there were some clear indications that the war was coming to an end. Rania and Phina were to stay in Montmartre and Robert in an official residence. At the time of this visit the front line had moved further away again and the threat to Paris had lifted. Nonetheless, Aunt Rania was disappointed with her experience. There had been a sequence of strikes, food shortages, rationing and influenza outbreaks. Even Aunt Rania's favourite breads and brioche were forbidden – only large stale loaves were available, and so unpalatable, she had lamented.

Aunt Rania had written to my mother from Paris. Having described the living conditions she went on to complain that Montmartre was reduced, the artists, writers and "all the interesting people" having migrated to Montparnasse. She also expressed her anxieties about Phina, who she described as an unoriginal child. She regretted how very much like her husband she was – dull, dutiful to her father, and censorious towards her mother. "My God, Kate, I do believe she is embarrassed about me. Can you believe this?". Aunt Rania advised my mother to value me, a far more interesting and creative child, a potential bohemian if ever there was one. Mother was sharing this with me now, all these years afterwards.

Back to our summers in Montmartre. In retrospect, each of

these summers had its own special character. In the summer 1935 we'd taken to joining our crowd at Bricktop's nightclub, The Monaco. Cole Porter had a special table reserved there. No-one was allowed to sit at his table. It was said he'd written "Miss Otis Regrets" for Bricktop. I loved that song. Bricktop became Miss Otis when she performed it. The song of a rich woman taking revenge on the lover who deserted her was thrilling to me. Perhaps it was a premonition of what was to come. The pulling of the gun from the velvet gown was such an evocative, exquisite image.

The Spanish Civil War broke out in July 1936 and this brought a general feeling of apprehension to our circle of friends. The Nationalists, Franco's forces, were brutally repressing Republican sympathisers. They were executing intellectuals, artists, teachers and unionists. People were fleeing to France and friends of friends were joining our circle in Paris. They told us about the torture, rape and murder that was being inflicted on the people.

Polio, pneumonia and poverty still prowled across Europe, but still the party went on. Until it didn't.

In the summer of 1937, the shadows began to lengthen even more. I started again to taste the terror of the zeppelin. It felt as if something or somethings were closing in on Ida and me and that both, or one, of us would be picked off. This was the summer of Le Baron.

Thinking back to those times, our troubles were heralded by the abdication. On 11th December 1936, at one minute past ten in the evening, Sir Jonathan Reith introduced a live radio broadcast. We were gathered at The Mount. Ida and I sat together on the sofa. Father was in his large leather winged chair and Mother was perched on a more modest model.

"This is Windsor Castle."

The Prince of Wales, or, as announced by the BBC's Director General, His Royal Highness Prince Edward, was to address the nation. A drama. The prince wanted to be free to marry the woman he loved, a Mrs Wallace Simpson.

"It may be some time before I return to my native land."

As Menston, and the nation reeled, regretted, and mourned, Ida and I rejoiced. How brave and how bold of him to prioritise passion.

After this, Father and I locked horns repeatedly. His words about the prince were unprintable. My support for the man and his love were unshakeable. Tensions rose that Christmas. Mother and little Andrew kept their heads down. This latest locking of horns spilled over into the following months.

Wallace Simpson became our heroine, our style icon, our muse. Ida and I devoured all the articles about her. Perhaps I misjudged the mood of the times by writing a piece for the Telegraph and Argus entitled "Would Wallace have worn it?" It was a style guide, really a bit of fun for the New Year. It certainly provoked an avalanche of angry responses. The editor asked me to pen an apology to the readers. I wrote a guarded response. When it was published, I was dismayed, cross even, to see that it had been both heavily edited and embellished by the editor. The editor made it sound as if I'd capitulated to public pressure, been humbled and that I was full of remorse. I was none of these.

Father was beside himself with anger. I had shown my hand publicly. I had supported a man who had put himself before the nation. I might as well have aligned myself with the Devil. He declared he was ashamed of me. I had brought shame on the family, on the very name of Atha.

And I didn't give a damn.

But "would Wallace have worn it?" became my own touchstone to taste. And in Paris, no two ways, Wallace was fast becoming an arbiter of fashion.

The couple married in France on 3rd June that fateful summer, after the finalisation of Wallace's second divorce. Ida and I were thrilled for the couple. Shortly after their marriage, we saw them in the beautiful Bagatelle rose gardens. We'd taken morning coffee outdoors by the Orangery, enveloped in the fragrance of roses. There had been a short, sharp rain shower and then the sun emerged. It back lit jewel drops on the buds. Then there they were. We gawped and waved like two gauche girls. They acknowledged us, smiling. Wallace waved back and the prince blew us a kiss. I think it was the first and only time a man made my heart lurch. Except my darling Andrew, of course.

Just before we left for Paris, Father had finally decided to talk to me again. He was unhappy about our planned trip and begged us not to go.

'There's a war coming, believe you me. You don't want to be caught on the wrong side of the English Channel.'

Ida and I had giggled. What tosh, we thought. We should have heeded his advice, even though the war he so rightly anticipated would take another couple of years.

Chapter 17

J'ai Deaux Amours

More turbulence. The purser takes away my glass and plate. I check my lips in my compact mirror for any hint of juice or crumb. It is then that a dark shape surfaces from the recesses of my memory. Le Baron will not be blocked.

One night we were clustered with our friends in a bar close to the apartment. The music started. It was the snake charmer song, "The Streets of Cairo", sometimes known as "The Poor Little Country Maid" – how ironic. It was being belted out on the piano. Ida had demanded the Tape Worm story - for the hundredth time! Instead, I mounted the table and, well, I don't know what possessed me, I started to dance along to the music. 'This is the tape worm dance,' I announced. 'A homage to my father.' I enjoyed every move I made. My body swayed and slithered like a snake, and everybody around us convulsed with appreciative laughter, delight and cheers.

But something changed that night, I'll swear it. It was the first time I'd really noticed him. All other eyes were on me. His eyes were locked on Ida. She appeared oblivious, or so I believed at the time.

"Le Baron" was his nickname amongst our circle. It was his father who held this title, a member of the "hobereaux" – "the old birds". Those lesser members of the French nobility, with little land and lots of arrogance. His son had already inherited the latter.

The title "baron" had always made me snigger. It transported me to The Alhambra in Bradford. One pantomime included a character called Baron Danglers, who strutted around the stage with two balloons between his legs. It was lost on me for I was still an innocent, but was clearly very risqué judging by the restrained simpering of the ladies, and the roars of the men.

Back to Paris, one of our circle, an American called Tom, called this man Baron Hardup because he never stood a round of drinks. Later I would link him to Baron Danglars, from *The Count of Monte Cristo*, the greedy and ruthless character who only cared about his own welfare and good fortune.

When I'd finished my dance and retaken my seat, Le Baron made a slow handclap. He shot me a glance and sneered, 'A male impersonator, impersonating a female, impersonating a snake. How droll. How complex. How very confusing. How very, very silly.'

I was stung. Ida went pink with discomfort. Le Baron had a most unpleasant, knowing smirk. I looked through him and decided he did not exist. In retrospect this was a mistake. I should have watched him carefully from that moment on.

It was around this time I realised that I was becoming more frequently unkind to Ida. I think the hedonistic life had begun to take its toll on both of us. I certainly felt a dark mood descending. Most mornings, once we had risen, I would write, or try to, exploring some design ideas. Ida would leave the apartment, to shop, to enjoy the boutiques, and the markets. Sometimes, she said, she met our friends for coffee. She would return with something for our lunch. This pleasant pattern continued for the early weeks of our stay. Then one day Ida came back and said she had to talk to me. She seemed unusually agitated and serious.

I put down my pen.

'Yes? We can talk. What's wrong? Are you unhappy?'

'No, indeed I am happy. But something has happened, and I fear you are going to be very upset about it.'

I went cold. I got up from my desk and sat beside her. I attempted to take her hand but she pulled away from me.

'Ida, what on earth is wrong? It can't be so bad, surely?'

There was silence. I waited. Finally she had collected herself enough to say, 'I am engaged to be married.'

I sat and stared at her. I was incredulous. The enormity, the brutality of what she had just said was like a claw constricting my heart, and I found it difficult to breath. I was unable to speak.

There was silence, an empty space between us.

Ida spoke first. 'It's no good, you and me. I can't go on like this. I want children. I've had an offer of marriage and I've accepted it.'

I was immediately aware how English she sounded. I realise now that I was focusing on this rather than what she was saying, to delay the pain of properly digesting her words.

I am a proud person. I do not like to be perceived as a victim. Throughout my life I've hidden my hurts, and withdrawn. My heart was breaking but still I could not speak. I just stared at her. It was as if she was already miles away from me and moving further, and I had not noticed her go.

Finally, I managed to ask, 'Who?'

'Robert.'

'Robert?' I was incredulous. Could another Robert have been sent to blight my life.

'Robert, Le Baron, as you all call him. He loves me.'

'I love you.' I stammered. 'I've loved you since I first saw you from the stairs.'

'But listen to me, your love isn't going to give me a child.

We can't go any further. I'm truly sorry Amba, but this is how it must be. If I'm ever to have children, I need to act now.'

'Act? How appropriate. How long has this been going on?'

Now she was crying. My question hung for a while. She blew her nose, then, 'Since we arrived this time. I'd noticed him watching me. Robert and I, well, we've been meeting at cafés. He is so nice to me.'

'If I haven't been nice to you, I'm sorry. I can do better.'

'But you can't give me what I want. I want the life he has offered me, not the life we have. We have two months of the year properly together. When we are home, we must hide, pretend, deceive even our closest and our families.'

I remained silent. She blew her nose on her lace handkerchief, and then continued. 'He has an ancient château and a vineyard in Bordeaux. It has been in his family since the early eighteenth century. The castle overlooks the vineyard and the lake. It is a perfect place to raise a family.'

Anger, outrage, misery and disgust waged war within me.

'Does he know what we are to each other? What we have been? What I fondly and foolishly imagined we would always be?'

'No, of course not. You have to see, I want us to remain friends, you and me. How could that happen if he knew about us? He wouldn't want you to come and see me. He wouldn't want you anywhere near me.'

'Ida, perhaps he just wouldn't want you at all.'

'Amba, Amba, please, never, ever tell anyone. You wouldn't spoil my chances, would you? You could not be so cruel to me? You are supposed to love me.'

The room was tilting. The sands were shifting. The very chandelier started to swing. The kaleidoscope images of our life together spiralled down on a collision course with the hard ground. And I held on tight to the ruby velvet chaise longue. I sat and stared at the ornate gilt mirror and the green river gravel fireplace – "Verdi Marinace", the green seashore - such a beautiful intricacy of colour and shape. Rania came into my head. Was she ever thus betrayed; let down? This was excruciating.

I sighed heavily. I could not look at Ida. I was not prepared to make a proper response. My mind was trying to take in what she was saying to me, what it would mean, what it would mean for me. The foundations of my world had just given way. What was I supposed to say?

But Ida had not done with me. 'The thing is, I've missed my period.'

'What? You are telling me that you have been copulating with that odious man?'

'Amba! Don't be so crude.'

'You've let him fuck you and then come back to my bed?' My voice was thick with disgust.

There was a further silence. Then she spoke, quietly at first, imploringly. 'I've accepted his proposal, and he wants to celebrate tonight. He's hosting an impromptu party. Please, Amba, you must come.'

I imagined her eyes were imploring too, but still, I would not look at her. She continued; she was becoming relentless. 'For you not to be there, as my best friend, it would look suspicious. It would be entirely wrong. Please Amba, do say you will come.'

'So, I'm your best friend, in his eyes?'

'Of course. You will always be my best friend, Amba. Always. You know that.'

'I have to go out. I need to think. I need to take all of this in. It's just too much for me, too sudden, and too profoundly upsetting.'

I stood abruptly. She started to rise too.

'No, you can't come with me, so don't even ask.'

And I was gone from her. I made my way down to the Seine and walked for miles, or so it seemed, along the embankments, crossing the river at the Pont de la Tournelle. I took in the view of the chevet of Notre Dame and tried to pray, but the right words wouldn't form. Snatches of familiar tunes seeped from the cafés along the way and licked the ornate lamp posts. How could the beauty of Paris have become so tarnished?

I crossed back by the Pont Marie to the Quai des Célestins, lingering on the bridge and begging the river spirit to help me. I visualised L'Inconnue de la Seine, the unknown drowned woman with the serene face and perfect lips. She was so like Ida. In my mind I kissed those death mask lips. I begged her to protect us both. I prayed for our love to be kept intact.

Finally, exhausted, I returned to the apartment.

Ida was still there. Each time she tried to speak to me, I turned away. I remained unmoved by her beseeching eyes. I would not make things easy for her. How could she think she could keep me after such treachery. Let her go to him. Let her have her home and babies and her unpleasant, pretentious husband. It was over.

The night was warm and sultry. Robert came to collect her. I watched them out of the corner of my eye. Ida was flirtatious. I had never seen her like this. Was this my Ida?

Ida wore the simple, slinky, glittering silver sheaf dress that I had designed and made for her last birthday. She looked so beautiful as she left, it crushed my heart. I told her I would make my own way to the party. And I did. I was determined that I would carry myself with dignity. I wrapped my hurt like a wound and hid it from view. No-one would be allowed to draw satisfaction from my loss. When Robert made his announcement to our friends, all eyes swivelled sharply towards me, and I smiled with such grace and inclined my head as if in benediction. There seemed to be a collective exhalation. Then we toasted the happy couple.

That night I danced. I sank myself into the rhythms, or rather they penetrated me. The new song was playing. "Let's Face the Music and Dance" by Irving Berlin. Perhaps I drank a little too much, but no-one would have guessed the excruciating hurt I was quelling. The enormity of Ida's betrayal was hitting me harder and harder as the night progressed, but still, I would not crack.

It was much later when someone suggested a celebratory swim in the Seine. We had done it before, even though it was forbidden by law. Ida and Robert were eager. We headed off in the cars for our favourite bathing place by the steps. Night bathing is a bad idea at the best of times. Night bathing in the murky waters of the Seine was a foolish escapade, especially considering how much wine and absinthe we had all drunk. I saw Ida swimming out in the oil-black water, way beyond Robert. I stood on the steps and saw her crumpled, cast aside dress, the dress I had so lovingly made for her. I picked it up, smoothed it and folded it properly. Despite my resolve, tears spilled from my eyes. I looked for her across the water. There she was with her pale, perfect flesh picked out by moon light. I saw her throw back her head, laughing. I believed in that moment she was laughing at me. Then she was gone.

Robert turned sharply and screamed at us all.

'La sauver! Pour l'amour de Dieu, sauvez-la!'

I am a strong swimmer. I made for the spot where I had last seen her head above water. I reached the place, took a deep breath, and dived down. I dived repeatedly. Each time I broke the surface, the frenzied shouts, screams and sirens hit me like a hammer. I dived for the peace of the depths, I dived for solace. But did I dive for Ida?

Hearing the commotion, the gendarmerie had arrived. Robert, our friends, and divers from the force were desperately seeking Ida. I regained my breath and rejoined the search. By the time Ida was found and brought to the Quai du Louvre, attempts to resuscitate her were futile.

At first light, Ida's wrapped body was taken away to la morgue. The rest of us parted and went our separate ways.

I sat alone on the concrete steps for a while. There, next to me was Ida's dress. I rolled it up, tucked it under my arm, and returned to the apartment. I could not sleep. I kept rerunning scenes from the previous twenty-four hours, trying to make sense, to understand. Things had moved at a pace beyond my comprehension. Waves of grief engulfed me. I was too devastated to cry. I'd lost my love twice that day. Once to Robert. Once to the river. I wanted my mother.

A few lost days later, Robert arrived at my apartment. He asked me to help him with the arrangements to return Ida's body to Menston. I agreed to do this. Our conversation was formal, clipped you might say.

I packed up Ida's belongings, then my own, closed the shutters, moth-balled the wardrobes, draped the elegant furniture in dust sheets and locked up the apartment. As I boarded the night ferry train at the Gard du Nord for Dunkirk, and onto London, I didn't imagine that it would be nine years before I would return to Paris.

I travelled in a first-class sleeping car to give me peace and privacy. It was just as well. My tears fell properly for the first time. I sobbed. I had never felt so alone in my life. I couldn't even bear to be near myself.

Eleven hours later I emerged from my carriage onto the platform at Victoria Station. I'd cried myself out. From there, across London to King's Cross and then onto Leeds.

Poor timing, I reflected. The posters declared the new

L.N.E.R. streamlined train for the fastest service ever between the towns of the West Riding and London. The journey was to take two hours and forty-four minutes. Unfortunately, I was three weeks too early. My journey seemed long and tedious. When I finally reached The Mount, Mother and Father greeted me with hugs, sympathy, and much kindness. They treated my long silences with respect. My parents were there for me, listening when I chose to talk. Mainly I chose not to.

Shortly after my return, Father sat beside me by the lake, and rubbed my wrist with his thumb, in such a kind and comforting way.

'I'm so deeply sorry, Amba. I know Ida meant the world to you.'

I was surprised at this. I nodded and took his hand in mine and squeezed it tight. A rare show of intimacy between us. Strange, but I became conscious of the wood pigeons' calls. It was as if they were hooting, "I love you, Daddy." Once I became aware of this, I wanted to giggle. It seemed so outrageous, so very inappropriate.

The hardest thing was meeting Ida's parents. Mrs Rose hugged me tightly and wept.

'Oh Amba,' she sighed, over and over again.

When she calmed herself, she said I'd been a brilliant friend to Ida and how Ida had thought the world of me. But she soon introduced the marriage topic. I fought to keep my composure and set my smile. She said that Ida had written to her about Robert's proposal, asking them to come to the château to meet his parents, hopefully to approve her choice. The Roses had been so thrilled for her, so excited. They knew I'd have shared their enthusiasm.

I nodded my head bleakly.

But what she said next stunned me. She revealed that

Ida's letter had arrived a fortnight before her death. The implications of this, the full extent of Ida's betrayal, hit me like a wave. Ida had agreed to marry her Darling Danglers and kept it from me for days and days. Piecing together the clues, I realised that all our dear friends knew too. I was the last to know. My bitterness and hurt intensified. How could she be so duplicitous? So cruel?

'The pity of it, the sheer pity of it. Not only have we lost our beloved daughter, but we've also lost the only chance we had of becoming grandparents. Ida was desperate to become a mother. Before she left for France this last time, she told me that it was more important to her than anything, anything or anyone.'

This hit me hard. I thought of Ida's unborn baby. Of course, Ida's parents had no idea about her pregnancy, nor had Robert. I was processing this as Ida's mother delivered her next blow.

'You see, Ida's father and me, we were a little bit worried that you and Ida were too close. But now we know you were just very good friends.'

I felt so outraged at this. How dare she presume to know what Ida and I had been to each other. I looked away, perhaps a little too sharply. Ida's mother let the matter of our closeness drop.

We parted with a stiff hug. As I walked down The Gables' tree-lined drive, a horrible image came into my mind, an image I'd once seen on my travels. It was in a disused Benedictine chapel in Bavaria. The plasterwork had a curious image, a memento mori, a seated skeleton puffing through a bubble pipe. Part of a sequence of skeleton pieces, this was the one that haunted me. I thought of the fun Ida and I had had, blowing bubbles for my baby brother. I thought about this innocent joy, the fragility of life, and how quickly time and the choices we make can rob us of what we hold most precious. Death blowing bubbles.

I tried to surface from such thoughts.

It was a short walk back to The Mount. The words of the Cole Porter song played in my head: "Miss Otis Regrets". I think I might have been singing them out loud.

Ida's funeral at St John's Menston was a sombre affair. Few speak ill of the dead, but my own thoughts were far from kind. My tears were real enough, but they were not shed for Ida or her unborn child.

Robert did not attend. Later, Ida's parents were dismayed when Robert forwarded the invoice for the transporting of their daughter's body back home to Menston. The last I heard of him was from our Parisienne artist friend, Adeline. It was about a year after the occupation began. She wrote to tell me that he had been killed in France, although for which side he'd been fighting remained unclear.

Chapter 18

Come On, Amba!

I stretch. I love flying, but you do get stiff. I'm tempted to kick off my shoes and wiggle my toes.

I've dwelt too long in the darkness of Ida's betrayal.

Now I'm thinking about Andrew, my sweet young brother.

'Come on Amba!' This was his rallying call. Some scheme, some quest, some piece of childish idiocy, and I was hooked and raring to go.

It is hard to skulk in the shadows of a broken heart and a bereavement with a nine-year-old boy determined to haul you back to life. He was patient, but he was watching my every move, sensitive to each shift in mood. This boy was my salvation.

Andrew Horatio Atha became my sole companion and my confidant. Soon he became my new world. And he has remained so since. My brother, my boy, my dearest and beautiful Andrew.

Andrew has always been hungry to learn. He's looked to me for guidance, and I always wanted to shape him in my own image, and to pass on all that I had learnt in life. Why should Father have him? I wanted him to find his sensitive side, his creativity, style, taste, discernment, the very poetry within his soul. I wanted him to be a different sort of man to our father.

But basically, I wanted him to adore me to the exclusion of all others.

And so I set to work on him. In the first instance, I turned my attention to Andrew's education. In those early days, I assumed he would be sent away to Father's old school, Marlborough. I'd calculated I had two years before this would happen, but we could cover a lot of ground by then. And after that there would be the holidays. Yes, Andrew truly would become my creature. We would be everything to each other. And so we have been.

Mercifully, Andrew never went to Marlborough. Father changed his mind. I recall one breakfast when Father started to fume and rage:

'Damned silly scheme. How the hell will this work?'

He shook out the Yorkshire Post with some violence.

'They are intent on moving the whole of the City of London School into Marlborough. George Turner, The Master of Marlborough has come to an agreement with Francis Dale, Headmaster of the City of London School, that they will box and cox in the same buildings. Lessons for one school in the morning, and sport in the afternoon, and then vice versa. Damned silly scheme, indeed! I'm not throwing good money at that.'

Mother, Andrew and I rarely found ourselves entirely in agreement with Father, but on this occasion, we all managed to look suitably shocked, and we three nodded sagely.

As it worked out, the year before Andrew would have been packed off, there were initial negotiations to take the Marlborough site for the Ministry of Aircraft. These came to nothing, but Father used it as further evidence that it was right to keep his boy at home, and his money in the bank.

Instead, Andrew started to attend the Leeds Grammar School and travelled daily from Menston, just as his big sister had done before him.

Through Andrew, my grief for Ida softened, and my anger dissipated, well almost. To hold on to such poisonous thoughts would have destroyed my equanimity, my life and made me very ill. Of course, the shadows remained, the oily black river and what lay beneath. I consciously blocked that last day, those final moments. My Andrew had led me home.

Before the outbreak of war, the two of us embarked on our projects. Fun was the touchstone. Andrew and I agreed a programme of exploration. We began with the railways.

Andrew was obsessed with trains, so we planned an excursion to London on the new high speed passenger service with the sleek, green, black and gold A4 locomotive – the train with the sloping nose as Andrew called it. I was able to charm my way to getting Andrew into the cab before it set off. The glorious glow and heat of the coals, and the all-enveloping choking cloud of cream steam. How could you not catch the mood of the moment?

I treated Andrew to the full breakfast in the Pullman coach. We were going to see the Science Museum, and *The Good Earth*, the new movie about farmers in rural China. These were both Andrew's choices. I was surprised by the movie, but there was always something mystifying and slightly eccentric about Andrew's choices, and I suspected he might have selected it for me, knowing my passion for the wider world, other cultures - other ways of going on. We took afternoon tea in The Regent Palace Hotel's Rotunda Court, Piccadilly before catching the train for home. We passed through the Winter Garden vestibule, with its marble, palms and rattan chairs. I loved the place. It was so much less fussy and stuffy than the Ritz – far more democratic in spirit. Andrew was all mouth and eyes when the cake trolley was wheeled to our table.

As Andrew made his choices, I froze. A familiar figure caught my attention. Then I became aware that Andrew and the waitress were looking at me.

'And for your mother?' asked the waitress, pad in hand and pencil cocked.

'Amba is my sister!' Andrew laughed at the lady's mistake. This wasn't the first time it had happened to us.

I smiled: 'Cinnamon toast for me, thank you.'

As Andrew took in the lavish palmed interior, my eyes swivelled straight back to the man. I had to be sure.

This man was sitting at a table with his back to me. He exuded entitlement. The broad bent shoulders, too long at a mahogany desk. The excellent tailoring of the suit. The cloth of highest quality. The thick grizzled hair, greyer than I remembered.

Sitting opposite this man was a girl of around eighteen years of age. I turned my attention to her. She was on the cusp of womanhood, pretty but pasty. Her appearance was redeemed a little by the expense of the outfit. So, I mused, this is what Cousin Phina might have looked like if she had been spared the Spanish flu. Father and daughter. How sweet. How very touching.

'Amba, are you alright? Your eyes look angry, and you have gone so pale. Has something upset you? Was it the lady thinking you were my mother?'

'No silly. What's the saying? Someone just walked over my grave, yes? You know how it is, when you remember something that happened way back in the past that caused you displeasure and pain. Lots of pain and trouble.'

'Well, you're with me now, and these cakes are smashing. Get stuck in, as Cook would say. Would you like a piece of mine?'

This was Andrew's not so subtle way of securing a slice of

my cinnamon toast. Of course, I handed some fragrant and dripping toast triangles over to him. My own appetite had waned.

Andrew wielded his cake fork with enthusiasm. I nibbled my toast. It was sugary, buttery and delicious, but I might as well have been eating stale bread. My mind was elsewhere and working quickly. I was conceiving a plan. She who was not Phina, was making for the powder room. Opportunity beckoned.

I finished my cinnamon toast. Andrew was setting about his next bun, a very fancy fondant.

'Andrew, I'm just going to powder my nose. I shall not be long.'

A record was playing – familiar music from Adam Sandler's Palm Court Orchestra. It was Henry Geehl's *For You Alone*. A favourite of mine. I hummed along.

Inside the powder room the young woman was sitting at an ornate dressing table. This had elaborate salmon pink ruched skirts and emerald tassels. She was applying her lipstick in a self-conscious, unpractised way. I acknowledged her and she smiled sweetly. So artless, I reflected. I sat down at the dressing table adjacent to hers. We had the room to ourselves. I took out my compact and caught her eye in the mirror.

'I believe we are related, my dear.'

'Oh, my goodness! Really?' She smiled again and swivelled to face me. I continued, my expression slowly falling towards sorrow.

'Yes, my late Aunt Urania was your father's first wife.'

'Oh, I think I've heard a little about her.' It was as if a guard had dropped over her face, like a portcullis. She suddenly looked very uncertain.

'Hmm. Yes, indeed.' I sighed and adopted a confiding, "elder sister" demeanour.

'Well, I hope you had a good childhood. I hope nothing untoward ever happened to you.'

I looked into the poor young woman's eyes and smiled sadly, but as sympathetically as I could.

'You see, your father, my Uncle Robert...' I broke off, seemingly overcome with profound emotional turmoil, as if I was weighing whether I should proceed.

My wringing hands relaxed a little and crossed over my throat. I swallowed with effort.

She gave me a few moments to compose myself.

'My father? You were saying?' She nodded slightly, torn between whether she wanted me to continue, or not. I had certainly caught her full attention.

'He interfered with me. He came into my bedroom at night. I was eleven.'

I exhaled as if still in trauma, reliving those moments, but I summoned the strength to go on.

'His hands, that strange swan neck twist of the middle finger of his right hand, and that other thing, from down below. Horrible. He hurt me.'

It was as if she was paralysed. Her mouth was gaping. I noticed her lipstick was on her teeth, the ones that were biting into her bottom lip.

'Truly, my dear, I hope nothing like that ever happened to you. If you are ever a mother yourself, watch him near your daughters, their cousins and their friends. He is not to be trusted. I tell you this from the best possible motive - for their protection. Be on your guard. Remember my words.'

I placed my compact carefully in my handbag.

It was then that she found her voice. 'I don't believe you. You are a hateful liar. My daddy would never...' She trailed off.

I took no offence at this, just smiled at her sadly. 'Of course, if he has managed to restrain himself, you are the lucky one. Naturally, you will be angry with me. My revelation might come as a terrible surprise. What I advise you to do is this. Reflect on your own childhood. Ask yourself 'Did anything ever happen to me? Did Daddy ever do anything untoward?"

'No!' This filtered through her fingers. Her hand was clamped over her mouth.

'Of course, you might just have banished the memory. Blanked it. This may be how you learned to live with it.'

'Daddy didn't! Stop these lies!'

She was shaking. Her hands were now attempting to cover her ears. She looked quite wild.

Another exhalation. I shook my head. 'His infidelities broke my poor Aunt Rania's heart. I hope he has been more constant to your own mother, Winifred as I recall. I wish you well, my dear. Good day.'

I left her sitting at the dressing table. She was dumbfounded, trembling and in shock.

I noted the rather lovely shell lamps either side of the mirror – le style moderne – and how the soft peach light caught the tears pooling, then falling over her lower lids.

On the way back to the table I asked our waitress to make haste with the bill for we had a train to catch.

Andrew beamed when he saw me. 'Afternoon tea at The Regent Palace. The best thing ever, Amba! Wait till I tell Mother. She will be so envious.'

'I'm glad you enjoyed it, my darling. Come, we must hurry to the station.'

I gave the waitress a very generous tip. My brother and I had enjoyed our visit immensely, I told her.

Uncle Robert was looking at his fob watch as I breezed by his back. His daughter had yet to emerge from the powder room.

I felt a glow of satisfaction. Let the punishment fit the crime.

On the journey back to Leeds, Andrew was worn out. He soon fell asleep, leaning into me. I put my arm around his shoulders and held him close. It was a sweet sensation. I watched the fleeting fields, the skeletons of trees against a darkening sky. And then, as dusk descended further, I saw my face own reflected. I engaged eye contact with my reflection.

I must have dozed a little myself. I awoke with a judder. There looking at me through the glass was Ida. Her eyes were reproachful and full of hurt. I was filled with loss and longing and then, an overpowering sense of guilt and shame. I looked again and this time caught my own eyes in the glass again. I told myself firmly that this was the time of the living, not the dead. Ida had made her choice. I would not be stalked by her ghost.

This trip to London was the first of many adventures. I promised myself I would enjoy these and not be dogged by anything or anyone from the past. To see the world through the eyes of a child is to experience it again as new. And thus, through my Andrew, I was determined to be reborn.

Chapter 19

The War Effort

In that time before the outbreak of war, I felt compelled to travel again. I managed to visit New York and Peru. I avoided Europe and looked to the west. I suppose I finally heeded Father's war warnings. My choice of destination was a subtle combination of inclination, interests and instinct – or 'nose' as I called it. My fashion writing was a cloak for my more general curiosity. Was I seeking or fleeing? Without a doubt, movement and novelty helped keep those shadows at bay. There were times like now when I spied that patch of blue between the clouds, that patch of blue we call the sky.

Then war was declared in September 1939, the war that Father had been predicting for twenty years. How he'd always scoffed at the very concept of "the war to end all wars".

'Have I not said so all along?'

Andrew and I mumbled in acknowledgement of his wisdom. Mother was more loquacious, massaging his ego and applauding his foresight.

My travelling stopped for the duration. Even the Phoney War curtailed my schemes. At first, we called it the Bore War, because nothing much seemed to happen, but everyone prepared. The term the 'war effort' became common parlance at The Mount. Father wanted to know what I intended to do to contribute. I told him that we each had our callings, and

I would continue to help women dress themselves stylishly even in adverse conditions. Morale on the home front is as essential as wielding a gun, I told him.

I knew there would be clothing shortages. I had visions of women tearing apart, or rather, un-picking garments to re-style into new outfits. Ideas about reuses, recycling, remakes, twists and tweaks bubbled through my teeming brain and I wrote articles along these lines to prepare my readers. I urged them to discard nothing – off-cuts of material, thread, elastic, even sacking and linen bags. Zips should be unpicked and reused. Buttons snipped off, popped in a tin and then recycled. I suggested even the humble press stud might enjoy many lives,

My articles advocating thrift and frugality were months ahead of their time, appearing from the late autumn of 1939. At the time it was conjecture on my part because no-one had any idea of how long the war would last. I never imagined that even now, in the summer of 1948, clothes rationing would still be in place. Rumour has it that it might be lifted next year.

Early in 1940, the Government started to promote the need for recycling, rejuvenation and reconditioning too. Soon Government specifications would limit how much material could be used for any item, even down to how many buttons were allowed. Pockets were restricted, turn-ups abolished.

By the Spring of 1940, material shortages were starting to bite. Factories, including my father's, had switched from producing fabric for civilian clothes to uniforms. Leather was in increasingly short supply, and silk was unavailable.

In the April, Vogue embraced the noble cause and urged the readers to be ready to welcome home heroes on leave. "Beauty is a duty," was the rallying cry. The theme of the article was that, no matter what privations were being experienced on the home front, it was essential to make an effort with your appearance. Later issues would show models in utility suits with fitted jackets, knee length skirts and kick pleats picking their way nimbly through the rubble and the wrecks of bombed-out homes. They were such evocative images; romantic almost. They made me think about my own efforts to live again after Ida.

The Government wanted to keep the fashion industry going and brought together the cream of designers to devise the Utility wardrobe. Simple lines, minimal trimmings, austerity with creativity. There was a new emphasis on accessories. In 1941, CC41 came in to regulate and try to ensure good quality clothes for your coupons.

I designed a pattern for a siren suit, and it became popular. I like to think my design was chic, warm, stylish and easy to slip on when the sirens sounded. I realised that, for a woman or child, the key challenge of any one-piece garment was the necessity to go to the lavatory. My design was the first to include a toilet flap. Function and flair in action. William Morris's utility and beauty; the recipe for harmony.

I embraced the new rules. For me, excess was unpatriotic, and counterproductive to the war effort. The challenge for a designer like myself was exciting. I felt glad that fashion had become more democratic.

But how different things were in Paris under the army of occupation. I had heard from Adeline that haute couture was flourishing under the Nazis. How could this be? She wrote that one hundred salons had been allowed to stay open and that wealthy women in Paris, wives of collaborators, were keeping the industry alive. These people were enjoying luxurious lifestyles. The outfits designed and made for them were opulent and extravagant. Silk was still being produced in Lyon for the fashion houses. Imogen, my dear tutor, also kept in touch with me and she had mentioned that the trade links were still open for Parisienne haute couture to Scandinavia, Switzerland, Portugal and Brazil.

I found all these things shocking. I was hit by the contrast of the Utility approaches and styles of this country and America to what appeared to be happening in Paris. But this was not the full story. Surely, for the ordinary women of Paris, privations would have been as severe as here. And how dreadful to live under an army of occupation.

Thinking of Paris led me, as ever, to Ida and our summers in the thirties in Montmartre. I could almost taste the joy and freedoms of the life we had there. Ghosts. And I thought of The Glow Worm cut from Aunt Rania's opera gloves. I mused that this was an early example of the reusing for which I had become so adept. I thought of all those beautiful clothes in Aunt Rania's wardrobes, and how I could do with them, and what I would do with them. I wondered what had become of the apartment. Was a Nazi officer enjoying our bed? Had he found The Teaser Box?

Mainly, I remembered the innocence of our love, before we fell from grace.

Even our old heroes had fallen from grace. Rumours abounded about Edward and Wallace. It was alleged by many that they were sympathetic to the Third Reich. Was he a Nazi puppet? Edward had made imprudent comments in support of Germany's foreign policies, and had spoken out against the French, characterising them as impossible and impetuous. He had made anti-Semitic remarks, remarks that had fallen on some receptive ears in Britain. The Nazis regarded him as "half-German". Edward felt there was greater peril from Soviet communism, than from Hitler.

But thoughts, disappointments and resulting reappraisals such as these were fleeting. I could not afford to let myself linger on them. Our past would weigh heavily upon me, holding me down, stopping me resurfacing as surely as if there was a manacle clasped around my ankle. Such thoughts distressed me. I banished them for the sake of my sanity.

I return in my musings to the summer of 1940. Mother, Andrew and I enjoyed a rare day out. We went over to Manchester on the train to see Gone with the Wind at the Gaiety. Bliss. We made a day of it, of course we did. Father wouldn't come. The thought of a film lasting for three hours and forty minutes was an anathema to him. But we were desperate to see it. It wouldn't be shown elsewhere, outside London, until mid-Autumn.

How pleased I was to see Scarlet O'Hara cutting up Tara's green velvet curtains to style a new outfit. Needs must. I was able to weave this into my classes for women at The Shipley Institute. Make do and mend in action. Be like the beautiful Vivien Leigh. Dig deep and channel our inner Scarlet, girls.

Back to Father and his desire to know what I was really going to do to help the war effort. I sat there in contemplation.

'What can I do, Father?' piped up Andrew. Andrew's voice always called me back from my reveries.

'Well, my son, you're way too young to fight, but you can wield a spade. Our household needs protection and you're the man. We will be needing an air raid shelter soon enough.'

'Ambrose, that odious Hitler man won't be after bombing The Mount, surely?'

'My dear, when the Luftwaffe bombs start dropping, there will be homes damaged outside the key targets. Leeds will be hit, mark my words. But bombs are notoriously hit and miss. Nowhere even near Leeds will be safe.'

'Oh my God Ambrose, now you're frightening me.'

'We should all be afraid this time, my dear. This war will come closer to home than The Great War did. We need to prepare properly. I've been reading about these Air Raid Shelters that Sir John Anderson has been promoting. We're way too rich for a free one, but for payment of seven pounds I believe I can get hold of one for the garden.'

'But if there was a raid, why wouldn't we go into the cellar dear?'

'Too risky in the face of a direct hit. You wouldn't want The Mount collapsing on top of us. We'd never see daylight again.'

'So why do I need a spade, Father? From what I understand, it won't be underground.'

'Ideally it needs to be buried half-underground. It's made of strong corrugated sheets, bolted together with steel plates at each end. They aren't too difficult to put together. But first we need a hole in the ground, six and a half feet by four and a quarter. I've worked out the ideal spot.'

'It still won't save us if there's a direct hit,' I said, reaching for another slice of toast.

Father shot me a look that would have put ice on the surface of the lake. I instantly felt I'd better redeem myself.

'Well, I'm good with a spade too. I'll join Andrew. Show us the chosen spot, Father, and don't forget that famous tape measure of yours.'

But Father's question about what I intended to do kept me thinking. Those women from The Women's Auxiliary Army Corp marched through my memory. At thirty-two I had no excuse. This time round, I would do something truly useful.

Chapter 20

Miss Sapho

'What would you do if an air raid warning sounded tonight? Preparedness, complete preparedness, is our best protection, and our only insurance against attack!'

I worked hard to keep my composure, not to let shock register on my face. The A.R.P. recruiter had woven her spell. Well, what would I do?

Yes, I'd designed a siren suit with a toilet flap, but this didn't seem enough. Clearly, I needed to volunteer, train, secure a role. I fancied fighting fires most of all. I didn't want to work in a factory, especially not Father's. He'd already moved over to manufacturing uniforms. I wasn't going to work for him.

First aid and nursing held little appeal. Too physical, and far too much to do with men. But I was a competent driver. I could race to the fire sub-station and drive one of those new auxiliary pumps. I could command a Godiva, my own appliance. That would be one in the eye for Father.

The romance versus the reality, eh? There was a chasm between this vision and my own experience. With firefighting, women were entering hostile territory, whether on the frontline or as clerical support.

The A.R.P. woman in that hall in Menston hadn't been entirely honest. They wanted clerks, not hands-on firefighters. Well, this is how it was at first, before things hotted up and more men were needed for active service at the front.

To be useful, I had to work in Leeds. I took digs in a terrace of small houses just to the north of the city centre, on Blandford Gardens. There were several young women lodging there. They had come from all over Yorkshire, mostly involved in war related activities. I became quite close to a girl in her early twenties called Phyllis. There was something special about her, I thought. I realise now that I was looking for Ida, and Phyllis had just a little of Ida about her - given the right light. Perhaps it was the sweet tilt of her head, and the expression in her eyes when she looked at me.

Phyllis had come up from Doncaster and was glad to be away from her family. She said she preferred making shells to facing her mother at breakfast every morning. She spoke little about her work, but I got the sense that it was highly skilled, requiring precision and physical strength. It was also extremely dangerous. She worked in the ROF Factory that had been built before the war on the site of the Barnbow Munitions Factory. She told me about the Barnbow Lasses, the victims of the explosion there in the Great War. Thirty-five women were killed outright, in Room 42. Some could only be identified by the tags they wore round their necks for this very purpose. Many more were injured and maimed.

I was surprised that such a terrible accident hadn't made the Yorkshire Evening Post.

'Security.' Phyllis tapped her nose. 'There's so much we aren't told in wartime, and any other time too.'

The mention of these women chilled me to my core.

The sub-station I was attached to posed a challenge in itself. The control room was insanitary with less than basic facilities. On shift, we had to sleep there, and cook our own meals with only rats for company.

When I was finally allowed to fight fires, I was partnered

with Freddy.

'Well, Miss Sapho, seems it will be a busy night tonight.'

Freddy could never bring himself to call me Amba, nor could he get used to Miss Atha. He managed to corrupt the latter to Miss Sapho. I learned to accept this with good grace, for it did seem appropriate, a private and personal joke, for Freddy, of course, would not have realised my preferences.

'It's you I want. It's you I want.'

That was Freddy's way of preparing us for action. He'd rock at the wheel of our Godiva, chanting it over and over. It's what the German bombers' engines seemed to be saying. The closer they came, the more pronounced this sounded.

'It's you I want.'

Freddy knew I found this disquieting, and he revelled in my discomfort.

Mid-March 1941, and a beautifully clear night. Freddy pointed up at the gibbous moon. He contorted his face, under-lit by his torch, into a manic leer.

'The Jerries will look down and see you, Miss Sapho, and they'll think me the luckiest man alive. Me, my Godiva and my posh girl, Miss Sapho. Who could ask for anything more?'

'Well, let's hope we don't have to roll out your old hose tonight, Freddy.'

Famous last words. This was the night the Jerries nearly got us both. Forty bombers were on their way to Leeds. We were directed out to the ROF munitions factory and were parked up as the blitz began. I started to worry about Phyllis, but then remembered it wasn't her shift tonight. I realised I was becoming rather too fond of her.

The first bombs dropped about 9.00 p.m., and they were still dropping in the early hours.

At first Freddy and I felt quite confident that we could cope. We were tackling incendiary bombs, dousing fires as the high explosive bombs were falling close by. The ground shook. The very sky was on fire. Flashes, thuds and crashes. The Leeds skyline became its own firework show. Each flash illuminated a changing city.

We were taken by surprise by the delayed action bombs. You were never sure where the next explosion would come from. The munitions factory was hit by an incendiary bomb.

Freddy was hurt helping some young women out. The sleeve of his uniform was burned right through, and his forearm looked raw. There was a strong smell of burning flesh and cordite. He was in agony so I treated him with a syrette of morphine and dressed his arm as best I could from the kit we always carried. I persuaded him to wait for me in the Godiva. He didn't need too much persuading.

Then I went back in.

The damaged part of the factory was in chaos. But we soon regrouped and established order. I held onto the hose, and I was joined by a host of women workers. Some were in overalls with their goggles still strapped round their heads. Some were in coats and headscarves, their bangs beginning to flop. Some were just in dresses and pinnies. Perhaps it was because I was female, but these women sprang to help me. They organised themselves efficiently. Along with the hose, we had human chains of women carrying buckets to douse the flames. The acrid smell, the soot and the choking smoke got to us all. We were filthy, shaken and soaked, but determined to keep on fighting. Too much was at risk to flee the scene for safety.

More Godivas arrived and their crews joined us. Gradually we got on top of the blaze.

Then the last bomber departed, and we drew breath. I went to check on Freddy who was sound asleep, slumped over the wheel. I gently eased him across to the passenger side and for the first time, drove our Godiva back to the sub-station. Ours was the last one back. A group of firefighters were waiting anxiously. They clocked the fact that it was me, a mere woman, at the wheel, and there was Freddy, sleeping and soaked in blood. They broke into applause.

My stock rose that night. There was even a photo of me in the Yorkshire Evening Post, descending from our Godiva, no doubt to encourage more women recruits. I made a pretty speech to the reporter, praising the women of the munitions factory and insisting that all credit was due to them. And it was the truth. These women went beyond the call of duty that night, but that thought would never have crossed their own minds. I chose not to tell the reporter that my own bravery was an act of atonement. Who wants to hear such a thing amidst the turmoil of war?

Andrew was thrilled to hear about my night of excitement. I could tell that even Father was impressed. He couldn't say so to my face, but I overheard him talking on the telephone to some of our friends and acquaintances. But I had to ask myself why Father's approval counted for anything.

The war sometimes seems a blur, but this was my standout night. They never struck medals for firefighters, but Freddy and I both claimed our Defence Medals. I still have mine now in the trunk. I suppose I keep it with me to reassure myself that once in my life, I did do something worthwhile.

Chapter 21

My Sin Comes Seeking

I'm now at The Mount. A summer's morning following my night of fire.

'Amba my dear, can you help me with a mystery?'

'Ah, you're reading Patricia Wentworth. I'll help if I can.'

Mother and I were enjoying morning coffee. A rare moment of peace in the household. Father had left early for Bradford, and Andrew for school in Leeds. I was resting after my exhausting fire watch shift. Patricia Wentworth's *Grey Mask* was next to Mother's cup.

'No, not in a novel, my dear. But then, perhaps, it should be.'

She was looking at me in that curious way, quizzical but hoping for the best. I felt as if I was a child again. I knew I might be in trouble.

'You went to London with Andrew, just before this awful war business started.'

'I did.' I didn't like where this was going at all.

'You went to The Rotunda Court for afternoon tea. Andrew was full of it, as I recall.'

'Yes.' I smiled. I was working hard to appear calm.

'Shortly after that visit, a letter arrived here. It was addressed to your father. I recognised the writing. Your Uncle Robert's. Have you any idea what this letter might have been about?'

'Mother, our own experience is that nothing pleasant ever

comes from that man. His correspondence has always caused us both distress and dismay.'

'Indeed. That is why I did something for which I should be ashamed. I intercepted the letter.'

I could feel my shoulders dropping.

'Did you burn it?'

'I did, but I read it first.'

'What did he have to say?'

'First I want to hear from you what happened.'

I was thinking fast.

'Come on Amba, what happened during your afternoon tea? I need to hear it from your own lips.'

I could feel my face flushing.

'It was like this. I saw him. At first, I couldn't be sure, but then I knew it was him.'

'And?'

'He had this girl with him, about eighteen, pale and pasty. She was so like Phina. She just had to be his daughter. Mother, I felt angry, furious in truth. I remembered everything – how he'd upset Aunt Rania, how he'd been horrible to you and so hostile to me, how he had wrecked my dancing career, sowed the seeds of distrust and ruined my relationship with Father. He had accused Aunt Rania of corrupting me, that I'd done awful things with her to get the apartment and her money. Poisonous Uncle Robert…'

I was warming to my theme.

'Darling don't upset yourself. Just tell me what you did.'

'A brief interchange in the powder room. That's all.'

'Where was Andrew whilst this brief exchange was happening?'

'He found the space for a lemon and lavender fondant fancy – his fourth cake, as I recall.'

'The details of your exchange, please.'

'I told the girl what I thought of her father. I said that he'd interfered with my life. I said he'd damaged me.'

'Hmm. The bare bones of the story match. Did you say that there had been element of sexual interference?'

'Mother! I used the word "interfere". But I suppose I might not have been specific about the context.'

'Amba, did that man ever touch you?'

'No, Mother, he didn't touch me.'

'That's all I needed to know.'

Mother sat back in her chair with relief. She took a deep breath. Silence. Then she spoke again. 'It seems the daughter hasn't spoken to him since. She shuns him. He learned of the interchange from his second wife, Winifred. Winifred had to be summoned by the manager of The Regent Palace Hotel to accompany her daughter home. The girl refused to leave the powder room. A waitress had been sent in by Robert to see what was happening.

The poor girl has suffered some sort of depression since. She claims you warned her that her father was a danger to children – to all young girls. A child abuser, no less. She can't bear him near her now.'

Mother braced herself.

'Amba, since reading that letter, I have been so worried there was something you weren't telling me about that last stay at Cadogan Square, all those years ago.'

'Mother, look at me. Would I make things up about Uncle Robert?'

'He lied about you. It seemed logical you might have tried to get even. That's what I'd hoped. But I was being eaten away by the thought he might have actually interfered with you.'

'You'd "hoped?"'

Mother was beginning to smile. I couldn't believe it.

'Did you write back?'

'Oh yes. I wrote back all right. I didn't want him writing again. He'd threatened legal action, defamation, slander, and that he was going to seek substantial damages. I wrote back and told him my husband was unwell and that you were no longer "with us". Two can play at ambiguity, my darling. It's in the genes.'

'Mother, you implied I was dead!'

'Hmm. You were in Leeds at the time I wrote.'

We were both laughing now. Hugging each other and laughing.

'Magical Child indeed! Monster Child more like.'

'Avenging angel perhaps?' I suggested, tentatively.

'Close to the mark. Closer than you might have realised. You see, I had to fight Robert off on several occasions.'

'After you were married?'

'Most certainly. Rania's resistance left him a very frustrated man.'

This revelation stunned me. How dare he? My mother. I hated him even more.

Resting in my mother's arms, I was transported back twenty-three years to our final return from Cadogan Square, that delicious train journey when I snuggled up to her. These days it was rare to get the chance to be so close to her. I was savouring every moment.

'I love you, my darling,' she whispered. 'I've tried to keep the peace between you and your father over the years. But I must confess, the more difficult you have become, the more I have loved and admired you. It was always the same with Rania. You are my sister's double.'

She kissed my brow.

'My beautiful, vindictive Monster Child. Yes Amba, I shall always love you, no matter what. But what on earth will become of you?'

Chapter 22

But We Don't Talk About That

I stretch my spine and wriggle my toes. We can't be far off RAF Northolt now, surely? Well, back to remembering.

When I wasn't putting out fires in Leeds, I was lighting new ones on the home front. I'm trying to remember when Andrew first became my dresser.

Andrew was eleven when the war was declared. We spent much of our time at home in each other's company. Andrew retreated to my suite in the evenings. He was eager to keep out of Father's way. In joining me upstairs, he entered a woman's world, a world so different to our father's. I began to teach him about all things feminine.

If his destiny was to be wool, worsted, then I reasoned he needed to know everything about style, design, textiles, and textures. I revisited many elements of my art and design course with him. We sat side by side and I shared my portfolios of designs and swatches.

Sitting with Andrew evoked for me those heady times in Cadogan Square. Why, I would have been just his age, a formative time in one's life. I vividly remembered sitting with Rania, gazing at Maud. What an initiation it was. I would become to Andrew what Rania had been to me. But this time, there would be no Uncle Robert to ruin things.

Andrew had an innate sense of style and great taste. His

approach to colour combinations sometimes astonished me. His ideas were fresh. But they worked, even though they were audacious. Not only did he clash colours, but he also ignored conventions and combined disparate elements to great effect.

Andrew became my dresser on his thirteenth birthday. It was a Sunday, the seventh of December,1941. He had progressed so well with his appreciation of style that I decided that he could put together an outfit for me to wear for his birthday luncheon. He was to go through my wardrobe, outfits, accessories, jewellery and make-up. He was in charge, I told him.

Andrew took this commission very seriously. It was a strange yet delicious sensation to see him going through my clothes – wardrobes and drawers. He treated every item with reverence. He was transported.

What Andrew came up with was impressive, elegant, with just the right amount of flamboyance. He favoured green and found my slinky emerald crepe de chine trousers. Above he added a lime silk wrap-round blouse that fell across my chest in dramatic folds and was nipped in at the waist with a tie. He insisted on tying the bow for me. At first I was a little disconcerted when he stroked the silk over my breasts. It felt intimate, but not in a base physical sense. It was more elevated than this. He was like a sculptor finishing his creation. He fetched my emerald earrings but then rejected them.

'Too obvious,' he muttered, shaking his head.

He then picked out my Deep Siberian amethyst ones, predominantly purple with blue and red hues. He added my matching amethyst choker. For shoes he chose a pair of crimson velvet pointed ballerinas with satin laces.

I was surprised when he insisted that he would do my make-up. Luckily, I'd stock-piled my favourite items of make-up at the outbreak of war. I instructed Andrew to use it sparingly. Nonetheless, we had such fun. The lips in deepest dark crimson took three applications, but he soon got the hang of it. Then he swept my hair right off my face. My beloved kiss curls went skywards.

When the gong sounded, the two of us descended the stairs for luncheon arm in arm. Father complimented Andrew on what a fine young fellow he was for thirteen. He ignored me. Mother studied my outfit for a little while with a quizzical expression, and then turned her attention back to the supervision of the birthday meal.

Dressing for dinner became our favourite thing; a tradition if you like. Andrew was always on hand. The actual meals became more frugal as the war rumbled on, but this didn't compromise our style explorations and adventures. We enjoyed an exalted intimacy, sharing ideas, impressions, and sensations. I like to think our mutual experiences were sensuous rather than sensual. Of course we touched, but not in a carnal, sexual way. Nothing unseemly or gross ever happened between us.

Each night, after the evening meal, Father would tune into the Home Service, or The Forces Programme. He loved Vera Lynn's "Sincerely Yours", her songs and the messages to the troops from their loved ones that she read out. His tastes were wide, ranging from the comedy "ITMA" to the Brains Trust. Most of all he loved to keep up to date with the news.

Mother, Andrew and I were not allowed to speak whilst the radio was on. When Father wasn't listening, he would be reading his newspapers, keeping abreast he called it. If we were present he would insist on reading out long reports of the fighting, the losses at sea, in the air, on the ground, and at home. We were not invited to comment. This drove Andrew and I back upstairs to my suite.

In my suite we had a new portable HMV 102 gramophone

and our favourite 78s. I taught Andrew to dance to these – Glenn Miller's "Chattanooga Choo Choo", Billy Holiday's "God Bless the Child", and Duke Ellington's "Take The 'A' Train". We ended each session with a slow foxtrot to our own special song, Jimmy Dorsey's "My Sister & I".

Chapter 23

It's You I Want

I'm nearing the end of my flight. It's coming up to 3.00 p.m. and it looks as if we'll be on time. It's funny but I've always loved take-off. The sheer exhilaration of rising at speed. But the descending and the landing always make me a little nervous. Today is no exception. I feel apprehensive and anxious.

The weather is grim with heavy rain. July in England, eh? Who'd want to be anywhere else? And for once, for me, this is true. Perhaps, for the first time, this strange longing I'm feeling is homesickness.

I hope Father has brought Andrew to meet me. Perhaps, tomorrow night, Andrew will dress me for dinner. Later I might dance in his arms again. We'll play our favourite 78s. I'm trying to remember the words from Jimmy Dorsey's "My Sister and I", something about learning to forget the fear that came from a troubled sky.

Yes, I long to be home in Menston, safe, at The Mount, with Mother waiting, eager to hear my latest adventures. I see the drive, the panelled entrance hall and the lilies in my mother's favourite vase. Their heady scent mingles with the aroma of coffee seeping from the kitchen. I see the lake, Leda and Lilith. I can see the rain on the water. I can hear Ida's laughter…

No, I have never forgotten Ida. I have recurring dreams. My Ida is Leda, assailed, enveloped by the malevolent swan. This bird has the eyes of Le Baron. Ida is the true L'Inconnue de la Seine, the unknown woman with the Mona Lisa smile and the eerie calm.

And then, in my dreams, she spies me and transforms before my eyes. Now she is holding her baby. No Madonna and child this. She dangles the baby by one leg. It bumps against her thigh. She points at me with her other hand, her finger jabbing. Her beautiful face contorts. She becomes hideously ugly and moves round the rim of the lake with a mechanical Fritz Lang style gait. There's a malevolent gleam in her eyes and her teeth are bared. She casts the baby into the water and lunges towards me, grabs my wrists tightly until they hurt. She forces me down under the surface. She holds me there until life leaves me. And I know I have no fight left in me. I know I have no right to life.

Always I wake, sweating, terrified, and I try to acknowledge that I have done wrong, and yet I cannot. Because I know that if I could be back in that moment, and choose again, I would still do as I did then. You see, the truth about that fateful night by the Seine cannot be denied. I must face myself and what I am.

That night, the surface of the Seine was like an oil slick. The water was heavy, dense and cloudy. As I dived down. I thought I saw a shape. I swam closer. I could make out her silhouette. One of her legs seemed to have been caught by something below. Her arms and free leg were frantically trying to push; to swim to the surface. I saw her hair spreading in a swirling halo. Our eyes met, hers imploring, mine full of fury. Death blowing bubbles, the strangest thought. I saw the stream of bubbles thinning. The silence pulsed in my ears.

I looked away. I turned and pushed upwards. Yes, I left her

to die. I swam to the surface. I left her alone. Truly, I believe I could have saved her. I made my choice.

The rain is heavier now, clawing against the glass. The cloud low and dense. I gaze out of the window, along the wing. Something is wrong. There's a huge dark shape too close and rising towards us. A malevolent rising bulk. Doesn't the pilot see it? It's another plane. For God's sake!

The crash of collision, the tilting, spiralling down. I cannot breathe. Trees press against what is left of us, and then … fire. People are screaming. Some are upside down. The children are squealing.

Then, all I can hear is Ida's laughter. 'It's you I want. Amba. It's you I want.'

'No.'

PART 2

After Amba

Chapter 1

Andrew

I saw the crash that took my sister on a Pathé newsreel. I had to leave the cinema. I made it to the alley beside the building and vomited. I had been caught completely off guard.

A swirling string accompaniment. The vision of the mangled remains of a plane, still smouldering in the wood. The clipped commentary. No, it wasn't the DC-6, *Agnar Viking*. They led the story with the other plane, the RAF *Avro York*, dwelling on the six crew members and especially the High Commissioner for the Federation of Malaya, Sir Edward Gent. Then: 'A mile away lay the remains ...'

A mile away lay the incinerated remains of Ambrosia Atha, my beautiful and extraordinary sister. She had been travelling on what was glibly dismissed as a commercial flight from Stockholm. Of the *Agnar Viking*, all that remained was the rudder and tailplane.

Father and I had arrived in good time to meet Amba at RAF Northolt. We couldn't understand the delay. Then all those waiting to meet passengers from that flight were called together and led to a place of greater privacy. A priest appeared – on hand to comfort the bereaved.

All I remember is the dreadful, dawning, devastating realisation that Amba was dead. It was as if some force was choking the breath out of me.

Father held his composure but I knew he was broken. We felt compelled to drive on to Northwood, to get as close as possible to the spot Amba left the planet. We stayed locally overnight just to be near her. There was no hope, yet still we hoped. When we were finally allowed to approach the scene, the enormity of what had happened hit us even harder.

We edged as close as we were allowed into the woods. The crash site was roped off. Something caught my eye. I stooped as if to retie my lace and carefully secreted a small object into the palm of my hand. I surreptitiously pocketed my treasure. Later I would retrieve it and wonder at the chances. Did she direct me to it? A small owl hewn from the grey volcanic rocks near Reykjavik. I recognised it immediately.

I carry it with me always.

Father and I decided to go home to Menston. We completed whatever formalities were required and set off for the north. We drove in silence. Both of us needed to see Mother, and we knew she would so desperately need to see us.

Chapter 2

Frasey Hannah Fisher

Part of me is asking what I'm doing here. Why am I sitting in the elegant garden room at The Mount listening to this elderly man recall the time of his greatest pain and loss? He's talking to me with an intimacy that makes me feel privileged. On one level I feel I am unworthy of his confidences. But even I cannot deny the strong sense of empathy and compassion, soul connection if you will. Yes, that's what we share.

This is not my world. But it has become my world.

Truly, in my life so far, I have always felt misplaced as if somehow I ended up in the wrong family. Wishful thinking? Once, in the turmoil of my adolescence, I checked my birth certificate, to see if there was any indication of adoption. Foul play? Infant theft? For how else could I ever begin to explain my sense of isolation from my parents, and younger sister? How is it possible to long for home, when you are at home, unless it isn't your real home. Oh, this must sound ridiculous.

Let's start at the beginning. I want to tell you about how I met Andrew Horatio Atha.

Miss Claxton, my boss, was responsible. I think it was one of the few good turns she ever did me. She started sounding off one break-time:

'Well, the Librarian calls me in and introduces me to this elderly man. "May I introduce Mr Andrew Atha," he says.

"He has a potential project for one of our research librarians." It was all about letters, and papers – boxes of it – and some unpublished novel. "We haven't got the capacity for this type of stuff. We've been cut to the bone." I told them both, in no uncertain terms.'

Miss Claxton sipped her coffee through her tight, colourless lips and frowned: 'Oh I told them both, be assured. I laid it on the line.'

'Wasn't he going to pay?' I ventured.

'Of course, he would pay. But we can't say yes to every Tom and Dick who comes along waving wads of notes.'

'Still, I would have been interested. I really would.'

'Well, you go after him. He's probably still in the building. Spend your Saturdays and Sundays on some old man's dead sister's papers. Personally, I'd shred the lot. But what you want to do with your own time is entirely up to you, lady. Some of us have lives to live. It's not my idea of quality leisure time.'

I made my excuses and left the room.

Miss Claxton was warming to her theme as I went.

'Stick to your stats, Frasey. Play to your strengths. These old men can be such a pain in the arse,' she called to my receding back.

I was making rapid calculations. Working weekends in the run up to this infernal end of February wedding – perfect. Celine my mother, and Phoebe my younger sister, were driving me insane. They'd certainly lost the plot themselves. As for me, I had kept trying to rein in my temper. My mother had already accused me of being crabbit – a crabbit old spinster no less. Phoebe dismissed my disdain as jealousy – the older sister left on the shelf. And what the hell is "the shelf"? I was desperately trying to remain cheerful, to all outward appearances at least.

The "favours" were the last straw.

'What the fuck are favours?' I blurted out.

Too late. Phoebe burst into tears, and Celine banished me from the lounge. Bloody lollipops and paint-sprayed plastic toys. Give me strength. It could only get worse.

I shot up the cold stone steps to Mrs Felix's room.

Patricia Felix was the Librarian's Administrator: 'Sorry. Mr Atha has left the building. Ooh, I make him sound like Elvis. Don't get your hopes up, Frasey. Elvis he is not, but they must have been born about the same time. Well, give or take a few years. Still, he seemed a nice enough old giffer. Very polite anyway.'

Patricia looked out of the plate glass window, pointing down with a half-eaten greasy baked sausage: 'That's him down there, silver hair, matching moustache, walking with a stick – making his way across the car park. You might catch him if you sprint. I certainly couldn't.' Patricia giggled as she slapped her midriff, then embarked upon her mid-morning bacon-stuffed croissant with an exaggerated relish. She used the bag to catch the crumbs.

Luckily, I'm lean, athletic and determined. I caught up with Mr Atha as he opened the door of his Mercedes.

'Mr Atha, forgive me! Oh!' I recall pressing my hand to my chest. Stitch.

'My dear, please, draw breath.'

'Thank you, I will. I must be out of shape. I used to run for Yorkshire when I was at school.'

Mr Atha was amused. 'It's a long time since I was pursued by a young lady, and such an attractive one. Oh, forgive me, I'm not to be encouraged to make comments like that anymore. I know it's not the thing for nowadays. "Me Too" and all that. I keep up with these things, you know.'

'No Mr Atha, please forgive me if I'm the one who sounds inappropriate, impertinent even, but Miss Claxton mentioned your project. I know I must seem forward, but I am a qualified and experienced research librarian, and I wondered – would you consider me, to work on your collection at weekends? It sounds a fascinating project. Would you like to interview me? I can send you a CV. I have excellent references; you can inspect my credentials.'

I'll never forget the way Mr Atha looked at me. He sized me up and down, albeit discretely. He nodded, and his smile broadened. An inscrutable smile. I swear I felt his eyes dancing over my face, his clear eyes of harebell blue. I was struck by the whites. They had the palest blue tinge and were not at all rheumy – remarkable for such an aged man.

A silence followed, as if we were both suspended in the moment, in the car park. I conducted a further furtive assessment of Mr Atha. My nostrils quivered as I inhaled his cologne. Citrus and vetiver, with woody undertones. Probably Guerlain, I guessed. I felt my nose drawn to his neck just to check. I love to identify scents. I've never understood why I am so passionate about perfume. Get a grip, I told myself.

Mr Atha reminded me of someone famous. A politician of the past perhaps? Harold McMillan? Not really, but the same colouring and a fine head of silver hair and luxuriant moustache. He was thin and angular, charmingly awkward but then, that could be his arthritis. He was a bit like Bill Nighy. But no, it eventually came to me, it was Peter O'Toole – in his later years. I love vintage films and I've seen this actor in quite a few. Yes, there seemed to be something of a latent decadence lurking in Mr Atha too – a sorrowful, reluctant decadence. This was a fleeting reflection. I was undeterred.

Mr Atha broke the silence:

'Perhaps you and I should discuss your most kind offer. Can you join me at The Mount, Menston, this Saturday? Would 11.00 am suit?'

'I'll be there. I know The Mount – the gates at the end of the drive at least, for I've passed it on my bike – it's that large, secluded house behind the trees – Edwardian, I think.'

'The house is indeed Edwardian. It has been the home of the Athas since 1902. But I forget my manners again.' He held out his hand to me. 'I am Andrew Horatio Atha, and…?' A pause. His un-put question floated between us.

I caught it. 'Frasey Hannah Fisher. Delighted to meet you, Mr Atha.'

'Andrew, please, do call me Andrew. Until Saturday, Frasey.'

I nodded, then watched and waved as Mr Atha reversed his Mercedes with caution and care from the parking space. My knees were wobbly. Seriously out of condition, I thought. But I felt also that my world had tilted on its axis. If I had acted impulsively, I reflected, I had time to change my mind. But it also occurred to me that I had been driven to pursue this opportunity, almost compelled by a force, a force far stronger than the desire to avoid my family. What had come over me. And no, I would not be telling Celine or Phoebe that this was not part of my regular work role.

Chapter 3

The Mount, Menston

If only all interviews were as delightful and delicious as this one.

I cycled to The Mount. I tethered my bike to some elegant railings, just inside the gates, shielded from the house by an ancient beech tree. I took a few deep breaths to calm myself, then walked up the curving drive to the house.

The drive was delightful. It rose gently through mature specimen trees, shrubs and an evergreen floor-cover in a well-manicured woodland setting. The church clock was sounding eleven chimes as I pressed the front doorbell of The Mount.

A rather stolid, "I'll have none of your nonsense" woman, early-sixties, opened the elaborately carved oak door. I would soon know her as Mrs Eleanor Tordoff, the housekeeper. I remember wondering how long it was since that mouth stretched to a smile.

'Miss Fisher? You are expected. Follow me.'

Mrs Tordoff led me past oak panels and portraits into a light-filled room. French doors, wide open, drew my eye into a formal garden with Yorkshire flag stones and elegant urns with miscellaneous faces and figures, Bacchanalian, full-lipped men and Beardsley style women. Beyond, a stone rimmed pool with a pair of statues.

Mr Atha was standing by the doors, smiling warmly at me.

Sun picked out the ripples on the water.

'How totally beautiful,' I whispered. I hadn't meant to drop my guard so easily, but I was overwhelmed with a strange excitement. Enchantment? 'Is that a Lilith? This one's obviously Leda.'

'Ah, you recognise Lilith. Impressive, Frasey.'

'Well, the serpent wrapped round her body is a bit of a give-away, a little like Leda's swan.'

'Have you read much about Aleister Crowley?'

'Oh yes, I find him fascinating. And his father is one of the Plymouth Brethren! But I can't believe he deserved his notoriety. Libertine, social critic, drug dependent and bi-sexual, okay, they weren't quite the thing then, but the press called him the wickedest man in the world, which given the violence and corruption of those times, I find rather baffling. Exasperating, even.'

'Indeed. Me too.'

'But why do you ask?'

'All will become clear. You will find some brief correspondence between my sister Ambrosia and Mr Crowley after our aunt's death. Our Aunt Rania was one of his women. Oh, that sounds a little crude. Forgive me. Aunt Rania moved in rather different circles to our mother. I understand Crowley chose Rania as one of his harem. It was a project to conceive a Magical Child. Satan was supposed to be on hand too. The whole caper appalled our mother, but Ambrosia seemed to find the episode hysterically funny. Of course, Crowley was much, much older than Aunt Rania. But at that time, a decade or more before my birth, she was one of his neophytes.'

'OMG.'

'Indeed, Frasey, OMG indeed.'

Mr Atha's eyes lit up with amusement, but then he

straightened his face, and his tone became brisk. 'Now, Mrs Tordoff will bring us our mid-morning refreshments in about half an hour. Your Miss Claxton at the university gave me short shrift. I hardly had chance to tell anything about the project. So perhaps, first things first, I ought to tell you a little about Ambrosia. You might decide she's not your "cup of tea". I'll try to keep it brief for I don't wish to bore you. In truth, her notes, her diaries, her writings and her unpublished novel will speak for her. You will be able to piece her together.'

'Is this Ambrosia?' A portrait of a young woman was positioned over the huge marble fireplace.

'Yes, this is my sister Ambrosia aged twenty-one. A coming-of-age birthday portrait. It would be 1928.'

I was transfixed. It was as if I locked eyes with the subject. The connection was tangible. I would not have called Ambrosia conventionally beautiful. The eyes a little too wide, the smile a little too broad, the cheek bones perhaps a little too sharp, but there was something in her face that was extremely attractive, beguiling, and yet, so familiar.

'She was about your height and build. Your colouring too in truth. Tall for then. I must show you her wardrobe one day. I've kept everything, clothes, shoes, personal items, etcetera and her jewellery. She loved exquisite things.'

'Her eyes are mesmeric. They seem to draw you in. It is a wonderful portrait.'

'Art, paint, these could never do her justice. Her eyes were the most captivating I have ever encountered.'

Mr Atha looked lost in a different time.

'As a small child I adored Ambrosia. I have this hazy, early image of her. I'm on her knee. She's laughing and teasing me. I smell her perfume. I hear the rattle of her bracelets. I'm trying to pull her earrings and she's throwing back her head: "Yum-Yum, no!"'

'Yum-Yum?'

'Oh, my dear, do forgive me, please, I was miles away. Yum-Yum was her name for me. I was an avid thumb sucker and Ambrosia found it hilarious, especially the grunting, 'yumming' noise I was wont to make. She threatened to confiscate my thumb.'

'That must have been troubling. How old were you?'

'Almost three, I think. You never knew if she was serious. But I adored her. I was so much younger than her. She was brilliant, mercurial, truly original. She was my education. Sometimes, when the wind rattles the surface of the water out there, I swear I hear her crystal laughter's effervescence breaking through. Then the water swirls with the cadence and depth of the voice of a woman. I like to believe this is her voice.'

Mr Atha's gaze turned back to the portrait.

'Ambrosia has decided that you are to call her Amba. I think she likes you.'

'That's encouraging,' I said.

He smiled mischievously, then turned abruptly away. 'But come, I'll show you the collection. It's all in her own suite of rooms. I've kept everything as she left it. Mrs Tordoff knows the rules.'

There never was any question as to whether I was hired. Mr Atha assumed from the start that I was the one, and I wasn't inclined to ask him why. Mrs Tordoff would hand me an envelope at each calendar month's end. "For Frasey – our private arrangement" was hand-written on the front, in a semi-Bellissima script. I remember being concerned about the tax I should be paying, so I made my own calculation, and handed the sum to a different charity each month.

On these terms, I began to work through the Amba collection. I soon began to 'piece her together', as Mr Atha had suggested I would. Amba's letters were engrossing. They became increasingly frank, and her diary entries more confiding as the years passed. The letters of the young Amba dwelt on subjects such as the superiority of the shingle over the soft wave bob, the right length for a skirt, how she would die for an ivory cigarette holder with a gold mouthpiece, the need for her own car as soon as possible, and then, how she had perfected the jitterbug on a rainy afternoon with new dear friend, Ida. It was clear from the letters that Amba's mother had become uneasy. Ida's mother became increasingly concerned. The affection between the two friends was electric. Both mothers were shocked. Their two daughters were very tactile.

'There will be talk,' complained Amba's mother. 'No man will want you, hanging off that girl's arm like that. Girls don't do this in Menston.'

'But men are so tedious, mother, and Menston men the most boring of the lot. Andrew, my angel boy excepted. He'll never be boring, not by the time I've finished with him.'

'Of course, my sister was a lesbian,' confided Andrew, early in our acquaintanceship. 'It was particularly difficult for my father to accept this. He wished her to make an advantageous marriage. He wanted grandchildren. To him, his daughter's inclinations were unnatural and as such, entirely unacceptable. He enquired about conversion therapy at High Royds. They were doing some pioneering work with hypnosis. But Mother would not allow hypnosis, and certainly not at the local institution. Mother always believed it was a phase that Amba would grow out of. As if.'

Andrew recalled the Sunday lunch when things began to turn truly challenging. The family was assembled around the mahogany table. Ida was present, seated next to Amba. Father was at the head. Amba, lavish as ever with her endearments turned to Ida and gazed at her.

'Ida, Ida, my sweet, so soft, eider duck.'

'Fuck, more like,' boomed Father, puce of face and outraged.

'Ambrose, please, your language, in front of the girls, and your son.' Mother was becoming the mediator.

'All young girls have crushes on each other. They grow out of it.'

'She's in her sodding thirties, Kate, for fuck's sake. You all need to grow up, that's the bloody truth of it. Grow up and wake up.'

Amba and Ida were planning another holiday in Paris.

'Paris!' snarled Father. 'High Royds bound, more like, for the pair of them. Families have incarcerated girls for less. And that's a one-way ticket, is High Royds.' He addressed this to Mother because he'd stopped speaking to Amba by this time. Father pressed on.

'What's more, there's another war coming, you mark my words. They'd be better advised to stick to Menston. Stay off the continent; stay this side of the channel. You tell 'em. Silly, spoilt bitches.'

The young Andrew heard his father's censure, and watched his sister's fall from grace, in a mute sadness. Amba squared up to their father, but Ida shrank into herself. Ida hated conflict. She was desperate for approval. Andrew found it hard to remember an occasion when Ida wasn't smiling.

Andrew recalled his own sorrow. Amba was his world, and this world, his inspiration, was planning to leave home again.

I photocopied the unpublished novel and took it home to read. It was a lesbian novel set in the Yorkshire Dales. Its title: 'Lilith and Leda'. Its plot was based loosely on the famous Ilkley Moor Baht'at song. It was a tale of the love of two women, one catching her death of cold on the moors – a thinly veiled metaphor for the shunning and ostracism by the families and society – worms eating the victim, ducks eating the worms. But it was clever, funny, satirical, brave, bold and bitter. Ida was Mary Jane.

In one of those examples of life imitating art, Ida was to die in Paris, after a frivolous, abandoned and licentious evening. It was always party time for the girls in Paris. At some point during the early hours, the revellers took a moonlit dip from the steps on the banks of the Seine. The West Yorkshire papers made much of the tragedy, as they would nowadays. The yellowing newspaper articles had all been saved. I was baffled by one concluding paragraph that dwelt on the fact that Ida had announced her engagement to a French baron's son that very evening, and a very advantageous marriage it would have been for a Menston girl, even an affluent one like Ida.

How could that be, I wondered, when Amba and Ida were such an item? How could Ida be getting engaged? What on earth was going on?

After Ida's death, Amba returned to her family, heartbroken and in deep depression. Andrew recalled that time of darkness.

'Amba was haunted by something beyond raw grief. Even Father conceded she had taken her friend's death very badly. We all tried to call her back from those depths. Perhaps I was the most successful. Children have a certain way with them.'

Andrew explained how he became her sole companion and 'project' through these dark times, and he became her salvation. She went through so many different phases following Ida's death. Mood swings. Her brittle gaiety was perhaps the hardest, he said, for that was when she became least like herself.

Then came the war.

Amba's contribution to the war effort was to join the fire service. After the war had ended, she resumed her travels.

She returned to her fashion journalism, and wrote some fine travel pieces, all of which were published.

'I was twenty when she died,' sighed Andrew. 'She was only forty-one. So young. So much promise.'

I asked how she died. Was she ill?

Andrew shook his head.

'She was well, and as happy as I'd seen her since the heady days of Ida. Such a tragic accident. She died in the terrible Northwood plane crash. Mid-air collision. She was on the DC-6 "Agnar Viking" − scheduled flight from Stockholm via Schiphol to London. The other plane was RAF − 99 Squadron. She was coming home to me, but the skies took her − 1948 was the year.'

'I'm so sorry, Andrew.' This was the first time I used his first name.

This is when he told me about seeing the crash on the Pathé News in the cinema.

'It's funny. Amba and I shared a love of the cinema. She nurtured my love of films. We could lose ourselves in them. Different lives, different worlds. It was such a shock to me to have my own personal tragedy up there on the big screen. It was as if it was an entertainment. I was traumatised, yes, mortified and traumatised.

You know Frasey, when you love someone so much, as I loved Amba, and that person is taken from you without warning, it is almost impossible to let them go. I have never been able to release her, and I'm not sure she has ever been willing to let me go either.'

My eyes were drawn to the portrait of Amba, and I understood what he was saying. How those eyes held me. It was as if my very soul was being sucked away by a force far stronger than me.

Andrew sighed softly. I turned to him.

'Some people aren't here to grow old.' he said as his eyes dropped and moistened; he looked away and swallowed hard. His hands locked tighter around the chrome Fritz handle of his dark beechwood cane. Then his eyes turned to me and our eyes seemed looked together in what seemed an eternity of silence.

Chapter 4

To the Core of My Pelvic Floor

'Everything changed from that time onwards.'

Andrew exhaled, slowly, deeply.

'I'll tell you a little about my life, my life after Amba died. Well, the bare bones. My father never recovered. Amba's death was like a catalyst. I can tell you about his death later. Suffice it to say he went into a sharp decline. He died in 1950 in High Royds, our mental asylum here in Menston.

In the mid-fifties Mother developed angina. I remember she used to have these episodes. She used to go a translucent blue round her mouth. Eventually her pain was excruciating. She went onto the nitro glycerine medication. A tiny pill under the tongue when she had one of her dos. As they got more severe, she needed morphine.

The night she died will be with me forever. She'd been feeling unwell. We'd persuaded her to go to bed. Something stopped me leaving her, I was propped up on her bed, massaging her neck and shoulders. She used to love that. Suddenly she raised both arms high. It was all up with her.

Mother had suffered a major heart attack. She died in my arms.'

Andrew seemed lost in the moment. I waited until he was ready to continue.

'By this time, 1958, I was approaching thirty. It was time to take stock. I had no family, no-one to please. Amba, the only person I had ever wanted to be with, had been taken from me, but her influence continued.

I asked her what I should do and she urged me to travel. She had always told me travel freed the mind and, believe me, my mind was in sore need of freedom.

I did so much thinking at this time. I decided that the time was right to sell the mill and the factories.'

'That must have been a tough decision.' I ventured.

'Not really. They gave me no joy. I'd followed Father's wishes and had taken over, but it was dawning on me that it was all over with wool. Our wealth, and Bradford's wealth, were built on wool and by this time the more astute could see that the writing was on the wall. Our mill and factories had been dedicated to worsted, from raw fleece to woven cloth. I sold our whole concern to a rival family at a very favourable price. Some might say a killing. It certainly looked like it ten years later. My father would never have sold. What happened to worsted would have broken his heart, and our wealth.

I have never seen myself as entrepreneurial, but every investment I have made has been sound. I have finely tuned antennae and I always knew when to jump in, and when to step out. I suppose I have been lucky in this respect at least.'

'So what did you do next?'

'Don't laugh, Frasey. I followed the beatnik trail. I set off for Benares. Varanasi is what they call it now. Then on to southern India, to Trivandrum, now Kerala, and on to Kathmandu. In India I was initiated into the Tantra, a weaving of the physical with the spiritual — a bit like worsted really.'

Andrew grinned at the silliness of his own simile.

I asked him more about the Tantra. I told him I'd heard of it but mainly in relation to long drawn-out sex sessions endorsed by rock celebrities.

'Of course, Frasey, Tantra philosophy encompasses and intertwines spirituality, sexuality and mindfulness. It's about celebrating your body and feeling heightened sensuality.'

'So it is more than just sex?' Half of me couldn't believe I was having this conversation with an elderly man. It felt novel, a little edgy but quite natural. Yes, it was okay, I decided.

'In a relationship between two people, the aim is to achieve a higher level of connection. This can be an end in itself. Breathing, meditation, yoga are all important. The mind, the spirit and the body make a tantric experience. This can transcend or enhance the sexual.'

'I like the sound of it.' It was occurring to me that heightened arousal as an end in itself was an intriguing and pleasing idea. It was so less messy than the furtive fumblings that had characterised my previously abortive relationships with much younger men than Andrew.

Andrew was watching me intently.

'You know Frasey, human sexuality presents itself in so many different behaviours. Amba taught me this. Most of these are recreative rather than procreative. The recreative can be so much more interesting, complex and pleasurable.'

Caution took command and I steered us away with a question.

'So, did you find what you were looking for on the beatnik trail?

'If I'm honest, I was looking for Amba. It's only now, after all these years, I think I might have found her.'

Our eyes locked. The pressure of the portrait to our side was quite tangible. I dared not turn my head to her. Back to the beatnik trail.

'So were you away for a long time?'

'Four years, perhaps longer.'

'And what brought you back to Menston?'

'It was the strangest thing. It happened one night in Uttar Pradesh. Frasey, I remember it like yesterday. I was travelling with a man of about my own age, a man called Christopher. We'd hired a car. We came to this village, a small place strung out along a dusty road. It looked as if all the families were outside. Fires were burning, faces illuminated by the flames. Merriment, music and laughter. There was an overwhelming sense of community, of family and of friends together. A type of neighbourliness I'd never encountered. Everyone was friendly. They must have been intrigued by these two somewhat flamboyant young English men. But I had such a sense of being on the outside looking in.

I had so much, and yet so little. Where was my family? What was my family? I wanted Amba, and I knew I wouldn't find her there. At that moment of desolation, I could almost hear her voice: 'Come home.' That's what she was saying, I was convinced.

The next morning I made my arrangements. I had decided to return to Menston. I would take up residence again in The Mount. And here I've been ever since.

It was a good decision. I have felt closer to her here, but never closer than now, Frasey.

As to the Tantra, I've kept up the practices throughout the rest of my life. And they have proved a solace and a fulfilment.'

The next question was out before I'd thought it through.

'Would you tell me more about these tantric practices?'

How I felt Amba's eyes upon me. But Andrew seemed quite eager to continue.

'It's quite simple Frasey. First you have to be at one with your surroundings. Take time to become aware of what is around you. Use each of your senses. Relax. This is so important. If you are with the partner of your choice, lock eyes, explore touch, what sensations give you pleasure, synchronise your breathing and develop a mutual rhythm. Breathe deeply. Breathe down to the very core of your pelvic floor.'

I sat back in my chair. I filled my lungs, but I suspected I had to go much deeper.

'Go beyond the diaphragm Frasey. You will need to engage your stomach muscles. Take your time. You won't get it immediately.'

'I've done some Pilates in the past.'

'Well that won't be wasted.' His smile was beautiful, something about his eyes. 'Keep breathing Frasey, steady and deep. Let's breathe together. Follow me.'

We remained there for a while, eyes locked and breathing deeply together. Through repetition I found I was breathing more deeply. I was confident sharing a rhythm with Andrew. And over the following days I found myself breathing much more deeply.

Gradually, I started to experience a quickening, from the very core of my pelvic floor. And one thing led to another.

Chapter 5

Dressing Up

My mind slips forward a few months. I'd been working on the research project since the beginning of the autumn term. I'm now recalling a Sunday in early December 2017, a significant date for both Andrew and me.

How can I explain the toe-curling joy of escaping from my house, Celine and Phoebe, and cycling up to The Mount. Wind in my hair, folders in my basket and hope in my heart. Truly, this was going home. Mrs Tordoff let me in. Even she was beginning to thaw, I could tell. She nodded now, and tried not to smile, but her eyes gave her away. I felt she was accepting me.

This day had begun as a normal working weekend Sunday. I'd done two hours on Amba's diaries, cross referencing them with her writings, notes and finished novel. I was developing an interesting timeline and was looking forward to sharing my latest insights with Andrew. Often, when I did this, it proved a trigger to his own reminiscences. The essence of his recollections I then added as footnotes. I could feel a biography coming on, but I hadn't yet shared this with Andrew.

The gong sounded to summon me to morning coffee.

Andrew was in the morning room. He was particularly cheerful.

'Frasey, you look lovely this morning. All this cycling is the antidote to your research endeavours. It brings a delightful peach blush to your cheeks and a new vivacity to your beautiful eyes.'

'Thank you, Andrew.' I felt flattered, for Andrew was a man of taste and discernment: 'Shall I pour?' I felt the need for caffeine.

'Please do. Mrs Tordoff has done some macaroons. A treat for me. It's my birthday week.'

'Andrew, I had no idea. Why, I …'

'You know, my dear, you get to my age you try to give up counting. Each year is a plus. Well. I'm eighty-nine, thus, entering my ninetieth year. Scary stuff, eh?'

'You look so much younger.'

'What does any age look like? But, no, Frasey, I don't.'

'Well, I would have bought you a card, at least.'

'You know my dear, there is something you could do for me, much better than a card. But please, if the suggestion embarrasses you, just dismiss it.'

'Okay. What would you like me to do?'

'Well, you'll be taking lunch with me − duck with the livers wrapped in bacon and sizzled in the pan − Amba's favourite. What would give me immense pleasure is this. But please, if this suggestion gives you any anxiety, discomfort, embarrassment, you must say no − it will not be mentioned again.'

'Of course.' I was intrigued.

'I wondered if you might consider wearing one of Amba's outfits. There is one I think would be most becoming. Your complexion, your colouring, even your eyes − a little − actually, so like my lovely sister's. Might you dress as Amba for lunch?'

I glanced up at the portrait, and could have sworn that the lips moved, subtly forming a smile, a far from innocent smile.

I could swear I heard a sultry voice whispering 'Do it!' in my head.

I felt a turmoil of emotions. Amba's spell was certainly drawing me in. It was impossible to read those diaries without experiencing the pulse, and the pull of her personality and the life she chose to lead. Was it such an unreasonable request for an eighty-nine-year-old man to ask a twenty-six-year-old woman to dress up in the clothes of his long dead sister? Nigh on seventy years dead too, she was.

Yes, I was disconcerted, but I was also excited and strangely aroused. In truth, I was attracted by this proposal. I tried to rationalise my inclinations. Dressing as Amba would help me into role. Look at Lucy Worsley, I reasoned. She dresses up to immerse herself in a different world. She's fun; she has fun. Lucy is clearly in control. She isn't being used or abused. And I do so love vintage clothing, especially of the 1930s and 40s.

And that is how it started. I would do my work from 9.00 – 12.00. Thirty minutes break with Andrew for morning coffee and catch-up. At noon, I would enter Amba's suite with Mrs Tordoff, and choose an outfit. Both Amba and I were perfect size 10s, and both size five and a half shoes, slender fit. Mrs Tordoff would help me put on the jewellery – bracelets and earrings. I would pull my long dark hair into a discrete, tight bun, to reveal the nape of my neck. I was cultivating a soft, short fringe round my face – just like the portrait.

Sometimes I found myself lingering on the stool in front of the mirror. It was easy to slip into a semi-trance-like mood. I could almost feel Amba around me, enveloping me. Sometimes I had this weird feeling I was becoming Amba, that she was starting to inhabit me. It was the strangest thing, both a cerebral and a physical sensation.

Towards the end of term, I had my long hair cropped close to my head. I'd borrowed a photograph to show the hairdresser. I wanted a replica. I wanted the two kiss-curls just like the later photos of Amba. Andrew became emotional when he saw my new style. He raised my head, his hand cradling my chin, and just gazed into my eyes. He brushed my forehead with a kiss right between the two curls. We stood together in a rapture of recognition for some moments. Mrs Tordoff's entry with the morning coffee tray broke the spell.

Back home, Celine and Phoebe were furious. They knew very little about my weekend work. They accused me of trying, single-handedly, to sabotage the wedding photos.

'Maxine says you'll look like a dyke!' protested Phoebe. Maxine was the lead bridesmaid.

'Excellent! I have to say that would please me. Many might suggest that I'll redeem the bridal group snaps. I don't get this modern compulsion to have hair spilling all over the place, over your shoulders and down to your bum, even to the point where if you haven't got enough of your own by nature, you stick on some other poor bugger's – from Eastern Europe, no doubt, and relinquished through necessity.'

Mrs Tordoff was disapproving – censorious, of "all this dressing-up malarkey". She'd loved my longer hair and felt I was pandering to Mr Atha's fantasies. How could I tell her they were becoming mine too.

'Are you sure you should indulge him, Miss? You don't know where this will lead. Hornet's nest you might be unleashing. He's always slept with her shoes under the bed, and her silk stockings and French knickers under his pillow. And they aren't in their packets. Funny business alright.'

'I'm happy to wear these outfits – honoured. I think it prompts Mr Atha to remember, and for me to get the feel of the times.'

'As long as that's all you get to feel.'

'Mrs Tordoff, Mr Atha is the perfect gentleman.'

'Well. I've said my piece. You've been warned. Keep your wits about you and run if you need to. One thing's for certain – he couldn't catch up with you. Bikers' thighs yours, Miss. Remember, I'm here, push the bell if you need me.'

'Thank you, Mrs Tordoff. Hopefully, not necessary, but thank you, anyway. I feel safe with you here.' I grinned. Mrs Tordoff pruned her lips in response and shook her head. I was beginning to like her. It might well be reciprocal.

I confess I found it interesting, the unexpected and not unwelcome effect that adjusting suspenders on silk stocking tops had on me. I felt as if I was getting in touch with an element of my personality that I had never explored. A desire for beautiful clothes, gowns, exquisite materials, perfume. Perhaps I'd been too eager to embrace utility. Now I felt as if I had an innate appreciation of style, gorgeousness and an inexplicable connection to a period almost one hundred years previous. What on earth was happening to me?

My mind slips forward a little further into the festive season at The Mount.

Christmas Lunch was to be a splendid affair. Even Mrs. Tordoff caught the mood of the moment. Indeed, she smiled warmly at my gift to her. It was Gervase Phinn's "Over Hill and Dale". I had secured a signed copy. This would be Mrs. Tordoff's cup of tea, I thought, and I was right. It certainly wouldn't have done for Andrew. I had something else in mind for him.

Andrew smiled at my gift for Mrs. Tordoff.

'Well, I wasn't sure if "Lilith and Leda" would be quite her thing.'

'No indeed. Well, my present to Mrs Tordoff is always the same. A year's subscription to "The Dalesman" and a table for two, premier dining on the steam train, Skipton to Carlisle and back, over Ribblehead viaduct. Pullman carriage, first class and partner of her choice. She always takes her sister Janine. She says it's the highlight of her year.'

I had felt a little mean telling my parents and Phoebe that I wouldn't be taking Christmas lunch with them this year. There were the usual reproaches from my mother: 'Your sister's last Christmas at home. The very last Christmas we could all be together as a family.'

Thank heavens for that, I'd thought. They'd be happier without me, I reasoned. Anyway, my place at the table was snapped up by the groom to be.

Christmas lunch, prepared by Mrs Tordoff with me as her willing assistant, was lavish. I had found a diary entry from the early 1930s, just when the country was getting back on its feet, well almost. Not that the Atha household had ever lost its footing. The entry was simply headed: Christmas Lunch at The Mount.

The menu was described in detail, for Amba loved good food. Some of the ingredients for the re-enactment had challenged even the Otley Waitrose, but a posh emporium in Harrogate, under-pinned by Amazon, had met any deficit. The family meal followed the classical order of formal French table service from earlier centuries – soup, hors d'oeuvres, entre, roast, salad, entremets, and dessert – or cheese, or both. We went for both.

Roast Goose was a favourite of the whole family, with a prune stuffing, along with a game pie. Amba was quite specific about the preparation of the vegetables, roast potatoes, sauces and gravy. She could not abide Christmas pudding, and would only countenance a chilled black chocolate, cherry and brandy yule log, with clotted cream and the slightest dusting of icing sugar, to suggest snow. Amba had recorded that the log was topped with a stag rampant. Mrs Tordoff had come across this cake decoration when she cleaned out the pantry. It was in an old and rusty "Bless This House" tin. Strange, but I'd happened to mention this detail I'd come across in the diary. It seemed Amba loved the stag. It rang a bell with Mrs Tordoff, for something had stopped her throwing it out. Mrs Tordoff was so gratified, embarrassed almost, at the delight showed by both Mr Atha and me, when she retrieved her find from the pantry.

Wensleydale was the cheese of choice, but there were alternatives on the board, including a fine Stilton. My own preference for Creamy Lancashire caused Andrew and Mrs Tordoff some disquiet, but they indulged me. The oatcakes came from north of the border.

Just scanning the wine list made me feel quite tipsy. There was a different wine for each stage of the meal. As I organised the three place settings, I struggled to place the different crystal glasses in the right order. Mrs Tordoff was a stickler for propriety and etiquette. I was a knife, fork and spoon girl with a coaster for the drink on the right. Mrs Tordoff said Mr Atha wanted swan serviette sculptures, for Amba had always insisted on these. I researched the folding method from an ancient Mrs Beeton.

I had always had simple tastes. For me, lunch was usually a salad sandwich, or a home-made rice and lentil concoction taken to work in a Tupperware box. I wasn't being abstemious; I just hadn't ever been conditioned to excess.

But something had shifted and I was warmed by this new mantle of sophistication. I was beginning to enjoy fine dining.

The Christmas meal re-enactment seemed to last for hours. In truth, it did last for three hours and twenty-four minutes. I felt the extraordinary glow of over-eating, and over drinking. Even Mrs Tordoff went pink and let out the odd discrete burp. Andrew smiled throughout, always in command of his senses. Truth is, I had never seen him so happy.

On the production of the yule log, topped with stag rampant, I felt Mr Atha's hand on my thigh – just over my suspenders. It lingered there for a little longer than might have been expected.

'Frasey, you make an old man very happy.' This was delivered in a re-assuring, almost avuncular voice.

'Andrew, I couldn't be happier myself.' This was the truth.

Mrs Tordoff was looking away.

I'd never really taken notice of the ancient, portable, hand-cranked record player – the Victorola. It was in a wooden case, covered in blue fabric, with gold-plated hardware.

'It's positively steam-punk, Andrew!'

He looked bewildered.

'Kinetic, no steam nor electricity required, my dear.'

A selection of 78s was sitting beside it. Top of the pile was "I can't give you anything but love, Baby".

'Let's go for it. Turn that handle!'

That's when we started to dance.

By the end of the evening we were, as Andrew termed it, quite "tol-hol." Mrs Tordoff had kept an eye on us both and it was she who decided I was in no shape to pedal home.

'You'll be all over the road, Miss Frasey. You'll end up in LGI. Now listen to me. You let your mother know you're staying over. I've made you up the bed in Miss Ida's bedroom, adjacent to Miss Amba's suite.

I must have made some half-hearted protest. But I texted Celine and Phoebe to say the Christmas celebrations continued, and my presence was required at The Mount. I told them it was my duty to be there.

Christmas Day night was a mild one, and at midnight, after Mrs Tordoff had gone to bed, Andrew and I stood by the lake, our fingers interlocked. I felt truly whole, and home, for the first time in my life.

At midnight, Andrew and I mounted the panelled stairs arm in arm, kissed demurely on the landing and we 'repaired' to our separate rooms. I entered Ida's boudoir.

Boudoir? Where did that come from. I've never used such a word. But boudoir felt right in the circumstances for the room seemed a little over the top for a bedroom. It was distinctly Art Deco. It might have been the surfeit of alcohol and fine food, the dressing up in Amba's clothes, but I felt Ida's presence in the very fabric of the room, even down to the long-handled, silver paddle hairbrush with a green enamel guilloché back, resting on the glass tray. I found myself examining this brush and pulling out a short fair hair. Was it one of Ida's? It had to be. I brushed my own hair and felt a current pass through my body. I concluded I was drunk. I removed Amba's clothing and slipped naked between the pale, blush pink silk sheets.

Sleep proved elusive. The house creaked. Old houses do. But then the adjoining door between Amba's suite and Ida's room opened silently and a lithe female form stood silhouetted against the moonlight that was flooding Amba's room. Then she entered. I knew who she was. She cast her robe, pulled back the covers and joined me. I thought of Leda, assailed by the swan, enveloped and taken, totally. I have never ever imagined I could feel such exquisite fulfilment. Was this happening to me? Was it a dream or a re-enactment of some scene from nigh on ninety years ago. Whatever, I wanted it to go on and on. I reached a level of erotic fulfilment beyond anything I'd ever imagined, ever believed possible. I cleaved a ghost to my body, and I could not, would not let her go. I felt I could never let her go.

When I awoke on Boxing Day morning, I didn't feel quite myself. Why in history was I here?

I took in the room and the wrecked bed. At first, I just wanted to burrow back into my dream. Whatever had possessed me? Whoever had possessed me? But no victim me. I could not pretend I wasn't party to whatever had happened. But then, had anything really happened? I lay between the cool silk sheets and started to persuade myself it was all a dream. After all, I have occasionally enjoyed erotic dreams. They can happen to anyone, surely? It probably was the alcohol, and the very weirdness of the night and the heightened emotions between Andrew and me. All this cerebral stuff was forced to seep into your subconscious. I was thinking about the sound of the Victorola and the old 78s, when the words of Tom Waits' *Innocent When You Dream* came into my mind. The man was right. Absolutely, you are innocent when you dream.

I gave myself a good talking to and prepared myself for breakfast. I would meet Andrew and Mrs Tordoff with full composure and good humour. And I reminded myself, I needed to ask for the early February weekend off for my sister's Hen Party.

'You have a sister? Frasey, you never said. I have been so selfish. I have never asked about you or your life. I forget there is life beyond the gates of The Mount. I so rarely venture out.'

'Andrew, you have been wise not to, to ask that is.'

'Tell me about your sister, her wedding, your family.'

'Are you sure you wish to know?'

'Of course. I am fascinated.'

And so, I began my tale. I tried to explain my relationship with my sister Phoebe, my mother Celine, the enmity between myself and Maxine, the lead bridesmaid and best friend to the bride-to-be. I also described my close but sometimes difficult relationship with my reclusive and singular father. I said the planned Hen Party excursion was an anathema to me, but that I felt obliged to go, and to take care of my sister who was easily led astray, especially by Maxine. I had promised my mother that nothing bad would happen. Foolish, in retrospect.

Andrew smiled ruefully. 'You know Frasey, we're all damaged goods. But point me to the person who dares send us back. Of course, you must go and protect Phoebe. Oh Frasey, take care of yourself too. During these last few months, you have opened a casement for me. I no longer feel entombed in this place. You have come in like a fresh breeze in my face, a fresh breeze off the moor, bringing the perfume of heather and the scent of the honey to come. I can spare you for a weekend, but I cannot live without you now. You know that, don't you? Promise you will come home to me.'

'Andrew, I have no intention of disappearing. I promise you faithfully. My time with you here at The Mount has been the most precious in my life. It has felt like coming home.'

'So where is the hen party bound?'

'Iceland. Akureyri.'

'No! Frasey, Iceland was Amba's favourite place. She loved Reykjavik. She adored Akureyri. What a coincidence that you should be going there. Amba always said she could have made her home in Iceland. She found it such a magical, mystical place. She was intrigued by its history and awed by the volcanoes. You'll find some of her travel pieces explore Akureyri. She was entranced by a church there. I forget its name. You must find these pieces and read them before you go. Why, she was in Reykjavik and Akureyri before travelling on to Stockholm on her return in 1948. Oh Frasey, my dear, do take care. I shall worry about you, you know. More than ever now I know where you are bound.'

After the Boxing Day lunch, we sat back in our chairs in Andrew's study and regarded each other. Our eyes were locked together. We breathed deeply, in harmony. From eight feet apart, it was as if we were making love. This cerebral, spiritual coupling rekindled the intense erotic encounter of the evening before. These were the first of many such experiences. The rub of his hand on my silk underwear, the pressing of his palm across my breast to smooth a gown. Whenever I was in his presence I entered a state of arousal, as if some force outside of me had taken possession of my senses. I didn't understand what was happening, but I felt no objection. Quite the contrary.

It was hard to recall exactly when I dispensed with Mrs. Tordoff's assistance in dressing for lunch. Mrs. Tordoff didn't approve anyway, and it interrupted her culinary preparations. She hated putting the gravy on hold; she loathed a skin on a sauce. 'The dressing-up malarkey put everything on hold,' she complained.

I assured Mrs Tordoff that I was perfectly capable of dressing myself without assistance and promised faithfully to place everything back exactly where it had been taken from – house rules.

It was from this time Andrew joined me in Amba's suite. He happened to be passing the door when I emerged having jammed the zip. My intent was to summon Mrs. Tordoff from the kitchen to assist. Andrew insisted he was up to the task. Then he settled himself in the old deep buttoned plum velvet armchair and watched me with a smile.

'I used to sit like this and watch Amba prepare for dinner. She liked me to help her.' He wore a faraway, wistful look. He stroked the chair arms and then looked straight into my eyes. 'I could be on hand to assist you, Frasey.'

'I would like that.' I meant it. I became increasingly aware that when I was in Amba's suite, wearing Amba's clothing, even down to her most intimate garments, my reactions, my feelings, my very instincts, were no longer my own. Or were they? I enjoyed a delicious confusion. I felt out of control, like on a ride at the fair. I felt I had out-Lucy-ed Lucy Worsely. I was becoming the part itself.

'How old were you when you started to assist Amba to dress?' I was genuinely curious.

'From about twelve, or a little later. There was a war raging. The war was so male and Amba's suite was female territory. Nothing seemed to matter when I was with her. Just me and Amba. As I properly entered my early teens, the experience with Amba became more and more intense; I lived to be with her. It was a form of possession, I suppose.'

From that encounter onwards, Andrew would enter the study, accompany me to Amba's dressing room and help me select the outfit for day. He would wind-up Amba's gramophone and place on Borodin's 'Gliding Dance of the Maidens' from Prince Igor.

I loved to remove my clothing to this music. He would sit in the velvet armchair and watch as I undressed. I would cast off Frasey and become Amba. His expression would be rapt at the transformation. When I was ready, he would stand and approach me, and he would smooth down the silk over my body, stroking me gently – my neck, breasts, arms, thighs, even my groin area if I was wearing Amba's loose silk Crepe de Chine trousers.

On Andrew's suggestion, I would spritz Joy by Jean Patou onto my neck, and, lightly, onto the inside of my wrists. Andrew had corrected me when he watched me spray onto my left wrist then rub that onto my right. He quoted Amba as expert – spray, don't rub. Friction changes the notes of the perfume. Especially a floral parfum such as Joy. And remember, never leave the bottle in the sun, and always keep it at room temperature, or cooler.'

'You make it sound like champagne, Andrew.'

'Ah, but the effect is more potent; it has a far greater power to lift the spirit. Amba had no time for champagne, you know. She always called it "the tapeworm tipple."'

'What did she mean?'

Andrew went on to tell me about their father's Great War affliction. He came back with a tapeworm.

'You know Frasey, there was a streak of cruelty lurking within my sister. This very rarely showed itself. She never once turned it on me, and certainly never on Mother. But my father didn't fare so well. She enjoyed seeing him thwarted and reduced. I do know she resented him. As I understand it, my parents handled his return from the Great War with a singular lack of sensitivity towards Amba. Sound parenting it was not. Amba found herself suddenly cast adrift from Mother. Our mother had been her world until the day Father returned. She told me that, from that moment onwards, she felt on the outside looking in.'

Andrew looked so sad. Then he smiled and continued, 'Amba came to view the tapeworm as an avenging serpent. And in a way it was. It was the tapeworm and the plane crash together that precipitated my father's decline and death. Mother told me that she had been warned by the family doctor way back in 1919 that there were dangers of dementia arising from the tapeworm. It was something to do with cysts dying, and the brain starting to swell. Well in 1949, within a year of the crash, Father went rapidly downhill. In the end we had to have him admitted to the High Royds asylum. If he wasn't reliving the Battle of Megiddo, he was calling for Amba. He also had this recurrent and terrifying vision of pigs. He said they were coming for him, coming to eat him. It was horrible to witness when he was like this. And it was truly sad. In a relatively short period, he started seeing people who weren't there.

I was with him one day when he insisted T. E Lawrence had entered the room. I think he mistook the nurse's white cap for Lawrence's keffiyeh. Who knows? Mother and I had all on persuading him that the nurse hadn't come in with evil intent. He hated Lawrence. He also endured unwelcome visits from his sister-in-law Rania.

"Bloody woman, get her out of here!"

'This was brought on every time one rather stunning nurse entered the room. I suppose she was a little like the pictures I've seen of Rania. Oh, but it was hard for Mother to be losing her husband and have her beloved, long dead sister exhumed and abused. He also became quite violent and very unpredictable. But even towards the end he enjoyed odd moments of lucidity. I say enjoyed. Hardly enjoyment. It's hard to come to your senses, and to find yourself in High Royds.'

Back to our pre-lunch preparations.

'Joy' had been Amba's favourite perfume – jasmine and roses. It had been created the year that Wall Street crashed. It was billed as the most expensive perfume in the world back then and stood in stark contrast to the feel of the times.

I loved wearing it; it was a trigger. Andrew would lightly snuffle my neck, and then select jewellery. He was very adept with intricate clasps – surprising for a man with such arthritic misshapen fingers.

When I was ready, Andrew would stand back, regard me and brush my hand with his moustache-veiled lips. We ate lunch in a state of heightened desire.

After lunch, Andrew liked to take a nap. Mrs Tordoff would clear away, and I would transform back into myself. I needed no assistance for this.

As I worked on into the afternoon, I rested my eyes. I caught myself smiling. It hit me how much I was going to miss Andrew on the weekend of the hen party. A song came into my mind, a song from long ago. "Stranger in Paradise" from Kismet. Then I realised – it was so like the "Gliding Dance". I would have to check this out, but then, I checked myself. Why? Who cares? The devil might be in the detail, as the saying went, but for me, the thing I most sought was the energy of elation and euphoria in the risk, the reverie and the rapture of desire. Desire became the end, an exquisite emotion sufficient unto itself.

This was such new territory for me.

Chapter 6

Taking Off

Past the Leeds Bradford Airport's industrial estates, in a layby near the Otley turn, Andrew Atha joins the plane spotters. He eases himself out, slowly and stiffly, from his Mercedes. He leans his weight on his black beechwood cane with a chrome Fritz handle and collar. He checks his watch. He sees the plane lifting. He follows its progress, its rising, with something akin to a prayer to the sky:

'Please don't take her away from me again,' he whispers. 'Please keep her safe.'

This plane carries the Menston Hen Party. It's flying the young women to the north of Iceland, to Akureyri. The members are strapped in, five rows down. The plane rises through the dense cloud, higher and higher.

Frasey watches the landscape surrounding the airport. She thinks of Andrew, somewhere below her. She then focuses on the white wing tips through the windows crisp against the pure blue sky.

The seat belt light goes off. There is a general unbuckling, sighing and stretching.

Either side of the aisle are three seats, but there are seven hens, so they spill over. Maxine, lead bridesmaid, has organised the seating plan and she has placed Frasey on the row in front, on her own. We know that Maxine is in charge because it says so on her tee-shirt. Maxine's had a boob job, so the message stands out. Its content is endorsed by a more than risqué image of a dominatrix in bondage, straddling and whipping a man.

Frasey does not mind this demotion to the row in front, for she finds her own company a lot more agreeable, intelligent and rewarding than her companion hens' half-hearted attempts to engage her. She is relieved the hens have removed their 'fun' headpieces for the flight. Again, these were Maxine's choice. She found them on-line on a dodgy site. Frasey has steadfastly refused to wear hers; it remains, pristine, in its box.

Next to Frasey is an elderly couple, George and Mary. Pleasantries have been exchanged. Frasey has always enjoyed brief encounters with strangers.

Over the aisle from Frasey is an empty seat – a rare thing for this airline. An absent friend, perhaps? Then, there's Belinda, who can't believe her luck to have a free seat next to her. She can spread out now the seat belt signs have gone off. Next to Belinda is Patch, her eight-year-old son. Patch is glued to the window. He's considering the nature of clouds.

When Belinda leaves her seat to use the toilet, she steps into the aisle and turns to Frasey.

'Just need to nip to the loo. Might you keep your eye on my son for a moment?'

'My pleasure,' says Frasey. She watches Belinda move forward with a slight stagger.

The captain comes on to warn of turbulence. George is securing the remains of his tea. Patch is sidling and shuffling along the seat towards Frasey.

'Do you know about clouds?' Patch's earnest eyes look

directly into Frasey's.

'A little. What about you?'

'Our teacher says they are made of water. They don't look as though they are, not from the window.'

'She's right though. They are made up of droplets of water, or ice crystals. It depends on how high they are, and the temperature of the atmosphere. Because of the height of the plane, and that we are flying northwest, these are probably made of ice crystals.'

'Do you know anything else about clouds?'

'I know the four main types – each has a name.'

'What names do they have?'

'Stratus – flat – like the ones we've just come through. Then there's cumulus – think cauliflowers; cirrus are wispy and nimbus are dark and threatening – rain bearing.'

Patch asks Frasey to say these again. She can tell he's memorising. She feels a strange affinity with the child.

'My mum's coming back. Can you tell me one more thing about clouds?'

'They're beautiful.' Frasey smiles.

'I think so too. I think clouds are brilliant. These glitter in the sun like jewels.'

'Then they must be made up of particles of ice.'

'Ice clouds, clouds of ice.' Patch roles the concept round his mind, smiles and turns his attention back to the window.

Frasey sits back and thinks – to see through the science, to find the joy, the poetry in the data, the music in the maths, the unexpected and inexplicable within the explainable. It can be done, otherwise there is no point.

As Belinda returns, she sees Patch deep in conversation with Frasey across the aisle.

'This lady has told me things about clouds.'

Belinda turns to Frasey. 'That's so good. But I hope he

hasn't been a nuisance.'

'Not at all. He has, I suspect, a serious mind. Bright boy. Lucky you.'

'I think I am.'

Yes, I am lucky. It's good to have come away, thinks Belinda.

The seat belt sign is illuminated again. The captain announces the descent into Akureyri – right on time, he adds. The weather report – sunny, cold and crisp. Adverse weather on the way, but not until tomorrow.

Patch looks out again, now they are through the clouds.

'What can you see, Patch?' Belinda has moved back to the seat next to Patch for the descent.

Patch sees the azure, blue sky that fades gently to the palest iced lemon at the point where sky meets land. He sees the iced mountainous landscape. He sees, he gasps, yes, he sees a crater, a volcano's crater.

'Mum, I'm looking down a volcano!'

The sun is picking out the inside of the crater. Belinda, sceptical, leans over him.

'My God Patch. You are! Imagine that!'

Patch takes a photo on his iPhone.

'Show this to the cloud lady. She can't see from where she's sitting.'

Belinda stretches over with the phone to show Frasey.

'Patch wants you to see the volcano. I think you've made a deep impression on my son!'

Frasey beams. She sees Patch's eager eyes waiting for her response. She nods to him and puts her thumb up.

'My very first volcano!' she says. 'Thank you, Patch. There I was, dreaming away. I had no idea I was flying over a volcano.'

Belinda and Patch hold hands for the final descent. The plane bumps a little on the landing, then glides along.

'Quite a soft landing, Patch, considering. Let's let them

all get off. No-one is going anywhere fast and the man we're meeting won't drive off without us, that's for sure.'

The seat belt light is switched off. People are stirring in their seats. Frasey is daydreaming about Andrew and the nature of the desire they both feel for each other. She wonders if she will ever be able to confide in anyone about her relationship with him. She wants to tell the world, but shrinks at the thought. Who could ever understand? Her mother, Phoebe, Maxine, spare me she thought, Miss Claxton? Even Mrs Tordoff was hoping it wasn't really happening.

George turns to Frasey:

'You must have dropped off love. You didn't even notice the bump.'

'I was dreaming, dreaming, remembering and wondering.'

'Pleasant things, I suspect. You were smiling. Are you one of these hens behind us?'

The Hens were now shrill with anticipation and adjusting their hen headpieces. Hysterical laughter, each egging the other on.

'I'm afraid I am. I'm sister of the bride. My mother thinks I'll make them all behave themselves. As if.'

Frasey rolls her eyes skywards.

'Poor you. You'll have your hands full, love. What made you choose Iceland rather than somewhere warm?'

'It was my sister's choice. She'd read that Iceland was the safest place in the world for women.'

'Will it be safe for the men though? That's what I want to know.'

'Most likely not. Have you seen what they're wearing on their heads. I categorically refused to put one on mine.'

George looked round his headrest.

'Well. I've seen it all now. Mary, cop these girls on the row behind. In my born days, I would never have imagined such.'

The Hens are now swaying in the aisle, clamouring to get off. They pass the cabin crew, who look up above their heads, in mild surprise. Frasey hangs back to let George get his hand luggage down, and she gives Mary a hand to sidle out of the seat. Belinda and Patch follow.

Our travellers take their first steps on Iceland's frozen tarmac, and make their way, with caution, to the terminal building.

Chapter 7

The Long, Long Weekend

Gunnar the Tour Guide sits beneath the window of Porgeir the Lawspeaker in the Akureyrarkirkja – The Church of Akureyri. He calms himself. He checks his watch. In twenty minutes' time, he will stride, with seeming confidence, down the steep steps towards the water, collect his tour minibus from the designated parking area by the hotel, and drive along the shore of the Eyjafjorour Fjord to the airport. He has travellers to meet, greet and keep safe.

Steady deep breathing helps. Gunnar feels his nerves jangle before each new group arrives. He is not yet seasoned in his role. Until he meets this new group and gets their measure, he will experience tension, apprehension and, possibly, a mild migraine.

Gunnar's eyes seek those of Porgeir the Lawspeaker, who is set in stained glass. Porgeir is one of his early and enduring heroes. He was and is the stuff of boys' comics. Lawspeakers were chosen for their wisdom and eloquence.

'You would take all of this in your stride, old fellow.' Gunnar locks eyes with Porgeir and tastes his own inadequacy.

Porgeir is not at liberty to answer, being set in lead and glass, but it doesn't stop him feeling a degree of sympathy for this pleasant young warrior. To take on the great white bird is big, by anyone's standards.

Þorgeir carried the well-being of his people in his own hands – their spiritual well-being, that is. Well over a thousand years ago it was. He led them from the old gods to the new one. But he honoured the old ones. He himself was a heathen, to begin with. He respectfully cast the relics of the Aesir – of Odin, Frigg, Thor and the others – into the large and beautiful waterfall near his farm at Ljdsavatn. This became known as Godafoss – the Falls of the Gods.

Gunnar Gunnarsson is charged with the physical well-being of a party from Menston, near Leeds. Their spiritual well-being? Well, that would be a truly big ask. But he wants them to have a nice time, tell their friends, and drum up more business for Gunnarsson's North of Iceland Getaways. Þorgeir wanted to ensure his people went to heaven. Gunnar just wants them to get back to Leeds Bradford Airport in one piece – each one of them. Intact, with happy memories and lots of good pictures – digital are better but do have a care for the cold conditions, he will tell them, will screw up their batteries. "Keep your camera in your pocket, unless you are using it." He works to a well-thought out and rehearsed script. He'd polished his English via his passion for Hollywood blockbusters and Netflix boxed sets. His English was enough.

'Time to throw off the old cloak again, Þorgeir. Let's go meet these Brits.'

Þorgeir the Lawspeaker watched him leave the church. He wanted to shout after him: 'Be lucky!' but his words were locked in his throat.

Gunnar waits by the arrivals gate. His green Gunnarsson's Getaways board in his hand, his first glimpse of his new charges is as they cluster together, pointing up towards a screen. He looks up. 'Oh God' he's thinking. 'The Iceland Phallological Museum.' It's causing them great mirth. The young women are cackling into their palms. Then he realises the seven young women are an English hen party. Six of the seven are wearing pink horned helmets. A nod to the Viking warriors no doubt, thinks Gunnar. He will have to tell them there is no evidence Vikings wore horned helmets. Then there's the elderly couple, and finally a young mother and child, hanging back a little. Eleven members – nine female, one man, one boy aged eight. As they draw closer he sees the pink horns are in fact erect penises on fluffy headbands.

'Give me strength, Porgeir. I'm going to need it. This looks a toughie. It's going to be a long, long weekend.'

Flight Number ENT501 – Departs Leeds Bradford 8.20. Arriving Akureyri 11.00

'Right on time, Mary. Now we need to find our guide. Perhaps he'll be waiting at the gate with something in his hand.'

'Look at that, George! Up there, on the screen.'

'What's it saying, lass?' George peers over his glasses, reads slowly and articulates carefully: 'The Iceland Penis Museum. Good God, our Mary. What next?'

'These folk here, they have no shame, George. Where have we come? What are they like?'

Mary and George have this inclusive way of talking. All those near them are now drawn in, alert to the screen and engaged in speculation. The Menston Hen Party is convulsed in giggles, members suggesting great specimens they have encountered, and which they would like to see exhibited in the museum, so long as they took their owners with them.

A quieter and yet more authoritative voice speaks out.

'As far as I can see, that's where most of them belong! Sorry Hens, no disrespect meant.'

All eyes turn to Belinda and her young son. These two are bringing up the rear, behind the Hen Party.

'Are you one of them there feminists?' asks George, in troubled disapproval. He's studying her through his varifocal lenses.

Belinda's smile is enigmatic and evasive. She closes this line of enquiry with a furrowing of her brows. But she does not look away.

Most of the Hens are losing steam and interest. Attention span is spent, except for Frasey. The concept of The Iceland Penis Museum intrigues her.

'It says here The Icelandic Phallological Museum is probably the only museum in the world to contain a collection of phallic specimens belonging to all the types of mammals found in a single country. TripAdvisor ranks it at No 40 amongst 183 attractions in Reykjavik. That's not a bad score.'

'Reykjavik is in the south, and we're in the north. So, we can't go anyway. And put your tablet away Frasey. The cold will screw up your battery. It warned us about that in the trip notes.'

Frasey squares up to Maxine: 'The notes referred to conditions outdoors, not in the airport building itself.'

Phoebe's doubts about the personality mix between her studious sister Frasey and her own more licentious friends are mounting. Maxine, chief bridesmaid-to-be, projects tangible contempt towards Frasey – the antipathy of an opposite. Maxine might be a beauty, but she has hard eyes, and a disdainful mouth: 'It's a shame your sister's never discovered Smirnoff,' whispers Maxine to Phoebe, with a sneer.

Belinda's son Patch is also troubled:

'Mum, we don't have to go to see these dicks, do we?'

'No Patch, it's the Northern Lights for us. We're here to see The Merry Dancers. No dicks, and no more dickheads, eh?' Belinda shoots a look at George's disappearing back and rolls her eyes.

Gunnar is waiting for his new group at the arrivals gate. They cluster around him and he ticks them off on the list on his clipboard. All accounted for, he leads them to the mini tour bus. Once on board, he introduces himself in slightly off-kilter English and a heavy accent. He says he's called Gunnar and he welcomes the group to the long week-end in Akureyri: 'First we go get our hotel!'

The tour minibus traverses a lunar landscape. Patch looks back to Frasey who mouths 'volcanic' and they exchange smiles. It is hard to tell who is the more excited.

Later, Frasey settles into her hotel room. The window looks out on a long flight of steps that leads up to the church doors. There is a light sprinkling of snow. The black cast iron handrails jut up in stark contrast. The sparse trees fractionate the dying light, ice silver blue smoothly merging into the deepest midnight hue. The church's columned, Art Deco twin towers are illuminated in a comforting yellow light, and beneath the central cross is a bold clock showing five to six in roman numerals, black against a cream background. Frasey feels this moment through her core.

Sometimes, Frasey reflects, being alone is delicious, exciting and highly conducive to stretching each moment. She has that strange feeling of having been in this place before. The clock strikes six with jangly chimes. As these notes cease, a figure appears to the right and starts to mount the steps. A female, Frasey has no doubt of this. A black sable cape envelops her form, a tight turban pulled down over her head, and wide dark trousers sway. Her walk is so elegant she almost glides. She doesn't take the rails. At the top of the steps the figure halts and turns, slowly. She turns to look directly down. It is as if she is staring straight into Frasey's window, even into her eyes. The figure inclines her head graciously. Frasey begins to raise her hand to wave, but there's a knocking at the door. Frasey turns sharply.

It's Gunnar checking that she's happy with her room. Of course she is.

When she returns to the window, the sky has swallowed the light, and the figure has gone.

Three hours later, after dinner, Patch and Belinda descend the hotel stairs well-wrapped and muffled against the plummeting evening temperature. Patch listens to the church bell chiming nine. To him, the sequence sounds like a skeleton plucking the strings of an ice harp.

It's a bit past his bedtime, the boy being barely eight. It's a treat to be up so late. He's trying to remember not to put his thumb in. He is the man now, that's what his mum has told him.

'Will they dance for us tonight?'

'We travel in hope,' sighs Belinda.

Patch thinks that's what she's saying, but she's so well scarfed up it's hard to tell. They climb onto the tour bus, which is raised high above the ground on massive broad tyres with deep tread.

Gunnar greets his group again and reminds them that the quest this first evening is to go and find the Northern Lights.

'But before we set off we must toilet think.'

The Hens have spent the last hour in the hotel bar and toilet think hasn't been top of their agenda. They greet Gunnar's thoughts with mirth.

'Seriously, my sweet travellers – no toilets. Not on bus, not where we go, so if you need toilet, you go on snow. Okay? So, now you know – you go now or forever hold your piss.'

Belinda starts to giggle. She thinks Gunnar might be fun, then kills the thought, and her smile, shortly afterwards.

The Hens retreat to the ground floor toilets of the hotel, followed by George, who ducks into the adjacent door.

'Old waterworks – that's his problem,' announces Mary to all who have remained in their seats.

When everyone is back onboard, Gunnar begins to describe the evening's trip, but is interrupted by Maxine:

'Hey Gunnar, so is it Jon Snow's cave tomorrow?'

The rest of the Hens pile in:

'You know – the place where he lost his cherry.'

'Yeh, he might have lost his cherry, but he kept his kit on, even his furry mitts.'

'She didn't. I wish my arse was as trim as hers. I won't be presenting mine to camera.'

'Don't worry yourself on that score – they'd pay you to keep it under wraps.'

'Still, I'd love to do it with a man in furs.'

'He must have taken something off…'

'Anyway, never mind all this, is it tomorrow?' Maxine presses on, losing patience.

Frasey is sinking lower and lower into her quilted coat, and down further in her seat.

'Yes ladies, the Jon and Ygritte Cave is in tomorrow plan. But first we have tonight Northern Light trip.'

Gunnar tries to recapture his thread – the route to be taken, timings, where best to see the Lights, and the likely chances of a sighting.

'Who's this Jon Snow, Mum? Why was he eating his cherries in a cave? Was it a picnic?'

'Always a possibility Patch. It's all about a series on the telly. I didn't watch it.' Belinda shrugs.

Gunnar struggles on with his commentary.

Patch continues: 'Now what's the man saying?' Patch is eager not to miss a moment, but he's having a bit of trouble with Gunnar's English, his accent and the Hens' constant cackling.

Belinda whispers:

'He's saying that the conditions are good. No moon – that's a plus – 'cos it's all about avoiding light pollution. And it's a clear night. So, we've got a lot going for us. They saw some good ones, last night. This means the Dancers know their way here.'

Patch has been trying to imagine the Merry Dancers.

'But, how will we know if we've seen them?'

'Tricky, and yet not tricky at all. Sometimes they're like curtains in a breeze. Sometimes they're like light rain showers on the horizon, or smoke. And sometimes they're like a great rainbow reforming. But you'll know, Patch. Of this I have no doubt.'

Patch curls into his mother's side. He raises his thumb, then pulls it back sharply. Oscar is his proper name. But Belinda always calls him Patch, or her Patch of Blue, when they have a cuddle. The name has stuck. Belinda tries to explain; she says it's Reading Gaol meets Mary Newland Carson. Oscar doesn't care where it comes from. He likes Patch. It makes him think of pirates, especially Pugwash. He's got a full set of the books – in a special presentation box. It sits on his bedroom shelf in their bedsit.

'Ah yes, and they change colours. They might start out cream, but then pink or magenta creeps in, then to red, and green and many shades of blue – your colour Patch.'

They drive the darkness, high above the fjord, along the side of the mountain and park by the road. The group descends the coach steps, climbs over the mini hill of snow pushed up by the plough along the road's edge and shuffle along to take up a viewing spot. Gunnar struggles off with a telescope on a tripod. He calls to the group:

'Don't wander too far off – there's big drop. And keep your bodies off road. Keep this thought – cars can't brake fast here.'

'Breakfast?' interjects George, confused. The Hens cackle. They are beginning to bond with George since the 'toilet think' incident.

Belinda touches her son's sleeve: 'Look Patch, over there. No Dancers yet, but the sky is starting to shimmer.'

His eyes fly. He sees the stars as he's never seen them before. There is something wobbling above, and within him.

Gunnar is on to it too. There's a 'v' in the mountain range opposite. He's pointing to it. Something is coming up like smoke.

'OMG! Seen it, tick it off. But it's bloody freezing.' Phoebe, Maxine and the Hens, minus Frasey, retreat to the minibus in triumph. Mary follows too. The door closes behind them with a soft sucking sound, sealing in the warmth. But those who board must sit in darkness. The inside lights would ruin the viewing for those who stay outside.

Belinda gets her tablet out of her rucksack and points the lens, steady, towards the emerging lights.

'It won't make much of a picture.' says George.

She blanks him. She's undeterred. She kneels on the achingly iced ground.

'Give it thirty seconds, Patch. It takes that long to collect the light. She holds the tablet in front of him, so he needn't take off his gloves.

'Mum, it's Lyra's dust. There's red particles flying in!' Belinda thinks the look on Patch's face at this moment makes this trip worthwhile.

Then the turquoise spirits rise above the mountain, over the fjord. A broad band of Dancers arc the sky, in a rearing rainbow.

Belinda and her Patch of Blue, arms around each other for warmth, stand and stare. They stand so long, so chilled, so thrilled, and the shutters in their heads click and the spirits enter. There they will dance forever.

Gunnar stands slightly to the side, a little behind them. He's watching the mother and her son intently.

Frasey stands close too, gazing across the fjord, her gaze moving up gradually with the Dancers, higher and higher, until her neck seems to set rigid on her shoulders. She turns to Gunnar. 'How would you score tonight's showing?'

Gunnar turns to her and smiles broadly, 'Eight out of ten – we have been lucky.' Then he looks up again, and bethinks himself:

'Wow, better and better by moment – possibly, yep, a definite nine.'

Right arm extended, Gunnar traces the pulsing, broad and complete bridge of the Lights. 'Full sweep from both sides – rare thing – now time to make a wish. Tell Dancers what hope you hope for most.'

'Load of complete tosh,' grumbles George. 'I bet there isn't a Bloody Dancer up there that can stop Guiseley going down. It's been in the stars since sodding Christmas.'

Gunnar smiles, unphased by George's scepticism. Gunnar's a football fan too and knows how frustrating this can be. Finger to frosted lips, he whispers 'Keep wish secret.'

Patch, Belinda, Frasey, Gunnar and even George gaze upwards, each measuring the heights of their own hopes.

'Really better than last night?' asks Patch.

'Yes, my little man, better than any sighting this year. Full force of the ten. They must have known you were coming.'

The last Lights gazers, weary, frozen stiff and elated, climb back on board.

'That driver lad – Gunnerside, or whatever his name – says

you should make a wish when you get the full curve of the lights like them up there.'

Mary nods, looks out through the steaming glass and, silently, makes her wish: 'Twelve more months and a soft landing, Girls.' For politeness, she adds 'Please.' She shifts in her seat for a more comfortable position.

Phoebe gazes at Frasey as her sister moves down the aisle to take up her seat. Frasey has just pulled off her beanie, on entering the bus. With her hair cropped tightly to her head and her wide dark eyes, she reminds Phoebe of a fawn. It has occurred to her, regularly in fact, that Celine, her mother, might have played away at the time of her Frasey's conception. There seems no strand of similarity between herself and Frasey. Their faces bear no element of resemblance. Frasey is tall and angular, and somehow off the pace. She herself is ash blonde, pretty, petite, and curvaceous. She likes to live in the present, have friends, laughs, fun, frivolity. Her husband to be, Jim, has been her boyfriend since they were both sixteen, in the same class at school. She feels that she and Jim follow a map, and that the path is clear. They have found a flat, they will save for a house with a garden, and have kids Yes, there will be children one day soon, sooner than anyone might imagine, she smiles to herself. She likes to pick names in anticipation. She would like girl babies and dress them up in pretty outfits.

Frasey smiles down at her sister: 'So glad I've come; these Lights are brilliant. I had no idea. You should have stayed out there. They got better and better, stronger and stronger. You missed the best bits.'

Phoebe shrugs: 'We'd seen enough, and we were frozen stiff. Still, I'm glad you liked them.' Maxine nudges Phoebe surreptitiously, smirks and raises her pencilled eyebrows. Not only is Maxine Phoebe's friend, but she's also Eric's girlfriend.

Eric is to be best man at the wedding. He and Jim have been best friends since nursery school. The two couples anticipate their friendship will last forever.

Frasey's thoughts are running along different tracks. The hen party trip is already defying her own expectations. When the issue of a hen party was first raised by Phoebe, Frasey froze. She anticipated the cringing embarrassment of being corralled with Phoebe's friends. She expected it would be all "I'll show my muff at Magaluf" and that kind of stuff. The choice of Iceland surprised, pleased and intrigued her. It seems, Phoebe had set her heart on Iceland, the north of Iceland too. When Frasey asked why, Phoebe had told her it was the safest place on earth for women. What Phoebe omitted to say was that it was driven by her obsession with Game of Thrones. Phoebe has the hots for Jon Snow, and so have the other Hens. Frasey hasn't a clue who this man is. Still, Frasey finds she herself is taking different pleasures from the experience.

Frasey snuggles into her seat, arms wrapped across her chest. She wipes the back of her fur-lined mitten across the steamed glass. She looks down at the deep dark fjord and tries to imagine the temperature of the water. But then she confuses herself with thoughts about the volcanic nature of Iceland, geothermal factors, and what if, yes, what if, warmer water changes things. What if those seemingly frozen depths are as warm as Ilkley lido on a hot August afternoon? She makes a mental note of this for later research, or to check with Gunnar. She thinks she needs to know.

Then, as Frasey stares at the fjord, she has one of those rare insights – the sort you get when you are travelling far away from home. At that moment she sees that so much in life is about chance, and chance can be capricious, and yet can be emancipating. Phoebe tells her repeatedly to loosen up, to let herself go a little, but then Phoebe has no inkling of her other life, her life at The Mount. Frasey would acknowledge that, until the advent of Andrew, she had conducted her own life, largely, to mitigate chance. She had tried to impose a discipline and calculation on everything that she did. She took her joys from knowledge, facts and stats. But where had that got her? And she also knows she's not done yet. Something is happening to her, and wherever it is leading her, it is freeing her from her former herself.

What is the line about the best laid plans, Frasey wonders. Surreptitiously, she takes out her tablet and googles it. From Steinbeck she clicks on to Robbie Burns, but it is schemes not plans that go wrong. "Gang aft agley" – "Go oft awry". She rolls "gang aft agley" round her mouth. She thinks she might enjoy it – to "gang aft agley", properly "agley", over and over again. She already has started to enjoy it, immensely. In her head she sees Andrew's enraptured face as he sits in the velvet chair, watching her undress to Borodin. She's aware she is warming up; she smiles to herself. She whispers goodnight for now to him. She'll email him when she gets back to the hotel. The heat from the coach's blowers now envelops her too and she pulls off her down jacket. After the icy night with its visions and mysteries, she will allow herself the luxury of a nap.

'Seriously underwhelmed, Mary,' says George.

'Well, worth seeing, but not worth the trip, eh?' Mary laughs. She smiles fondly at her husband and continues: 'Someone famous said something like that about somewhere – Scotland I think. Well, it's true here – not when you add up the costs, and the cold. I'll be glad to get back to the hotel. But, in fairness, it is a lovely hotel. Wonder what they eat for breakfast?'

'I'd put money on a buffet, Mary. As much as you can eat. I always like that. I'll be disappointed if it is a menu thingy. I hate it when they put it out for you on your plate.'

'George, the principle behind the buffet is that the average person is too polite to load up and go back again and again.'

'More fools them.'

Mary squeezes her husband's hand and gazes out the window. The stars battle the darkness above the fleeting, snow encrusted caps of pines. When to tell him, that is the question. Lumps and tests. The prognosis is not good. She too tries to clear a patch on the misting glass. The last of the lights waves her goodnight. She shudders with the chill and the eternal darkness up above her:

'Remember my wish, Merry Dancers.' Mary channels her thoughts to the firmament, then crosses herself as a second security. I'll wait till we get back home to Leeds, she thinks. I hope to make it to the summer. And I'm not spoiling his trip.

The travellers fall quiet. The coach's headlamps eat up the night. The return drive to the hotel seems so much shorter. Gunnar pulls the coach into the drop off area, with all the skill, elegance and certainty of a person used to driving on thick ice. He assists each traveller down the icy steps, modifying the level of intervention subtly, to each according to their need. Then he climbs back to check the coach is empty. He sees Belinda standing, gazing down towards the seat.

'Okay?'

'My son, Patch, he's sound asleep. It's a shame. I'd better wake him.'

Gunnar nods, takes in the scene.

'Stand back.' Gunnar lifts the sleeping Patch in his arms. 'Sleep on, little man,' he whispers. 'Which room?'

'Room 413.'

Belinda opens the lift and lets them in. She steps in too.

She sees her son from a different angle. His floppy mid-brown hair is hanging down – his trapper hat has come off, secured only by the ties. His arms and legs hang down too, inert, unlike Gunnar whose body and stance exude strength and energy. Out of the lift, and at the door, she fumbles her card into the slot – the door swings open.

'Bed by the window.'

Gunnar lays down the still sleeping Patch onto the bed with unexpected gentleness. He unties the hat and pulls off the boy's heavy snow boots, parka and gloves.

'I think little man had a good time tonight, yes?'

'Gunnar, he loved tonight. I thank you.'

And Gunnar is gone. Belinda loosens Patch's belt and carefully winds off his scarf. She covers him with the quilt.

'My sweet Patch of Blue,' she whispers. Her lips gently brush the boy's brow.

Belinda sits on her own bed, watching the soft rise and fall of Patch's quilt. She feels overwhelmed with sadness, sorrow, so overcome she chokes with tearless sobs. She breathes deeply and pushes away her thoughts. Kindness, that's what does it, she thinks. Kindness can be harder than cruelty, when you are used to clenching your jaws firmly against a blow.

She opens the minibar for solace, gin and tonic, and a small sachet of roasted cashew nuts. Best not to drain the lot, she thinks. But then again?

'Stop that now. Low self-esteem – your father's gift to you, and so totally endorsed by your husband, your ex I should say. We'll be having no more of that!' Her counsellor cum life coach lives on in her mind. This way, the counsellor keeps Belinda on track to recovery.

Belinda props herself up on her bed and focuses on Patch's

breathing. She tries to match her own with his. When she finally emerges from this state of abstraction, she realises she is crying, silently. Breathe, she tells herself, as she pours herself another G&T.

Chapter 8

One of the Good Guys

Gunnar is in turmoil. Since he left Belinda and the sleeping Patch at speed, he has been racked with anxiety and self-recrimination. Should he be in a female guest's room? Okay, his motives were honourable. He wanted to help the young mother. He had lifted her sleeping child from his bus and carried him to the hotel bed. But, for a man to carry a woman's child – was this a significant thing? No doubt it was tantamount to marriage in some cultures. No, he is being silly, taking on. He was there to ensure his travellers were happy, safe and well-catered for. He should help when required. But should he have entered her hotel bedroom?

What Gunnar is trying not to acknowledge to himself is that he has been experiencing a high voltage attraction to the mother all evening, and once in her room, a strong, almost overwhelming impulse to throw her onto the bed and ravish her. She is gorgeous. She seems to be bringing out the long-buried Viking in him. Well, something is stirring, he's thinking. But that isn't her fault. He's the one who harbours inappropriate thoughts.

'Come on,' says the Porgeir in his head. 'You didn't do it, boy. You resisted the temptation – top man!' By some strange shift in Gunnar's sub-conscious, Porgeir speaks in Gunnar's dreams and in his head, in a Brooklyn accent – think Harvey

Keitel in 'Reservoir Dogs'. Gunnar himself has tried to style his own accent and delivery on Barack Obama. He can't always pull this off.

Still, thinks Gunnar, I'm sinning in my head, and heart, and elsewhere. It's not very professional, is it? I am an ethical tour operator. I don't eat puffins and recently, I've even rejected whale meat, my favourite. Well, I might have had the odd slip. I'm a good guide to my beautiful country, not a cheap opportunist gigolo. I've got to get a grip.

Gunnar has been unlucky in love, and in life in general. His role as tour operator was prompted by a sequence of disasters. The financial crisis of 2008 – 2011 resulted in Gunnar losing his job at the University of Iceland in Reykjavik. He'd been taken on, albeit in a temporary post, at the Northern Volcanological Centre, but the resulting economic depression meant job losses, and he had no security. He lost his partner, Birta, to his best friend and former colleague, at the Centre. His friend had been kept on.

Unemployed and heartbroken he retreated to the family sheep farm, only to face further devastation when the impact of the 2010 eruption hit the farm, and left work for only one son – his elder brother.

Aftershocks continued – one a year. Birta and his ex-best friend kept producing babies. This could have been us, lamented Gunnar. He was haunted by the vision of the beautiful blond Birta, babies at her voluptuous breasts, toddlers tugging at her trousers. This could have been us.

Now is the time to panic, thought Gunnar. Like Porgeir, a thousand years before him, he spent a night and a day under the cloak, wrestling with his own demons, to reach a key decision about his future life. Like Porgeir, he, Gunnar, was a pragmatist. He itemised his skills, strengths and knowledge. He knew about farming, nature, history, geology, geomorphology and he certainly knew a lot about volcanoes. He sold his flat in Reykjavik and bought a small tour bus.

Gunnar hasn't looked at another woman until this night. Belinda has blown Birta out of the water, so it's another night under the cloak. Gunnar falls into a fitful slumber. He walks by the waters of the Godafoss. Porgeir approaches resplendent in his clasped scarlet cloak and green robe. The jewels of his clasp glint in the sun. The sky glows blue behind the mauve tinged hills and mountains. They exchange words:

'Win the kid and you've halfway won the broad.'

'Really?'

'Truly. You're off to a flyer. You carried the kid to bed, then vamoosed. You left her wanting more. You are one of the good guys.'

Before dawn breaks, he's decided to win the woman's heart – a reputable quest indeed. And the way to her heart …

Chapter 9

Frasey

In her room, a little further down the corridor, Frasey takes out her tablet and types:

Dear Andrew,

I'm here and safe so please don't worry.

I have a comfortable room with a fine view of the Akureyrarkirkja – The Church of Akureyri. I look out onto the steps. This was Amba's favourite church – the one she wrote about.

Things have been so strange since we parted. So many sensations; so many emotions. The Hen Party is such an embarrassment. It is so odd to be part of a group, and yet remain isolated. Maxine, the lead bridesmaid, finds it impossible to conceal her dislike for me. I don't really understand where this came from. I have never willingly offended her. But she has such a face on her, as my mother would say, every time she looks at me. Phoebe has softened a little. I suspect she feels sorry for me because she sees I'm out on a limb. Truly, I reckon I have more reason to feel sorry for her.

In our small tour group I gravitate to those outside the Hens. I am particularly drawn to a young woman called Belinda. I don't know Belinda's story, but sadness lives in her eyes. She intrigues me. I suspect she might be divorced. She has an adorable son called Patch. I assume this is a nickname. Patch is eight. On the plane, Belinda left Patch in my care whilst she went to the toilet. We bonded over clouds, and then volcanoes. He is a singular child, curious, sweet natured and very intelligent. The two make pleasing companions for me. And then there is an older couple, George and Mary. They are from Guiseley and at first, I thought they would be rather narrow minded, but I think they are going to be fun. They are very "Yorkshire" – cut from the same cloth as Mrs Tordoff.

But enough of them all. What happened tonight was amazing. I saw The Northern Lights. Amba had prepared me for The Merrie Dancers in her writings, but the showing tonight exceeded all my expectations. How I wished that you had been by my side to see this vision.

How I wish you were by my side now. We are giving up one of our precious weekends for me to be here. I know I promised Celine to keep my eye on Phoebe, but I have to confess, I have already departed from my brief. After the trip tonight, I ducked out of going out again. The Hens have gone clubbing. I just couldn't face it. I ordered a cocoa and toast in my room and attempted to make sense of Icelandic news on the TV. Luckily there was a fair bit in English with sub-titles for the locals.

I'll report back tomorrow evening. We are off on a full day's excursion to Pingeyjarsveit in the mountains. It promises to be a spectacular drive.
My love to you, Andrew. I miss you so much.
Frasey

Chapter 10

The Best Laid Plans

It is the next morning, and George is not underwhelmed by his breakfast; the invading Norse hoards had nothing on him. He plunders the buffet. Mary goes continental. Her appetite isn't what it was once.

Second day familiarity softens Belinda, who greets George and Mary as if they are her elderly, distant family members – the sort you humour at weddings, funerals and the occasional big family birthday. Patch shows their room key to the lady with the list. Belinda has assigned this task to him.

'How are you this morning Patch? You were out for the count last night.' Mary asks, and then to Belinda: 'Did you manage alright, love? George tipped Gunnar off you might need a bit of a hand.'

'Yes, thank you. Gunnar carried him to our room. He was so kind. And Patch didn't come to until 8:00 this morning. He was exhausted – the plane, the lights – too much excitement by half.'

'I wasn't really asleep.'

'Patch, you fibber! You were comatose.' Belinda's eyes shoot into her head with incredulity. George and Mary join in the laughter, and George recommends the pancakes, bacon and maple syrup to Patch. '5 stars Patch, fill your snow boots. I'm going to go back for more, so you better get in there quick before I lay waste.'

Frasey enters alone.

'Where's your fellow Hens?' asks Mary.

'The girls are skipping breakfast. I'm not sure what time they came back from that nightclub down the main street, but it was well past my bedtime. I hope they didn't disturb you all. They can be raucous.'

'Ah, the piper must be paid. But get yourself over here and joins us four. The more the merrier. George is 'o.d.-ing' on pancakes, and he's encouraging young Patch here to do the same.'

George takes in this information with a sly and satisfied smile. He whispers to Patch: 'If all the Hens are gippy, Patch, there's more for us. Result! What say you, old chap? Let's go for it.'

Patch enters the conspiracy and grunts his approval. His mother tells him to chew nicely and not to eat too fast, or too much. There is a long coach ride ahead.

'You'll get the collywobbles on the coach We don't want you chucking,' she warns him.

Gunnar enters and sits down with the group. He has an air of ice and energy.

'How are we doing? Patch, you're awake, and I see you're no worse for wear. Now, about today.' Gunnar sighs and pulls a face of comic sorrow. 'It is regretful, but I must report heavy snow making its way towards us. Weather warnings severe. Roads closing. Bad news or good news, Patch?'

'Bad news first.'

'Good man. Always best to know. So …'

Gunnar holds the moment until he has everyone's attention.

'The bad news is this – the big trip is off. No Myvatn Nature Baths. And no cave where Jon Snow lost the cherry. Airport is closed. Even our president is trapped here in Akureyri, today. See – we are equal society here in Iceland.'

'And the good news?' asks Patch, trying to conceal his disappointment. He didn't know anything about Jon Snow, but he'd packed his trunks for this special trip, and his mum had bought a new swimsuit on-line.

'Sundlaug!' says Gunnar, with a mix of pride and respect.

'Sun what? Come again?' George is perplexed and is already thinking compensation – big compensation – from the travel firm.

'Sundlaug!' Gunnar's grin is wide: 'Sundlaug is our own celebrated public swimming pool here in Akureyri. Geothermal! Forget Myvatn. Forget the Blue Lagoon. Sundlaug is the place, trust me!'

During this brief interchange, Frasey has been tapping her tablet keys.

'Ranked Number 1 out of the 5 spas and wellness centres in Akureyri. It holds the Certificate of Wellness.'

'I could do with a bit of wellness,' mutters Mary, under her breath.

Gunnar continues to extol the merits of Sundlaug: 'Geothermal waters heal. They heal mind, body, soul and –' Gunnar places his hand on his chest, 'The Heart! Think of this, ladies.' He catches Belinda's eye.

'I have the heart of the Ice Queen, trust me!' replies Belinda. She tries not to laugh, but she has a strange compulsion to crease with giggles each time Gunnar speaks to her.

'Then geothermal experience is must for you! Sundlaug waters melt Ice Queen.'

'Brill! Mum, can we go? You're coming – you are, aren't you Gunnar?'

'You try stop me, Patch. You and me, we do The Slide – if Mum says okay?' He casts a tentative glance across at

Belinda: 'I take care of him, I promise, on my life and future breathings.'

Belinda smiles, nods, and then she turns to Frasey: 'But, what about your sister Hens?'

Frasey is taking in all the TripAdvisor reviews for Sundlaug and barely looks up: 'Consistently five stars. Oh, them? They can sleep off last night. They are a special breed of hen – nocturnal – a bit like owls and bats, but they make a lot more noise with their hooting, and they really get in your hair.' She grimaces. 'I should warn you, Gunnar, those Hens will be peed off about Jon Snow's Cherry Cave though. I wouldn't like to be in your shoes.'

Gunnar is uneasy:

'Ah, Frasey, you must at least give them choice. I can do nothing about Jon Snow, but, please do let Hens know that the flower of Akureyri manhood will be on display. On a day when no-one can leave the town, our public bath is the hot spot, especially for the young dudes.'

Then, as an afterthought, Gunnar adds:

'Tell them our guys won't be wearing furs. They won't be wearing much at all.'

'Well, I'm not putting my manhood on display!' George pulled a face of mock terror: 'Some bugger would make off with my tackle and put it in a glass cabinet down in Reykjavik.'

Gunnar looks perplexed, but Mary chimes in: 'Don't kid yourself, George. They'd have to find it first, under that big paunch. Believe me, you've got nothing worth writing home about down below, and don't swear in front of Patch and the ladies.'

'My apologies to one and all. But I intend to hang onto to my equipment for the duration. And as for it not being special, well Mary, that's not what you used to say.' George guffaws at his own joke.

'Well, that's true George. You never needed a length of Lou Reed's pipe stuck down your pants.'

Belinda, too, tries not to laugh, and Frasey snaps her tablet case and hurries to change the subject: 'Okay, Gunnar, I'll let the Hens know there will be gorgeous guys galore. It might revive them and make up for the Game of Thrones experience. I could tell them Jon Snow used the pool. I'm up for it anyway.'

'Us too, aren't we mum?'

'Yes.' Belinda turns to George: 'And George, we'll protect you – fight off all assailants – just in case the museum has sent some scouts out.'

Gunnar shakes his head. He watches his charges leave for their rooms to get themselves ready for Sundlaug. Then, he draws himself a cup of coffee from the machine and pinches a sausage from the hotplate. He reflects quietly, that no matter how charming they are, this group of Brits is slightly bonkers.

The snow is falling fast as the group climb the steps from the hotel to the Akureyrarkirkja. The church looms above them in monochrome, an imposing structure, polka-dotted with the thick swirling snow that's dropping briskly from a gun metal sky. It's hard to even find the steps. Mary hangs onto George's arm with a grim determination. She's wondering now if this escapade was a wise move.

'Wow! The church! It's just like the top of the Chrysler Building. I spent a while just looking at it yesterday evening, but it is even more impressive in the daylight.' Frasey is entranced. 'Come on Gunnar. What can you tell us about it?'

'I'm no big churchy guy, but it makes the people here very proud. It was designed in 1940 by Gudjon Samuelson, the man who did the Hallgrimskirkja in Reykjavik. They are alike, but we like ours much the best.'

'How strange.' Belinda stops to take it in. 'Frasey's right, it looks just like a 1920s New York sky-scraper. Art Deco? What's it like inside?'

'You must go in, but not just now. Patch will have big interest. Norse ship hangs down from the ceiling. Our tradition – to make offering for safety of those on waves. The window's rainbow glass is amazing. My special window stars Porgeir, the Lawspeaker – great man. He holds Odin tight. Odin is wooden totem – is that right? Wood statue? Odin's ravens, Hugin and Munin sit on shoulder. Hugin is memory. Munin means thought. Soon Porgeir will cast relic to water, but still he holds on. Behind is the water, with waterfall entering. Above, patch of blue sky. They are all set in fish net web of lead. There is Bishop Jon Arason, a monk, axe men, poets, farmers with animals – all aspects of Nordic life, life here, then and now – all on different windows.'

'I'll go back and look at the stained glass, Mary. It sounds interesting. I'll photograph it for my collection.'

'George has spent his life in glass, Gunnar,' says Mary, with pride. 'Stained glass is what he does. He repairs the ancient windows. He's a craftsman.'

'Well you have to make admire, George, simple, yet striking. Check them out.'

They skirt the church. The pavements are feet deep in snow. It is impossible to tell road from path. Parked cars are disappearing; they are fast transforming into igloos, clustered along the roadside. But ahead of them, through the mists of falling snow, the group can make out the strange structure of Sundlaug.

A person could be forgiven for mistaking the Sundlaug public baths for a power station. Clouds of warm steam drift upwards to meet the snow. A high metal tower rises, encased in a tall glass tube, along with enclosed shoots snaking round and down. These are the slides. The whole complex is protected by a high grille fence. The entry is through a low building. Here, at reception, the group divides - men from women, Patch abandoning his mother to join Gunnar and George. Belinda lingers to watch her son go off. She feels that mixture of anxiety and relief. He's growing, growing in height and independence. Eight years old is getting too old to take him into the ladies' changing rooms, but too young to let him go off into the men's, with total confidence for his safety. She's relieved he's with Gunnar, and George, of course. She banishes a thought about what Gunnar might look like in his trunks. Then she smiles at herself – honestly, behave yourself!

Once changed, their lockers secured, bodies showered, the party members regroup within the bath complex. It seems the whole population of Akureyri has turned out, this morning, to embrace the snow and steam experience, and have some fun. Here there is a unique sense of a community celebrating – all ages, all shapes and sizes, all states of health. All sadness and problems shelved.

'My god, it's like a communal baptism,' gasps Frasey. 'It's brilliant.'

Gunnar gives a brief introduction to the pool area, the two large outdoor pools, the indoor pool, the slides, icy splash pools, hot pots and steam baths and water jets.

'Hotpots?' asks George, 'As in Betty's Hotpot?'

Again, Gunnar looks confused. Mary helps out, explaining to George:

'What we would call a hot tub back home. And you just forget your stomach for once George.'

'Okay, everyone? Enjoy!' With a broad grin, Gunnar turns to Patch and cries 'Man or mouse?'

'Man!' shrieks Patch and they race each other to the tall tower, the stairway to the big slide. Belinda's heart is in her mouth. She takes in the height of the tower and the length of the long shoot – a coiled red and yellow worm. She isn't sure at all that this is the right thing for Patch. He can swim, yes, but how will he be in such a claustrophobic space? The walls of the worm are not transparent. What if he gets one of his anxiety attacks? He's never been in such a situation. And with a man he hardly knows …

It's as if Mary reads her thoughts. 'He'll be fine love. It's what he needs, a young lad without a dad. Men have their uses. And you must learn to let go, and trust, just a little. Come on, Frasey and me, we've spotted the hot pot – the really hot one.'

George senses this is a girl thing and decides he's doing a few lengths of the indoor pool to earn some cake. 'I'll catch you later,' he says to the disappearing backs of his wife and the two women. He strokes his ample, hairy paunch and hopes his new trunks stay up below it. He couldn't see to tie the knot.

The three women descend the steps, Belinda turning to offer Mary a steadying hand. They take up seats on the side bench of the hottest of the hot pots.

'Oh, it's paradise,' says Mary. 'To think I nearly passed on this. Breathe deep girls. We'll remember this back in Leeds.'

'Funny thing is, I can't imagine doing this in Leeds,' says Belinda. 'For if I was sitting in a hot tub anywhere at home, I'd be worried about how I looked, were my stretch marks showing, did I have too much cellulite, bingo wings, had I removed all body hair, was my hair going frizzy, was my cozzie the right choice. Here, no-one gives a shit. And no-one should.'

'I was thinking that too,' adds Frasey. 'It's as if we've been brain-washed, back home. We've been force fed these ridiculous glossy images, and notions of what people should look like. We don't stop to consider what people feel like, or how it feels if we can't keep up – like don't have the money or the natural attributes, or we are just too old or physically challenged. Does it matter if we aren't conventionally beautiful?'

A strange look came across Mary's face. It was if she was weighing something up:

'Listen. Girls like you, you shouldn't worry about any of these things. On the plane to Iceland I was reading this article in one of the free papers about all the treatments you can have now back home. Oh, it did make me mad. Did you know you can fat-freeze your bingo wings? You can have radio frequency to zap your crêpey inner thighs, micro injections on your outer thighs, thermal treatment on your neck and décolletage – wherever that may be. You know, I'm not even sure I've got one. Even women my age are having this stuff, silly old mares. The cost for one op would feed a refugee camp for a week. It's obscene.'

Mary pauses, collects herself, and continues: 'Look, girls, before we left for here, I got some results back. I haven't told George, so this is between the three of us – top secret. I have a tumour. It's malignant. It's inoperable. There are a few interventions to be made, but ... I have however long I have. And when I read about these silly ... and when they've got nothing wrong with them –' She broke off.

Frasey and Belinda sandwich Mary – their arms encircle her. She draws strength from them. Frasey's eyes fill first: 'Is there really nothing to be done?'

'Nothing, well not much. They say that they'll zap it with this and that. Chemo might give me a bit longer. I'd settle gladly for a bit longer – a few weeks, months, anything the Almighty can spare me.'

They listen to the water, the mini waves lapping the tiled

sides, the gurgle of the filter. They hear the calls of joy, jokes and laughter. They breathe in the geothermal sulphur scent. Snow settles on their hair, eyelids and cools their eyes. Eventually, Belinda breaks the silence. Her voice has a tremble:

'People have it so wrong back home. They starve the health service, begrudge paying taxes and live to indulge themselves. They don't see the needy. They look down on people sleeping on the streets as eyesores, useless at best, criminals at worst, not people. They see them as a problem, not a responsibility. They stuff a tin of beans in a foodbank and think they've saved the universe. And then you look at this place; it's like before the Fall.' Belinda sighs. Her attention comes back to Mary: 'I'm truly sorry.' She takes Mary's hand.

'Please don't tell George. This will be our last holiday. I couldn't spoil it for him. He'd set his heart on Iceland – it's one of those places he's always wanted to see. What's that silly phrase they use now? Bucket list! Well, it's top of his bucket list. Silly old sod. Sometimes I'd like to put a bucket over his head. But I love the old bugger. And listen, thanks girls. I didn't mean to upset you both, but, if it's any consolation, I feel so much better for sharing it with you two. It's in my mind most of the time. Thank you, very, very much, for your kindness, and for being here with me, in this weird, wonderful and ridiculous place.'

Mary, Belinda and Frasey sit in quiet reflection – serene and sisterly – each immersed in their own thoughts. Frasey straightens herself a little. Her arms stretch out along the edge of the pool. Her fingers trace the curve of the tiles:

'Can I ask you something, Belinda, something a bit personal? It's about Patch. Did you choose to be a single mother?'

Belinda hesitates. She's thinking that it's hard to raise your guard when you are almost naked in a hot pot, and after all, Mary has been so honest and trusting. Belinda has been determined not to 'spill her guts' on this holiday, but … she sees that this is a genuine enquiry. She senses Frasey's good intentions.

'Well, it took some courage to leave Patch's dad and go it alone.'

'What went wrong?' asks Mary. 'Just fell out of love? But tell me if it's none of my business.'

'I try not to talk about it. Perhaps it's time I did. Mary, you give me courage. So, here goes – again, all lips sealed?'

'Of course!' Mary and Frasey speak almost in unison.

'My partner, my ex-partner, I don't want to say his name, was an attractive man in a good job. Well, I suppose he is still good looking and in well-paid employment. A respectable man, eh? If you met him, you'd be charmed. Most were. We had a nice home. He's still in it – but not for long, I hope. I'll try and get to the essence of what happened – not get mired in the ugliness. I know I have much to let go. My counsellor tells me so, at least.'

Belinda pauses: 'Now I can see my partner was a bully. But bullies make you think it's you – that's how it works. He was, is, twelve years older than me. He was undermining, coercive, abusive – ultimately violent, very violent. Gaslighting plus. Well, they're the words they use in court. For me, living with this man was like tiptoeing through hell – on eggshells.'

Belinda breaks off, takes some deep steam breaths, and continues: 'Mood swings, they call it. Patch was only little when he first asked me about Daddy's Moose Wings. It would have been comic if it wasn't so bloody tragic.'

She swallows hard: 'The swings got more extreme. He knew how to hit, where to hit. He was big on shaking. He'd throw me to the floor, scald me – straight from the cafetière.

Yes, he wouldn't have instant coffee in the house.'

Belinda winces and her mouth tightens. She's haunted by her memories.

'I put up with a lot, for several years, for Patch's sake. I had my own landscape design business, although he always called it garden maintenance. Some days I had to ring my customers to give my apologies – he'd done me so much damage I couldn't even lift a spade. The mistakes we make, eh? When he turned on Patch too, well that was that.'

Belinda's voice changes. Suddenly she seethes with raw anger: 'He hurt my Patch, and quite badly. I packed up and left – case in one hand, my boy's hand in the other. What had held me back was the notion that I couldn't provide Patch with the posh home he was used to. But you must ask yourself, what is a home? Being safe is the foundation stone, surely?'

It's now the turn for Belinda to be comforted by Frasey and Mary.

'You must have been through terrible times,' says Frasey.

'There were the refuges – I don't know what I'd have done without them. There are some brilliant women out there. Patch and me, we had to move a lot. We thought we'd escaped him, but then there was the tech abuse. He kept on coming after us, tracking us. I couldn't understand how, wherever we went, there he was walking by the window, or standing over the other side of the street. But he was into my emails. I've never been that clued up. He was tracking Patch too – his laptop. Every time the poor kid tried to find out about something, his father was stalking him on-line, tracking him. The refuge advisors sorted us out and showed us how to stop him.' Belinda sighed and began again: 'We had so little money to get by. But it has been a lot easier since I legged it – after the court slapped a restraining order on him, that is. Then there was the court case, and the compensation… Blood money, eh? That's how we can afford this holiday.'

'You did right luv,' says Mary.

Frasey asks: 'But it must be hard to be on your own with a child?'

'It's kind of lonely, especially in the evening, when Patch has gone to bed. And I feel I can never be enough for him. You see how Patch responds to Gunnar. Why, Mary, you pointed it out too?'

'Better no man than a bad man. And yours sounds a belter!' Mary squeezed Belinda's wrist. 'No pun intended love. I could never make light of what you have been through, God forgive me if I could; I've been so lucky with George.'

'You know, I often consider having a child on my own.' Frasey's looks from Belinda to Mary. 'I'm not joking. I would adopt if I could. I'd love a child, a 'project' of my own.'

Mary nods: 'Well you girls can do so much more on your own, these days. You have so much freedom. You are not judged and labelled like we were. Well, not so much. But there's a price Frasey. Belinda will tell you that. It's not like taking on a pet. The word you used – 'project' – well, I don't think I would see it in a term such as that. A child is a lifetime commitment. It has to be unselfish.' Mary looks reflective: 'George and me, we never had kids. We felt we were sufficient for each other. Well, if I'm honest, that's how we see it now. We tried, but nothing came of it. We didn't gel, as they used to say, well, not in the fertility way. Sex was good though – brilliant in fact. Oh, we gelled in that department, definitely!'

Frasey's attention is caught by squeals and hilarity from the entrance area. She groans, 'Oh no! Oh shit!'

'Well he wasn't all that bad Frasey! He didn't have that paunch then. He was always up for it and so was I.'

'No, not your George, Mary. It's the Hens, and they're coming this way! Oh, bollocks!" Frasey sinks further into the steamy depths. Her face is a picture of despair and embarrassment.

The three women watch in morbid fascination the approach of the Hens. The Hens are sashaying down the central corridor between the two main pools, shrieking with giggles. It's a glorious carnival conga – not out of place in Magaluf, but incongruous in snowy Sundlaug. The locals are smiling indulgently; they seem to be enjoying the spectacle. The Hens are singing:

'*We came, we saw, we conga-ed! We came we saw we conga-ed! Da, daa, daa, da! Da, daa, daa, da!*'

The Hens' bodies are plucked, oiled and seemingly part-roast – each with an even, gleaming, golden tan. Phoebe leads in a high-legged, one shouldered swimsuit in indigo blue, extravagantly tasselled from chest to hip. Elegant though this is, our bride-to-be is upstaged by her first bridesmaid. Maxine has chosen a stunning white suit, the Cuba mesh plunge model. Frasey fights away the gory image from Macbeth – 'unseemed from nave to chops.' Despite the 'modest' white gauze lower midriff cover, Maxine reveals much breast, more and more as she raises her arms in a triumphant, insolent wave to Frasey. Frasey hopes it's a wave, anyway. The middle finger is raised on each hand.

'Oh God,' she gasps. Frasey's thinking she wouldn't mind if someone 'unseemed' Maxine. She's hoping they'll do it quickly.

But the conga passes by the hot pot. It's making for a group of young men who are beckoning and whooping with encouragement. It's the young men from the night before, and clearly, there is a deep level of familiarity, no, intimacy, between the Hens and these young men. Today's reunion clinches are enthusiastic and well-practised.

'My mum sent me out here to police that lot,' groans Frasey. 'How can you police what you can't even bear to be near?'

Belinda and Mary emit long, sympathetic sighs.

'I'm glad I'm not responsible for them. I don't think your mother could expect you to make an intervention,' says Mary. 'There's only so much you can do, Frasey. They are all adults.'

'You haven't met my mother. I wonder what the rules are on poolside copulation?'

'Well they'd never let you away with it at Wilsthorpe,' reflects Mary, 'or at Withernsea.'

'Perhaps the lifeguards will eject them. I do hope so. I'm pinking up with embarrassment!'

'Frasey! They won't go that far?' asks Belinda. 'Or will they?' Belinda's eyes are on stalks. She's wondering if the lifeguards will intervene. After all, there are families here, with young children. There might be a decency issue.

'I have no idea. I'm not trying to defend my sister – if she's old enough to marry, she's old enough to behave herself, but she's led by the nose by that dreadful Maxine.'

'Hmm, nasty piece of work, is she?' Mary shakes her head: 'I don't like the cut of her gib, I must say.'

'It's possibly sour grapes on my part. Phoebe asked me to be lead bridesmaid, but Maxine persuaded her to dispense with my services. She said I was too old and plain and she questioned my sexuality. I'm only twenty-six, for God's sake.'

'And you're pretty! But you are not done up – you're natural. Loads of blokes would choose you over Maxine. She'd terrify most of them. She'd certainly fit the bill for one of those penis museum scouts.'

'It's sweet of you to say that Belinda. I wish it were true – that I am attractive, I mean.'

Frasey takes a deep breath:

'And I do have a love interest, but our relationship isn't what one might call conventional.'

Belinda and Mary look at Frasey, encouraging further revelation.

Their discussion is interrupted by the fast slapping of small, wet feet on the path.

'Mum! We did the slide, and it was brill. And Gunnar's been teaching me how to float. I can do it. It's so cool. He said we had to come back and tell you I'm still alive. Which I am! Mum, isn't this the best place ever?'

'Well, I've never been anywhere quite like it!' says Belinda, and she holds Gunnar's eye for a long moment.

'Is he being a nuisance, Gunnar? You are very kind, very patient.'

'Patch is my friend. And he's my excuse to do Slide.'

'Gunnar's also taught me this, too.' Patch raised his arms, claps his hands above his head and emits a ferocious roar.

'What? What is this?' Belinda looks askance.

Gunnar, laughing: 'He's got it!'

'And what is "it" supposed to be?'

'It's Viking Cry. We celebrate the national team's win with this. And we prepare ourselves at the top of the Slide. It's for courage!'

'Man, or mouse, Gunnar? First to the Slide.' And they fly off again.

'He's not much more than a big kid himself, is Gunnar.' Belinda smiles and watches them sprinting towards the Slide.

'He's alright, I have to say,' says Mary and she and Frasey exchange knowing glances. 'And fit,' adds Frasey, as Gunnar disappears.

'Budge up girls – there's room for a little 'un, surely?' George has had enough swimming for one day. He wants warming-up before he goes to change. He's set his eyes, and his heart, on the cake selection in the pool's café. He's fancying the special hot chocolate, with whipped cream too. The doctor's told George he's going to have to tackle that paunch, but he keeps putting it off until tomorrow.

'By heck, I saw them Hens a bit ago, over by the pool. I thought it was the invading Norsemen who were supposed to ravish and rape our women – not t'other way round. Nice to see our girls turn the tables on 'em. One or two of the local lovelies were looking right put out. Faces like slapped bottoms. Tears before bedtime, eh?'

'Oh George, I hope not. My sister and Maxine. What are they like? And the others are no better. The sooner I get them back to Leeds Bradford the calmer I'll feel. I just hope my mum never finds out.'

As if on cue, the serenity of the steam blanket is torn by a scream.

'You bitch! You fucking cunt!'

'That's Phoebe!' Frasey staggers to her feet and climbs unsteadily the wet steps out of the hot pot. She dashes across the long, raised pavement towards the voice. It's coming from the changing rooms. Her companions do their best to follow close behind, although George stops at the door, hanging well back.

Naked Hens, gloriously polished, tanned and toned are hurrying to wrap themselves in towels. Phoebe and Maxine are facing up to each other beside the lockers.

'You nasty, vile, hateful fucking bitch!' Phoebe, distraught, is still screaming at Maxine. 'You've spoiled everything. You've ruined my life!'

'What? What am I supposed to have done?' Maxine, hands between heaving, enhanced breasts, affects innocence, hurt and surprise, but she isn't quite a practised enough liar to banish the residue of malice and treachery from her expression.

Phoebe collapses into her sister's arms, shaking with sobs. Belinda empties Maxine's locker contents into the girl's basket and says: 'Go, lose yourself for a while, sister.' There's something in the tone of the older woman that brooks no opposition. Maxine withdraws, with a sulky yet satisfied expression, leaving the other Hens craning to look at Phoebe, as if a glimpse of her face could explain everything.

Mary sends off the remaining Hens to the other side of the changing rooms. Gradually, through sobs, snot, and gasps for breath, the story emerges from Phoebe. Frasey holds her sister, as Mary wraps her in extra towels, and Belinda fetches a beaker of chilled water.

'Maxine put up a video of our night out last night and sent Eric the link. He forwarded it to Jim. It's off. She's fucked everything up for me, totally.'

'But what was on it?' Frasey's consternation is mounting. She has a vision of her mother in full on accusatory mode.

Phoebe's bottom lip trembles. Tears fall fast.

'Jim just didn't need to see it … Why did she do it? She knew he'd share it. They've always shared everything.'

'How bad was it Fee? What were you doing?'

'It – with Bjarki - in his car. And Maxine was at it with Sigi in the front. I bet she didn't post a clip of that on her Facebook page.'

'Right. Dear God, girl. I don't know what to say.' But Frasey still holds on to her sister tightly.

'Help her get dressed. She'll be in shock, and needs to keep warm,' advises Belinda. 'We'll get her a cup of strong tea.'

Mary and Belinda withdraw, as Frasey gradually persuades Phoebe to put on some clothes.

Þorgeir the Lawspeaker looks down, his helmet framed by a patch of blue sky. His chiselled brow forms furrows. He's still hanging on to Odin and the ravens. He wishes he could step down from the stained-glass window, to offer comfort to the sobbing maiden. Instead it is the pastor who hurries down the aisle.

'Grievous lady, let me help?'

He means 'grieving' thinks Frasey but quells her impulse to put him right. Phoebe sobs, wails and swears through snot. Frasey explains to the pastor: 'Broken heart – little to be done. She needs to cry.'

'I can pray,' offers the pastor.

'That should do the trick.'

'What she call herself?'

'Phoebe.'

'Fee-bee?'

Phoebe's swollen eyes look up at him in trust.

He smiles:

'Bless you my child.'

'She's shafted me, and he's ripped my heart out!' shouts Phoebe, at the pastor, who scurries off as quickly as he came. Frasey stares at his retreating back, mildly surprised. She'd assumed clergy men were made of sterner stuff.

'Oh, I know. Come on, come on.' Frasey soothes and strokes her sister's head. She's rocking Phoebe in her arms. It reminds her of their childhood – grazed knee, broken doll, mean friends, losing at Monopoly – the only times her sister ever really wanted her near. Mean friends? Her thoughts turn to Maxine. I just need to get my sister home, thinks Frasey. It's a mercy the plane is tomorrow. I hope to God the airport is open again. Perhaps the pastor could add that to the prayer list.

Frasey is also reflecting that forty-two percent of UK

marriages end in divorce, so this outcome is probably a mercy. She holds this fact back. Possibly she'll share it with Phoebe later. Then she feels a gentle touch on her shoulder.

'How is she?' whispers Belinda. 'Tell me what I can do. Gunnar's looking after Patch, along with Mary and George.'

Belinda takes out a hip flask of brandy.

'Gunnar sent this across, just for you Phoebe. He says it's very special, with herbs – he says it will calm you, then knock you out. I don't know what he's put in it?'

Phoebe can't help but smile. She takes a big swig, hiccups and grimaces.

'Jees, that stuff's strong.'

Belinda looks at Phoebe with kindness in her eyes: 'The Hens are so upset. Maxine has been cancelled – she's lurking upstairs in the hotel, pretending to read. The girls say she just doesn't get it, that she's to blame. They are incredulous. You have good friends there. They really care about you. Devastated they are. They all send their love.'

Phoebe nods and snuffles. Frasey hands her another dry tissue.

Belinda starts: 'Look, I know you won't want to hear this, but there will come a day that you will thank your guardian angel for this one.'

Phoebe's haunted, hurt red eyes look up at Belinda. Porgeir the Lawspeaker is listening intently too. He'd like to nod.

Belinda continues: 'Me, I wouldn't put the clock right back, but perhaps to the week before my wedding. You see, I was already expecting Patch. The thought of being without Patch is totally unacceptable. But if I could have dumped the bloke, my God, I'd have jumped at the chance. And that's before he started making me feel worthless and knocking me about.'

Phoebe looks at Belinda, then at Frasey. She bites her bottom lip:

'I'm pregnant too!'

'Gang aft effing agley!' gasps Frasey.

'What?'

'Nothing – just Robbie Burns.' Frasey's face is a picture now – of concern, love, joy, shock and, yes, of calculation:

'Oh Fee! You've kept this quiet. This baby is more important than the man. Why Fee, we'll raise him. We'll raise him – or her – together. Oh God, we might have a girl!'

'What's Mum going to say?'

'Fee, I don't give a flying fuck about Mum. It's you and the baby. That's what's important now. I'm going to take care of you both.'

Phoebe raises her head and rests it on Frasey's chest. Her breathing is steadying. She's looking a little unfocussed.

'Let's get her back to her room, for a sleep. I think Gunnar's magic potion is kicking in,' says Belinda. 'We'll take an arm each. The path down those steps is treacherous.'

As they retreat down the aisle, Phoebe's eyes are drawn up to the stained-glass window – the one with the Norseman. It might be her sedated state, for the walls are stretching and the aisle is tilting, but Phoebe is sure that the man in the glass window smiles and nods his head to her. She thinks his left-hand slips from beneath his heavy red cloak and that he blows her a kiss. How can this be? But she takes some strength and comfort from this perceived chivalrous gesture.

Frasey turns too, but she is not looking at the stained-glass window. Her eyes are drawn to the front of the church. It's the lady in the turban and black sable cape again. She's sitting on a pew, her arm draped languidly over the back. She's half-turned and staring directly at Frasey. She's smiling. They lock eyes and the woman nods and smiles slowly.

Through this secret interchange, Frasey is overcome with conviction, confidence and courage. Hard to describe, but it is as if she has been told that these events are part of a pattern, and that all will be well.

'It's her,' says Frasey, to no-one but herself.

'Who?' asks Belinda, but their attention is called back to Phoebe who sighs and stumbles. As Belinda and Frasey flank Phoebe down the steps to the hotel, they meet George and Gunnar coming up the steps.

'Mary is with Patch. They are by the fireside. Patch is snoozing. All that Slide activity has knocked him for six,' says George. 'Gunnar and me, we're going to see the stained glass in the church next door. Gunnar says he is going to introduce me to Þorgeir, and his friends.'

'We'll be back for afternoon tea. Meet in lounge by fire,' adds Gunnar.

Gunnar and George enter the church. Gunnar is watching George's reaction to the stained-glass windows, his head tilting with pride. George studies them intently.

'I like these windows. You said it – 'simple and striking' – they tell you about people and how they lived – the good, the great, the flawed and the ordinary folk. Every window should have a story you know, or at least, a lovely pattern or a bit of nature. Yes, I like them.

Gunnar is gratified.

'It's alright to photograph them, isn't it? For my collection. The pastor won't mind, will he? I've seen him lurking up by the altar, edging behind a pillar. He's keeping an eye on us. You know, I keep a photo of every window I've ever worked on, along with the ones that catch my fancy. Glass has been a big part of my life.'

Gunnar smiles in satisfaction, and George adds, as an after-thought: 'If you ever get yourself to Yorkshire, I'll take you to York Minster. You can come and meet my brilliant Five Sisters.'

'I'd love to meet your family, George. Thank you.'

George slips up to their room to check on Mary. He opens the door softly.

He watches her full soft bosom rise and fall. Her eyes are flickering towards closed. He's praying she's okay. He's hoping she's happy. He suspects she might be tearful, but it's hard to tell from the side.

'A life in glass.' George muses, and sighs. 'That's the life I've led, and it hasn't been a bad one. Still, not the one I'd intended.' His mind slips back to the summer of '62.

George has never known how it was for them, his parents. It's like a film that he runs, runs and runs again. He's more than the script writer. He directs this film, a remake of the original. The dialogue has evolved over the years – inspired by his recollections of tea-times long gone. Their images flicker. It's so long ago, he summons them in black and white on the 8mm cine spool he keeps in his brain – just for them. Just for the memory of them both, Dan and Clemmie, his mam and dad.

He remembers the doorbell and the looming silhouette of kindly constable who addressed him as "Master". At sixteen, he'd never been called that before.

The constable asked if he could come in.

'Sit down lad. This is the bit of the job I hate.' Constable emphasised the "the". 'There's no way to say this right. Your mam and dad, they're dead son. Lorry jack-knifed, just north of Scotch Corner. Oil spill on the south-bound carriageway. Back-end went right though the central reservation. If it's any consolation, they won't have known nothing about it. Ford Anglia squashed like a tin of sardines. I never liked those back windows – slanting inwards. Car just crumpled. Poor buggers.'

Better not to dwell in the past. He leaves Mary to rest and

returns to Gunnar and Patch.

As George leaves the room, Mary's eyes snap open.

Mary had resisted this trip to Iceland for a long time. When George first suggested it, she thought he was wanting to stock-up the freezer. She only agreed to come for his sake.

George was desperate to see the Northern Lights. She'd warned him – it's not Blackpool. 'There's an element of uncertainty, George. Be prepared for disappointment. No guarantees, eh? Even the brochure says they don't always show.'

'We'll travel in hope,' said George. 'It's in my genes. My dad said always look north. He'd seen the Northern Lights off Reykjavik, on watch, on the bridge of his destroyer, the HMS Nyasaland, during the Second World War. My dad said: "When I saw those lights, I knew I would live, survive like". He survived the war all right. He didn't survive the bleeding peace. But few leave this world alive. Untimely, nonetheless.'

'No need to get emotional, George. Language. The past is exactly what it says on the tin.'

Mary's response may have sounded brusque, but that was just her way. She knew that for George, the very word holiday opened the possibility of dying. Well, he'd seen the Northern Lights now. He may not have been too impressed, but since that night things had started to change for both of them, a quickening, a pulse, a sense of experiencing something beyond the holiday brochure.

Chapter 11

The End of the Long Weekend

After their visit to the Akureyrarkirkja, Gunnar and George have spent a lot of the afternoon with Patch. They have introduced him to the rules of chess. They play in front of the roaring log fire. The chess pieces are all in the shapes of Norsemen and their ships. These figures will live on in Patch's mind, long after the holiday. They will fire his imagination, and his pre-sleep reveries. They are his keys to a memory of great pleasure. Then there is pop and cakes, to 'tide them over till tea'. George makes sure of this. In later life Patch will recall this day as a totally golden one – the change day.

This last night's meal at the hotel should have been a celebration – the last night before the home flight to Leeds Bradford. Instead, well, what was it like? No-one at the table has that much to say about what has happened. It is as if they've each been washed up on a beach – survivors of a shipwreck, but still uncertain about how to get off the island, and then, what might lie ahead. Each is alone with their own thoughts; but that doesn't seem to affect their appetites.

George, Mary, Patch and Belinda sit down together to break bread, enjoy starters, mains and puddings, lubricated with a bottle of dry white, followed with a good burgundy and some diet coke for Patch, as a special treat. Belinda doesn't really approve of that sort of fizzy drink. Frasey will join them when she's certain Phoebe is asleep. Mary has magicked some more sedatives, for Gunnar's potion had worn off, and the bride-not-to-be is now deep in slumber. Gunnar himself wouldn't dream of intruding; he prides himself on knowing when to disappear, and when to re-appear.

The Hens minus Maxine, and of course, Phoebe, have left the hotel on a quest to find their evening meal. They have been subdued since the Sundlaug fall out. No wedding, no last night knees-up. The flaccid penis head-dresses are now packed away in their suitcases in preparation for the trip home tomorrow. The Hens are experiencing a feeling of seismic shift in their own small circle. A circle of friends ruptured forever. They are now making their way, quietly, towards the fish restaurant that Gunnar recommended, down near the harbour. The snow is still deep. The depleted Hens have lost their appetites but know they need to keep body and soul together.

Maxine? Her appetite is not diminished. She's ordered a slap-up dinner from room service. She's subscribed to a rather raunchy video – one that's she's seen the reviews for and has wanted to watch for ages. She thinks she'll shift the bridesmaid's dress on eBay.

Mary and George? Well, they feel useful. They are players in an Icelandic saga. Mary has risen to the role of confidante, counsellor, and comforter. George has acquired a grandson. More than this, George sees Mary in a new light. She has come into her own this holiday he feels. She is normally reticent, shy, conservative and cautious. But now he sees his wife is seeing things through an altered lens. She has become calm, philosophical, open-minded, and caring towards others beyond the two of them. He sees she is cautious to judge. She is trying to grasp everything from everyone's point of view. It as if she has found new wisdom.

George remembers how much he loves Mary, has always loved her. And the surge of love brings its own perils. Suddenly he is overtaken by a deep fear, a profound anxiety that he will lose her. He has a presentiment, a thought followed by a full-on foreboding – for what will he do without her? It seems to come from nowhere and it hits him like a blow, a body blow. And now he vows, whatever is going on, whenever it happens, he will be with her, care for her. For suddenly he is quite certain his wife is going to die.

Mary? Well, she feels she's found the family she never had and has always missed. Prickly Belinda, that's what George called her on the first day. But since Sundlaug, Mary knows Belinda's been damaged, and is swimming to the surface for her son's sake. You never know what lays beneath the surface, Mary reflects. But somewhere in the steam, when they all dropped their guard, Belinda, young Patch, Frasey the funny librarian who deals in facts but longs for something beyond the obvious, and finally poor promiscuous Phoebe, the bride not-to-be, have all become members of her family, the one she never had. And she has found a reservoir of love to be channelled towards each one of them.

Over the evening meal, Patch keeps them going – as children often do in such situations. He knows something has gone off, for that's how Gunnar has described it. Gunnar calls it a "love situation".

'Things can kick off when you live with volcanoes.' That's what Gunnar says, and George nods his head. George says, for the blokes – Gunnar, Patch and he, himself – well, they'd best lay low.

Gunnar suggests the three of them will be ready for a night "under the cloak." They need time to take it all in, to reflect on matters.

After dinner, and coffee, Belinda takes Patch up to his bed.

She hugs him, tucks him in and soon he is sound asleep.

The minibar beckons – a nightcap for herself perhaps. She's wondering if she's had enough for one day. The slippery slope, she's thinking, but then she is still on holiday, and she may not pass this way again.

Then there is a soft tap on the door.

'Belinda are you there?' It's Gunnar.

Gunnar's voice is having an effect on Belinda. She feels a quickening - as well as a giggling. She smiles to herself and lets him in. He carries a flat parcel, and a bottle.

'Patch's asleep.'

'I can see. He'll be knackered, I guess. This is for him.'

'Gunnar, this is so kind.' She takes the parcel of him.

'He may want to wear it tomorrow. I worry about your case weight.'

'Wear?' She's intrigued.

'It's the Iceland National team strip. It's blue – his colour he says, with a red and white trim. You will see "fyrir Island" on the collar. It means "for Iceland". There is no point in doing the Viking Cry without the strip.'

'Gunnar – I don't know what to say. You have been so kind. You have restored my faith in mankind. I mean by that – the kindness of men. This is something I have little experience of, and nor does Patch.'

'Perhaps, Belinda, you will restore my faith in the kindness of the women, yes?'

The couple move towards each other, embrace, kiss, and then Belinda whispers in Gunnar's ear, 'I hope it's a screw top.'

Down the corridor, Frasey opens her tablet. How best to explain all this to Andrew. The difference a day makes.

Dear Andrew.

So much has happened in the past hours, I hardly know where to begin. It is the sort of tale better told in person. But I feel I need to unburden myself and who else can I confide in but you, dear friend, my love.

Today we have been snowbound, and events have played out against a backdrop of deep snow, ice, and steam – in a public pool, a church and a hotel. This is not the day we had planned, but it has been as memorable as the mountains, glacier and waterfalls we have missed. I think a number of our lives have changed direction today.

Tomorrow, when I return Phoebe home to my mother, I fear I will be in deep disgrace. My brief was to keep her safe. Well, it hasn't worked out that way. The wedding is off. My mother is going to be incandescent with rage and, be assured, I will be to blame. I always am.

Last night, whilst I took refuge in my hotel room, with cocoa and hot buttered toast, the Hens, led by Maxine, took Akureyri by storm. Their night of clubbing ended in pre-nuptial infidelities. Maxine captured Phoebe behaving promiscuously, on her mobile, and posted footage of this on Facebook, alerting her boyfriend to view. Maxine's boyfriend is the groom's best friend, and he shared this with the groom. Need I say more?

Added to my dereliction of duty last night, the situation is further complicated by the fact that my sister is pregnant. In truth, this piece of news gave me great joy. In the face of Phoebe's grief, I found myself making plans. I know this might be construed as selfish, but I know my mother well enough to know she will not be kind to Phoebe. Outward appearances are hugely important to Celine. She will be embarrassed about the fact that her younger daughter has been abandoned by the man she was to marry and is pregnant. She will urge termination.

I have been thinking about the best way forward. I intend

to find a flat, or small rented house, and will set up home with Phoebe and her baby. I must support my sister. I will let you know how the plot unfolds. When we arrive back at Leeds Bradford, I intend to take Phoebe home to face the music, but any dancing will be on hot coals. I hope to be with you next weekend, and that we can resume our precious time together.

Until then, my dearest Andrew,

Frasey

Frasey presses send and switches off her tablet. She decides to look in on Phoebe to check her sister is still okay. Phoebe's room is like a freezer. The bed is empty. The window is wide.

Frasey screams in horror as she takes in the scene. She sees Phoebe's anorak is still hanging behind the door, drying off from earlier. All of her sister's outdoor clothes are neatly piled in the chair at the end of the bed. Frasey's mind and imagination are working overtime, together. She is trying to calculate how long a person could stay alive in these sub-zero temperatures. She knows that Phoebe is probably still wearing her white silk pyjamas, a present from the Hens.

Is this self-harm, wonders Frasey? Has her heart broken to the point of self-annihilation? Frasey remembers a scene from their childhood. Phoebe had been so upset about some friend's silly and unkind jibe; she'd tried to stick the point of a compass in her arm. Celine had told Frasey off for having such an offensive weapon in her Maths set. She had dismissed this incident as Phoebe being highly strung, but Frasey knew her sister better. Please God , no, she prays.

Frasey abandons caution and logic. She climbs out of the window in pursuit. At least she has the presence of mind to grab the duvet from Phoebe's bed, just in case.

Phoebe's footprints are still clear. Frasey can see from these that her sister had slipped her boots on, a relief indeed. The footprints lead in the direction of the church steps. The step lights are still illuminated, and Frasey looks up towards the church entrance. There, by the huge wooden doors, she sees a dark shape. It looks as if someone has shot a bear. No, as her eyes adjust to the strange orange light, she makes out a figure, two figures in fact, in a strange huddle.

It's the woman in sable, and she has enveloped Phoebe in her long dark cape. She is gently rocking Phoebe in her arms. When the woman sees Frasey, she and beckons her to join them. There's a contained urgency in this gesture. Frasey takes the steps, now deeply covered in snow, as best she can. She didn't stop to dress for this outing. The cold is penetrating. Nonetheless she soldiers on up to the two of them.

'We need to get your sister back to the hotel. She's shivering, slurring her words and confused. Come on now.' The woman's voice has a strange authority. Frasey does as she is told. This is not the time to ask questions. With one either side of Phoebe, they begin the slow and difficult descent.

Another figure is joining the scene. It's Gunnar. He heard Frasey's scream and had left Belinda's bed to see what was happening. Then he followed Frasey through the open window.

Gunnar can see the three figures struggling down through the snow. He trips and catches the black metal handrail. When he looks up again, it is only Frasey, with Phoebe enveloped in a hotel quilt. Both women look perished. He lifts Phoebe and the small group finally arrive back in Frasey's room.

Gunnar summons a member of the hotel night staff. More quilts and a hot pack are conjured up. Frasey removes Phoebe's wet pyjamas, towels her off and finds some dry clothes. She begins to chafe the feeling back into her sister's body, especially her extremities. She wraps herself round Phoebe, under a pile of duvets. A doctor arrives and takes Phoebe's pulse and blood pressure. Her heart rate and breathing are coming down. He checks her reflexes. The doctor concludes she is experiencing mild hypothermia. They cover her up with every item of clothing, duvets and blankets to hand.

'It's a good job you found her as quickly as you did. She could easily have lost her life tonight. What on earth was she doing out there in silk pyjamas? You are her sister, no? You keep your eye on her, lady.'

Frasey has no intention of letting Phoebe out of her sight, ever again she thinks.

The doctor administers yet another sedative. He leaves, and as do the hotel staff. The drama appears to be over.

'Have you any idea what she was doing?' asks Gunnar softly. 'Could she have been trying to, you know…?'

'I'll find out Gunnar, but tonight we'd better just count our blessings she's still with us. Oh God, it could have been so different. I am so thankful you were still here to get things organised.'

'All part of the service.' Gunnar does look a little sheepish at this, but Frasey's attention is elsewhere so she misses his blush and his bashful smile.

Frasey lolls back on the bed and gazes down at her sedated sister who is now sound asleep. What a shit I have been to her, she reflects. How harmless painted plastic animals now seem. How sad that all Phoebe's dreams and hopes have been crushed, and on my watch.

Gradually, Frasey herself nods off to sleep.

It's very early next morning. Frasey feels Phoebe move in her arms. Her eyes snap open.

'What on earth got into you, Phoebe? Why would you go

out, through a window, in deep snow? And in your white silk pyjamas? White pyjamas against the snow. We might never have found you. We couldn't even have seen you! I could have lost both of you. Now you must think about baby too. I just can't believe you did that. It's a miracle you are alive.'

'I wanted to see the man in the window, the one who blew me a kiss. He was kind to me. I needed to see him again. I trust him and want to tell him things.'

Gunnar taps softly on the door.

'I heard your voices. Is she okay?'

'She seems to be. Although she might still be rambling a little. Phoebe says she needed to see the man in the window again, to tell him things. What is she like?'

Gunnar sits down carefully on the side of the bed next to Phoebe. He gently lifts her hand.

'Phoebe, I understand. It is Porgeir in the window. He will speak to you every time you call his name, wherever you are. He speaks to me, gives me the good advice. He comforts me. He will do this for you too, now he's in your head. Porgeir will talk to you. He's always got your back. He's that kind of guy. You have to believe this.'

Frasey wonders if Gunnar has lost the plot too, but she notices the calming effect he's having on Phoebe.

'Frasey, a question. When I followed you, I saw you by the church door. The two of you weren't alone. Who was that woman in the long fur cloak? And how come she disappeared? It was as if she just vaporised?'

Frasey wonders how to answer him, but Phoebe speaks first.

'She was standing by the church door as I struggled up. She was wearing this funny turban like Sujjan at work. By this time, I was beginning to feel very blurry and beyond frozen. She scooped me up into her cloak. It was so warm and brilliant. I know it's wrong to wear real fur like she was doing, but it's bloody warm when you need it. Then she said something really weird. She said it wasn't my time yet. She went on to say something that sounded like it was taken from the bible. It was that 'Blessed are they' thingy we used to have to say in church, the list, you know…something like: "the meek shall inherit the mount". Strange or what? Frasey, you know about that sort of stuff. What can she have meant? She was old fashioned, but lovely. Yeh, and she knew I was pregnant. She told me to take care of him. Him, like she knew what it would be. When she saw you, she said: 'Here's Frasey'. So how come she knows your name? And who is she?'

Frasey's jaw drops open.

Gunnar begins to explain that even with mild hypothermia some people can start to hallucinate.

Frasey cuts in:

'She said what?'

'The meek shall inherit the mount. Perhaps she meant the top of the steps?'

'There's no way she meant that. Holy fuck, Fee, what have I drawn you into?'

This is departure day. Gunnar lifts the luggage into the coach's hold. He checked early doors – the airport is open. The snow ploughs have been out since dawn, clearing up after the storm.

The airport's only a short trip from the centre of Akureyri. At the airport, our group stands beneath the Penis Museum promotion screen. Nobody takes any heed, makes any comment – except George. When Mary says: 'I always worry they'll lose our luggage.' George replies: 'Worse things happen, lass. At least I'm coming away with my tackle intact. You always have to prioritise what's important.'

George has agreed to swap seats with Phoebe. He will position himself next to Maxine, who drank too much last night and is looking less coiffed and composed than when she arrived. She's drawn on one of her eyebrows at a curious tilt. This causes a mild consternation at passport control.

Gunnar is trying to conceal his joy, as well as sorrow, as he says goodbye to Belinda and Patch. His impulse is to grab Belinda and tell the world they've found each other. They have enjoyed a night of unbridled passion, albeit with one interruption. Luckily Patch enjoyed a sound night's sleep throughout.

Patch is wearing the Iceland National strip. At the Gate, Patch turns back towards Gunnar, raises his arms, claps and starts the Viking Cry. Gunnar responds with his own version. Another victory for Iceland, thinks Gunnar, and in truth, it's a victory for the three of them.

Frasey pauses as she passes through the gate. She takes in the airport concourse. She notices the black sable cape lady at the entrance. Again, she looks directly at Frasey and raises an elegant cigarette holder to her ruby lips. Frasey is perplexed. Surely smoking isn't permitted. But she reasons, it isn't her concern. Their smiles meet across the concourse.

The lady is gliding closer all the time. Frasey waves, and the lady removes the holder, exhales and blows her a kiss. Frasey knows exactly who this is, and, as the figure vaporises, it hits Frasey like a revelation. Amba is taking possession of her.

The strangest thing is that Frasey isn't even troubled by this thought.

Frasey and Phoebe take up seats together. Baby talk is the order of the day. Six months to go and so many preparations.

Their excitement is tangible.

As the plane rises over Akureyri, Porgeir the Lawspeaker looks up. He's still hanging on to the wooden relic of Odin and the ravens. He often thanks his own god, as another great white bird takes off with a group of English folk. But he'll miss this set of invaders, especially the girl who weeps. He wonders what will become of her, and her serious sister and their friend who seems to care. He's never had much time for the pastor. Give me that old time religion, he reflects, then catches himself on. Did he emerge from the cloak with the wrong decision all those centuries ago? Holy shit!

Chapter 12

Frasey

Once back at Leeds Bradford, the Hens disperse. As the flight progressed, they became more subdued, as if the enormity of what had happened finally dawned on them. There will be no wedding, no going back. Even I feel a little glum, deflated perhaps, and Phoebe is becoming agitated and tearful again. Perhaps the prospect of confronting Celine with the cancellation of the wedding is overwhelming her. As for me, I feel grimly determined. Let the pieces fall. I square my shoulders for battle.

But oh joy, I can barely believe it. Andrew is waiting at the Arrivals Gate. He's come to collect me. In a rare show of public affection, I throw my arms around him. I kiss him. I introduce him to Phoebe. He bows to her and takes her hand and raises it to his lips. He is such a gentleman. We secure a trolley for our bags and make for the car park. The spring is back in my step.

We have already swapped contact details with our new friends. Gunnar organised this. We see them as they go their separate ways and wave. We have promised to keep in touch, for we want to know how their stories unfold, just as they want to know about ours.

Andrew says he just couldn't resist surprising me, and Phoebe. When he read my email, he thought we might need rescuing. We are driven in style in the Mercedes, back to

The Mount. Mrs Tordoff makes such a great fuss of me, and Phoebe. She confesses that it wasn't the same without me, and that Mr Atha has been positively dejected.

'He's been like an ill-sitting hen. Oops – no pun intended.'

We are to have a late lunch – a Mrs Tordoff special. No dressing up on this occasion, and as our eyes meet, it is clear Andrew and I are thinking along similar lines. There will be lots of time for dressing up later, lots and lots.

I can tell that Phoebe is a little in awe of this place, and these people. The Mount has become such an important part of my life now, it is easy to forget how it might strike a young woman like my sister – how it struck me at first. But Andrew and Mrs. Tordoff could not be kinder to her. How much of the situation Andrew has shared with Mrs. Tordoff, I do not know. But there is nothing censorious in her treatment of Phoebe, far from it.

Perhaps we are all changing, I wonder.

When Andrew hears the full story of the break-up after lunch, his mouth drops slightly ajar; he closes it only to suppress his mirth. Phoebe and I drop into a double act. Me with my clipped, considered and accurate descriptions of events, embellished at each key point by Phoebe, who excels at hyperbole. Phoebe's mood brightens considerably. She glows in the warmth of his wisdom and take on events. I can tell he is going out of his way to prepare her for the encounter to come.

Then we can delay no longer. Andrew drives us home to face the music, or rather, Celine.

'Always better to do battle on a full stomach,' he tells us.

It is as if there is a tacit agreement between Phoebe and me not to mention the business about my sister's late night snow episode. Nor do either of us mention the woman in the sable cloak and stylish turban. Phoebe seems to want to draw a veil over the incident, and I am happy with this. I am still baffled by the meaning of Amba's words to Phoebe, the bizarre beatitude.

The following Saturday Andrew demands an update. He barely gives me time to enter the Garden Room.

'How's Phoebe? What did Celine say? Come on Frasey, I can't wait for my second instalment!'

'Well Andrew, we've had histrionics galore from Celine. My father hasn't engaged at all. He gave a grunt to begin with, then silence. I've had reproach showered upon me – the marriage called off on my watch, you can just imagine. But then I've been down at the University Library mostly and I've taken on two extra nights' over-time to keep out the way. Cowardly behaviour, I know, but Celine in full-flight fury is insupportable. She keeps on and on about how she'll never get to be mother-of-the bride. Phoebe was priceless. She said to me: 'Celine's like that daft batty mother in the Jane Austen box set you rate so highly, Frasey – the one with all the daughters. Celine's only got us two, and she keeps lamenting that she'll never get to wear the hat!'

Andrew loves to hear these nuggets. I warm to my theme:

'Perpetually 'Baht'at' in fact. Seriously, Celine needs to move on. So, I've started to look for somewhere for the two of us to live – Phoebe and me. I've got to rescue my sister and her unborn child. I promised Phoebe this in Akureyri. I thought I'd rent, but perhaps I've saved enough for a deposit on a small terrace – I'm to look at one near the football ground in the week. And, if this house is okay, I will be closer to The Mount.'

'Now listen, for I have a plan,' Andrew has a new note of firmness in his voice. 'Take time to think about this. My proposal is this. I want you both to come and live here. I've discussed it with Mrs Tordoff, and she agrees it would be an ideal development. The north wing is never used these days. It would be easy to convert it to an apartment for Phoebe and the baby, and of course you Frasey can take over Amba's suite on a permanent basis. We can refurbish the rooms, create a nursery, install a kitchen and an additional bathroom.'

I stare at Andrew, speechless. Eventually, words come:

'You would do that for us? But why?'

'Because you are you, Frasey, and you are also my Amba, and you have brought light and life to me, and you will bring Little Horatio here too, or possibly a Little Amba. And he or she will be ours Frasey, our family, and I'm sure there's room in my heart for Phoebe too. I must confess; your sister is rather comical and truly entertaining. Even Mrs Tordoff said your Phoebe is "a case".'

A silence. Then I remind Andrew how he has always kept Amba's suite exactly as it was on the day of her death.

'But Frasey, life has to go on, until it doesn't. I have had such complex thoughts whilst you were away. I know it was only a long weekend, but it brought it home to me how precious our time is together. I want as much of you as I can have before I die. I had determined to invite you to move in. I told Mrs Tordoff that this was my plan, and she thoroughly approves. Now I'm enjoying visions of an instant family, of a new lease of life for us all. I am a rich man. I can do good here. Don't deny me Frasey. You have given me a zest for life I never ever thought I could feel again.'

I have to look away. When I turn back to Andrew, my eyes will be brimming with tears.

'I have these strange and alien feelings, Andrew. I feel emotional. I feel joy. A circle complete, eternal – "Giotto's O", the perfect circle. I don't know what to say.'

'Well, I suppose you'll have to persuade Phoebe. She might have reservations about moving in with an octogenarian, soon to be a nonagenarian, along with his elderly housekeeper.'

'We'll pay our way, I promise, and Phoebe – she'll have to agree not to be loud, crude or silly – or all three at the same time.'

Andrew holds up his hand. 'You'll do no such thing to Phoebe. And do you think I want for money? I'll tell you what, we'll work out some sum, and you can open a trust for the little one – a nest egg.'

Andrew, smiling affably, added a caveat: 'But, I think Phoebe will need to take baby home to see the grandparents each weekend, for you and me, we still have much to do, much to explore and much to achieve. The weekends will always be our time.'

We sit for some minutes, just gazing, breathing deeply and smiling at each other.

Later that afternoon, I take a break. I wrap myself up in my quilted coat and slip out of the Garden Room doors onto the patio. I feel I need some air and I'm drawn to the lake. I stand and take in the scene. My hand strokes Lilith's cold smooth brow.

It's a sharp late February day. The drifts of snowdrops are only just beginning to fade – leggy leaves, bowing stalks and dimming flowers. The clouds, heavier earlier, are breaking up. The sun is trying to break through. As I gaze at the surface, a patch of blue, a reflection of the break in the clouds, catches the ripples. A light breeze stirs the surface, and I can hear a woman's light laughter. I know it is her and I know that my present good fortune would not have come to pass without her, my lady in the sable cape.

I muse on. When I have been dressing up, I reflect, I've never come across this cape. But then the shocking realisation hits me – that the cape no longer exists. Of course it doesn't. The sable cape was consumed in the fire in the wood nigh on seventy years ago.

I swallow hard. I listen to the laughter and form my words of thanks. For she is the force who has forged my new life, and she is here with me always. I do truly believe this. And I know that I have her blessing. For all that I have read and heard makes me believe that Amba would have wanted happiness for her younger brother, and she has chosen me as her embodiment. She told him in her last letter that she was coming home. I have no reason to doubt that she was a woman of her word.

I return from the lake to my desk in Amba's suite, and open another ribbon bound bundle of her letters. What I find astonishes me. The address on the deep cream deckle-edged sheet is Regent's Park and the date is late January 1919.

My dear Ambrosia,

How kind and thoughtful you have been to let me know of Urania's death. My first emotion was shock. I must confess your letter has also revived the most joyful and tender memories of your aunt. I am left torn between tears of sorrow and smiles of gratitude. Yes, gratitude for the very privilege of knowing her. She was a beautiful, whole, and amazing person. A woman so perfect should never grow old.

When I think of Rania, I recall that time before my recent fall from grace – pushed over the edge by that odious, vile Pemberton Billing man and his baying hounds. If I lower my lids and inhale, I can almost smell the violets she loved so much. Violets have such a moist and earthy perfume, lifted skywards by a spritz of the divine. Rania always kept a simple bunch in her opulent boudoir at Cadogan Square. Oh, I see her eyes now, lit by love and rapture, the passion we shared. Our eyes made words redundant. Our souls spoke freely to each other.

When Rania commissioned the painting you mention, I was

her more than willing subject. So often she sat with me, as the artist worked her magic. As time passed, we almost became one.

It grieves me to say our joy was short lived. Men can have such a crude understanding of the superior relationship that two women can share – woman to woman. A man's hostility to this closeness, and his impulse to destroy is a defence mechanism. Men are compelled to spoil what they fail to comprehend.

I was no threat to your Uncle Robert. Truly, there was no contest at all. When Rania and I shared tender moments and intimacies, he counted for nothing, less than nothing.

It thrills me that the picture still exists, for it is a testimony to our time together. I am relieved too that you and your mother are removing me to Paris. I shudder to think of being locked in Robert's attic or subjected to a fate more fearful. Your aunt would have wished me away from him, her so-called husband.

There is a great satisfaction too in knowing that the picture will hang in Rania's apartment in Montmartre. We enjoyed such freedoms and delicious intimacies there, cocooned from the censorious eyes of the judgemental, the prudish and the ignorant.

Now I live a reduced life here in London, and am soon to leave for my homeland, to stay awhile with my mother. She needs me, and this trial has taken such a toll. I am indebted to my friend and supporter Margot Asquith for providing this apartment for my use whenever I am inclined to reside in London. I will return, be assured, and when I am back, I will let you know. When you are in London, do please come to me.

Do give my sincere condolences to your mother. I met her once, you know. A rare beauty she was then. The sisters were quite different but each glorious in their own way. Is it impertinent of me to suggest that the two sisters married beneath themselves, in the sphere of the spirit and their sensibilities? No, I believe not. There are things that wealth cannot buy.

Such exquisite, tender moments were ours, my child. I hope

I bound down the stairs.

'Andrew, you must read this. This is fascinating. What a
bizarre letter to write to a twelve-year-old girl.'

Andrew takes out his reading glasses and begins to read.
He rereads the letter and sits back in his chair.

'I haven't told you much about Paris, have I? You know,
Aunt Rania had an apartment in Montmartre. It allowed her
certain freedoms, as I understand. The sort of freedoms that
might have been denied to her here. But, before I begin, I
think we both need a glass of Viognier. It was Rania's favourite
tipple, and Amba's too. Time for an aperitif my dear?'

'It sounds as if I'm going to need it.'

Chapter 13

Paris

I sit back in my chair and admire the elegant way Andrew pours the Viognier. He too settles himself and we toast each other.

'Now, about Paris.' Andrew smiles.

'There was a period of four years in the mid '30s when Amba and Ida spent each summer in Paris. Rania had left her Montmartre apartment to Amba, and, as I understand it, quite a substantial sum of money in trust. She also left a large painting of Maud Allan.

Well, who else would she leave it all too? Her husband, by my mother's account, was an unpleasant man who had turned against his wife before her death. Rania's own daughter Seraphina, died in the Spanish Flu outbreak at the end of The Great War, and Rania succumbed too. Rania had never left her daughter's bedside. To leave her personal fortune and her beloved apartment to my mother would have benefited my father. Rania despised Father almost as much as her husband. Amba was my aunt's favourite, so really there was no mystery to the bequest.'

'So how old was Amba when she inherited the apartment?'

'Twelve. Actually, eleven because Rania died in the late autumn of 1918. The apartment and the money were left in trust until Amba reached the age of twenty-one.'

Andrew sighed and looked out over the lake. It was as if he was weighing how much to tell me, or how best to explain.

'This all happened about ten years before my own birth. I wasn't there; I depend on reminiscences from my mother and Amba. Recollections vary. I have tried to piece together what happened. What I did witness was my father's hostility to Rania. He would not let her ghost rest. He took every opportunity to vilify her, much to my mother's dismay and distress. Mother confided in me that Uncle Robert had made the most appalling accusations about Rania. She said this was provoked by his deep resentment over Rania's will. He suggested that Amba had been the beneficiary because she had allowed herself to be seduced by her aunt. Robert took the extreme step of writing to Father whilst he was away in Palestine, to warn him that his wife had corrupted Amba. To poison Father's mind was unforgivable. Amba was only a child, for heaven's sake. But Father always believed that Rania had ruined Amba. He cited Amba's relationship with Ida as evidence.'

'Robert wrote to your father after the will business?'

'Of yes, immediately after.'

'My goodness, that sounds like spite. But in fairness Andrew, the letter I've just found does sound as if Rania preferred women. One doesn't have to read too deeply beneath Maud's words to get a real sense of the intimacy of their relationship.'

'Indeed. Rania was a lesbian. For her, Robert was a flag of convenience. There has been much speculation about Maud Allan's sexual orientation too. It seems Maud preferred women, but the times were such that neither women could disclose. Amba once told me that Robert had found Rania and Maud in a very compromising situation in Rania's boudoir at Cadogan Square. Rania had become infatuated with Maud and had commissioned the painting. Clearly this gave Rania and Maud the time and place to enjoy the intimacy Maud refers to. When the trial of Maud Allan began, Robert insisted that Maud's painting be removed to the attic. He felt it could be politically compromising. Maud had become a political hot potato.'

I start to giggle at this metaphor, and Andrew joins in. I collect myself:

'Did Amba ever talk to you about her relationship with Rania?'

'Only positive things. She used to tell me about the time they decided to recreate Maud Allan's Salome dance. Fired by Rania's enthusiasm, Amba was desperate to go to see Maud perform, but Mother insisted she was too young. To make up for her disappointment, Rania cajoled Mother into a home show – a recreation. It seems Uncle Robert put a stop to this too.'

'So, what happened to the apartment, and what happened to the painting of Maud?

'Well, this is what I was coming to.' Andrew is sinking back in time. He has that faraway look. I determine to stop interrupting his flow. This is hard as there are so many things I am desperate to ask him.

'Those summers when Amba left for Paris with Ida caused me such sadness. In truth. Amba and Ida had raised me in my early years, I can even remember them pushing my pram out in Menston, fooling round by the lake, dancing for me, helping me build a snowman. I have such golden memories of them. I loved them dearly. They were such good fun. Their laughter was so infectious. It used to ripple over the lake. Sometimes, Frasey, I think I hear it now. Sometimes I see her.'

I've vowed not to interrupt but I long to tell him that I

hear it too. I see Amba too. Andrew takes a deep breath and continues:

'I used to beg to go with them. Amba said that one day, when I was old enough, she would take me and we would be together in Aunt Rania's apartment. She said she would introduce me to Montmartre, to the markets, the clubs, the pâtisseries, cafés, the freedoms of Paris. But then Ida died, the war came, and after the war, Amba had lost her appetite for Paris. She kept promising we would go, but even when things started to get back to normal, she always thought of a reason why we had to wait.'

Andrew looked profoundly sad.

'I finally got my wish in 1950. Mother had been uneasy about the apartment. She felt we needed to visit, to see how it had survived the army of occupation. She needn't have worried. It was just as Amba had left it after Ida's death, thirteen years earlier. It was hard for Mother and me to go there – particularly hard for Mother because she had such wonderful memories of a visit with Amba, Ida and Ida's mother. They had made a twenty first birthday trip, for Amba to claim her inheritance. Mother felt Rania's presence, Amba's and Ida's. Ghosts. We both were overwhelmed with sorrow. Post war Paris was dismal, people desperately trying to breathe life back into the city. We decided the best way forward was to sell the apartment.

'Shouldn't you have given yourselves more time?'

'In retrospect, yes. But we both felt so profoundly sad, we just wanted to turn the key in the door for the last time, walk away and come home.'

Andrew is deep in thought.

'Yes, Mother found it depressing. She rested whilst I organised the packing – any precious items of furniture, lamps, glassware, art, jewellery, some exquisite vintage gowns belonging to Rania. I have to admit, the apartment still felt more Rania's than Amba's. It had a real Belle Époque vibe. There were some priceless pieces. We shipped home what we could. Mother insisted that the picture of Maud Allan came back.'

Andrew begins to smile.

'Let me tell you about "The Teaser Box".'

'What on earth was that?'

'Well, I'd persuaded Mother to attend an exclusive Christian Dior event. Paris had at least resumed its leadership of haute couture. Mother left and I tackled one of the ornate armoires – the bonnetière. I found a locked wooden box in the base. It was rather beautiful with carved flowers. In the absence of a key, I decided to force the lock.

What I beheld amazed me. What had Aunt Rania been up to? I'm sure all the stuff was hers, and not Amba's. It was not my sister's style at all. You could tell by the nature of the risqué lingerie, and what I can best describe as items for female sexual gratification. There was even a manual with illustrations on how to use these items, not that anyone with an iota of imagination would need help. And there were two true curiosities. Both items were made from green kid leather. One was quite futuristic in a way, but with a petal trim. A bit like a green water lily with an elephant's trunk. Quite bizarre. The other – dear God. It wouldn't have been out of place in the basement of a museum – the area they usually reserve for archaeological remains. It was a crusty item that might be labelled "leather chest expander" – except it obviously wasn't. This one had had a lot more use than the elephant's trunk. I think I concluded it was a, yes, a double dildo.

Frasey, I have never seen such a collection. I was a young man of twenty-one, and relatively inexperienced in such matters. My face must have been a picture. Puce wouldn't begin to describe it.'

Andrew pauses. I turn and catch the eye of Amba in the portrait. I try to read her smile and have a clear presentiment the Amba knew exactly what was in the Teaser Box. Where this knowledge came from, I could only speculate. I probed further:

'How intriguing. What did you do?'

'Well, I thought it better that Mother knew nothing about the box and its contents. I decided to take it with me for a walk by the Seine. I confess I abandoned it by a bench near Notre Dame. Imagine. I just dumped it. Mass had just finished and people were streaming down the steps. Nowadays passers-by would think it was a bomb. Luckily no-one noticed me walking away. No-one came running after me to return it, thank heavens.'

Andrew and I enjoy some speculation about the box's fate.

'I wonder if the contents were ever used again?'

'Oh Frasey, I hope not. It's not the sort of stuff you'd want to use second hand. It would be like using someone else's ancient enema apparatus. You'd know where it had been, and you wouldn't be happy.'

'And the picture of Maud. Where is it now?'

'Ah yes, I've digressed. She's up in the attic. From what we've just read, she won't be happy.'

'Do you think we should bring her down?' I ask.

'I wonder, is there a wall to receive her in Amba's suite? I'm afraid it is quite a substantial painting. Let's go and look. We might be able to weave it into the refurbishment plans.'

Up in the attic Andrew draws the dust sheet away from a huge canvas. We stare at the stunning image of the dancer. The painting has a strange effect on me. I'm beginning to feel a little warm. It is both exotic and erotic.

As we gaze on it together, a strong Yorkshire voice booms

out behind us, 'That lass needs a warmer pair of knickers!'

Eleanor heard us moving above and wanted to know what was going on.

'She's coming downstairs, Eleanor.'

Eleanor's mouth takes on a censorious pout. 'A picture of a belly dancer, eh? My days Frasey. I hope you won't be dressing up as this one.'

As Eleanor leaves us, Andrew gasps and moves over to a small trunk tucked away in a corner.

'It's here. I was thinking about this earlier, and I wouldn't have known where to look. I can't believe it.'

'Andrew, are you okay? What's the matter? You look as if you've seen a ghost.'

'Well, it feels a bit like that. This relates to what I was telling you earlier. I must have digressed. If I'm not mistaken, Aunt Rania's legendary Salome costume is in this trunk. Mother and I found it in Montmartre when we were packing up the apartment. Mother became emotional when we found it.'

'Andrew, it was my fault. I interrupted you. You were about to tell me about a home performance, and Rania's husband Robert putting a stop to it.'

'Indeed. Well, it seems that Rania persuaded Mother and Cousin Seraphina to help her recreate Maud Allan's Salome dance. Amba, of course, didn't need any persuading. She was desperate to see it. Rania became very close to Amba whilst they were involved in this project. Mother confessed to me her fears that aunt and niece had become too close. Of course, Mother was very discreet, but you could tell her anxieties had lingered over the years. It seems that Rania rather monopolised my sister during this period and involved her in costume creation. Amba had to sew on sequins and jewels and make Aunt Rania's pantaloons. Mother feared the fittings had become a little out of hand.'

'Well, can we have a look at it?' I am growing impatient.

The trunk lid opens easily, and Andrew invites me to take out the costume. He says his joints are too stiff with arthritis.

Holding this outfit against my body gives me the strangest sensation. I feel the pulse and pain of past preoccupations, passions and ruptured dreams. Suddenly, hot tears sting my eyes. Andrew is watching me with the saddest of expressions. He wraps his arms around me, and we weep together. This moment of raw grief seems to stretch into eternity.

Chapter 14

Life Goes On

My sister Phoebe didn't need a lot of persuading to move into The Mount. Almost six months after our long weekend in Akureyri, with the refurbishment complete, the two of us moved in on a permanent basis. Mrs Tordoff and Phoebe hit it off from the start – Mrs Tordoff becoming Aunt Eleanor to Phoebe, and it soon became clear that Eleanor preferred Phoebe to me. I have never minded this.

'A lovely, open-hearted girl, and none of that dressing-up malarkey, but I'm saying nowt about that to the nice young lass. I suppose folk do what they feel they have to.'

I well remember Mrs Tordoff's withering glance as she delivered this to me.

New house rules were agreed, a little more relaxed than previously. Eleanor was softening. She softened even more when Phoebe's baby arrived.

It was a Sunday night when Phoebe's waters broke. I shall never forget it.

'Frasey!'

A strangely urgent summons from the bathroom, like a loud whisper.

'Frasey, I think I'm dying. I can't stop pissing. This is fucking embarrassing.'

Mrs Tordoff was passing and immediately took command

of the situation. I was so relieved for I was wrecked with panic.

'You've got to get your sister to hospital straight away. We can't delay now her waters have gone. Her bag is already packed. I'll ring the maternity ward to say she's coming in. Come on Frasey, action stations.' She clapped her hands together.

As Phoebe and I descended the stairs, Andrew was waiting in the hall. His face was a picture of excitement, anticipation and apprehension. He handed over the keys to the Mercedes with a trembling hand.

'No time for a taxi. Off you go. Good luck, my darling girls.' He went on. 'Frasey, you will ring as soon as there is news.' This was more a command than a question.

I had never driven Andrew's Mercedes before. I am not a confident driver at the best of times, and to be handed the keys of a large, top of the range Mercedes was genuinely daunting. I've always preferred my bike as a means of transport. But the urgency of the situation was such that there was no choice. Luckily the streets were empty, the road over the moor quiet and even the hospital car park had large empty spaces. I craned to read the noticeboards to locate the maternity wing.

Horatio Porgeir Fisher was born in Airedale Hospital on the evening of 1st October 2018. I was allowed to be in attendance for the birth. It was, to say the least, emotional – my kid sister as I have never seen her, hair all sweaty and stuck to her head, eyes wild yet determined. She made no fuss and never complained, even as the hours passed by and the contractions became more severe and more frequent. Fee was so brave and never gave up. Grunts, groans aplenty but no self-pity. Horatio was a fine baby boy of ten pounds in weight, so giving birth to him was no mean feat. I felt incredibly proud of her, and I told her so.

Phoebe took to motherhood immediately. My sister is a

natural. She seemed to transform into earth mother overnight.

The name Horatio came from the man who helped her reshape her life in a way she could never have imagined. It is Andrew's middle name. Phoebe learnt the name of her Nordic guardian from Gunnar – Porgeir, the man in the glass window who blew her a kiss. Porgeir was her comforter in her darkest hours.

I'm embarrassed to say that I am responsible for Horatio's nickname. Phoebe was crowing that she had chosen a name that couldn't be shortened. Andrew agreed. But it was quite a mouthful, and in an unguarded moment I called him 'Ratio'. Somehow this stuck. Andrew told me it said more about me than the baby, but he too has been heard to use it.

Over these recent times, Phoebe and I have come back together stronger and closer than we have ever been. Andrew, Phoebe, Baby Horatio and even Eleanor – this is my true family. They say you can choose friends but not family. I can only speak from experience, and I don't agree. But then, there's a quiet, female voice in my head saying, 'Remember - I chose you.'

We have kept in touch with our friends, Belinda. Patch, Gunnar, George and Mary and even one or two of the Hens. Those few days cocooned in Akureyri's deepening snow proved transformative for each member of our small group. Birth, marriage and death followed our long weekend.

The Hens brought news of Maxine. It seems that once Maxine was back in Leeds, word, or video footage, got back to her boyfriend Eric about her own wayward behaviour. Eric broke off their engagement. Instead, Maxine married Phoebe's ex, Jim – both on the rebound. She claimed she'd always fancied Jim more anyway. The Hens suspected that she'd engineered the whole thing. Did the pair live happily ever after? Well, for five and a half weeks at least. Then they joined the forty-two percent.

Belinda and Gunnar were married at Menston Parish Church, St John the Divine, that summer. Belinda told me that Gunnar had checked an on-line etiquette guide on the subject of marriage proposals. He then asked Patch for his mother's hand. Patch was perplexed.

'Tie the knot? Get hitched?' offered Gunnar, by way of explanation. Finally it dawned on Patch.

'Oh, you want to marry Mum. Why didn't you say so?'

'Well, is it okay by you?'

'Man or mouse? Go for it.' Patch may have tutted, rolled his eyes skyward, but he laughed in delight when Gunnar reported back that it was mission accomplished.

George was thrilled and proud to be asked to give the bride away. Patch was the page boy. He was kitted out in the latest incarnation of the Iceland National Team strip - "Fyrir Island".

On Andrew's insistence, the reception was held at The Mount. A sumptuous yet informal affair it was too, thanks to Mrs Tordoff and her team. Belinda had made a most divine cake. The sun shone on the couple and spangled the lake. They were photographed betwixt Lilith and Leda, along with their beaming page, Patch.

Phoebe stands out on the wedding photos, so proud of her growing baby bump. Her face is prettier than ever. Mary's face looks chiselled, and we had to bring her a seat to sit down. She was so tired, but she's smiling with delight. Everyone is.

When we studied the photos later, Andrew and I noticed a translucent shape in the shrubbery, a female form, appearing in some of the photos. A trick of the light perhaps? Or over-exposure?

At the end of the year there was a second celebration at The Mount. A naming ceremony for Horatio. Phoebe consulted Andrew on whether it should be a Christening or a naming ceremony, and his advice was to go for the latter: 'Ratio will make his own mind up when he's older. It will be his call.'

The celebrant was a delightful woman called Jennifer. She had advised Phoebe that she could have as many guide parents as she liked. Each one of these should make an individual promise to the child. Phoebe was taken with the idea of guide parents. She asked Andrew first.

'But Phoebe, my guide parent role might well be a time limited one.'

'Quality not quantity, that's what counts, Andrew,' Phoebe insisted. I marvelled at the confidence motherhood had showered on my sister.

I was proud to accept this role too, as was Eleanor. Celine and my father were asked as well – an olive branch perhaps. Phoebe always was the more diplomatic of the two of us.

And so it was Viognier, a table weighed down with delicacies and, as centrepiece, a chilled black chocolate, cherry and brandy yule log, with clotted cream and the slightest dusting of icing sugar to suggest snow. The log was topped with the stag rampant, as Atha tradition demanded.

Then something strange happened. In the merriment and general happiness that followed the informal celebrations, I found myself sitting between Belinda and Mary on the big squishy sofa at the back of The Garden Room..

'It's just like the Sundlaug public baths,' said Belinda.

'The hottest hotpot on earth,' I added.

'I could just do with a dip in there now,' Mary sighed and then she asked, 'Frasey, are you and Mr Atha an item?'

I was caught, a Brie and chive straw poised to enter my mouth. I started to choke.

'Sorry, I shouldn't have asked. It was impertinent.'

'But,' said Belinda, 'we have wondered.'

Images of steaming Sundlaug, and my companions' revelations came into my head. But my own revelation had remained shrouded, thanks to Maxine, the Hens, my distraught sister and her broken bridal dreams. I had thought that my own revelation moment had passed forever.

Mary continued, 'He looks at you as if you've just dropped off the Christmas tree, Frasey. And you are as bad. Folk will talk. It's only natural.'

Mary was teasing me, her wide smile full of wisdom and kindness.

I had regained my composure. 'I must be honest with you both. You are my friends and I trust you. Andrew and I are very close. Yes, we are in a relationship. It is, and it isn't what you think. We love each other so much. I know the difference in our ages would make most people censorious, incredulous, disgusted even. But ours is a different sort of love affair. It is love of a different order. You might call it cerebral, not physical, but it doesn't mean it isn't sensual. It is certainly consensual. Do know this, we completely satisfy each other, whatever it is we get up to.'

'So who are you hurting? Whose joy are you stealing?' asked Belinda. She too is smiling broadly.

And Mary followed on. 'What is love? Who dares to stipulate the pattern? You need to grasp the love and friendship that is on offer. Believe me, it's in short supply out there, Frasey.'

Both my friends hugged me and there may have been tears.

I shook my head. 'Age, eh? The last taboo.' I smiled – joy and relief. It felt good to come out. The Viognier flowed forth freely.

Mary defied the consultant's prediction. She lived on until

well into the New Year. She died in George's arms – a soft landing.

Belinda, Gunnar, Patch, Phoebe and I rallied round and were there for George. Patch and Gunnar kept him going with chess, and football talk, especially Guiseley FC. Belinda and I shopped and cleaned for him and made sure his freezer was filled with pre-cooked meals. And George felt blessed, but it wasn't enough. It could never be enough.

Less than two years after Mary died, George followed her. At this point, I could quote the statistics for the longevity of the bereaved partners within closely woven couples, but I won't. Instead, I find myself marvelling at relationships, their infinite diversity and the nature of love. We friends knew that for George the light had dimmed when Mary died, and he was killing time, no matter how we cared, included, and encouraged him.

Covid took George in late November 2020. Having felt unwell, he started to experience breathing difficulties. I called round. Covid restrictions meant I had to speak to him through the bay window of his home. We stood either side of the window, smiling at each other as we talked into our mobile phones.

'A life in glass eh, Frasey. And now I'm stuck in here behind glass. What is this all about?'

I'd taken George his shopping, to leave at the door. But I was so concerned at George's frail appearance, and thready breathing, that I called an ambulance there and then.

George was taken off to the newly opened Covid Ward in Harrogate. I was the last of the friends to see George alive. When the ambulance came, the crew stretchered George out. I stood by and George waved and gave me the thumbs up, and that was it. As George's condition worsened, the hospital tried every treatment and approach available at that time.

Then George experienced failure of all vital organs.

Our close-knit group was the less for Mary and George's passing. We felt it was almost like being orphaned. It was as if we'd taken down our umbrellas and shaken them out, but the rain hadn't really stopped.

George was buried in a sealed coffin next to Mary. Our small group stood together, masked and socially distanced. It was a subdued affair until the party reached the church gate to return home. Gunnar and Patch held back and then, beating their chests and looking skyward, they delivered the Viking Cry. Belinda, Phoebe and I exchanged knowing glances, and followed suit. In those awful circumstances, it was the best send-off we could muster. Covid rules – we weren't even allowed to have a wake. But our tribute wouldn't have been wasted on George, or his waiting Mary.

And then our friends Belinda, Gunnar and Patch left us. Although Gunnar loved living in Yorkshire, he always had plans to move back to Iceland. He used the Covid years to improve his English – invaluable for career advancement in the leisure industry back home. He'd fallen in love with the Yorkshire coast, especially the area around Bempton Cliffs and Flamborough Head. He marvelled at the sea bird colonies and explored bird migration, and the links between Iceland and Britain. He started to plan niche nature tours – birds first, then perhaps an Icelandic horse experience and a volcano tour.

Just over a year ago, Gunnar, Belinda and Patch migrated back to Akureyri on the big white bird. Gunnarsson's Getaways are back in business, with bird watching extensions. Belinda decided to pick up where she left off, adjusting her landscape gardening activities to a more challenging climate and environment. She is developing a new specialism for indoor gardening and is already in high demand to work for the proliferation of hotels for the ever-increasing tourist trade over in Iceland.

Andrew, Phoebe and I have followed their fortunes with fascination as the years fly. Their latest news gave us joy. The Gunnarssons have welcomed a daughter – Belle Star. The name Belle is Gunnar's choice. Belinda has added Star, to give the name a bit more edge, for she'd like her daughter to have edge, a little anyway. The name is also a nod to the westerns that Gunnar loves so much. I have just heard from Belinda that Belle Star has been baptised in the Akureyrarkirkja, under the approving and protective eye of Porgeir the Lawspeaker. She writes that Gunnar is proving a proud and caring father to both his children and that in his eyes, Belle will outshine all the Merry Dancers together – she'll score ten plus.

And Patch is thrilled to have a sister. When the time comes, he says he's going to introduce Belle to the Viking Cry. And Saturdays will be football, and Sundays, Sundlaug – whatever life and the volcanoes lob at them as our world goes wrong.

Chapter 15

Five Candles for Horatio

Back home, The Mount remains our sanctuary.

On 1st October 2023, Horatio's fifth birthday, Phoebe changed his family name to Atha, on Andrew's request. Horatio Porgeir Atha - a fine name indeed.

Andrew has told Phoebe and me that Horatio Porgeir Atha will be left a very rich young man. His fortune will be held in trust until an age when he can appreciate the finer things. Andrew also says that Eleanor, Phoebe and especially me will be left wanting for nothing. There is to be a generous settlement for each of us, and a luxurious home for life.

"Blessed are the meek..."

Horatio's fifth birthday also saw a new addition to our household. Eleanor presented him with a wicker carrying basket. Inside was an adorable grey kitten. This creature was an instant hit with us all. His coat was the softest grey — a blue shorthair. He had long back legs. Eleanor said this meant he would be a big cat when he was full grown.

'His name is Aubrey.'

Eleanor was quite emphatic on this point.

'Aubrey? An unusual choice. Why Aubrey, Eleanor?' Mr Atha was curious, but he was also thinking Ratio should name his own cat. Her answer shocked Andrew and me.

'Miss Amba had a great big grey cat called Aubrey. It was

a fifth birthday present from her aunt in London. I heard about this cat from my gran, who was Cook when Miss Amba was a girl. Gran loved to reminisce. She'd tell the tale with embellishments, I'm sure. She was that way. Aubrey the cat became something of a legend at The Mount. He was quite a character.

Gran told me the staff here loved Miss Amba. I think they felt sorry for her because she was a solitary and singular child. Gran said it would break your heart the way she used to sit on the stairs hoping to see her mother. Your father had no time for her. So, Aubrey was her companion. She loved that cat and he always slept on her bed.'

Eleanor stopped.

'Perhaps I'm saying too much? This isn't a nice story and the dead can't speak up for themselves.'

Not so sure about that, I thought.

'No, please tell us. I'm not sure I've ever heard about Aubrey.' Andrew looked lost in the past as he so often did when Amba's name was mentioned.

'Something dreadful happened. Just after you were born, Mr Atha, your father decided Aubrey was a danger to you. People said that cats could smother babies. So he took a notion to get rid of the creature. Miss Amba saw her father holding the cat underwater, over there, between those two statues. She was distraught, like a person possessed. She attempted to stop him and had to be pulled off her father's back because she was punching him so hard. She tried to throttle her own father.

Gran said the cat was far too old and arthritic to pose any threat to you. He was sixteen and was probably getting to the end of his life anyway. He spent most of his days curled up in the kitchen by the fire. Your father had come into the kitchen and lifted him out of his basket. Gran said it wasn't right at all. Proper cruel it was. The household was shocked.'

Eleanor shrugged. 'Long ago and far away. Anyway, I thought young Horatio would love the wee kitten. It's a nod to Miss Amba too if you like. It squares the circle as they say.'

Eleanor, Phoebe and Horatio left us. They wanted to make sure Aubrey settled into life at The Mount. Andrew and I sat together in silence for what seemed a long time, just breathing and taking things in. Then he spoke. 'I had no idea about any of that.' He looked shaken and moved. 'My poor Amba. She never said. And she never held it against me.'

'But Andrew, it wasn't your fault. You were an innocent baby. You didn't kill the cat. What Amba was determined to do was to protect you from your father, and stop you being moulded by him into that sort of man. She shaped you into the man you are, kind, considerate and loveable.'

'But Frasey, it makes me feel awful that my birth occasioned such a cruel act.'

'These things are beyond our control. It is certainly true that Amba loved Aubrey. She refers to him a lot in her earlier diaries as her true friend and confidante. But she never mentions the drowning.'

'It was probably too painful. Well, Eleanor's story certainly sounds plausible. It would be just like Aunt Rania to call the cat Aubrey. She was a great fan of Beardsley. They shared a taste for grotesque erotica along with an enthusiasm for Salome and her dance.'

There was a pause. It was as if Andrew was taking stock.

'Frasey, Father was no monster. It would be wrong to judge him too harshly. We have no idea of the privations and pressures he was or had been under. We tend to rewrite the past through the prism of the present and try to impose our values on times beyond our grasp. But one thing is for sure, Father had little time for Amba, that is, until after her death.

We both stared at the painting. Then Andrew continued, 'Why, there is Amba at twenty-one. She looks so joyous and eager to start out in life. Eleven months later, she's leaping on Father's back and raining punches on his head, trying to save her cat. I have to ask myself, what sort of family were we Athas?'

Leda and Lilith is published.

I wrote the foreword. I made some light-touch edits, but only with Amba's approval. It has been very well-received. The publisher is pressing me for Amba's biography. She says there is a real market for this book, especially by those who are fascinated by lesbian lives in the inter-was years. But I'm not finding this easy. Progress has slowed. I find it hard to separate myself from my subject.

It is strange but true that each time I think I've finished my work on Amba, some new incident or insight occurs to me. I cannot let her go. Perhaps the truth of it is, she will not release me. Each letter I read makes my senses quicken. It is as though I was there and part of it, as if I'm reading my own past.

Some days I settle at her desk and nothing comes. On a good day I feel I know the real Amba and my writing flows. On a very good day I become her, and when I read what I have written I do not remember writing those words. But I don't dare change them. Can it be normal for a biographer to fall in love with their subject, to the point at which they become so immersed they lose their own self?

I have started to ask myself this question. Should my research even be presented as a biography? Andrew has told me that the biography is an irrelevance now. He said, 'Frasey, this was only ever about me finding Amba, and I have found Amba through you, my love.'

Did Amba propel me to sprint across the university car

park in pursuit of her brother? Working for Andrew and loving Andrew has transformed my life. Am I a pawn, a puppet or a player? Like my darling Andrew, I have grown to love Amba too, and I ask myself if it even matters who pulls the strings. I would change nothing about my life.

We are a minor triad, three notes in tune and time, a trinity of eternity, love and connection. Rather than a biography I think I shall write the story of Amba, Andrew and me.

Epilogue

Coming Home

On 4th April 2027, a heart attack takes Andrew. He's ninety-eight. He passes away in the velvet chair, just after his lunch, his left hand falling suddenly and heavily. Frasey is standing by his side in Amba's emerald crepe de chine trousers. She leans down to stroke, then kiss his brow.

After Andrew's death, Frasey never enjoys the same appetite for anything. She knows she will miss him forever. She will never forget him. Nor will she be allowed to. The wind whipping up the ripples on the lake will reveal new, lower notes, more contained, restrained, yet an appreciative laugh alongside Amba's.

Frasey will sit in Andrew's velvet chair, breathe deeply, and relax into her surroundings, just as he taught her. She will watch the lake and listen to the intermingling laughter of Amba and Andrew. She longs to laugh with them.

The lake mirrors the fleeting seasons as six years pass.

One summer morning, Frasey hears faint music. She opens the French doors and is drawn to the lake. She listens and smiles as she recognises Jimmy Dorsey's "My Sister & I". A crackly 78 sound, a slow and seductive fox trot. She sighs and then she sees them. A young man in a cream dinner jacket holds an elegant woman in his arms. The woman wears a golden Grecian gown.

Amba and Andrew are dancing together along the lake's rim.

The words of the song tell of a brother and sister away from home. They think about friends who had to stay behind. Finally, Amba and Andrew become aware of Frasey. They look towards her. Then, beaming, they gently pull apart. Their arms open and they beckon her over. She moves towards them and the three sway to the music until the song is almost done.

As the orchestra swells to the finale, the three slip beneath the water together.